Deep in a secret, underground laboratory, a group of scientists find themselves in danger. Achieving cutting-edge breakthroughs in genetic engineering, they have created powerful viruses, the likes of which the world has never seen. But their creations have the power to turn on them—and do.

The scientists work for the U.S. military, developing biological weapons of mass destruction in direct violation of federal and international law. But it's a necessary evil, for while these dedicated men and women create microscopic monsters, they work even harder to try to develop antidotes to stop them.

Some monsters can't be contained, though. Or stopped.

When an accident unleashes one of their creations, Craig Leland, commander of the underground laboratory, and his team watch helplessly as the virus kills one of their own. They reel, struggling to come to grips with their loss. But their nightmare is just beginning, and all is not as it seems. In a race against time, with no way out, Craig must fight for his team's survival—and the woman he secretly loves.

Keres' Eyes

Michael Curtis

Steele Press
Chicago

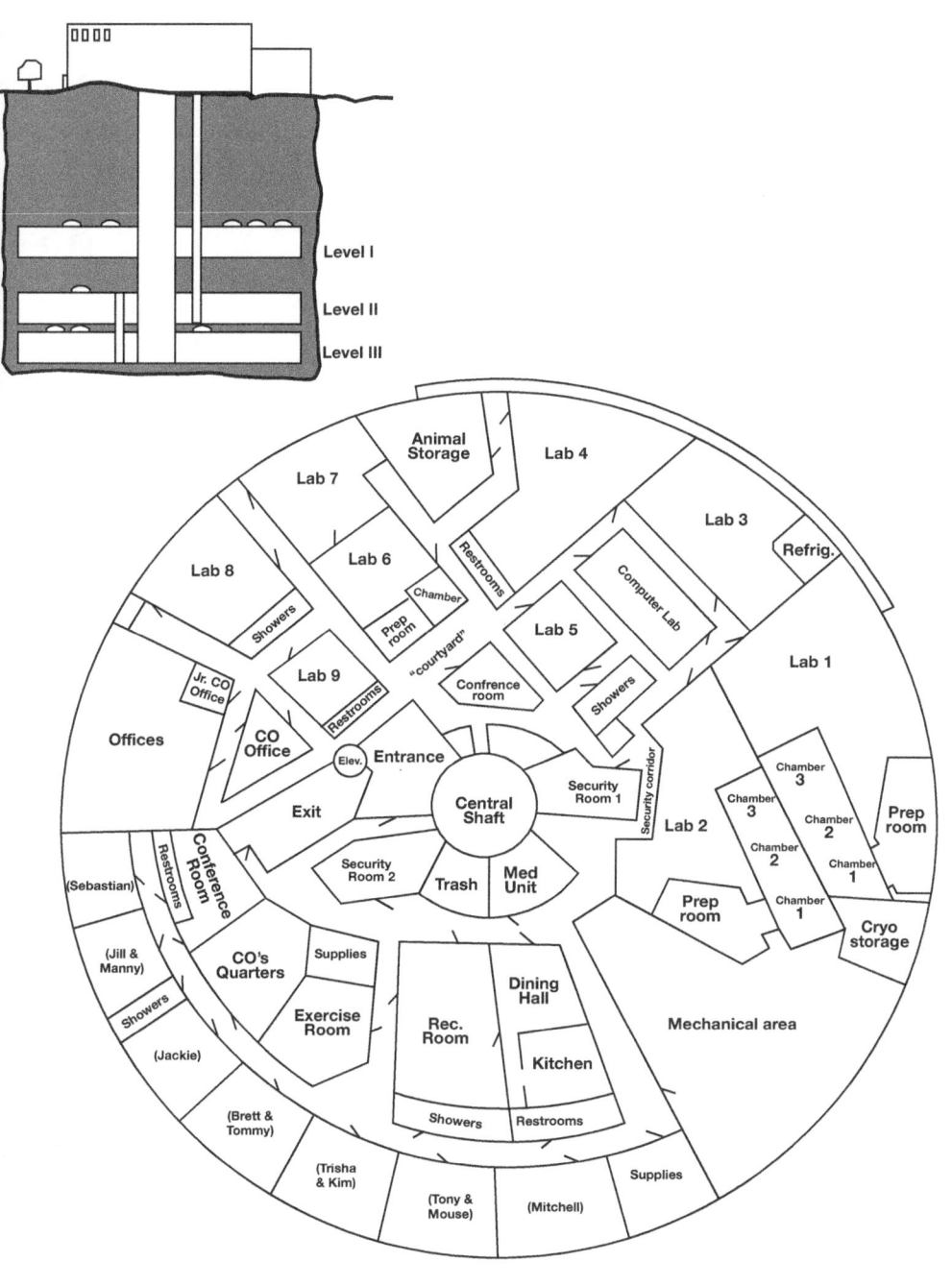

CHAPTER 1

The test subject screamed in anger and frustration.

Danny Neumann did his best to ignore the screams as he prepared the syringe, but it wasn't easy. They were deafening, echoing in his ears as they bounced off the walls of the sealed room.

When he couldn't take it anymore, he shot the animal a glare. "Stop your bitching. We're not gonna kill you today."

The monkey fell silent, as if it understood. But then it started shrieking again, its tiny hands wrapped around the bars of its cage.

Danny gritted his teeth. Where was Craig? Danny couldn't start without him. Not only was it against protocol, but he needed help strapping the beast down. It was the only way he'd safely be able to draw blood to see how the antibodies were doing.

At least the monkey hadn't been infected with anything. It was being prepped to be exposed to the new virus, the latest in a line of biological monsters that had been created down here in this cold, underground womb. Danny hated having to infect these animals—the facility had a number of them: monkeys, rabbits, etc.—but there was no use complaining about it. Sacrifices had to be made.

He shot an impatient glance towards the door. He wanted to get this over with. The monkey was driving him batshit.

He grabbed the syringe, hesitated, and put it back down. "Don't be stupid, Danny," he thought aloud.

He glanced at the door again but the pressure-sealed door remained closed. The thick glass embedded in the door allowed him to see the hallway beyond. Empty. He turned and looked at the door to Lab 7, but it was dark.

He shook his head. The CO was always on time. This wasn't like him.

Captain Craig Leland sat in his darkened office, oblivious to the hustle and flow of the level as he stared at the communiqué in his hands. He read it over and over, understanding the message even as his mind struggled to accept it. He hadn't expected it to come this quickly—

The phone rang.

Without taking his eyes off the document, he picked up the receiver. "Yes?"

"Sir? Are you coming?"

"Yeah," Craig replied. "I ... I'll be right there."

He was only dimly aware that Danny was still talking as he hung up. His hazel eyes remained locked on the communiqué, traveling over the terse words until they hammered in his brain. He tried to convince himself that it was good news, that it was what he wanted, but the pit in his stomach spoke otherwise.

What makes you happy?" her voice whispered, that fateful conversation from two years ago slipping through his thoughts. He knew what made him happy. She did. Trisha Foster. His sub-ordinate—which was the problem.

The paper in his hand resolved the conflict inside him, although not for the better. He didn't have a choice. It would change everything. Things already were different, though no one knew it. Not yet. This communiqué announced the end.

It had to be this way.

He thought of the others down here, men and women he considered family. He was the leader of a group of talented scientists dedicated to the creation of and subsequent protection from the deadliest viruses in the world. It was a dangerous, delicate job that required massive support and massive protection—both of which were provided by a government that knew little of its existence.

Craig's team worked in one of the most secret military installations ever devised. Buried deep underground, the laboratory had been built in the 1950s to keep pace with the world in terms of chemical and biological weapons. Now, however, they focused strictly on biological agents.

It was difficult working in a place like this, cut off from the rest of the world, handling some of the most dangerous agents known to mankind. People's quirks and personality traits flared brightly in this restricted environment, far from the comforting rays of the sun. With the extreme conditions and constant pressure, he was forced to coddle his people to make sure they all got along. At times, it made for delicate situations.

Their reactions to the bomb in his hand would be terrible to witness.

He glanced at the clock. No wonder Danny had called. Craig should've been there twenty minutes ago.

He searched for a place to put the communiqué, opened his desk drawer and jammed it inside. As he began to close the drawer, he spotted the other messages piled on his desk, left forgotten as he'd stared at the communiqué, and with an arm swiped them into the drawer before closing it.

He stood to go. In frustration, he picked up a dart and threw it with a practiced turn of his wrist at the dartboard hanging on the opposite wall of his office, wedged in between motivational posters that had been all the rage a few years back—posters he didn't even glance at anymore.

He didn't have to look to know where it landed. He had been throwing darts for years and was a master champion. The dart landed square in the center of the board, piercing its red heart.

Bullseye.

Danny washed his hands as the toilet filled behind him, humming to himself as he meticulously scrubbed them clean. When he finished, he looked at his reflection in the mirror. He was in no rush to return to the lab. The monkey's screams had been like daggers assaulting his ears.

He primped for a few moments, gave himself a sly grin, and finally turned to leave. He couldn't wait to make his announcement. It was going to be huge. Man was his life gonna change. He wouldn't be just another worker bee after this. He would get the respect he deserved, that he'd longed for so long.

Still humming, he walked out of the bathroom, back towards Lab 6—but then stopped. Something was wrong. He wondered if he'd made a big mistake. The little shit was screeching its head off.

But it was more than that. The doors to the labs sealed airtight and very little sound escaped. He shouldn't have been able to hear the creature in the first place.

Suddenly, alarms erupted around him. He flinched with the sheer volume of sound, the electronic noise jabbing straight through his eardrums and into the center of his brain. Before he could react, doors appeared as if out of nowhere. He stared at them dumbly as they slid out of the wall and quickly, efficiently, slid across the hallway. The doors—which he hadn't known even existed—blocked off the hallway leading to the "courtyard", as well as the side hallway that led to Lab 4 and Animal Storage.

He was trapped.

The monkey continued to scream.

In a state of near panic, Danny turned back to Lab 6. He wasn't cut off from the door that led into the Lab. He had a way out.

He'd only taken one step when a burning sensation swept through him.

*   *   *

After locking his office—something he rarely did—Craig turned and started down the hallway. To his relief, no one was around. He was in no mood for idle chitchat.

A quick glance at his watch caused him to quicken his pace.

He was trying to remember which test the virologist was running today when a siren went off. He jerked in surprise, as he'd never heard that kind of alarm before. But he only paused for a moment. His training quickly took over and he broke into a run, scrambling towards the source of the alarm.

He raced past the conference room, across the "courtyard", turned the corner to Lab 6—and nearly collided with a door. He managed to stop in time, although his confusion remained. He didn't know where it had come from. It had to be a form of protection, a means to contain a potential outbreak, as it filled the entire hallway, blocking his path. Made up primarily of thick glass, it enabled Craig to see the hallway on the other side.

To his horror, he watched as Danny struggled to remain on his feet, trapped inside the sudden containment area.

A dozen questions leapt to Craig's mind but his first concern was his subordinate's safety. He pounded on the glass, trying to get to Danny, but the glass, set tightly within the metal-composite frame, didn't budge.

In the flashing light that accompanied the alarm, Craig watched Danny struggle to take a step.

Craig heard the others running towards him, responding to the alert. He glanced behind him and saw equal looks of surprise and trepidation. Tony was the first to arrive, followed by Sebastian Bierg. Sebastian was the Senior Scientist and the smartest man Craig had ever met. Craig looked at him hopefully, but the look in Sebastian's eyes told him what he already feared: they had no hope of getting to Danny.

The rest of the team quickly showed up. Besides Craig, there were eleven people who worked on this level: six scientists, three technicians, a biomedical engineer and a maintenance worker. Even Mouse, the maintenance worker, responded.

Kim Sook Chang, one of four women in the group, pushed her way forward and put her hands on the glass. "Danny!"

Craig doubted Danny could hear her. The glass was too thick. Even so, Danny turned around and smiled at her—or, tried to smile. He shuffled towards the door, his terror-filled eyes locked onto hers.

The entire staff watched in silent horror as he stumbled and fell.

He stretched out his hand and pressed it against the glass. Stifling a sob, Kim moved her hand to the same spot. His eyes remained locked on hers as his body began to convulse, his face turning pale.

Then his eyes began to change.

Gray splotches appeared in the whites of his eyes, rapidly growing and overlapping. Within moments, his pupils were islands in a sea of black. Danny's mouth opened in a scream, the thick door muffling most of his primal cry of fear and pain. Then his body convulsed violently once, twice, and he collapsed to the floor, dead.

CHAPTER 2

Banks sat in the far corner of one of the bars that lined the con-course, nursing a drink and wondering how his life had become such a mess. He took another drink, only dimly feeling the burn as the alcohol rolled down his throat, and thought of getting rip-roaring drunk. Maybe then he could forget what he was supposed to do.

He suddenly realized he wasn't alone. He jerked his eyes up—and almost leapt out of his chair.

"Easy," the man said.

"Wha—What are you doing here?"

"I wanted to make sure everything's on schedule."

"How did you know where I was?"

"Come now, Christopher, you don't think we'd just take your word for it, did you? My employer wants me to keep an eye on you."

Banks' eyes darted around the nearly empty bar. "Is he here?"

The associate laughed. "Don't be foolish."

Banks picked up his glass and took another drink. A long one. "You shouldn't be here. Someone might recognize you."

"You have other things to worry about."

Banks tried to formulate a reply as the loudspeaker overhead announced a final boarding call. "We told you we'd get—"

"I know what you told us. The retainer we gave you is substantial. We want to make sure you deliver. The details weren't made clear to us—"

"Don't worry about how. That's our problem."

The associate leaned forward. "Yes, it is."

Banks lifted his glass again only to find it empty. He desperately wanted another but didn't dare risk it. He set the glass down, avoiding the man's gaze, and began to rub the back of his hand. The man noticed this, smiled, and Banks quickly stopped. They even knew about that. He could feel his cheeks flush.

"So everything's on schedule?"

Banks nodded.

"Good. Then I believe you have a plane to catch."

*　　　*　　　*

Tony Vasquez, the Security Officer and one of the Lab Technicians, stared at the body in disbelief. This couldn't be happening.

For a few moments, no one moved. No one spoke. They were in too much shock, too much amazement and bewilderment, to react. The only sound came from the siren's constant braying.

As he stood motionless, his CO turned on Mouse. "Shut off the alarm."

Mouse blinked. "I don't think I can override the safety procedures—"

"At least turn off that damn noise."

"Yes sir."

Mouse scampered down the hallway.

Trisha and Jill pushed past Tony to reach Kim, who was clawing at the glass and calling Danny's name. He wasn't surprised at her reaction, although it barely had the power to break through the fog that seemed to paralyze his heart.

"What do you need me to do?" Sebastian asked.

"Find out what happened," Craig said through clenched teeth. "I need to know."

"Of course."

The alarm suddenly cut off, but the sound continued to echo in Tony's ears.

Craig turned to Jackie, the Jr. CO. "Set up a perimeter. I want this area off-limits."

"Right away."

Looking at Tony, Craig said, "Initiate the security controls. You know the drill, right?"

Tony nodded reluctantly. "Yes."

"Then do it."

Tony turned and headed back through the level. At the first intersection, though, he stopped as soon as he was out of sight. His legs felt like they were about to give out. He leaned against the wall, silently chastising himself as he struggled to catch his breath. The alarm still wailed in his mind, taunting him, accusing him. After a moment, he pushed away from the wall and forced himself onward.

He had always been creeped out working down here, but Danny's sudden death magnified his uneasiness. He felt all three hundred feet of rock and earth pressing down on him from above, trying to squash him like a bug.

When he had first come here, Tony had been impressed. The underground facility had three levels, accessed via elevator. Level I was located two hundred feet underground. Level II, which handled more dangerous agents, was located eighty feet further down, and Level III, which handled the deadliest weapons, was below that. Entry to or exit from a level required a series of steps designed to prevent contamination from one level to the next. It was a lengthy process, however. To get from Level III to the surface required almost a day of sterilization, testing, and more sterilization.

He wasn't impressed anymore. He felt like a rat in a maze, and the absence of sunlight or even fresh air added to the unsettled feeling that always hounded him, magnified by the low ceilings and cramped quarters.

He couldn't believe Danny had died, he thought with a rising anger as he stepped through the security corridor and headed towards the exit. Security had been breached in some way—and his friend had died because of it. He tried to ignore the tears in his eyes as he continued towards Security Room 2, located at the entrance to the Level. At least he was away from the others. A man had the right to be alone with his pain.

When he had first taken this assignment, he'd believed it was a stepping stone towards a greater position. He was career military, in fact the only 'true' military man down here in his eyes. All of the rest—except for Craig and Jackie—were civilians. Now, all he wanted to do was find out why Danny had died. It was the right thing to do—and possibly the only way Tony could redeem himself.

He entered the security room. It was familiar, but now it felt cold. Impersonal. Hostile.

He went over to the control panel and pulled out a laminated card. He knew most of the steps but used the card anyway, reluctantly following procedure. He barely remembered doing each step, though, as he was still reeling from the loss.

As he pressed the final series of buttons, locking the entrance and exit to the Level, he realized the implications of his actions. One seal had failed, which meant they all could fail. He and his coworkers were in mortal danger. The next "failure" could kill them in one strike, so locking the place down was the last thing he should've been doing ... but he had to follow procedure. He was a soldier. He would do as he was commanded.

But that didn't mean he was an idiot. He knew the regs weren't designed to protect them. They were designed to protect everyone else. He and his coworkers were all guinea pigs waiting to die, sealed in here as tightly as Danny had been sealed in that hallway.

The image of Danny's ravaged body rose in his mind—and Tony froze as a terrible realization hit him.

*　　*　　*

Craig was back in his office, struggling to write a report to his superiors. He had told the others to return to their work and had stood in front of the sealed hallway until they'd all left. Then he'd turned back to the glass.

He had stared at Danny's lifeless body for only a few moments before walking away—it's all he would allow himself—but he knew the image would stay with him for the rest of his life.

Craig frowned at the 'Incident Report' he was supposed to fill out. He found himself mulling over the weapons they worked on instead, and the blood and sweat that had gone into creating vaccines for many of those weapons. It was an important job that none of them were willing to trust to anyone else—especially considering some of the microscopic death machines they'd birthed.

Ironically, Keres' Eyes was a perfect example of their ideal weapon. In fact, it was one of the most lethal viruses ever devised, faster than Ebola and with a higher percentage of susceptibility—and there was no cure. Craig wasn't sure if they would ever be able to create one. It was that brutal, that fast of a killer. Having that sucker loose was beyond scary.

Craig and the others had recognized it immediately. Agent #V349230, a noncontagious microorganism, had been developed through a concerted effort of half of Craig's entire team. Unlike most viruses, Agent #V349230 did not attack through the skin, only through the nasal passages or the eyes—especially the eyes. As soon as the victim was infected, it multiplied at a mind-numbing rate, spewing copies of itself across the eyeball. This was the reason Danny's eyes had turned black. The microbe had multiplied, swelling to millions of copies within seconds. As it attacked the eyes, other copies of the bacterium shot through the optical nerve and into the brain, killing the victim.

When they first witnessed the deadly method of attack, Sebastian had given Agent #V349230 a nickname. He had called it Keres' Eyes. When Craig asked who Keres was, Sebastian had told him that Keres had been the name for goddesses in Greek mythology attributed to violent death, the personification of the horror witnessed on battlefields and in gruesome murders. He said he could imagine those goddesses with black eyes.

Craig suppressed a shudder. He had no idea how Danny had become infected—and couldn't imagine the horror Danny had suffered knowing that one of his own creations had escaped its bonds to kill him.

He shoved the Incident Report away. Not only did the form seem inappropriate, but he didn't know if he could write it. Craig couldn't believe one of his people was dead. He didn't know what to do.

He'd had about as "normal" a childhood as he could have hoped for in this day and age. He'd been fairly active in sports, enjoyed baseball and other feats of skill, and had the same love of comics and video games as the next kid. His parents had provided a roof over his head and clothes on his back, but they never took an interest in him, too wrapped up in their own lives and desires to spare time for their only child. It was one of many reasons why he didn't respect them or want anything to do with them.

He'd learned to be self-sufficient, paying his way through college via scholarships and money he made playing darts. After college, none of the job offers he received felt right—so in the end, he'd signed up for the military.

It had been the wrong move, he later decided, so when his four years came up, he bailed. He got a job with a bioengineering firm on the East Coast but was still unsatisfied, even though he received accolades for his work. It was only after the Army contacted him, luring him back into the fold, that he began to feel like he was making a difference. The Army put him on a fast track, steadily increasing his security clearance and rank. Bringing him deeper into the fold. Finally, he was dispatched to this underground world that was far different than the one above.

He still visited the outside world—breaks from the labs were regularly scheduled, thirty days up top, sixty days down here—but his life revolved around the laboratory. At least, it used to. He didn't know anymore. Didn't know who he was or what his life meant. The choices, mistakes, and capacity for hurting others were too much to contemplate.

How had everything turned out so badly?

He pulled out the communiqué and read it again, trying to convince himself that this was good news, that it's what he wanted, but he still felt troubled. Torn. His request had been granted—and they had decided to promote him as well, which surprised him. His transfer took effect next week, when he was to report to the Pentagon.

He heard her voice again, triggering a flush of guilt and desire. *"Have you ever done something you regretted?"* she'd purred.

He regretted that night ... or so he told himself.

It had started innocently enough, at a convention in Dallas. Some of the best minds in biological research, viruses and bioengineering had been there, meeting to discuss the latest and greatest advancements. Craig had been there at the Army's blessing, the last time he would attend a conference while an employee of the military.

He'd been ready to leave after the first day, but he'd been one of the speakers. He wished that he hadn't agreed to the organizers' request. He knew his work would sound hollow compared to the others—especially since there was a limit to what he could say.

But then something amazing had happened.

That first night, the organizers had arranged a social event so the attendees could meet and talk with the keynote speakers. These events were normally excruciating, filled with inane babble and blowhard proclamations. Craig had endured forty minutes of it before sneaking out the back—and had gotten caught. A ravishing woman with sparkling emerald eyes had been hurrying to the event, and initially assumed he was one of the attendees. When she saw his nametag, however, she chastised him for "bailing" the event.

He was surprised by her reaction, and felt more than a little guilty. Stalling for time, he asked her name. Trisha Foster, she told him with a smile.

He felt warm in her presence—but still didn't want to go back inside. "Can I buy you a drink?"

She hesitated.

Ordinarily, he would've backed off when he noticed her hesitation, but not this time. There was an attraction there. A strong one. He couldn't turn away. He pointed out that she would have his full attention—and that he'd be more entertaining than any of the blowhards inside.

With a giggle, she accepted.

The two talked for hours, each impressed with the other's knowledge, although Craig was forced to choose his words carefully, loathing every time he had to watch what he said, to avoid revealing any military secrets. He couldn't even tell her where he was stationed, but even that couldn't dampen the evening. Their specialties were similar, yet with enough differences that they were able to share insights with each other. And Craig felt the attraction intensify.

They ended up in her hotel room.

As soon as they were alone, they came together with a level of heat and desire that threatened to consume them both. It was an amazing night of passion, his body responding to hers in a way he hadn't experienced in years. They explored each other, teasing, stroking, kissing, and pleasing each other in every intimate way, bringing the other to the heights of pleasure over and over again until they collapsed in exhaustion, drained in the best possible way. It was a night that would've made the gods stop and watch.

Craig woke the next morning—after only a couple hours of sleep—deeply sated. Yet, as he watched her sleep beside him, her wonderful mane of hair spread across her pillow, he felt the need to run.

He left before she woke up.

Unfortunately, she showed up at his presentation.

After he finished, she approached the podium, greeting him with a radiant smile. They talked for a few moments as others moved around them. He could get lost in her presence, he realized, deliriously helpless to break free. He agreed to meet for dinner—

—but left town that afternoon, dropping off a message on his way out that told her "something came up". He didn't leave a number.

Now she was here.

She had arrived a year ago, turning his world upside down. Not only did he have to face his actions and lingering desire, but the moment she showed up, he became his father, the last thing he'd ever wanted.

A knock on the door interrupted his thoughts.

Craig quickly shoved the communiqué back in the drawer. "Come."

The door opened and Mouse hesitantly poked his head in. "Can I speak to you, sir?"

Craig motioned for him to enter. "Did you know about those safety doors?"

"Uh, you mean the ones that blocked off the hallway? No, I didn't. From what I can figure, they're hidden in the walls."

"How many are there? What triggers them, exactly?"

"I-I don't know, sir."

Craig forced himself to sit back. "Do me a favor. Find out about them, everything you can."

"Yes sir."

"So, what can I do for you?"

"Well, sir, I thought you'd want to know."

"Yes?" Craig asked, after Mouse grew quiet.

"Well, it's just that, sir, you need to talk to the others."

"What do you mean?"

Mouse took a deep breath. "I think ... I think they're ready to mutiny."

CHAPTER 3

Sebastian sat in front of one of five computer screens that lined the Computer Lab, oblivious to the mainframe looming behind him—as well as to the paperwork and cables strewn around the room. He was concentrated solely on the screen before him, rapidly moving through the various video camera programs. With each click of his mouse, a different video feed appeared. He scrolled through the images until he found the video camera for the hallway outside of Lab 6, then instructed the computer to rewind the video file, moving backwards in time.

He watched Danny's final moments. There was a time stamp in one corner of the image, so he could gauge how long Danny had been outside Lab 6 and how quickly he died. It didn't take long. Keres' Eyes moved amazingly fast, faster than any other biological weapon Sebastian had ever studied.

The angle of the video camera was perfect. He had a front-row seat to Danny's death.

The Computer Lab was Sebastian's domain, the central nexus for all work done on the Level. Located in the heart of the laboratory area, it allowed him to control virtually every piece of lab equipment via the integrated computer system, as well as many other aspects of the facility. From his perch, he could access any video camera on the floor, track the oxygen and carbon dioxide levels, and even control the temperature.

And he had conquered it all. The Lab had once been divided, with Manny overseeing the computers while Sebastian focused on the research. But the massive mainframe had been a constant nemesis, infringing on Sebastian's work at the most inopportune times. It had led to a number of heated arguments between Manny and Sebastian and had culminated with Sebastian bashing the sides of the mainframe with a metal rod in a fit of frustration. A couple of days later, Sebastian had started to learn the archaic and jumbled operating systems from Manny. Within weeks, Sebastian had surpassed Manny as well as the programmers on the surface.

The Computer Lab was all Sebastian's now. Manny had been relegated to a backup role, which was a good place for the Neanderthal.

A row of large, plate-glassed windows made up one wall of the room, with a couple extra windows thrown in for good measure on the adjoining walls. Due to corresponding windows in Labs 1 through 4, he was able to directly observe any and all activities in those labs from the Computer Lab—and with his mastery of the computer system, could track even the smallest event.

The next video feed appeared on Sebastian's computer screen. He noted the time, made a couple of copies of the footage, then switched to the camera inside Lab 6. The monkey was dead, all right. Sebastian was surprised the creature had been outside of its cage. He wondered what Danny had been thinking, letting it out and then leaving it unsupervised. The bloody fool.

He began to pull up data. A graph appeared on his screen, a rough bell curve that showed the intensity levels of detection for the viral outbreak. By moving backwards in time, Sebastian was able to calculate the speed in which the virus moved through the air. He watched the data slowly, over and over again, reluctantly impressed with the deadly efficiency of the manmade pathogen.

Craig was quiet as he followed Mouse to the Dining Hall. His pronouncement had been ominous, and Craig knew he had to handle the problem right away. But the news of his transfer was a shadow hanging over him. He would have to announce it. Soon.

When he entered the Hall, he found it empty, but he could hear yelling.

Like most of the facility, the walls of the Dining Hall were white. The military had tried to break up the monotony, however, by putting a 1950s design in the room complete with red leather and chrome bar stools that lined the seldom-used counter.

Craig quickly made his way around the Formica tables to the utilitarian-style kitchen. He went through the swinging doors into the kitchen and found his team members arguing with each other.

"You're full of shit and you know it," Mitchell was saying when he entered.

Jill opened her mouth to respond, but quickly closed it when she saw Craig. The others quieted as well, some even dropping their eyes to the floor. But he could tell by their body language that the argument wasn't over.

He was somewhat surprised to see that everyone—except for Sebastian—was here. Helpless to stop himself, his gaze went to her first.

Trisha Foster, sitting cross-legged on one of the stainless steel counters, was a biologist with a specialty in bioengineering. She was smart, decisive, and absolutely stunning, even when she had her auburn-highlighted hair pulled back in a ponytail. Her smile could light up a room—and take his breath away.

There were times Craig caught himself staring at her like a teenage boy drowning in hormones. He couldn't help it, although it only made matters worse. Even now, with the horror of what happened, he found himself drawn to her.

Manny and Jill were the only husband and wife team down here. Manny Turell, a scruffy-looking guy, was one of the lab techs. He was good at his job and proficient with a computer, so he acted as the backup programmer to Sebastian. He had a number of quirks, though, and was quick to anger. At least he loved his wife. She could always calm him down.

Jill Turell was older than Manny. An attractive woman, she was a little on the frumpy side but had a bright smile and a sharp mind. She was a virologist, bacteriologist and genetic engineer. Normally calm and cool, she had been deeply shaken by Danny's sudden death.

Mitchell Kelly, on the other hand, was anything but calm and cool. He was the jokester of the group, with a quick wit that never seemed to stop. A biologist/physiologist, he sometimes got in trouble by taking too many shortcuts in his work. He was tall, in shape from constantly using the weight machines, and had a quick grin. Craig hated to admit it, but the man was usually very funny. When he got on one of his rants, he sounded like a professional comic.

He was far from the military's ideal, however. He not only acted like the class clown, but he was best known for the extensive pornographic library he had on his computer. Craig wondered what the incoming CO would think about that.

Kim Sook Chang was the other lab technician. A slim, oriental woman, she was very proficient and generally seemed happy down here, away from the rest of the world. Normally bright and spunky, she was still visibly upset. Craig watched as she struggled not to break down again. She clung to Trisha, drawing strength from her.

Jacqueline "Jackie" DiScoli was Craig's second in command, a competent and efficient woman who seemed to have the initiative and the basic makeup needed to become a leader, although she was hardnosed and aloof at times.

These were Craig's people, men and women he cared about and trusted.

His gaze rested on the newcomer. Brett Collins was a biochemist, a recent addition to their team. His dossier claimed that he had only been in the Army for a short time but Craig wondered about the accuracy of the file. Brett had the bearing of a military man. He came across as friendly enough, but he played things real close to the vest.

Manny finally broke the silence. "Captain, my wife and I don't feel safe down here."

"I know you're upset by what happened," Craig told them. "So am I. And I understand your fear. But we have safety measures in place to protect you."

"Those 'safety measures' didn't protect Danny," Mitchell pointed out.

"What happened to Danny was an accident."

"The captain is correct," Jackie announced, her voice brisk and businesslike. "It was a tragedy, but it should also serve as a lesson. Follow all procedures at all times. They're there for a reason."

"Danny wasn't careless," Kim said. "He knew what he was doing."

"We don't know what happened," Craig said. "Sebastian's going through the data as we speak to see if he can find out what went wrong."

"I feel like we're not doing enough," Trisha said.

Jackie shook her head. "The procedure is to seal the area and not do anything. Once the quarantine period has passed, an investigation will be made."

"She's right," Craig said. "None of us are trained in this kind of work."

"So we're just supposed to sit around with our thumbs up our butts?" Manny asked. "That's bullshit!"

"He's right," Trisha said. "We need to do *something*."

"What do you think went wrong?" Brett spoke up tentatively.

Craig sighed. "He could have been careless. There could have been a tear of some kind, or he didn't check the seals on the vials. Some of the vials may have been old."

"The monkey could've turned on him," Mitchell said.

Craig forced himself not to snap at the tall biologist. This wasn't a joking matter.

"It couldn't have been a tear," Trisha pointed out. "He wasn't wearing a biohazard suit."

"Is it because it's an older facility and it's wearing out?" Kim asked. "Is that what killed Danny?"

Brett glared at Craig. "If that's the case, we shouldn't have sealed the exits."

Jackie replied before Craig had a chance to speak. "They're already sealed, and they will *stay* sealed until this is over. It's standard procedure."

"Great," Brett muttered in disgust.

"We all knew the risks working down here."

Tony, who had been quiet during the entire exchange, suddenly spoke up. "I don't think it was an accident. We all know which virus killed him. It was that bitch, Keres' Eyes. Only, no one had been working on Keres' Eyes in Lab 6—"

"Are you sure about that?" Craig asked.

"We can go back and check, but I'm almost positive. I think Danny was murdered."

Everybody began talking at once, their voices quickly rising in alarm. Craig's eyes had kept going back to Trisha, hypersensitive to her presence, but as the argument grew, Craig exchanged a glance with Mouse. This was what he had been referring to.

"That's enough," Craig said, forced to raise his voice in order to be heard. "He wasn't murdered. As tragic as it sounds, his death was an accident. Period."

"I sure hope you're right," Manny growled.

"Do we need to set up some sort of guard?" Jill asked.

"Stop, all of you," Craig said. "If we keep thinking this way, we're no longer going to be a 'team'—"

"You think I want to be a part of a killer's team?" Mitchell asked.

"Look, you need to calm down. You're smart people. So *think*. Danny had helped develop Keres' Eyes and had been working on a number of potential vaccines. He could have taken a vial in there with him, then either forgot about it, dropped it, or something else. Right now, we just don't know—but if you all start becoming too paranoid to work together, we'll never find out!"

The others grew quiet again as Craig's words echoed in the room. He took a deep breath and tried to calm down.

"What do you need us to do?" Trisha asked in a quiet voice.

"Focus on your work," he told them. "We have a number of projects underway in various stages. Don't abandon them because of Danny's death. But just to be safe, don't handle anything too dangerous right now. Finish up your existing projects, then focus on paperwork. I'm sure there are plenty of reports to write up."

"What about Danny?" Kim asked.

"We can't act like nothing happened," Jill said.

Craig felt everyone staring at him. This was the crux of it.

He swallowed.

CHAPTER 4

Craig followed the group as they walked out of the Dining Hall. Much to his relief, they split up, following his orders to return to their work.

He turned around and found Trisha approaching him. She looked incredible, as always. He smiled his first real smile since the alarms had gone off.

"Hi," he said.

She stole a quick glance around. "Hi."

"How are you holding up?"

"I was just about to ask you the same thing."

"I've been worried about you."

"Same here." She hesitated, but didn't say more.

Craig caught the hesitation, opened his mouth, but held back. This wasn't the time or place. *It never will be, for you.* Before he could say anything, he saw her tense.

"There you are," Mitchell cried as he emerged from the Dining Hall. "Ready to go tackle this green monster? I figured I'd use you as bait."

"What?" she asked.

"You know, to slay the dragon. You can play the damsel in distress. I figured you would look much better in a dress than I would."

A sigh escaped Craig's lips.

Mitchell heard the sigh. "Right. Well, let's get going before our slave master of a boss decides to whip us."

"OK." She turned to Craig. "See you later."

He nodded. "You hang in there." He cringed as soon as the words came out, turned and quickly walked away.

As he headed towards the security corridor that led to the lab area, he caught movement out of the corner of his eye. He turned his head in time to see Jackie at the other end of the lengthy hallway that ran between the Dining Hall/Kitchen and the Mechanical Room, ducking into the supply closet. He frowned, wondering what she was doing, but then put it out of his mind. Obviously she was getting supplies.

Danny's death was really messing with his head. He felt guilt for not being there for Danny, for requesting the transfer ... for a lot of things. It seemed as if he had let everybody down.

He entered the security corridor, a ridiculous design that had been integrated into the floor plan. The corridor was a narrow hallway between Security Room 1 and Lab 2, designed to be easily defendable—and could be sealed off at the touch of a button. Craig doubted they would ever have a security breach this far down. If someone made it down this far, then either the person was meant to be here or was too powerful to be stopped.

When he walked into the Computer Lab a few moments later, he found Sebastian hard at work. Craig depended on Sebastian immensely and was not ashamed to show it. Sebastian was not only their Senior Scientist, with more letters behind his name than seemed possible, but also their lead programmer—although he didn't look like a computer geek. In fact, he looked like a European actor, with flowing hair and flawless teeth. He even had a tan, an impressive feat when living underground the majority of the year.

He was also condescending and arrogant. The man could be impatient, snobbish and even rude, but he knew his field. He had been responsible for over half of the advancements the lab had made in the past five years.

"How's it coming?"

Sebastian paused only long enough to see who had come in. "Slow," he admitted in a distracted voice. "I have to weed out the data from each sensor, discount for the false-positives and then do an algorithm to determine the stream of infection."

Craig frowned as he rubbed the side of his jaw. "What will that show you?"

"It should give me a good idea of where the virus came from."

"What do you mean?"

"The assumption is that the virus came from Lab 6. I am making sure that this assumption is correct." He suddenly pushed his chair over to another monitor. With a flick of his wrist, he pointed at the screen. "I'm also running a database listing the location of every virus in the level. That way we'll know what was in Lab 6."

"You mean other than Keres' Eyes?"

"Are you sure that's what attacked Danny? It could have been another type of microbe, one that had somehow gotten out and then mutated, coincidentally mimicking Keres' Eyes. If we don't even know the type of microorganism, then we don't really know anything, do we?"

Craig crossed his arms. "Except for the fact that Danny's dead."

Sebastian paused and looked up at him again. "Of course."

Craig was glad to hear Sebastian's voice lose some of its haughtiness. "I understand what you're getting at, but I don't think it's a valid point. The odds of some other virus mutating into a mimic of Keres' Eyes are astronomical."

"I suppose—"

"Sebastian, I need to know what happened in there. You've reviewed the video, right? Did you see anything out of the ordinary?"

"No. I've thought of scanning the film for heat signatures, but that won't tell us anything."

"What about the sensors in Lab 6? Have you analyzed the air content and concentration of virus?"

Sebastian frowned. "Some of the readings I'm getting concern me. One sensor shows a high concentration, while another shows none."

"But the area is bathed in ultraviolet light, right?"

"It should be—the lights kicked on when the alarms went off—but either the light isn't blanketing the entire area or the microbe is immune."

"So the area still may be hot?"

"The sensors could be wrong. But yes, it appears so."

Craig leaned forward, his eyes blazing. "I need to know what happened. I need to know where the bug came from and whether it's safe."

Sebastian nodded.

"Also, check the sensors in the surrounding area; make sure the virus hasn't spread. And I want to know how Danny got infected in the hallway. He should have been infected in Lab 6, not out in the hall."

"I assume it followed him. Either that, or he became infected right before he walked out of the lab."

Craig leaned closer. "Find out."

*   *   *

"He thinks I'm a clown."

"Who does?"

Mitchell sighed. "Craig. He doesn't take me seriously. I feel like Rodney Dangerfield—no respect."

They turned past the conference room and entered the courtyard.

"Craig respects you."

Mitchell turned back to her. "Did you see the way he shut me down back there?"

"He's stressed out. We all are." She pushed him to get him moving again. "He gave you this assignment, didn't he?"

"That's just because of my good looks."

Trisha rolled her eyes as she followed him past Lab 9 and down the hallway towards the entrance to Lab 7. After a moment, she laughed. "I'm sure that's why the Army hired you, to brighten up our dungeon. And if you're buying that one, I've got some real estate to sell you."

Mitchell stopped so abruptly Trisha almost ran into him.

"What are you doing?" she asked as he stared through the glass into Lab 7.

"Looking at the sensors."

"Do you see any flashing?"

He hesitated. "Not that I can see ..."

With an impatient huff, she moved around him and slapped the doorplate.

Mitchell let out a yelp of surprise as the door began to open.

Each door in the laboratory-side of the facility was the same: reinforced steel with a thick window in it, designed to minimize the risks inherent in working with lethal viruses. To Trisha, they looked like something out of an old science fiction movie, but without them, she, Mitchell and everyone else would have to wear biohazard suits at all times.

When she hit the doorplate, the computers released the air pumped into the rubber tubing that ran along each edge and then the door slid open, like on a spaceship. They were crazy. Every time she triggered one of them, she expected to see Captain Kirk appear.

Mitchell complained—rather theatrically—that it was dangerous being in here as he followed her into the lab. Behind them, the door closed and the tubing inflated, resealing the room. "We have to find out why Danny died," she said.

"How do you know it's safe?"

"Do you hear any alarms?" When he didn't reply, she turned and made her way to the window set in the wall between Lab 6 and Lab 7.

She placed her hands on the window ledge as she leaned forward, her eyes taking in the scene before her.

The room looked like a tornado had touched down. Paper was scattered everywhere. Glass vials had been knocked off one of the tables, leaving the floor littered with broken glass. A stack of folders had been knocked over. A Bunsen burner, luckily unlit, dangled from a side counter and the microscope next to it, half covered with paper, laid on its side.

Trisha focused on those items as much as possible. She had spotted the monkey but couldn't bear looking at it. The animal, one of dozens kept down here for experiments, laid in a pool of its own blood, curled into a ball, its back twisted to the side in a final testament to the agony it had suffered. The chain, partly lying in the pool of blood, was still attached to its neck. Its cage had been knocked over, open and empty.

"You idiot, Danny," Mitchell muttered beside her. "You left the chain too long."

Trisha shuttered. They knew that Keres' Eyes affected humans and monkeys in the same way, with one exception: while an infected human would begin to convulse, as Danny had done, an infected monkey would become violent, destroying everything it could get its hands on before succumbing to the virus.

"Do you think the monkey inadvertently unleashed Keres' Eyes?"

"He had to have," Trisha said softly. "It's the only way it could've happened."

Mitchell sighed. "Poor bastard. He let the monkey go unsupervised, and the animal, probably pissed off from always being locked up started breaking things—"

"Including a vial containing Keres' Eyes?"

Mitchell shrugged.

Trisha glanced at him. "Danny wouldn't have left the virus sitting out though, right?"

"He left the monkey unsupervised. I never thought he would've done something like that. We've all been through enough training to know never to leave the animals unsupervised, especially the monkeys. They're clever bastards." Mitchell fell silent for a moment. "You think he was going to infect it?"

"Maybe it's worse than that. Maybe Danny didn't even realize Keres' Eyes was in the lab."

"I still don't know if it's safe in here."

"If it wasn't, we'd already be dead."

In a distracted voice, he asked, "How big is Keres' Eyes?"

"Two to three microns."

"Great."

She noticed that he was staring down at the caulking that sealed the window. She didn't see any visible cracks, but the caulking looked old, dingy. The entire place looked worn out.

She turned her attention back to Lab 6, struggling to figure out how the accident had happened. Everyone was depending on them.

*　　*　　*

Craig was walking towards the exit to the level, to check on the locks, when he heard Sebastian call his name. He stopped and turned around, expecting to see his friend, but he was alone in the hallway.

Her throaty laughter slipped into Craig's mind, the memory of her body making his hands ache for her.

Sebastian spoke again. "Are you there?"

Craig realized Sebastian's voice came from a nearby phone. "You used the cameras to find me, didn't you?"

"No. Tony told me where you were. We have a problem."

Craig lifted the handset, turning off the speaker. "What is it?"

"The seals were breached."

"Wait. What seals?"

"The ones for the door to Lab 6, the ones that are supposed to prevent anything from escaping," Sebastian told him in a quick, harried voice. "The seals were breached—which obviously allowed Keres' Eyes into the hallway where it attacked Danny."

Craig's mind was spinning. "How could that be? The computer monitors them, makes sure they inflate."

"The computer only inflates them to a predetermined level. It can monitor the air pressure, but it's not designed to compensate."

"Compensate for what?"

"For a hole."

Craig glanced down the hallway. Luckily, he was alone. "What are you telling me, Sebastian?"

"A hole must have formed in the seals, causing them to deflate. It wouldn't need to be big. It might be too small to see with the naked eye. But once the seals' integrity was breached, the virus could enter the hallway.

"I had a feeling that's how it happened," Sebastian went on. "It was the only reason I could come up with that explained why Danny had died in the hallway. So I checked the data, and it showed that the air pressure started to decrease moments after he left the lab."

"Wait. Are you saying that Keres' Eyes somehow *ate through* the rubber?"

"Pretty sure," Sebastian hedged. "It's how the numbers would look. I don't know how else the seals could have been breached."

"How could a virus eat through rubber?" Craig wondered aloud. He started to get angry. "None of the agents we work on can do that."

"The virus could have mutated, especially if it had been exposed to low levels of UV rays. Instead of breaking it down, the UV rays would have altered it. Remember, we're working with organic material here. Much more dangerous and unpredictable than chemical agents."

"That means Lab 7 could become infected. The seals on that door could fail as well."

CHAPTER 5

With a frown burrowing into his forehead, Tony typed the message again and hit ‹Send›. He stared intently at the screen, waiting for the computer to indicate that the message had been sent. He shook the mouse, hit the keyboard again, but the screen didn't change. He growled in frustration.

"What's the problem?"

Tony glanced at Brett, his eyes flickering with suspicion. "When did you come in?"

"Just in time to hear you swearing at the computer. Can I help?"

Tony glanced behind him, but the two men were alone in Security Room 1. "Not unless you're a computer whiz."

Brett's smile widened. "No more than the next guy. What's wrong with the system?"

Tony hesitated. "It keeps locking up. I've tried everything but I can't get it to work."

"You've rebooted?"

"Three times."

"Who are you trying to contact?"

"The security team on the surface. Every time I try, this stupid thing freezes. It's irritating as hell. The other programs seem to work, but I can't reach the surface."

"Still having problems?" Jackie asked as she entered the room. She paused when she saw Brett.

"Yeah," Tony grumbled. "I hate computers. They never do what you want."

Brett grinned at Jackie. "Do you know how to fix it?"

"What do I look like?" she asked, her glare forcing the smile from Brett's face. She turned back to Tony. "Have you asked Sebastian for help?"

"He said he was checking into it."

"Has this happened before?" Brett asked. Tony shook his head absently. "Maybe they're sending down a large file, which is interfering with the transmission."

Tony ignored him. "You complete the checklist?"

"Not yet," Jackie replied. "I'm going now to finish. Keep trying to reach the surface. They need to know what's going on."

"Right."

Brett followed Jackie out. "Can I help?"

She hesitated. "Sure." She walked through the security corridor without bothering to see if he was following.

When they entered the kitchen, Brett asked, "What are you doing?"

"Following protocol," she said as she approached the over-sized pantry.

"And protocol says you're to make a sandwich?" he joked.

"We need to make sure all food containers are properly sealed. Ones that aren't are to be thrown away."

"Why? And what's the big deal, anyway?"

"The food may be contaminated," she told him as patiently as she could manage. "Do you want to eat contaminated food?" When he shook his head, she turned and began to check the containers.

Brett joined her. He pointed out the ones that were questionnable and let her decide which ones to throw away. "I still don't understand why we're doing this," he blurted out a few minutes later.

"Because we're in lockdown. Protocol says we must ration all food to ensure we'll have enough to eat."

"And if we don't?"

"Then we're all going to get real hungry."

"You serious?'

"We take the incubation period of our slowest-acting agent and add an extra week. If after that time, no one shows signs of infection, we'll be able to leave. It's already programmed into the system."

"How long are we talking?"

"Two months."

He swallowed. "But there's some sort of emergency exit, right? Just in case?"

"No," she said. "Think of this place like a submarine, deep underwater. And submarines don't have emergency exits, do they? Neither do we."

*   *   *

Still disconcerted by Sebastian's news, Craig headed back through the labs towards his office.

Sebastian had checked the seals to Lab 7 while they had talked. He hadn't seen any change in pressure. "But I can't tell if the virus is attacking it," Sebastian had admitted. "The UV rays in the lab are too weak to destroy every strand. We're still getting some positive readings from a couple sensors."

Craig had let loose a string of expletives. There was a danger the virus could continue to spread, conceivably moving from room to room, eating through the rubber seals. Even if they managed to stop Keres' Eyes, another virus could break lose. There were so damn many weapons here. It was worse than working in a nitroglycerin factory. At least you could see that. These killers would slip inside you and sign your death warrant before you ever had a chance to react—

Just like they had been designed.

He was not in the mood to appreciate the irony.

As he turned down the hallway, he heard voices coming from the nearby Offices. The door was open and he was able to hear Manny and Jill talking to Kim. He was about to turn away when he heard Kim getting upset at the mention of Danny's name. As Craig listened, he discovered that she and Danny had been an item for the past few months.

No wonder she had reacted so strongly to Danny's death.

He grimaced. He was the boss, yet he didn't know everything that went on around here. Not a comforting thought.

He walked into the room—but before he could say anything, Manny spotted him. "Captain, have you learned any more about, um, the accident?"

Craig glanced at Kim, then turned to Manny and Jill. "Sebastian believes that the seals failed on the door to Lab 6," he said in a quiet voice. "He thinks that's why Danny died in the hallway."

"My god," Jill whispered.

"It's still safe, though, right?" Manny asked.

"I don't wanna alarm you, but we simply don't know. Sebastian is monitoring the situation as best he can."

"We should at least remove the animals, send them to the surface. We can't expose them unnecessarily."

"Manny, we have more important things to worry about right now, namely our own survival."

"But they've suffered enough! It's cruel to put them—"

"We can't. We're locked down here too. We have to worry about us for right now, and wait for the containment period to end."

"We can't stay here and not do anything," Jill spoke up as Manny turned away in disgust.

Kim nodded. "She's right. We need to figure out what happened."

Craig saw the determination on her face. "I know you want to help, but we need to be cautious."

"This is bullshit," Manny hollered, turning back. "We need to *do* something. We can't just sit around here with our thumbs up our asses!"

Kim frowned at Craig. "That doesn't make any sense. You let Mitchell and Trisha go into Lab 7. Why can't we get involved?"

"What did you say?" he asked incredulously.

"You told them to investigate, so they went into the adjoining lab. They're in there right now—"

"Get them on the phone," he ordered. "Tell them to get the hell out of there!"

Before they could respond, Craig whipped around and raced out of the room. How could he have been so stupid? He felt like he was in some sort of demented race that he'd lost with his first step.

He ran up to the door to Lab 7, pressed his face against the glass, and spotted Trisha and Mitchell staring through the window into Lab 6. He closed his eyes for a moment, relieved that she was all right—that *they* were all right. The seals were holding ... for now. He reached for the doorplate but stopped. He told himself to consider what was best for the group. He hated to think that way, but he had to.

The memory of Danny's death flashed through his mind, demanding an answer.

He was not the type to take unnecessary risks and blindly charge forward, but as he watched Trisha, inches away from a virus-infected room with only a pair of seals older than his car protecting her—seals that could be disintegrating—he felt something stir inside of him. He wasn't sure what it was, what had awoken. He was unable to identify it, but it made him uneasy.

He impatiently thrust his thoughts aside and slapped his hand against the doorplate. Trisha and Mitchell turned as the door opened and he walked into the lab.

"Hey boss," Mitchell said. Trisha smiled in greeting.

"Hey. How are things?" he asked, struggling to keep his voice level.

"You should check this out. The room's a mess."

The phone rang. It was Manny. Craig was amazed it had taken them so long to call. Then his cheeks flushed. They must've thought he had lost it. He'd been frantic to get Mitchell and Trisha out of the lab—yet here he was, standing beside them. Maybe he *was* losing it. "I'll take care of it."

He hung up and forced himself to walk up to the window. "Are you two OK?"

They both said they were. He nodded absently as his eyes scanned the sensors placed strategically throughout the room. He hoped to God that they were working—not that it would probably do any good.

He walked out of the lab without saying another word. He went around to where Danny had died, stopped in front of the emergency door and took in the grisly scene. Danny was sprawled on the floor, his body at an unnatural angle.

The feeling Craig had experienced came back, stronger than before. Still unable to identify it, he let it come unheeded; welcoming it in the hopes that it would break him out of his daze.

As the feeling pounded inside his brain, he realized that the rest of his team was just as frustrated and angry as he was. If he didn't do something soon, they would. He didn't think they would listen to him much longer anyway ...

"Are you sure about this?" he'd asked, words still echoing in his mind from that fateful night like a siren calling to him.

"I'm a grown woman. I make my own choices."

"I may not be the man you think."

"You saying I could regret it?"

"Everyone has secrets. I'm no different."

His warning had been too accurate. Unfortunately neither of them had listened. His reaction the morning after he'd slept with her had been deplorable, and he'd only made it worse by bailing on her the way he did. He couldn't stop thinking about how he'd run—and couldn't stop thinking about that night. It became a fantasy to him, a legend that lingered in his heart. When she'd first walked into his office a year later, the newest addition to his team, it was as if she'd walked out of his dreams. But it wasn't his mind playing tricks on him. It was really her. If there was any doubt, the look of hurt on her face when she saw him was proof that she was real. Hurt and something else. He didn't know what that other look was and knew he'd lost the right to ask. Staring at her, he wanted to say something, to explain his actions, but he didn't know the right words.

After he recovered from his shock, and as he was still trying to come to grips with the realization that his fantasy woman was now sleeping a few doors away from him every night, Craig discovered that the attraction between them, the delicious tension, was still there. Stronger than before. Torturing him. Calling to him.

He wasn't about to give in. He wasn't going to become his father.

He abruptly turned and began searching for his second-in-command. He found her in the hallway on the opposite side of the facility, heading towards the Med Unit.

"Stop what you're doing. I need you to set up a staging area in Lab 7. We'll need the portable shower brought in and clothing areas set up."

Jackie looked at him with wide eyes. "Are you serious? You're taking a huge risk—"

"I know," he said. "Set it up."

"What's going on?" Tony asked as he came over.

Craig turned to face him. "We're going in."

CHAPTER 6

Mouse stood in the shadows, quietly seething. "They have it out for me. Turned on me, cut me in the back."

Born William Poole, he had never been comfortable around people, so he had turned to machines. He was not blessed with any special talent, however, and had struggled to learn how things operated. He had finally learned how most machines worked, although he still struggled on occasion. And he still didn't understand people.

"How could they turn on me?" he whispered.

He wrung his hands. As a kid, he'd gnawed on his fingers whenever he got nervous. Years of working with machinery, with his hands coated in grease, had finally broken him of that habit, so now he wrung his hands instead.

Hidden from view, he watched the team with interest—and apprehension. A part of him wanted to tell Craig, to warn him, but he got nervous talking to people, Craig most of all. His fear used to be so bad he'd stutter every time he was forced to speak, and he still felt a bolt of fear on occasion. But these were his friends. That belief had enabled him to function more normally.

He didn't feel normal anymore.

His breath caught as he watched the scientists going in and out of Lab 7. They were in danger. They'd been betrayed.

From where he stood, he could see part of Danny's body. He couldn't stop staring at it. He'd never seen a corpse before. It didn't seem real to him, like it was a prop in a movie. He kept waiting for Danny to move, to stop pretending to be dead, but Danny hadn't moved for the past twenty minutes.

The thought that Danny might actually be dead scared him.

He heard a commotion and turned to look. Tony and Mitchell were dragging a contraption towards Lab 7, a chaotic bundle of tubes and plastic sheeting. Craig directed them into the lab and told them to set up near the door to Lab 6, then turned back to the phone. Mouse knew he was talking to Sebastian to get suggestions for setting up the room. Craig had told Mouse to gather as many portable viral sensors as possible, to act as another layer of alarm, but Mouse had forgotten. He was too upset.

He had poured his soul into this place. He knew it was struggling, that some parts of the lab should be replaced. The others didn't realize—or took for granted—all he did to keep them alive. But to be betrayed like this ...

Craig told Sebastian to positively pressurize Lab 7. Mouse jerked with surprise. That was smart. By pressurizing Lab 7, none of the air from Lab 6 would be able to escape into the adjoining lab when they opened the door. Since each room had its own separate air control, Mouse knew Sebastian could do as Craig asked. And that was part of the reason for the maze-like structure. Another reason was the huge tanks overhead, used to negatively pressurize the chambers that some labs had.

The vacuum and HVAC systems weren't the only controls down here, though. There were controls all over the place, much more than had originally been designed.

Mouse grew agitated as he looked at the emergency door that had materialized seemingly out of nowhere. He'd known about the doors in the security corridor that could seal off the lab area, but were there other emergency doors? Were they throughout the level? And if there was a major accident, would they all trigger, closing everyone off from each other, trapping them and leaving them helpless?

The thought made him shiver. He didn't want to die alone.

He knew he didn't know all of the secrets imbedded in this underground complex, but he thought he'd known the important ones.

Obviously, he'd been wrong. Wrong about a lot of things.

Still wringing his hands, he slipped into the shadows.

* * *

Thirty minutes later, the staging area was complete.

Craig immediately ordered Tony and Jill to leave. He didn't want his people in there any longer than necessary. Even though he'd decided to do this, he didn't trust the seals.

As Tony walked out, Mitchell came up to Craig. "You sure you want us to go in?"

Craig glared at him. "We've been through this."

Mitchell nodded and turned away.

The phone rang. Craig picked it up. "What?" he barked.

"I've finished pressurizing the room," Sebastian told him. "It's now at plus-forty percent."

Craig thanked him, hung up and, after Jill left, made sure everything was ready. The chemical shower was up and running, the dressing area was complete, and portable ultraviolet lights had been placed facing the door to Lab 6. The main labs had ultraviolet lights actually installed inside the rooms and tied into the alarm detection system, which would trigger at the first sign of detection, but the system was expensive and could be hazardous to scientists if they were exposed to the light for long periods of time. As a result, only Labs 1, 2 and 3 had the system, as did the Level entrance and exit. The portable lights Craig's team had brought in helped, but they didn't blanket the entire area like the installed lights did. Still, it was better than nothing.

Satisfied, Craig turned to Manny and Mitchell. "Get started."

The two men began to put on biohazard suits, pulling them on over their clothes. Craig had initially planned to go in himself, but he was still fuming over the argument he'd had with Trisha. He didn't think he would be able to focus on the task at hand.

He turned and left the room before they'd finished getting ready.

Jill stood in the hallway, nervously watching the two men dress. Jackie, standing next to her, opened her mouth when she saw Craig—but closed it again when he shot her a look of warning.

He turned his back on her and watched the two men through the window. Manny and Mitchell, fully suited in their biohazard gear, approached the door leading to Lab 6. After a moment of hesitation, Mitchell reached up and slapped the door-plate. The door opened and the two men cautiously walked inside.

*　　*　　*

Trisha was in Lab 3, her cheeks bright with anger. She wasn't helpless, dammit. She didn't deserve to be treated like that—and in front of everyone! She was mortified that so many people had witnessed their argument.

She banged on the keyboard, taking out her frustration on the computer.

She found herself on the verge of tears, which made her angrier. She wouldn't cry. She'd done enough of that in the past to last her a lifetime.

She finished inputting the search parameters and instructed the computer to begin. As the mainframe gathered the requested data, Trisha sat back and crossed her arms. She couldn't help thinking about Craig. He could infuriate her so badly at times—and this was a prime example. After deciding to send a team into Lab 6, he had declared that she wasn't allowed to participate. At first, she couldn't believe her ears. "Are you kidding?" She asked.

"No. I'll accompany Mitchell and provide whatever support he needs."

"I'm perfectly capable of helping Mitchell if he needs it," she told him, her shock turning to anger.

"We don't know what we'll find," he said. "It would be irresponsible of me to allow women into such a grisly scene."

"Oh please. Now you're forbidding my entire *gender*—?"

"Just at first."

"Fine," she said. "I'll be right outside. As soon as you come out, I'm going in. Or do you want to blindfold me so my delicate senses don't suffer?"

"That's enough," Craig said, his eyes flickering towards the others.

"No, it's not! Why can't I go in there? I'm just as much a part of this team as Mitchell."

"Because I said so."

She wanted to scream.

"Jill isn't allowed in there either," he added. "Neither is Jackie. I may be old-fashioned, but until I know it's safe, Mitchell and I will be the only two allowed in either lab."

"*Either* lab? You mean I can't even go into Lab 7!?"

"No, and that's final."

She almost *did* scream—but then she saw the fear in his eyes. It did little to calm her. She was scared too.

It was a familiar feeling.

She'd gotten married while still in college to a man who became threatened by her intelligence. He'd started drinking—and then became violent, as if his fists could make up for his lower IQ.

Trisha felt her mind drifting down the dark path of memories that made up her marriage and quickly pulled back. It had been bad enough going through it once. She didn't need to relive that horrific time.

The marriage ended two years later, but it took her a long time to get over the abuse she'd suffered. Left with nothing but scars—and an advanced degree in bioengineering and virology— she threw herself into her work. She felt safe there, able to control her life. Because of her looks, however, she still got hit on. She rebuffed every advance, determined to remain single.

She'd picked a lonely road to travel, but for the first few years, she was content. She didn't meet anyone who changed her mind—until she met the one man who did.

Like the rest of her life, that didn't go as she had hoped.

More determined than ever to focus on her career, she got into a unique specialty that brought her to the attention of some powerful people. But she hadn't done it for exposure. She'd had enough with unwanted attention.

The Army made her an interesting offer, and she accepted. After a few months of background checks and security clearances, she was sent down here to this secret, underground laboratory... where her life became excruciatingly complicated. She wasn't the type of woman to even think of sleeping with her boss. She wasn't that stupid, and positions of authority didn't attract her. But Craig did. Damn him for being her boss, for avoiding her when they'd first met, even though she understood now why he'd done it. Damn him.

Movement caught her eye. When she glanced up, she discovered that the computer had finished compiling the information she had requisitioned on Keres' Eyes. A three-dimensional computer model slowly rotated on the screen, showing her the design of the lethal virus.

She studied the image with a professional eye. She had seen it before, but that had been before it had struck down one of her colleagues. Looking at it now, it gave the impression of an evil and sinister creature.

She had wanted to see the virus not only out of morbid curiosity but because she was a believer in knowing her enemy—a lesson from her ex-husband.

According to the computer, the pathogen had been created in this very facility by a team led by Sebastian. No surprise there. Sebastian led virtually every team. The history on file stated that the microbe had been fashioned out of two other microorganisms, with a little organic magic thrown into the mix. By exposing the organic material to certain chemical agents, it had mutated into its present form.

She quickly scanned through the rest of the information, which mainly consisted of dense graphs that charted the strength and speed of the microbe. As soon as the team had created the virus and proved they could make billions of copies, they had set out to find a cure.

So far, they had been unsuccessful.

Bringing up the search program, she instructed the computer to list all known locations of the Keres' Eyes virus. The computer listed the cryogenic storage nestled in the rear of Lab 1, and Lab 3's refrigeration unit. There were small samples in two of the chambers in Lab 2, as well as a small amount being used in an experiment in Lab 1. But nothing in Lab 6.

She frowned as she leaned forward, her hair cascading over her shoulder. She had fully expected Lab 6 to be on the list, and had figured that even if Danny hadn't personally been working on Keres' Eyes, someone else had been. But the computer claimed that the pathogen was nowhere near Lab 6.

It had to be that the virus wasn't supposed to have been there. She couldn't think of any other conclusion.

If that was the case, then how had Danny gotten infected? Where had it come from?

What was going on around here?

CHAPTER 7

The two men cautiously entered Lab 6.

As the door closed behind them, Manny was nearly over-whelmed by the carnage. He hadn't realized the full extent of the damage to the room, the blood and debris. He stood there for a few moments, his mouth hanging open, as his mind absorbed the scene before them.

Mitchell lifted the portable gas chromatograph and activated its sensors. The miniature device pulled in a small sample of air, broke down the airborne particles and checked their biological makeup. Within moments, the results flashed on the LED display.

"The room is still hot," he broadcast.

Manny nodded to show that he'd heard the transmission. They both wore biohazard suits, complete with built-in radios, but he felt extremely vulnerable. One tiny hole in his suit and he was a dead man.

He glanced over at Mitchell and saw a bead of sweat rolling down the side of his face. Good. At least he wasn't the only one afraid.

As well they should be. Neither of them had experience in this sort of thing, going into an infected room to find the source of contamination. Glancing around, he wondered if they would ever figure it out.

"What a mess," he muttered to himself, sweating heavily.

"What did you say?"

"Nothing. Let's get this over with."

Mitchell cautioned him to wait, but Manny didn't listen. He wanted to get this done with and get the hell out of here. He could imagine the millions of deadly particles floating in the air around him, trying to penetrate the thin material of his suit to get to his eyes, to feast and multiply before shooting into his brain.

With forced bravado, he started forward—

"*Freeze!*"

The strength of Mitchell's voice, the panic, caused Manny's muscles to lock up. His foot hung in the air, a few inches above the floor.

Mitchell grabbed his shoulder and yanked him back.

As Manny regained his balance, he looked at the ground before him. A thick shard of glass gleamed from the spot where he'd almost brought his foot down. Although their biohazard suits had rubber soles, the shard of glass ended in a wicked point that would have easily punctured his suit.

The realization of what had almost happened hit him hard. "Thanks," he said in a shaky voice. He looked at the floor—really looked—and his heart began to pound in his chest. Broken glass coated the entire room.

"We need a friggin' broom," Mitchell said.

Manny managed to nod as Mitchell went back into Lab 7 to get one. He pictured using a leaf-blower to clear out the lab—and immediately regretted it as he imagined the bits of glass slamming into the far wall, flying up into the air and then swarming around him like a pack of angry wasps, cutting his suit in dozens of places.

Mitchell returned with a small broom and quickly began to make a path.

Manny was supposed to take photographs, as if this was a crime scene, but he couldn't. He felt like he had to go to the bathroom. This was a place of death—and the longer they stayed here, the greater they risked suffering Danny's fate.

*   *   *

Craig watched Mitchell return to Lab 6 with the broom. When Mitchell had suddenly reappeared, Craig had demanded to know what was going on, but he regretted it. Mitchell had been shaken—something had happened, although he insisted they were both fine—and jumping on him had been uncalled for.

Craig stood in the hallway for another minute, then forced himself to leave.

Five minutes later, he entered the Dining Hall and found Sebastian at one of the tables near the Kitchen. "Mind if I join you?"

Sebastian nodded as he bent over his food.

Craig sat down and watched him for a moment. "Leftovers?"

"I didn't want to waste time making anything."

"Good call." Craig grew silent as his thoughts churned in his mind. "I've got a bad feeling about all of this."

Sebastian glanced at him before returning to his food.

"The others are having a tough time—not that that's surprising. But the tension in this place is ridiculous. I ... I feel like I'm missing something, like I'm letting everybody down. I don't know. Maybe I'm just too wound up."

"Danny's death has affected you."

"I'm the Commanding Officer. I can't afford to screw up." He'd done so many things wrong already. He should be shot.

Her voice floated into his mind again, torturing him. *"Come here."*

Chewing thoughtfully, the lead scientist looked at Craig. After he swallowed, he said, "You've been adequate. No major mistakes as far as I can tell, although you could be doing a better job."

Craig nodded, temporarily distracted by her voice from long ago. Frowned. "Danny's death is going to hit everybody hard. I don't think we've even seen the tip of it yet. Keeping them busy only works for so long. It's going to get ugly, you know. It's hard enough living down here as it is." He waited for Sebastian to reply, and became concerned when Sebastian remained silent. "What's wrong? You seem upset."

"I saw the letter regarding your promotion. Congratulations."

"You saw it?"

"I had to decode the message before it could be printed. I must admit I'm disappointed, but I guess it makes sense. Axiomatic, in fact. I lack the military background required to be Commanding Officer."

"I'm sorry. I really am—"

"I was surprised Jackie did not get the promotion. She's next in line."

Still trying to come to grips with the fact that Sebastian knew about his transfer, Craig said, "She would have been good as CO. I recommended her for promotion at her last review."

"It would have been easier to accept if Jackie had gotten the job. Instead, the Army in their infinite wisdom has decided to send someone down here who is clueless about what we do."

"You know the guy replacing me?"

"Not directly," Sebastian hedged. "I looked into him."

Unable to help himself, Craig leaned forward. "What did you find?"

"I pulled his file. He's a lot more military than you are. More uptight."

"It said that?"

Sebastian smiled at the skeptical look on Craig's face. "I read between the lines. He's a straight shooter, if the file is accurate. He doesn't have the experience to work down here, though, nor the background. I doubt he knows what he's getting into." As Craig absorbed the information, Sebastian's gaze intensified. "I suspect morale will degenerate further after he arrives."

Craig wanted to tell Sebastian he wasn't sure if he wanted the transfer, but he knew Sebastian would laugh. Craig would be a fool to turn it down.

Sebastian looked down at his food. "It seems I've lost my appetite."

"I'm sorry," Craig said. "I was going to tell you, but with Danny's death ..."

"You were under no obligation to tell me." He stood up. "If you will excuse me."

"Wait. Don't leave on my account."

"When are you going to tell the others?"

Craig hesitated. "I want to figure out what happened with Danny before I say anything."

"Fair enough. I will let you spread the word. I hate being the bearer of unsettling news."

*   *   *

On the other side of the underground structure, Tony finished his surveillance of the floor. He had checked the exit, the security alarms and the backup systems, gradually moving from one end of the facility to the other. All seemed to be in working order.

Satisfied, he left the offices and traveled the corridors, heading back towards Security Room 1. When he reached the Conference Room, though, he stopped. After a moment, he turned and walked over to the sealed-off hallway. He was relieved to find that Danny's body had finally been moved.

Shadows moved across the doorway to Lab 6. He couldn't see into the lab from where he stood, but he knew Mitchell and Manny were inside, sifting through the shattered remains. They would have left Danny's body in the room somewhere, probably inside the small chamber. His corpse would be contagious, a breeding ground for the bastard virus.

Tony turned and continued his journey. After he rechecked the security monitors, he would volunteer to go into Lab 6. They would need the help. It would take hours to go through all of the debris.

He walked into Security Room 1—and jerked in surprise. "What are you doing?"

Sebastian stood up. "I heard the bell ring. I thought it might be encrypted."

Tony wondered.

The main security room had a large desk—Tony's desk—facing a two-way mirror. The mirror allowed Tony to watch anybody who approached from the living quarters without the person knowing he was being watched. The room also had a couple of chairs, some file cabinets, and a jumble of equipment.

The secured line, the one used for important security transmissions, sat on a squat table that butted up next to the desk. It rang whenever a new message arrived.

"Did you read it?" Tony demanded.

"Of course."

Tony snatched the communiqué from the scientist's hand. When he digested the short message, he grunted.

"I agree," Sebastian said.

Tony hit the intercom button. "Captain, please report to Security Room 1." He took his finger off the button and glanced at Sebastian. "Where're you going?"

"I need to check the labs." With a sardonic grin, he added, "Make sure we're following protocol, of course."

Tony grunted again but Sebastian ignored him, his grin dropping from his face as he left. Instead of going back to the lab, he turned down the security corridor towards the living quarters. He ran into Craig a moment later.

"We just got notice from the surface," he confided. "They're sending down an investigative team to find out what happened."

Craig blinked. "Now? But the quarantine was just initiated."

"Indeed."

"When are they coming?"

"They've started down already. Should be here within a few hours."

Craig rubbed the side of his jaw. "I don't like this. The Army may be looking for a scapegoat." And were willing to break the lockdown protocol to do it, he didn't add. When they got down here, they weren't going to be too happy about Craig gambling with Mitchell's and Manny's lives—although he suspected that was going to be the least of his problems.

"Or they might decide to sweep Danny's body under the rug, so to speak."

"I want this resolved before they get down here."

"I'll get back to the lab right away," Sebastian said.

"Do whatever it takes."

CHAPTER 8

A short time later, Jill got a chance to inspect Lab 6.

She walked gingerly across the room, following her husband as he took her into the chamber.

Manny reached down reluctantly, glanced at her, took a deep breath, then pulled back the sheet he and Mitchell had found to cover Danny's corpse.

As he turned away, Jill knelt beside the body, taking in all of the visual clues. After a couple of moments, she leaned in so close that she was nearly touching Danny's face with her faceplate. With a gloved hand, she gingerly pulled down one of his eyelids and discovered that the blackness extended back and underneath the eyeball. She then checked the nasal passageways and the mouth.

It certainly looked like Keres' Eyes. All of the signs were there.

"Are you finished?" Manny asked.

She lifted her gaze, alerted by the sound of his voice. He looked like he was about to vomit. "Yeah."

With a sigh of relief, Manny quickly covered the body and led the way back into the main room.

The husband and wife team went to work, going through the vial fragments, looking for clues.

"I don't understand it," she said in an exasperated tone some time later. "I don't see any experiments that involved Keres' Eyes. Not unless I'm missing something."

"What about the seals on the door?" he asked.

She tilted her head in thought. That was the other major question she had—and the one that was their immediate concern. "I wish I knew, hon."

"Could it have been some sort of chemical reaction that caused the holes?"

"No. None of the chemicals in here could do that." Almost as an afterthought, she added, "Although there *are* some chemicals on this level that could."

He blinked. "Other chemicals?"

She dismissed his concern with a wave of her hand. "Nothing that would trigger microscopic holes. Those seals would've had to have been exposed over a period of time before they lost integrity. They're pretty thick."

He fell quiet as he digested her statement.

Now that Manny had brought up the subject, Jill turned to the door leading to the hallway. She didn't expect to see any holes with the naked eye—and she wasn't about to check every square inch with a magnifying glass. She frowned as her eyes followed the outline of the door. They appeared to be fully inflated, although that didn't mean much.

She turned back and looked at the room, mentally going through the catalogue of items they'd found. Then she turned back to the door and slapped the doorplate. Manny let out a gasp as the door opened. Jill ignored him as she walked into the hallway where Danny had died.

She stopped just outside the lab, taking everything in. Manny joined her before the door closed and stood uncomfortably behind her. Before he could suggest they return to the lab, she headed slowly down the hallway, inspecting the floor as she walked. "Make sure you're not tracking anything."

Manny's eyebrows bunched together. "Why? What are you doing?"

"Did you or Mitchell track anything into the hallway? Or find anything?"

"Other than Dan ... other than the body? No."

She reached the end of the hall and examined the large glass door that blocked off the passageway.

Manny asked, "Can we go back now?"

"In a minute."

She faced the bathroom, hesitated, then walked inside.

Manny let out a squeak of surprise but it barely registered. At first glance, the bathroom appeared normal. Jill walked over to one of the urinals, trying to trace Danny's final moments, then turned towards the sink.

The door opened behind her.

"Never seen a Men's Room before?" Manny joked in a strained voice.

The area underneath the sink was covered in shadows—but there was something lying on the floor. She was sure of it. She bent down, her eyes straining to see in the darkness.

"What is that?"

"I don't know. Did you bring a flashlight?" she asked.

"No."

Before he could stop her, she reached down to grab whatever it was and brought it into the light. To their amazement, Jill was holding a piece of glass. It seemed to have a film to it.

"Give it to me," he whispered.

"Why?"

"I don't want it to cut your glove."

She gently placed the glass in his hand, then inspected her glove.

"Anything?"

"No," she said after a few moments.

He sighed. "Don't pick up anything else, OK?"

She nodded absently. "We need to find out what that is. There's more down there," she said as she glanced underneath the sink. "A lot of small pieces and a couple bigger ones."

"I can grab some forceps and a tray—"

"Not now," she said, cutting him off as she headed to the door.

"You think this is important?"

"Very."

"Why was it here?"

Jill stopped at the door and looked back. "Good question," she said. "Maybe Danny brought it in here and accidentally dropped it."

"That doesn't make much sense."

"I know. We'll have to take this a step at a time." With a gleam in her eye, she added, "But I think we're on the right track."

*   *   *

"I've been looking for you," Craig said in a subdued tone. "I wanted to apologize for earlier. I ... didn't mean to treat you like that."

Trisha was amazed to feel her anger dissipate. She didn't know if it was the fact that Craig had apologized or that he looked like a little boy when he did it. "It's OK."

"Really?"

She smiled. "Really. Just ... treat me like the rest of the group, OK?"

He opened his mouth, hesitated, then nodded. "I'm glad. I don't like you pissed at me."

God, he still had that little-boy look on his face.

Unaware that her cheeks were flushed, she said, "Then don't upset me."

"I'll try not to."

She turned back to the computer to collect herself. She had been wrapped up in the data on Keres' Eyes, and when she'd discovered him standing next to her, she had been thrown speechless.

He was so near her body was humming. She felt lightheaded.

"So, what are you doing?" she asked, turning back to him.

"Looking for you," he said, hanging his head. "Apologizing for being so crass."

She bit the side of her lip. "You've been a naughty boy," she said in a husky voice.

His head jerked up in surprise. "What?"

"Maybe I shouldn't let you off so easy," she said, her voice normal this time. "Make you work for my forgiveness." She watched him struggle to understand. He seemed to know she was flirting with him, yet doubted it at the same time.

What was wrong with her? This was totally inappropriate, and he was her boss! She'd made so many mistakes with men—but she couldn't help herself. Craig was mysterious in a lot of ways, which made him damn near irresistible. She couldn't stand being around him and not touching him. His closeness right now was so tempting.

Almost as if he could read her thoughts, he took a step back. "What would you want me to do?"

She couldn't dare say what was on her mind. "Well," she said, dragging out the word, "what did you have in mind?"

"I could be a cook, um, for a week," he blurted. The moment he said it, he looked as if he regretted it.

Her eyebrows shot up. "A cook?"

"Um, well, or I could cook something, you know."

She wasn't sure she did. She'd been about to throw herself at him, but his response confused her. A cook?

Before he could explain, there was a tap on the glass. The two looked around and found Brett standing outside the door. Trisha tensed. Craig glanced at her, and then motioned him inside.

Trisha made herself busy while the two men discussed Brett's latest experiment. "Can you sign off on the results?" he asked Craig.

"In a minute. I'll meet you there."

Brett left and Craig turned back to Trisha. She looked up expectedly, hoping he would do something. Danny's sudden death had reminded her that life was too short. She wanted Craig to hold her, to comfort her, to make her feel safe and warm.

She opened her mouth to tell him how she felt. She'd had enough. She couldn't stand it, Army regulations be damned, his hesitation be damned.

Craig spoke before she could get the words out. "I wanted to, um tell you something. Before you found out from someone else."

She blinked. The tone of his voice made her pull back. "About the inspection team coming down?"

"No."

"What? Is something wrong?"

"I guess it's how you look at it," he told her with another grin. The grin faded quickly, however, and she instinctively straightened. "I've been promoted."

"Really! That's great!" Before she could stop herself, she stood and gave him a hug.

When their bodies touched, it was so powerful—and so unexpected—it jolted both of them. They forgot everything as they stood in each other's arms.

Unfortunately, Craig recovered first. He stepped back. "Well, that's the good news. The bad is that, um—"

Manny's voice suddenly issued from the speakerphone. "Trisha, have you seen Craig?"

She sighed. Never a moment alone. Then she saw the look on Craig's face. She wasn't going to like the rest of his news. "It's for you."

"Wait, I need to tell you—"

"Trisha? You there?" Manny asked.

Trisha whipped her head around, using her hair to shield her face. She slammed her finger on the button triggering the microphone. "Yeah, Craig's here."

"Oh. Can I, uh, Craig? You there?"

Craig sighed. "What is it Manny?"

"Jill and I found something. It appears to be a piece of glass, only Jill thinks it might be more than just that."

In an annoyed tone, Craig asked, "What are you talking about?"

"Well, we need to do some tests, but it's really weird glass. Jill thinks she heard about it once, back when she went to a conference a couple years ago."

"I'm sure you've found all kinds of glass in there," Craig said. "I don't see—"

"The glass was found in the bathroom. Where Danny was right before he died."

Craig made sure they were alone, then leaned in closer. "You think the glass is imbedded with Keres' Eyes?"

"Yeah. Well, that's what Jill thinks."

"It would explain how the virus got there," Trisha said. She quickly told Craig about her fruitless search on the computer.

Craig turned pale. "If that's the case, then we've been thinking about this all wrong. *I've* been thinking about it wrong. This wasn't an accident."

"Someone did this on purpose."

"Tony suggested it, but I couldn't believe it." He sounded like he had been sucker-punched.

Manny's voice came back on the speakerphone. "Boss? Jill wanted me to tell you she's not certain. We need to do some tests before she knows for sure."

"Do it. You need anything, you let me know. We keep this between us for now, got it? Absolutely no one is to know."

"Right." They could hear Manny talking to Jill. He came back to the phone and said, "Jill thinks we should seal off the room. There's more glass in the bathroom. We didn't get all of it."

"I agree. Until further notice, no one goes in there. If anyone complains, tell 'em to talk to me."

Manny hung up, and Craig covered his face with his hands. "Are you OK?" Trisha asked.

"No. Not at all."

"Talk to me."

He lifted his head—and she winced at the pain in his eyes. "Maybe they're wrong," she said.

"No. I know in my gut they're right. I just have a hard time accepting it."

"Who would have done it?"

"Brett. It has to be. No one else would've turned like this. Besides, no one knows him, not really. No one trusts him."

She gave a half-shrug. "He's new. It takes time to trust someone."

"Have you seen the way he watches everyone? It's like he's waiting for them to make a mistake or something."

Craig sounded like a man trying to convince himself. But what if he was right? "What do we do?"

He reached for the phone. "We check him out." He punched in the Computer Lab. "Sebastian? I need you to do something for me. I want you to look into Brett's background. ... I know we got a file on him when he first came here, but it wasn't complete. Seriously, it was mostly fluff. Can you look into his background, get the whole story? Yeah? Good. How fast? OK, we'll be waiting."

When he hung up, Trisha asked, "Can he do it?"

"He's on it right now."

An idea hit her. "Isn't Brett waiting for you?"

"Shit. Uh, OK, I'll sign off on his experiment, then get him busy on something else. I want him distracted—and I wanna make sure he stays away from Lab 6."

*   *   *

Mouse moved through the Mechanical Room, snaking his way towards the back. It was a dark, dirty place, crammed with machinery. The air, which vibrated with noise, was filled with the sharp smell of oil and grease, the blood of the equipment that enabled the scientists to live so far underground. But none of it bothered him. He was in his element here, moving with a confidence he lacked elsewhere in the Level. He ducked around piping that hid in the shadows and casually brushed past electrical lines he knew were shielded.

As he returned to his workstation, his face was strained with aggravation. He had been busy for the past hour, following wires that ran through the walls to find out where they led. It had been a long, frustrating process, and he still didn't have all the answers.

He sat down heavily on the stool, his eyes unfocused as he recalled what he had learned. After a few moments, he shook himself out of it. He was situated between two large workbenches that served as his desk, work area, file cabinet and sometimes his lunch table. The workbenches were littered with equipment, tools, scraps of material and other odds and ends. Almost hidden among the rubbish was a computer hooked into the central system.

Mouse pulled the keyboard towards him and hit the keys a few times until the monitor brightened. He hated to use the thing, even for small tasks. It never seemed to make his job "easier", and when he used it to run diagnostics, he didn't always believe the results. There was something unnatural about a machine that acted like it could think and respond independently. He knew that was how it was programmed, but still, he didn't like it. The thing mimicked people too closely.

He began to type, unaware that he was sneering at the monitor. The system quickly and accurately showed him the data he requested, almost as if it was seeking his approval, but he was unimpressed.

He had been inspecting the alarm system, following the wires from the wall sensors through the computer to the alarms, and had found more emergency doors like the ones that had trapped Danny. They were scattered throughout the facility, over twenty in all. But even though he'd found them, Mouse was still frustrated. It came down to the fact that the entire system was controlled by the central computer. He had never been trained on the computer side—other than the basic commands needed to run diagnostics, set output levels, etc.—and he didn't know how to make it tell him how to stop the doors from operating. He'd seen movies where machines turned on humans. If that happened, they would all be in big trouble.

Grasping at straws, he typed in a command, but a message flashed on his monitor stating that he wasn't authorized to turn off the alarm system.

He shook his fist at the screen.

He headed out of the Mechanical Room, wanting to inspect those doors again. They looked pretty big. He didn't know if they could be moved once they slid into position—and that glass was too thick to break.

If what he'd heard was correct, the seals might finally be failing. The nasty viruses they created down here could come after them. They'd be helpless. If he didn't figure out how to control the alarm system, the emergency doors could end up trapping them rather than saving them.

*   *   *

Trisha and Craig waited for Sebastian to send Brett's file to their computer. There had been an awkward silence ever since Craig had returned, filled with words left unspoken.

Like a sadistic torturer, Craig's mind flashed to their night together, to when they'd connected in the bar. She had looked so vibrant, so alive. She seemed to draw everyone to her, including him. He'd been helpless to resist.

That had seemed like a lifetime ago. A dream, nothing more now. He wouldn't let it.

"I didn't get to finish what I was going to tell you," he finally managed to get out.

She turned to him expectantly.

He took a deep breath. "Like I said before, the good news is that I'm being promoted." He swallowed. "The bad news is that, um, it means a transfer."

"What?"

"I'm being transferred. To the Pentagon. I'll be some sort of liaison working with the CDC. They're bumping me up to Lt. Colonel."

She sat back. "You're serious?"

He nodded.

When she didn't say anything, he talked in a rush. "It might end up being for the good," he said, voicing the tiny bit of hope that lingered in the back of his mind. "There are a lot of opportunities, not only if I stay in the military, but also in the bio-engineering field, like what you're—"

"Why don't you fight for what you want?"

He blinked. "What do you mean?"

"If you want to stay, why don't you? Just tell the Army 'no thanks'. It's not like we're at war. You don't have to go, right?"

He was speechless.

"Well?" she asked in an angry voice. "Am I wrong? Do you *have* to go?"

"It *is* the Army ..."

She stood and headed for the door.

"Wait. Where are you going?"

"Don't talk to me."

"Trisha," he called out. "Please, stop."

She turned. "What?"

She had a way of throwing him out of rhythm with a single comment, even just a glance. But the look she gave him now was one of warning. She was furious.

He knew he deserved this—it was probably for the best anyway, considering what he'd done—but he was paralyzed between what he had to do and what he wanted to do.

Like many kids, he'd been shocked and wounded when his parents had announced their divorce. He'd resisted the truth, but had finally been forced to accept the fact that no matter what he did or said, his family was breaking apart. Even so, he still tried, using everything from anger to tears to try to persuade his parents to stay together, until one night when his father had been arrested for assault. Craig's father, a successful businessman, had used his position to coerce subordinates to have sex with him, until one of his victims had gone to the police. His father's defense was that Craig's mother had become "frigid" and wouldn't let him come near her, as if that justified his horrible actions. In response,

Craig's mother had revealed her own affair with one of his father's business associates.

Craig hadn't spoken to his father since then, disgusted at the man's actions. Even though his mother had also betrayed their vows, Craig blamed his father, suspecting that the claims of abuse ran far deeper and longer than anyone knew, especially when Craig saw the lack of remorse or shame on his father's face.

That had been years ago, when Craig was still in high school. He had been on his own ever since, determined not to repeat his parents' mistakes. But now, all these years later, Craig found himself attracted to his new subordinate. It was the worst thing that could've happened. He would never become his father, he'd sworn. Never. Every woman who worked for him was completely off limits, without exception ... yet, he wanted Trisha so badly he could barely think at times. He felt as if he was coming unhinged, ripped between desire for her and his overwhelming need to never become anything like his father, a cold, selfish man who didn't care whose life he destroyed.

Looking at Trisha, he didn't know how to explain it to her, didn't know if he had the right to tell her of his need, and didn't want to reveal his shame. But he knew he should try. She deserved to know the truth. He opened his mouth to try to explain, to describe the battle that had raged inside of him ... but the words wouldn't come, weighed down by too many repressed emotions.

She slapped the doorplate and stormed out.

He started after her, but Sebastian's voice erupted from the speakerphone. "Craig? Did you get the email?"

Swearing under his breath, Craig turned to the computer and clicked on the email, then opened the attachment.

"Yeah, it's here."

"Good." Sebastian severed the connection.

Craig stared at the door. In his mind, he imagined rushing after her, stopping her ... and then what? What could he say to her? Anything other than the truth would sound like a lame excuse—and he couldn't admit the truth. Not to her. He could barely admit it to himself.

Clenching his jaw, Craig turned back and forced himself to focus on the computer screen.

Staff Sergeant Brett Collins was on his third rotation of active duty with the Army. Originally from Nevada, he had shown an initial aptitude in science and espionage, a mixture of abilities that surprised Craig. The Army had quickly developed Brett's abilities, training him for the Army's Intelligence unit.

The more Craig read about Brett's actual history, the more he became concerned. Brett had experienced a unique career path, starting out at Los Alamos before heading overseas to Germany and then to the Middle East. His record listed commendations for work in quite a few Middle Eastern countries, as well as "actions" in two of the former republics of the Soviet Union.

Upon his return to the United States almost two years ago, Brett had trained with the Rapid Response team for six months, learning the latest cutting-edge techniques for handling biological and chemical threats—but then had been assigned to three different agencies after that, places Craig had never heard of before. Obviously, this wasn't the first black-ops outfit Brett had worked with. Craig didn't know if he liked that.

He called Sebastian back and asked about the other agencies, but Sebastian couldn't identify them.

"Is there any way to find out what they are?"

"Not without looking suspicious," Sebastian admitted. "Is it critical?"

Craig rubbed the side of his jaw as his eyes lingered on the screen. "I'm not sure. The file doesn't go into enough detail to really know what Brett's been up to. What I really don't understand is why someone with his background ended up here."

"What do you mean?"

"He was being groomed for something. The Army wouldn't have invested all of that time and training just to throw him down here. So what are we missing?"

Before Sebastian could reply, alarms erupted throughout the level.

CHAPTER 9

Craig's stomach dropped. His fears about the seals degrading—and the threat of one of their own turning on them—ignited as the alarm sounded. He bolted out the door and headed towards Lab 7, but stopped in confusion. When Danny had died, the alarm had been localized. Not this time. The sound was all around him. He didn't know where to go.

Tony came running up the hallway. "Where's it coming from?" he roared.

Kim was right behind him, her face white with fear.

Before they reached him, Craig spun towards the Computer Lab. As soon as he reached the door, he slapped his hand on the doorplate and raced inside.

Sebastian was bent over one of the computer screens, typing furiously.

"What's going on?" Craig bellowed.

"Type in your password," Sebastian directed, pointing at the terminal next to him without bothering to look up. "You have to counter-acknowledge the alarm if you want to turn it off."

Craig frowned at his friend. It wasn't the answer he'd expected. He typed in his password, hit ‹Enter› —and the sirens stopped.

Behind him, Tony sighed.

"Why did the alarm go off?" Kim demanded.

"Is it Lab 7?" Craig asked.

Sebastian swiveled in his chair to face him. Tony and Kim had followed Craig into the Computer Lab. As he opened his mouth to reply, Jackie entered as well, her jaw tight with concern.

"The warning wasn't for our Level," he explained. "It was for Level II. I'm not sure whether it was a breach of some kind, an accident or what, but the computer is saying that the Level is infected."

"The entire Level?" Craig asked incredulously.

"Most of it. The alarm went off as a precautionary move, to warn us."

Mouse squeezed into the crowded room. "What happened?"

As Kim told him, Craig glanced at the others. "OK, excitement's over. Everybody go back to what you were doing. We're fine down here, right?" he asked, glancing at Sebastian.

He nodded. "Our status has not changed."

As the team reluctantly began to leave, Craig leaned towards Jackie. "Would you spread the word, let the others know we're OK?"

"Try the Exit," Tony suggested. He stayed where he was, having ignored Craig's advice. "Whoever's not here probably bolted straight for the elevators, wanting the hell out of here."

"They're not the only ones," Kim said under her breath as she turned to leave. She followed Jackie out and the door shut behind them.

Craig turned back to Sebastian. "Talk to me."

"It has to be some sort of massive infection," Sebastian told him. He began typing again. "Everybody on the Level's being evacuated. They're going to be put in quarantine for the next few days so it must have been a major breach."

"Don't they have the same setup we do?" Tony asked. "How could an entire floor become infected at once?"

"Nothing's perfect. There is always the chance of a major failure of some kind. In this instance, their control systems were unable to handle it. I'm not sure why. It could be the location of the infection, or simply that their systems aren't as sophisticated as ours."

Craig blinked. "Their system isn't as sophisticated?"

"Not sure," Sebastian said, "but I suspect the Army incorporated the most extreme measures on our level, due to the nature of our work." Craig could tell Sebastian was rambling a bit. "Ah, here we go. A message from the surface."

Tony and Craig leaned over to look. A box had appeared on the computer screen, with a typed message from the surface commander. One of the "theories" that went into the design of the underground laboratory stated that due to the dangerous work they performed, the scientists should not be distracted. As a result, all communications were done via computer to avoid the risk of interrupting the scientists at the worst possible moment.

The message reiterated what Sebastian had told them about Level II's infection.

Sebastian leaned over the keyboard. "What about the investigative team that was coming down here?" he typed.

"Unable to proceed," came the terse reply. "Unknown when they will join you."

Craig straightened. "So we couldn't leave even if we wanted to."

Tony shook his head. "No. The elevators will be shut down."

"Well, with the lockdown, we weren't planning on leaving anytime soon," Sebastian pointed out.

"I don't like this," Craig said, remembering what Manny had told him. If Jill was right, it meant that they were trapped down here with a killer.

After the excitement died down, Mouse hesitantly approached the door to Lab 7. Mitchell stood in front of the door, casually blocking the way.

"Hi Mitchell," Mouse said, wringing his hands.

"Hey Mouse. What are you doing here?"

"I need to check something out. In Lab 7."

Mitchell laughed. "Sorry dude. No one goes in. Captain's orders."

"I'll only be a minute, really. I won't bother anything."

"I wish I could, but I can't."

Mouse looked at Mitchell's smiling face, uncomfortable with confrontation. He considered Mitchell a friend. He wasn't sure what to do. "I'll only be a minute."

"My hands are tied. Sorry."

"I need to get in there."

"I 'need' a lot of things," Mitchell quipped. "Seriously, I have to follow orders. Bites the big one, doesn't it?"

Mouse opened his mouth to reply but nothing came out. He was stumped. Desperate, he lunged for the doorplate.

Mitchell grabbed Mouse's wrist before he could trigger the plate. "I said no."

Mouse blinked at Mitchell's harsh tone. He backed away and Mitchell released his hold.

Defeated, Mouse turned to go. He didn't know what else to do. He began to shuffle back down the hallway, possibly to return to the Mechanical Room where he felt comfortable.

He was struck with a thought and froze. After a moment, he slowly turned back. "We are friends, right?"

"Yeah," Mitchell replied cautiously.

"I have to get in there. I have to see what happened. It's not for me, but for the whole team. I have to figure this out."

"I'm not supposed to let—"

"I'm asking you for a favor. Just like when I helped you, remember? You wanted me to install that cable for you. You couldn't do it yourself. You needed my help, and as a friend, I did it, even though it's against the rules."

"Are you trying to blackmail me?" Mitchell asked incredulously.

"I'm asking you to return a favor."

Mitchell shifted his weight as he glanced down the empty hallway.

"I'll only be a minute," Mouse assured him, going in for the kill.

Trisha consulted her printout as she ran her fingers over the grid of vials, but her hands began to tremble, blurring the words on the page.

She closed her eyes and took a deep breath. The alarm had really scared her—and on top of Craig's transfer, it had nearly driven her over the edge.

After a few moments, she opened her eyes and returned to her task, able to read the printout again.

She had decided to verify the location of all of the viruses and their corresponding vaccines. It was really Jackie's job, but Trisha wanted to check the information herself. She was still bothered by the Keres' Eye outbreak. She wanted to know the location of all microbes in play. It was better than crying in her room.

She couldn't think about Craig, not right now. Anything was better than that. Even killer germs.

As she'd expected, the majority of their stock was either in cryostorage or in one of the refrigeration units. She checked those briefly but didn't bother to count each individual vial. Instead, she focused on the vials that had been removed from the storage areas.

The printout listed all viruses and vaccines that were out of storage and their corresponding experiments. Labs 1 and 2 had the largest supplies, which didn't surprise her. She carefully checked each vial and made sure nothing was missing.

She continued her way through the facility, verifying the vials in every lab—except for Labs 6 and 7, of course. When she approached the last lab, she consulted her list and saw that a number of experiments were ongoing in Lab 9.

When she entered the room, she found Jackie leaning over one of the tables, her back to the door. Jackie jerked when she heard the door open.

Trisha paused. "Am I interrupting anything?"

"No," the second-in-command replied. She smiled sheepishly. "You just surprised me."

Trisha was startled to see Jackie smile. She was normally serious and direct, almost rude at times. "Do you need me to come back later?"

"No."

Trisha thought of leaving anyway.

"What have you got there?"

Trisha glanced at the printout in her hand. "It's a list of all current experiments."

"Checking to see where all of the viruses are?"

"Yeah. And the vaccines in stock. I hope you don't mind."

"Smart. In fact," Jackie admitted, "I was doing much the same thing."

Trisha smiled. "Really?"

"Great minds must think alike."

Trisha walked over to her. A large wire-frame container sat on the table, filled with over two dozen sealed vials. A barcoded label was attached to the side of each vial, along with a smaller piece of white tape with the vial's contents written on it.

"It looks like everything's here, but we should double check just to make sure," Jackie said.

Trisha began to go through the list, matching it with the corresponding vial. She had to stop for a moment when her hands started to shake again. "Sorry," she muttered as she tried to calm her nerves.

"I'm scared, too."

Trisha looked at her. "You are?"

"I'm human, just like everybody else. Yeah I'm scared. I'm supposed to be this tough commander, but sometimes it's hard to keep up the façade."

Trisha was so surprised her hands stopped trembling. "I never thought of it that way."

"What did you expect?" Jackie asked. "I have to be tough to be in the Army ... but with what happened, I'm not sure how much more I can take." She paused, then said, "I'm terrified of getting infected."

"Me too," Trisha whispered.

The women were silent for a moment. "Come on, let's finish this and get the hell out of here."

Trisha agreed and the two women quickly went through the list.

She found herself enjoying her time with Jackie. It was a nice break from the hardass persona the woman normally portrayed.

When they finished, Trisha said, "We should lock these up."

"Because of what Manny found?"

Trisha's eyebrows shot up. "You know about that?"

Jackie nodded. "Craig told me."

"So what do you think?"

"God I'd like to," Jackie sighed. "I don't think we can."

"It's not safe leaving them out."

"These are just vaccines, remember? All of the weapons are in the main labs or secured away."

Trisha hesitated.

"If we lock these up," Jackie explained, "we'll tip our hand to whomever's responsible. They'll know we're on to them."

"I still don't like it."

A bark of a laugh escaped Jackie's lips. "Welcome to management. Sucks, doesn't it?"

Mouse's breathing came out harsh and fast, the sound echoing in his helmet like a deep-sea diver. He felt awkward and stiff in the biosuit, which only added to his fear, but he forced himself to follow Mitchell into Lab 6.

The door shut behind them and Mouse looked around, his eyes wide in amazement. This was his first glimpse of the devastation. It was nearly overwhelming.

He realized Mitchell was looking at him. Before the scientist could stop him, Mouse got moving. He walked across the length of the room, trying not to think about the deadly air around him or the suit that kept the virus from getting to his eyes.

He approached the door that led into the hallway. This was what he had come to see.

"We're pushing our luck," Mitchell declared as Mouse shuffled closer to the door. "If Craig comes by here, we're both going to be busted—"

"Open the door."

"What?"

Mouse didn't turn around. "Open the door," he ordered. He was so close to the door his faceplate was almost touching it.

Mitchell argued with him but Mouse didn't move, didn't look at him.

Mitchell's voice thickened with anger. "This is ridiculous. We're not allowed—"

"Open the damn door," Mouse roared, his eyes transfixed on the black rubber seal.

In a rage, Mitchell slapped the doorplate.

The door hissed and slid open.

Mouse followed the door as it slid back, watching it glide into its resting place inside the wall. It stopped and Mouse waddled over to inspect the deflated seals. As he approached, a chill scurried down his back. He reached up and traced a pair of faint diagonal lines that ran down the seals. "Damn."

CHAPTER 10

"What is it?"

Mouse traced the lines again with his gloved hand. "You see this? It means the seals were deflated, then re-inflated."

"That's what they're supposed to do."

"Not like this," Mouse said. "The seals were deflated while the door was still closed, then re-inflated. That's not how they work. They deflate as the door opens, but they don't re-inflate until right before the door closes. That way they become fully inflated, to provide the best seal." He swallowed. "It means someone deflated the seal, letting the virus out, without opening the door. Unless you looked real close, you wouldn't realize the seal had been broken."

"Oh my God," Mitchell whispered.

"We need to tell Craig."

Mitchell grabbed him as he turned to leave. "Wait a second. Couldn't it have been caused by a virus eating at the rubber? That's what we were told."

"If that was the case, those holes would have widened."

"But ... maybe the door resealed itself and managed to cover them. Somehow."

"No. This was done deliberately. We're all in serious danger." Mouse began to shuffle towards the door to Lab 7. He wanted out of the biosuit as fast as possible. He didn't feel safe here—or anywhere in the facility for that matter.

"This is the proof Craig needs," he said as he approached the exit. "Someone killed Danny. I'm sure of it."

He was so focused on getting out of there that he didn't look back. If he had, he would have seen a disturbed and angry look on Mitchell's face. The scientist was clenching his fists, his eyes filled with loathing.

Brett watched from the shadows as Jill walked past. As soon as she turned the corner, he stepped into the hallway, checked both directions and silently followed.

She approached the door to Lab 2, triggered the doorplate and disappeared inside. Brett slipped past the open doorway while her back was turned and slipped into the shadows where the corridor turned.

His years of intelligence training served him well. Caution was the most important thing to remember, caution and patience. In this case, he was rewarded as Manny appeared in the hallway a few moments later and entered the lab.

Standing in the shadows, Brett knew he needed to get in there. He was not allowed inside Lab 6 or the adjoining hallway, and had not been ready to force the issue. When he had spotted Jill, however, he'd realized that he no longer needed to worry about Lab 6. He had seen the sealed container she had carried, the reinforced box used to carry infectious items. She had taken it into Lab 2, where she would certainly begin to analyze the object she'd discovered. She was a smart woman—hell, virtually everyone here was smart—and she would quickly discern its nature.

He already knew. The sealed box was made of a clear acrylic, enabling him to see the shard of glass lying inside.

He had almost charged in there without thinking but had held back. Now that Manny had joined her, Brett decided not to approach the lab. Not yet. But he had to move fast. He knew they would discover what the glass was and how it worked.

He slipped farther back into the shadows.

*   *   *

Mouse turned awkwardly in the temporary shower stall, trying to make sure the chemicals washing over him covered his entire suit. The liquid that ran down over his visor looked like tainted water. Radioactive water.

He washed off the chemicals, then hurried out of the temporary shower and pulled off his helmet. Mitchell was right behind him, watching him closely as he stepped into the spot Mouse had vacated and turned on the spray.

The air stank from the chemicals. Although not caustic enough to cause skin damage or eat at the biohazard suits, the mix of chemicals was lethal enough to destroy all biological pathogens and could cause damage if left on the skin too long. It also made Mouse's eyes burn. He blinked a few times as he stumbled over to the rack of biohazard suits, a sense of urgency hurrying his actions, the light from the portable ultraviolet lights casting a strange glow to the room. He struggled out of his suit, trying to make sure he didn't damage it, and haphazardly draped it over the metal hanger.

Mitchell loomed behind him, having come out of the showers, and quickly began to remove his suit. "Wait," he cried as Mouse slipped out of the changing area and disappeared.

Mouse hurried towards the door, a determined look pinching his face. "We have to find Craig. Right now," he insisted. "Come on."

"No. Wait a second."

He heard a grunt from the other side of the curtain, and the rattle of hangers. "I'll go find Craig—"

"Don't you dare leave. Hold—" another grunt "—on a second."

"We don't have time." He reached for the doorplate. "I'm going. Meet up when you can."

Mitchell suddenly lunged at Mouse, his long arm shooting out from behind the plastic curtains, and grabbed Mouse's shoulder. Mouse tried to pull away but froze when he saw the look on Mitchell's face.

Before either man could speak, Craig's voice came over the intercom. "Attention everyone. The three hours are up. Time to get together and review what we've learned. Meet me in the Rec Room in five minutes."

Brett ignored the announcement. He wasn't about to leave. He needed to get into Lab 2.

But Manny and Jill would answer Craig's call.

Brett slipped down the hall, went around the supply closet and circled around the shower area. As he approached the hallway that ran down the length of the Computer Lab, he heard the door to Lab 2 open, heard Jill and Manny talking. With a triumphant grin, he waited until they had started down the hallway towards the security corridor, then slipped around the corner. The door to Lab 2 was still open. He darted across the hallway and dove into the lab right before the door closed.

He pressed his body against the wall. The rest of the team would be heading to the Rec Room. He didn't want to risk being spotted as they walked by.

After a minute, he judged that it was safe to proceed. He wished he could cover the door's window, but that would immediately look suspicious—and Manny and Jill had left the lights on, so he didn't have any shadows to work with. But he had to get to the glass. If someone came in, he would just have to deal with them.

He quickly began to check the room. The sealed container had to be here somewhere.

The room was filled with laboratory equipment including computers, centrifuges, spectrographs, and microscopes. In addition, there were a number of work stations scattered throughout the large lab, and cabinets filled with various scientific equipment lined the back corner.

The largest portion of the lab, however, was occupied by the chambers.

The chambers were designed to handle the most dangerous elements. Negatively pressurized with double-sealed doors, the chambers allowed for open-air work of bioagents, detailed animal testing including dissection, and other sensitive handling of viruses under strictly controlled conditions. The only way into one of the chambers was through the Prep area, which stored the biohazard suits needed to work in such hostile environments.

Brett approached the string of chambers and peered through the immense windows. The chambers were dark so he didn't think Manny and Jill had gone inside. As he glanced at Chamber 2, however, he saw that a small lamp had been turned on. He stepped closer and spotted the acrylic container Jill had been carrying. It was attached to the side of the chamber, near the lamp. In an instant, Brett realized what they'd done. They had taken the container and, using the transferring mechanism integrated into the outside of the chamber, had opened the container inside Chamber 2. There were long, rubber gloves that allowed them to reach inside the Chamber and pull out the piece of glass.

He nodded his head in admiration. It allowed them to utilize the equipment inside the Chamber without having to go through the lengthy process of suiting up.

He extended his arms through the rubber gloves. With his face nearly pressed against the window, he found the specimen to his left. To the right and directly in front of him were various pieces of equipment including a sealed grinder and a modified microscope with a display screen attached to it.

He gingerly picked up the glass fragment and held it under the lamp. It was the same piece of glass, all right. He could tell by the way it caught the light, reflecting it in a distinct, wavy pattern. He stared at the glass for a few moments, watching the play of light as he tilted it back and forth, then got to work.

Most of the group had already gathered in the Rec Room when Mouse burst in. He spotted Craig and rushed up to him, with Mitchell reluctantly following behind. "We need to talk to you right away."

"Calm down," Craig said. "What's wrong?"

"We need to talk to you. Outside," Mouse added with a glance around.

"What about?"

Mouse didn't reply. He hurried to the door and motioned for Craig to follow. With a sigh of resignation, Craig followed the two men out. "Start talking."

The two men told him about the seals. "No one was supposed to go in that room, including you," Craig snarled at Mitchell.

Mitchell kept his face a mask. "Bust me later. This is important."

"Go on."

Mouse continued his story. "Someone purposefully deflated the seals, then re-inflated them," he concluded. "Danny was murdered."

Craig nodded grimly. This was the proof he'd been looking for, but it was so hard to accept.

"Tell him the rest," Mitchell said.

Mouse sighed. "There is one other possibility. The computer could be malfunctioning."

"Malfunctioning?" Craig scoffed. "It's the same system that has been running for years. It's been modified and improved to the point that it's as dependable as humanly possible."

"Then it's been tampered with," Mitchell said.

A shiver ran up Craig's spine. He looked at Mouse. "How easy would it be to tamper with it?"

Mouse shrugged. "I'm no expert."

"Whoever messed with it is the one responsible," Mitchell said.

That wasn't all. If Jill was right, whoever had murdered Danny had deflated the seals to confuse everyone, to make them think the infection had come from Lab 6. The murderer probably planned to sneak into the bathroom and remove the glass as soon as he or she got the chance, in order to hide the evidence.

Craig turned and walked back into the Rec Room, his thoughts tumbling together in his mind.

The moment he stepped inside the room, faces turned to him expectedly. His team was worried, suspicious. Some of them had made progress, he could tell by their expressions, and were eager to tell him. Others were confused and scared.

Sebastian hadn't arrived yet. With a hand, Craig asked for their patience, ducked back out and headed to a nearby phone where he dialed into the Computer Lab. "Sebastian?"

"Craig," the Senior Scientist replied. "I meant to call. Go ahead and start without me."

"Why?" Craig asked with a frown.

"I'm in the middle of running a diagnostic of the computer system. It'll be a while."

"Why are you running a diagnostic now?" He glanced at Mouse and Mitchell, who were watching him anxiously.

"I've run across some strange things. I'm not sure what the hell is going on."

"I'm not surprised." Cupping the mouthpiece, he turned to Mitchell. "Go grab Manny."

"Right."

Craig watched Mitchell disappear inside. "I think the computers have been tampered with," he told Sebastian. "I don't want to get into it right now, but I'm sending Manny over."

"Manny? What for?"

Mitchell returned to the hallway with Manny in tow. "I need you to go over to the Computer Lab," Craig told him. "There's something fishy with the computer system. Help Sebastian go through the programs and see what you can learn."

Manny nodded. "Fine. Sure."

Sebastian argued with Craig, trying to convince him that he could handle it alone, but Craig cut him off. "Manny's on his way over to help. I know the computers are your domain, but we need to know what's going on."

"I can be more productive—"

"That's an order."

*   *   *

Sebastian swore as he hung up the phone. Manny would figure everything out. He wasn't as knowledgeable as Sebastian was, but even so, it wouldn't take him long to discover what Sebastian had done.

He swore again, called up one of the computer programs and began to type furiously. He would have to show his hand early. He had tried to delay things a little further, but that was fine. With what he had planned, Craig and the others would be helpless.

CHAPTER 11

"OK, let's go through what we've learned," Craig said, struggling to keep his voice level. He was distracted, tense, but was determined to remain in control. "Who wants to start?"

His people sat on couches scattered throughout the room, but no one was relaxed. A sense of urgency and frustration filled the air, festering under the skin like an itch that couldn't be reached.

"What did Mouse and Mitchell talk to you about?" Jill asked him.

His eyes darted to Trisha as he debated whether to tell everyone. She had avoided him ever since he'd told her about his transfer, but now that she was here, he wanted to be near her, even if she wasn't talking to him.

He squared his shoulders. "They have reason to believe that our original theory was wrong, that the seals weren't compromised by the virus. They think the seals were deflated intentionally."

The room erupted in anger and disbelief.

It took him a few moments to calm them down. "Mouse, why don't you explain," he said.

The young man stood up and stared at the floor. "I could tell that the seals had been deflated without the door opening.

There are a series of faint lines that were made when they tried to re-inflate while still inside the door jam."

"Are you sure it's because of that?" Kim asked. "Couldn't those lines have already been there?"

"It's possible—"

"Did you inspect the seals before this happened?" Jackie asked in a curt voice.

"Uh, no."

"I still don't trust those seals," Tony grumbled.

Mitchell nodded. "Same here."

"But the seals were deflated on purpose," Mouse said.

Craig stepped in, but Jackie cut him off. "Face it, this place is a deathtrap. We're lucky we're all still alive."

He shot her a look as his people continued to argue. She kept her face expressionless, but she didn't fool him. She was pissed.

He swore silently. He had told her about his promotion right before calling the meeting. It had taken her a few moments to get control of herself, but overall she had taken the news better than he'd expected—or so he had thought.

"I understand what he said," Tony argued, pointing at Mouse, "but even if he's right, this place is old. Can it really protect against something like Keres' Eyes? Was it designed for that?"

"It was designed to prevent pathogens as small as one micron from spreading through the level," Craig said. "Regardless of which virus it was that killed Danny, this place was designed to keep us safe."

Tony opened his mouth to reply but never got the chance. The alarms went off again, the sound piercing their eardrums. It was all around them, the electronic warning of impending doom.

In what felt like an instant, Craig and the others were in the hallway, driven on by the insistent noise. Instinctively, they turned towards the Exit, even though it was already blocked. They raced down the hallway with Mitchell in the lead, past Supply and Security Room 2. Since the Exit door was blocked off, Mitchell turned down the hallway towards the Entrance, as if he could get out that way, but an emergency door suddenly appeared and slid across the hallway, cutting them off.

They stopped and turned back, their confusion adding to their anxiety as the alarms continued to blare. Craig hesitated, not sure if he wanted to go back towards the labs—but there was nowhere else to go. He glanced at Trisha; her face was white with fear. He instinctively grabbed her hand and headed towards the labs, the rest of the team in tow.

As they approached the security corridor, Manny rushed out, frantically searching for his wife. When he saw her, he stumbled to a halt in relief.

To everyone's horror, the security doors pulled out of the wall and slid across the narrow hallway behind him, sealing off the corridor. Manny tried to stop the first door from closing, but the motor driving it was too powerful. He almost lost his arm in the process. He roared in anger as the door closed, blocking the hallway.

They were cut off from the labs.

Craig ran to the nearest phone. He was unaware that he was still holding Trisha's hand and was nearly dragging her with him. He jabbed the intercom button and punched in the Computer Room. "What the hell is going on?" he yelled the instant he heard Sebastian pick up.

His heart froze when Sebastian laughed in response.

As the rest of the group gathered behind him, Craig yelled Sebastian's name. The alarms abruptly stopped.

"What the hell?" Tony whispered in the silence that followed.

Behind them, Craig heard something hissing. Letting go of Trisha's hand, he cautiously approached the sound, which came from behind one of the fake plants that were scattered throughout the facility. This one was located in front of Security Room 2, underneath the two-way mirror. With a sense of apprehension, Craig grabbed it and pulled it out of the way.

Behind the plant was a small device. Craig recognized it instantly. It was a remote-controlled biodispenser, designed by the U.S. Army to release biological weapons.

"I trust I have your attention," Sebastian's voice, smooth and confident, issued out of the speaker. "It's time to play a game."

Craig realized Sebastian could see them via the facility's security cameras. He looked up at the nearest one, which was nestled in the corner by the two-way mirror. "What are you talking about?"

"I have just infected you all with the Ebola virus. Lucky for you, I decided to use the weaponized strain, and I have the antidote. But you will have to earn it. Hence the game. If you don't cooperate, you will become sick within the next twenty-four hours and will be dead within forty-eight. Ebola is such a nasty way to die, don't you think?"

Craig was confused. "It was you? You were behind Danny's death? Behind all of this? Why?"

"Stay where you are," Sebastian ordered. "If you want to live, you will do exactly as I say."

He hung up, leaving the group of men and women in stunned silence.

CHAPTER 12

Banks sat in the darkness of the drab hotel room, rubbing the back of his hand. He didn't want to go, didn't want any part of this.

His life had turned into a nightmare.

He flinched when he heard a car pull up outside. Terrified, he got up and peaked through the thick curtains. It was only a young couple that occupied one of the units farther down. Just as he was about to pull away, he spotted a car parked across the street. Someone was inside, staring at the motel.

Banks quickly ducked back and closed the curtains. They were watching him.

He sat on the edge of the bed and scooped up the prescript-tion bottle but didn't open it. Not yet. He tried to fight the pull, his emotions raging inside his head. It had all gone so terribly wrong. Banks hadn't even become aware of it until it was too late. Sebastian had almost had to spell it out for him to get it. How pathetic. Banks could still remember that horrible day out on Sebastian's boat.

"What is this shit you've been telling my employer?" he'd asked.

"I only told him enough to ensure your cooperation."

"My 'cooperation'?"

Sebastian nodded. "You are going to help me with something. Don't worry. You'll be extremely well compensated. So well, in fact, that you can open your own pharmacy if you want when this is done. And of course you'll have the keys to all of those wonderful drugs—"

"How dare you! My boss has been watching me like a hawk ever since you talked to him."

"You should thank me. If I'd told him all of it, you wouldn't even be there anymore. Your career would be ruined."

"You asshole."

"It's not my fault you got yourself into this predicament. I'm merely taking advantage."

Banks would have stormed off—but they were miles from shore.

"It's quite simple, really," Sebastian continued. "You help me with this, you can keep your job, as well as your standing within the scientific community."

"You have no right."

"Yes, but I have proof. That trumps. Videos, a paper trial, and your pathetic attempts at covering your tracks. You didn't really think I wouldn't find out, did you? As Lead Scientist, I oversee everything—including your own destruction. The fact that I'm your only reference after dropping off the face of the earth for four years sweetens the pot, so to speak."

Banks was breathing heavily. "What do you want me to do?" he finally asked.

Sebastian explained his plan. By the time he'd finished, Banks' eyes were huge. "You monster."

Sebastian didn't even blink.

"I could turn you in."

"Do you think you'd live long enough, Christopher? That your family would live long enough? They know who you are. They knew before our first meeting. No, you're in this until the end."

Now, sitting in the hotel room, Banks knew Sebastian was right. There was no other choice. Sebastian was too smart to let Banks escape.

His hands trembling, Banks opened the prescription bottle and peered inside. There were only a handful of pills. Enough to take the sharpest edge off, but not enough to satisfy the beast inside of him. Sebastian had promised more afterwards.

Banks desperately hoped Sebastian had told the truth.

*　　*　　*

Craig couldn't believe it. Sebastian had locked them out of the lab area and taken control. Even more horrifying was the bio-dispenser. Without even a hint of remorse, Sebastian had infected them with weaponized Ebola. The modified virus had been created from the Ebola-Zaire strain, which in its natural form was ninety percent fatal.

Sebastian had signed their death warrants. In one stroke, he had killed them.

Craig's eyes glided over his team members, his family. They were all dead, murdered by one of their own.

This couldn't be happening!

He broke out of his paralysis and scrambled to Security Room 2. It served as a secondary guard post as well as a debriefing room for incoming visitors. The room didn't have all of the important equipment Tony needed to protect against a security breach, but it did have a communications terminal.

He pounced on the terminal and frantically began typing a message to the surface. Behind him, Tony came in and punched a large red button set in the wall. "Emergency alarm," he explained to Trisha, who had followed them inside. "At least the surface'll know something's wrong."

Craig hit the ‹Enter› key and waited impatiently for the surface to reply. Normally they would at least acknowledge receipt of a message, even before reading it. But after a few moments, he still hadn't received anything.

He tried a few more times, but never received a response. "Damn."

Jackie poked her head in the room. "Anything?"

"No. Did you try the exit?"

She nodded. "Sealed tight." The others gathered behind her, while Mitchell slipped past her to enter the room.

"What can we do?" Trisha asked in a frightened voice.

Craig looked at her, at Tony, at the rest of his team. He sighed. "Nothing. Sebastian is in control."

"You can't mean that—" Mitchell started to argue.

"He has access to the computer, the communications, the viruses and vaccines. Hell, he probably has all of the biosuits as well," Craig said.

"We have to have something though, right?"

"We have a taser," Tony answered. "That's it."

"This is unbelievable."

Craig looked at Mitchell with a grim expression. "The security measures were designed to prevent intruders from entering. They weren't designed to handle an internal problem."

"You mean a betrayal," Kim said from the doorway.

Craig nodded.

Mitchell shook his head in amazement and horror. "We're totally screwed."

Silence fell as the extent of their situation sunk in.

Tony finally broke the silence. "We do stand between Sebastian and the exit," he pointed out. "We could stop him before he leaves."

"How?" Jackie demanded. "With our bare hands?"

"All he has to do is wait two days and we'll be dead," Jill said.

Within seconds, virtually the entire group was arguing at once. "If what he said was true, we're all going to die," Manny shouted, his voice loud in the confined space.

"We should cooperate with him," Mouse spoke up.

"Oh?" Tony asked, rounding on him. "What makes you think he'll let us live? He's not going to give us the vaccine. Why would he? If we live, we'll tell the Army what happened and Sebastian'll be hunted around the globe. He's too smart for that."

Craig knew Tony spoke the truth, although it didn't slow the argument. As the battle raged around him, the realization of their situation hit him hard. He was furious that he had trusted Sebastian—that Sebastian had turned on him like this. He was also scared that Sebastian was the one behind this. He would be impossible to stop.

CHAPTER 13

"Are you OK?" Trisha asked.

"No I'm not," Craig said. "I'm furious with myself. I can't believe I didn't figure out what was going on—"

"It's not your fault—"

"Yes it is. I should've seen it. I'm sure there were signs. If only I'd paid attention."

"Sebastian fooled all of us."

"But I'm the Commanding Officer," Craig said. "I'm the one responsible. I should've discovered what he was planning and stopped him before it was too late."

They stood off to one side, away from the others. Manny, Mitchell, and Jackie were still arguing, although it was mostly out of fear rather than anger. The initial shock had worn off, replaced with despair and an impotent fear that made Craig feel like he was losing his mind.

At least Trisha was talking to him again.

Tony had gone back to the security room, but now he approached Craig. "We have a problem," he said in a low voice.

Craig's head snapped around. "Now what?"

Tony led Craig and Trisha to the security room. Once inside, he pointed to the emergency alarm. "This is hardwired to the surface. The moment I hit it, an alarm sounds up top. Even if they don't receive our messages, they'll hear the alarm."

"OK," Craig said, indicating for Tony to continue.

The security officer sighed. "When I didn't receive a response on the terminal, I started to get suspicious. Look." He reached for the emergency alarm button and pulled it out of the wall. Craig saw that Tony had removed the screws holding the alarm in place. When he pulled it out, a small bundle of wires came out of the wall—and ended abruptly. The line had been cut.

Craig swore under his breath. "What about a gun?" he asked. "Weren't you supplied with one?"

"Yeah. It's locked away in Security Room 1."

"Could Sebastian get to it?" Trisha asked.

"It's locked and the box is tamperproof. There's no way he could open it."

"I'm not so sure," Craig said. "It's obvious Sebastian had planned this for some time. He's probably booby-trapped the entire level, just like he did with the biodispenser that infected us. Who knows how long that bomb just sat there, waiting for Sebastian to trigger it."

Tony's frown was cutting a deep line in his forehead. "You're not making me feel real comfortable here."

"No kidding," Trisha said.

"We have to face what we're up against," Craig said. "He's been planning this for a while."

"So what do you think he wants?" Tony asked.

"It's obvious. He wants to steal one of the weapons we've developed, and I think I know which one: Keres' Eyes. It's the most effective and most dangerous. In the hands of an enemy, if done right, it could slaughter the vast majority of people in this country. No one would stand a chance."

"But we don't have a vaccine," Trisha argued. "He wouldn't want to unleash a virus he'd be vulnerable to."

"Maybe he created one but didn't tell anybody. If I'm right, Keres' Eyes would become that much more valuable. Enemies could inoculate themselves and then unleash Keres' Eyes without worrying about infecting themselves."

"You think he developed a vaccine?" Tony asked incredulously.

"It's just a hunch, but yeah, I do. Sebastian was the lead developer for the vaccine. He would have waited until he'd created one before betraying us."

Before Tony could respond, someone wailed in anguish.

Rushing out of the security room, they heard Kim crying in pain, her words almost incoherent as she wailed.

Craig ran for the security corridor. He found her pounding on the door blocking the hallway. "Why, you bastard? Why?"

With Trisha's help, Craig managed to pull Kim away from the door before she could hurt herself. He held her close, trying to calm her down, and she collapsed against him, sobbing so powerfully that her entire body shook.

He stroked her hair as she sobbed, silently chastising himself. She must've heard him talking about the vaccine Sebastian had probably developed, a vaccine that could have saved Danny.

A thought occurred to him. "Danny told you about working on Keres' Eyes, didn't he?" he whispered in her ear. "Helping Sebastian design it?"

Kim's sobs grew in strength at Craig's words.

"He did nothing wrong, you hear me? It wasn't his fault."

"But why?" she moaned in anguish. "Why did Sebastian kill him?"

"I don't know," Craig whispered. He looked at Trisha, unable to think of anything else to say. Trisha returned his gaze, her eyes filled with sorrow.

The rest of the group hovered around, offering their silent support. It was all they could do.

Kim pulled away from him. He let her go with a sad smile. She tried to return his smile, but then quickly buried her face in Trisha's neck.

His shirt still wet with Kim's tears, Craig had never felt so angry. He wanted to rip Sebastian's head off. Jackie, Tony, Manny and Jill, Mitchell, and Mouse stared at him, looking for guidance or at least a little bit of hope, but he was fresh out.

His anger came through his voice as he snapped at them. "Let this be a warning. Sebastian is a killer. He murdered Danny and has infected us all.

"He wants us for some reason," Craig continued, tired of being patient and sensitive to their needs. They all needed a good slap in the face. "If he didn't, he would have used the same virus he'd used on Danny and wiped us out. There *is* a game being played here. Our only chance is to figure out what it is and beat him. If we don't, if we fail to rise to the challenge, none of us will ever see daylight again."

"Where's Brett?" Jackie asked.

"Check this side, see if he's here," Craig ordered.

The team quickly scattered. They searched the private rooms, the bathrooms, kitchen, even the Mechanical Room, but he was nowhere to be found.

"Is he in on it with Sebastian?" Manny asked after they finished.

"He might be," Craig allowed. "If not, he could help—"

"Or he could accidentally infect us all with something else," Tony pointed out.

"He's got to be trapped in the labs somewhere," Trisha said

"Could that help?" Manny asked.

"I'm not sure what he could do—or what he *will* do when he finds out what happened," Craig told them. "For now, we don't know which side he's on. If anybody hears from him, if he calls, let me know. We have to watch what we say to him."

"I don't like this," Tony said. "The new guy just happens to avoid becoming infected? It's too convenient."

Craig had to give him that one—if Sebastian had told the truth about infecting them with weaponized Ebola. The modified strain they'd developed was non-transmittable. It had been designed to spread quickly and rapidly through the air, and its coat had been reinforced to allow the virus to survive longer in the open, but even so, the ultraviolet lights incorporated in the fluorescent lighting overhead would still degrade it. Brett could walk out of the security corridor right now and probably wouldn't become infected. Or Sebastian could just give him the vaccine.

Thinking of Sebastian, Craig glanced up at the camera set in the corner by the two-way mirror. "Tony. How easy is it to disable the cameras?"

He shrugged. "Pull out the wires and they go blind."

"How many cameras are there?"

"Thirty—but I'm not sure how many are on this side."

"You want to take them out?" Manny asked Craig.

"Yeah. Be quick, before Sebastian realizes what we're doing."

Tony set off immediately for the camera in the corner, while Mitchell and Manny split up to disable the others. He reached up, ripped the wires out of the back of the camera and then started down the hallway towards the Mechanical Room to take out another camera.

Before he'd made it halfway down the hallway, however, Sebastian's voice burst out of the intercom. "Take out another camera, you'll all bleed to death from the virus."

Tony faced the intercom. "You won't get away with this!"

"Back off," Craig said.

"Keep your boys in line," Sebastian warned Craig. "They almost ruined your one chance to live."

Before he could reply, Sebastian turned off the intercom.

"Two lousy cameras," Manny said bitterly. "We only managed to take out two lousy cameras."

Tony nodded absently but didn't say anything. He was staring at the camera he'd disabled, lost in thought.

* * *

The car rolled to a stop at the gate.

As the guard approached, Dr. Christopher Banks lowered his window.

"Hey Dr. Banks! What're you doing here? I thought you got transferred."

"I did," Banks replied, forcing a grin. "Never thought I'd be back, let me tell you. It's nice being on the surface full time."

"How long has it been?"

"Not long enough. I heard they already have a replacement for me."

"Yeah, guy by the name of Brett Collins."

"Collins. Haven't heard of him. Is he any good?"

"Oh, I don't know anything about science. I guess he's OK. So what are you doing here?"

"If you can believe it, they wanted to do a final debriefing. I flew into Scott Air Force Base last night."

"I don't know if you want to be here right now," the guard said with a worried expression. He hesitated to explain.

"You referring to the infection alerts?"

"You heard about that?" the young man asked.

"Of course. I still have friends here. That's why I came by, to see if I could help."

"Man, I wouldn't go in there if I were you. First they had the infection on Level III, then something about Level II being evacuated. They just brought up the last of the scientists from Levels I and II. I heard they're scared to death."

"I bet," Banks said under his breath. "Look, would it be possible for me to go in? I can come back later, after the excitement dies down, but I wanted to see if I could help."

"That's real brave of you," the guard said. "Yeah, sure, go on in. I'll let them know you're coming."

Banks only hesitated for a second. "Thanks. I appreciate that."

"You be careful," the guard said over his shoulder as he returned to his hut.

The veteran scientist hid a grimace as the gate rose up. "I'll try."

CHAPTER 14

The men and women who worked in the underground lab only focused on the most lethal of biological viruses. The U.S. Army wanted the strongest weapons, and since they paid the bills, Craig and his team focused on agents that had the most potential. In addition to finding cures for natures' smallest killers, they also created new biological weapons by taking pieces of different viruses and splicing them together. These new monsters were amazingly effective weapons, not only by design but by the simple fact that enemy countries had never encountered them before. They would be defenseless against them. It was a nasty truth, but as the saying went, it was the price of admission.

All of those pathogens now stood as weapons against Craig and his team. Sebastian had used one against them already and the clock was ticking. They were dying, with little hope of survival.

Craig was mortified by what Sebastian had done—and by what he planned to do. If he succeeded in stealing any of the weapons they'd developed, it would be catastrophic. Just one of those microbes could wipe out massive sections of a population.

Craig rubbed the side of his jaw. He needed to find a way to stop him.

He looked around the room. They had ended up in the Dining Hall, huddled together in small groups. Trisha was nearby, talking quietly with Kim, doing her best to keep Kim's mind off of Danny's death.

Craig recalled the layout of the floor. The door blocking off the security corridor effectively kept them from the other half of the facility, away from the Ebola vaccine. Unlike most vaccines, the one that had been developed for Ebola could be taken after infection—but it was only effective for a few hours. Once Ebola reached a certain point, the antidote would be unable to stop the virus's growth.

"We really need a biosuit," he heard Manny grumble.

No, we need to contact the surface, Craig thought. He glanced at the men and women around him, and his eyes settled on Mitchell.

Suddenly, he straightened. Trisha looked at him expectantly. "What is it?" Kim asked.

"Mitchell's computer is hooked to the internet, right?" he asked them.

"Yeah," Trisha said. "He's got some sort of high-speed access."

"Maybe we can contact the surface that way, send them an email. I know it sounds crazy, but it's worth a shot."

Mitchell came over. "Did I hear my name?"

"We want to use your computer," Craig told him.

"Sure. Oh, yeah, that might work," he replied, realizing what Craig was thinking.

Craig and Trisha stood up. "Do you want to come along?" she asked Kim.

Kim shook her head, her eyes dropping to the table.

Craig and Trisha followed Mitchell to his room. He didn't share it with anyone, so had felt free to decorate the place with posters of scantily clad women, as well as smaller pictures of women without any clothing at all.

Mitchell went to his computer. "What do you wanna try first? You want to dial 911, see if the local police department can send someone down here?"

"No. I want to send an email to the Pentagon. They'll be able to reach the base commander."

Mitchell pulled up the program.

As soon as it was up, Craig moved him out of the way, bent over the keyboard, and began to type.

Tony grunted as he set down the box. Wiping the sweat from his forehead, he walked back to the supply closet and returned with another one.

"What are you doing?" Jackie asked.

"Setting up a defensive perimeter."

"Isn't it a little late for that?"

"Better than nothing," he said. He went for another box as she surveyed the area. Tony had gathered up most of the fire extinguishers and placed them strategically around the area.

As he returned with another box, she asked, "Need some help?"

"I never turn away free labor."

Craig stared at the computer screen, waiting for a reply. Behind him, Mitchell and Trisha talked quietly, although they both kept an eye on the screen. Craig anxiously drummed his fingers, wondering how long it would take to get a response.

The door opened and Mouse stuck his head in. "Mitchell, can you help me for a minute?"

"I'm in the middle of something."

"It shouldn't take long," Mouse said. "Please?"

Mitchell hesitated, obviously unwilling to leave. He shot Trisha a glance, but when it became obvious that she wasn't going anywhere, he sighed in defeat and followed Mouse out.

As the door closed, Craig became acutely aware that he and Trisha were alone. He tried to think of something to say, but her proximity made it hard to think. The tension in the room was awkward, yet exciting. He started to have that push-pull feeling again. He wasn't sure what to do. He risked glancing at her, and returned her smile before looking back at the screen.

"Are you going to check his inbox?" she asked, startling him. When he asked her what she meant, she said, "When Mitchell opened the email program, he quickly minimized it so we wouldn't see what was in there."

"Maybe he has some private stuff he doesn't want us to see."

"Mitchell? Please," she scoffed. "Pull it up. I'm curious."

At least it was something to do. Craig brought the program back up and found a number of unopened emails, at least a dozen of them.

Trisha leaned over him, driving him to distraction. "Open that one."

He clicked on it. The message was from a girl named Tammy who claimed her boyfriend had taken some "exciting" new pictures of her. There was a link to a website.

"Click on it," Trisha said.

He had an uneasy feeling. "Are you sure? I mean, are you ... into that?"

"Like you said, we need answers."

He clicked on the site, but the computer had a problem loading the images. Craig was relieved.

"Hmm," Trisha said thoughtfully as he closed the window. "Are all of these emails the same thing?"

"Looks like it," he said ruefully as he read the subject lines.

Trisha took the mouse, shocking Craig with her touch as she slipped her hand over the device. He pulled back and watched as she began pulling up programs. "What are you doing?"

"It's a trick I learned. I want to see what sites he's gone to."

"Why?"

"I'm curious. Aren't you?" she asked, giving him a look before turning back to the screen. When she did, her hair slipped over her shoulder, blocking his view. He heard her clicking away with the mouse and leaned to the side in order to see.

He found her scrutinizing a list of entries, what he realized was a historical record of websites that had been visited. From his initial glance, it appeared they all were porn sites. He feared she would click on one of them. "Scroll down," he suggested in an attempt to distract her. She did, and the pattern continued.

"Certainly single-minded," Trisha muttered. Much to his relief, she closed the window. The email program was still up. She clicked on the Outbox.

Craig was about to ask what she was doing when she opened one of the emails. There was a compressed file attached to the email, and she clicked on it.

He gasped in mortification as a series of windows popped up, each containing a high-resolution picture of a naked couple in the throes of sex. A giggle escaped Trisha's lips as she pulled back from the screen. "Ooops."

Frantic, Craig reached over and turned off the video screen.

Her beautiful, green eyes went wide in surprise. Before she could say anything, Craig said, "Turn around."

"Are you serious?"

"Yes." He waited until she put her back to him before turning the screen back on. He quickly closed all of the windows. "OK, you can turn back around."

"You're blushing."

"Let's just leave the computer alone. I think we've gotten into enough trouble—"

"What's that?" she asked, pointing at the screen.

He looked. There were a couple of emails that were addressed differently. Rather than to an email account, the address line contained a series of numbers. "I don't know."

Trisha leaned in again. "They were sent out a couple of weeks ago. And they both have attachments."

"Maybe we should leave it alone."

She took the mouse and opened the first email. "That's weird. There's no message. Just the attachment."

His reluctance changed to concern. The attached file was a program. "Can you open the file?"

She clicked on it, but after a moment, the computer informed them that the file was missing. They tried to open the other file, but got the same message.

They shared a look. "Why do I have a bad feeling about this?"

"You're not the only one."

When he looked back at the screen, he saw another error message. The computer had been unable to send their email. "What the hell?" he whispered.

"Try dialing direct."

"Do you know the number to Scott Air Force Base?"

"No, but you can find it online."

Craig opened the internet browser, but the computer was unable to pull up anything. No matter what he did, he was unable to access any outside information. "The line's been cut, hasn't it?" Trisha asked.

With a growing sense of despair and suspicion, he nodded. They were cut off from the outside world. No one was going to save them. And the deception was deeper than he'd realized. He remembered how anxious Mitchell had been about leaving them alone with his computer.

Jill and Manny stood in the open area in front of the security checkpoint, talking about the biodispenser. Jill had a nagging feeling that she was missing something. That bothered her.

Behind her, Mouse and Mitchell appeared. She didn't pay attention to what they were doing at first, but when she heard them unscrewing one of the wall sensors, she spun around. The two men gingerly removed the sensor, careful not to pull the wires out of the electronic device. They made sure it was plugged in and did a self-test to verify it was operational.

"That's it!" she cried, rushing over.

Mouse smiled. "You figured it out too?"

"Not until I saw what you were doing. I can't believe I missed it."

Manny joined the group. "What are you talking about?"

"The sensors. They didn't go off when Sebastian triggered the bomb."

"Are you saying we aren't infected?"

"We're not sure yet," Mitchell cautioned. "Remember, Sebastian could have turned off the sensors."

Mouse shook his head. "The detection system runs on a different circuit. He shouldn't be able to turn them off—I think."

"So we're infected?" Manny asked.

"I don't know. Maybe." He flushed and dropped his gaze as the others stared at him. "Uh, well, what I mean is that the sensors might not have recognized the s-strain."

"What do you mean?" Jill asked, gently prodding him.

"The sensors are, um, updated at regular intervals, but they don't always have the latest viruses. I think it's been about three months since they were last updated."

"What viruses have we been working on?" Jill asked. Mitchell and Manny both started to name off the latest strains that had been created. They came up with three new ones. "That doesn't include the bugs in development," she added.

"Right," Mitchell agreed.

"What about the strain Sebastian said he used on us?" Mouse asked cautiously.

Jill thought for a moment. "The weaponized version of the Ebola-Zaire strain should be there, but since the sensors didn't go off, it couldn't be that."

"But we're infected with something?"

She nodded. "The biodispenser definitely contained some sort of pathogen. I found residue at the bottom of the chamber when I opened it."

As she talked, Mouse accessed the list of microbes downloaded to the sensor. "It's not listed," he said. Mitchell leaned over, looked at the tiny LED screen, and swore under his breath.

"It should have been," she said.

"He must have removed it."

"How?"

"He updates the system. So, I guess, he could have removed any virus he wanted."

"He removed more than just Ebola," Mitchell said as he scanned the list.

Jill's shoulders slumped. They were back where they started, infected with something, although they didn't know what. The fact that Sebastian had removed Ebola from the list reinforced the possibility that he'd told the truth—which meant they only had a short time to live.

"This sucks," Manny growled.

She looked at her husband, a savage protectiveness rising up inside of her. "We've got to identify which virus we've been infected with. That's the only chance we'll have."

"Captain. I'm glad you're here," she called out as Craig and Trisha approached.

"What's going on?" After they brought him up to speed, Craig agreed with Jill. "We need to isolate the microorganism first."

"You going to sample the residue?" Mitchell asked.

"No, we can get a sample from any of us," Jill said.

When she heard this, Trisha rubbed her arms.

"There's something else, too. We know which virus killed Danny, but we don't have a known cure. Sebastian had been working on one, and I suspect he found one that worked."

"You're kidding me," Manny exclaimed.

"You mean *Danny's* cure?" a voice said.

Jill spun around and found Kim glaring at her. "Danny's cure?"

"Yeah, he made it. That prick stole it from him."

"Are you sure of that?"

"Yes, I'm sure. Danny was killed for it. Don't you get it?"

Craig saw murder pacing impatiently in Kim's eyes. Her cheeks were wet with tears. "Were you there when he made the discovery?"

She shook her head. "He claimed I 'distracted' him too much."

Mitchell snickered. "So *that's* what you were doing when I walked in on you two—"

"Enough," Craig said.

Jackie was unable to keep quiet. "If what you're saying is true, then he went completely against protocol!"

Trisha hesitated. "I heard Danny slip once, talking about some sort of 'radically' different cure than would normally be expected—something that rapidly destroyed the virus—"

"It's true," Kim said. "He had been working on it with Sebastian, and he told me a few days ago that he thought they'd figured out the answer. They were going to surprise everyone with the news. I don't know how he did it, but Danny said the vaccine uses some of the same compounds they'd worked with before."

It explained why Sebastian had killed Danny. He'd been the only other person who knew how to create the vaccine.

Jill tilted her head thoughtfully. "If we can get to a lab, I wonder if we can recreate it, or at least start working on it."

Jackie frowned. "We can't even access the computers. How can we get to a lab? Sebastian's locked us out."

Craig turned to Kim. "I need you to do something for me, if you can. I need you to start going through Danny's room. See what you can find. He could have left notes, a journal, something that could help us."

It was obvious she was struggling with her emotions, hatred and sadness dueling for control of her heart. Some of the emotion left her eyes, however, as she imagined doing as Craig asked. Her shoulders slumped. "OK," she said in a resigned voice.

Craig watched her go before turning back. One problem down. Now for the hard one. He had to act fast, before more damage could be done.

CHAPTER 15

Craig found Tony in Security Room 2. He was staring at the computer screen, occasionally pounding on the keyboard in anger. "Anything?"

Tony shook his head.

"We need to have a talk with Mitchell."

Tony's eyes widened. He recognized the implication in Craig's voice. He opened his mouth, but then his expression went flat. "Where do you want me to take him?"

"His room."

Tony's face hardened as he left. He knew what was in Mitchell's room. It wasn't too difficult to connect the dots.

Craig found Jackie and Trisha in the Dining Hall and, wanting backup, he led them to Mitchell's room. When they walked in, Tony and Mitchell were already there.

Mitchell looked mildly surprised. "We having a party? I hope someone brought beer."

Craig was not amused. "We know what you did, Mitchell. If you come clean now, it'll be easier for you in the end."

Mitchell's eyes skipped over the group of people standing before him. "OK, I confess. I took the last of the chocolate chip cookies. I had the munchies and couldn't help myself."

"Mitchell—"

"What's this about? You're all acting like I just killed the Pope."

"You're on the right track," Tony said, his arms folded across his thick chest.

Craig stepped forward. "We have reason to believe that you have been in collusion with Sebastian and may have helped his efforts in taking over this lab."

Mitchell snorted. "Seems to me Sebastian was able to take over without anybody's help."

"What do you have to say about the charges against you?" Jackie asked.

"'Charges'? I think they're a load of crap, that's what I think—"

"What were the programs you emailed?" Craig asked, cutting him off. "The ones you sent out a couple of weeks ago, then erased."

"P-programs? What programs?"

Craig went to the computer and showed him the emails.

"Man, you got me. I have no idea what those are."

Craig rubbed the side of his jaw. After a few moments, he glanced at Trisha. "Find Manny and bring him here."

She nodded and left. "Manny?" Mitchell asked. "Why do you want him?"

"Why do you think? We need to get to the bottom of this."

"Is this because I let Mouse go into Lab 6? I *knew* I was gonna get burned for that!"

"No. This is much more serious. You're under suspicion for treason."

"Oh this is ridiculous. You're looking for a patsy, aren't you? Well, look somewhere else, Captain. You're barking up the wrong tree."

With a confident grin, Sebastian walked into Security Room 1. He spotted Trisha through the two-way mirror ducking into the Dining Hall and wondered what she was doing, although he wasn't worried. Only mildly curious. Dismissing them, he got to work.

He was pleased so far. Things were working out exactly as he'd planned. No one had a prayer of stopping him. That would teach them for mocking him and playing their pranks on him. How dare they, ignorant children. He was one of the greatest of their time. They should've treated him with respect. Adulation. Not as a victim of their cruel jokes. They deserved to suffer and die down here, trapped by their own devices and killed by their own creations. They were helpless to stop him or their demise.

It was the military's fault that they couldn't stop him, actually. He had to thank the upper brass for their paranoia. They had dictated the design of this place and its security systems. He had simply used what was available.

Craig and the others had been running around in circles ever since he'd cut them off. They couldn't change what had happened. He'd already won the contest with his first move. Not very exciting, but certainly gratifying.

Sebastian had gone to only the best schools. He deserved no less. He'd had the brightest future, for he knew he'd excel in whatever field he chose, but he discovered that he had little patience for authority and chains of command. They only bogged him down—or worse, tried to limit him.

He was American, although he had grown up in England and studied at Cambridge. The moment he'd begun his career, he had accomplished great things, but altercations with certain employers had interfered with his progress. He'd been forced to leave on more than one occasion—and rarely was the parting amicable.

The last place he'd worked, he'd trashed his laboratory and burned all of his notes before he'd left.

The military had liked what they saw. At least back then.

They took advantage of his precarious position, knowing full well that he would have a hard time finding gainful employment.

Not only did he despise authority, he found that he abhorred people in general. Limiting the number of coworkers he was forced to deal with had enticed him, and so he had agreed to their offer.

They hadn't fully trusted him at first, and had set him up in a legitimate branch of the Army's R&D division. But they'd been grooming him for this place, systematically increasing his security clearance—while keeping him under near constant surveillance. They knew he had international contacts, friends who operated in some of the darker corners of the world, but with his devotion to the Army's efforts and to his work, he had been cleared of any suspicion.

It had been five years since coming to this underground wonderland, this hellhole in the middle of farm country.

His freedom had been total. His imprisonment had been complete.

Although he was allowed to work on virtually whatever he wanted, the thrill of the chase had paled long ago. All it did was further confirm what he already knew: he was the best, untouchable.

Satisfied, he turned to leave the main security room.

He paused in the doorway and glanced back at the darkened window. All was quiet. The roaches were trapped on the other side, scurrying around helplessly.

His eyes were drawn to the curved wall on the far side of the security room. The central shaft was on the other side, stretching all the way to the surface. If Craig or the other scientists tried to use the shaft's elevator to get to the surface, he wouldn't be able to stop them. He wasn't concerned, though. They'd never think of it, because it wasn't supposed to be used like that. They weren't able to think that far outside of the 'box'.

Yes, things were definitely going his way.

Manny showed up a few minutes later with Jill in tow. Trisha wasn't with them. Seeing Jill, Mitchell asked, "What is this, an inquisition?"

Craig waved Manny over and pointed at the computer screen. "What are these files?"

Manny sat in the chair and tried to open them but was unable to. He switched over to DOS and tried to retrieve one of the files, rapidly entering commands. After a few moments, he sighed. "Whatever they were, they've been erased completely."

"Do you recognize the programs?" Tony asked.

He frowned. "No. They could've been anything, really. Without the actual files, it's anybody's guess."

Craig stifled a growl of frustration. "What about the emails? Do you know where they were sent?"

Manny backed out of DOS and looked at the email program. "Well, they weren't sent to an email address. They were sent directly to a website."

"A website?" Jackie asked, leaning over. "There's no name, just a series of numbers."

"That's the actual website location. Most people just know the name that's attached to a website, not the numerical address. Whoever sent the emails typed in the numerical address either to hide his tracks, or because the site doesn't have a registered name."

Craig's eyes drifted over to Mitchell, who seemed to be biting his tongue. "Do you know where the emails were sent?" he asked again.

"I have no ..." Manny began before lapsing into silence as he stared at the address. After a few moments, he faced the others. "I don't know for sure, but I think the files were sent to our own computer system."

The scientists in the room began talking at once, amazed by Manny's statement.

Craig waved for silence. "What do you mean?"

"Whoever sent this probably would have gone ahead and used the name of the website, if there was one, to make sure the emails went to the correct place. It's real easy to type in the wrong site if you're using the numerical address. So I bet it doesn't have a name. There are a lot of websites like that, although very few people know about it. It adds a level of security. If there's no way to find a particular site, it's harder to mess with. But," he said, turning back to the screen, "I think this is an Army website." He tapped the screen with his finger. "The beginning numbers are strictly military, kind of like the end of a published website indicates what kind it is: .com, .org, etc."

"That doesn't mean it went to our computer system," Jackie said.

"We're not connected with the outside at all," Tony agreed.

Manny spun back around. "Look, the code structure of that website tells me it's military. I don't have a lot of experience looking at numerical addresses, but this is one I've never seen before. It's more of a covert address, which is the kind of address I'd expect for this place." He looked at Tony. "I agree we're not connected directly with the internet—as far as we know. But think about this: we're connected to the surface. They share our data. All it'd take would be one computer up there to be connected to the internet for a hacker to gain access to our system."

"Are you serious?" Jill gasped.

He shrugged. "I don't know if any of you really look around when you're on the surface, but there's a lot of offices wedged in those nondescript buildings—and a lot of computers. I'll bet at least one is hooked to the 'net."

Craig felt sick to his stomach. "You're saying that someone sent our own system a set of programs."

Manny hesitated, then nodded. "God only knows what they're for."

The programs had been sent two weeks ago. Craig had suspected, but now he knew. Sebastian had planned to betray them for some time.

He could feel the anger building inside of him.

He looked at the others and saw that Tony looked as angry as he felt. But then Tony's expression changed, as if he'd been struck by an idea. Before Craig could ask, Tony abruptly left the room. Craig could hear him yelling Mouse's name as he ran down the hallway.

Craig looked back at Mitchell. "You ready to start talking?"

*   *   *

Lab 2 fell silent as Brett leaned towards the window, studying the monitor in Chamber 2. He scanned the results of his efforts, carefully searching for the answers he desperately needed.

He had become so focused on his search that he had stopped worrying about Jill's and Manny's return. His attention was on the glass, to the exclusion of all else.

After transferring the glass to a clean petri dish, he had carefully broken off a small piece. It was too thick to examine, however, so he had been forced to transfer the sliver of glass to the grinder. He had placed the piece inside, sealed it, and ground the piece to a fine dust. The grinder had been designed so he could take a small sample of the results while keeping the contents sealed, to avoid inadvertently releasing any deadly agents into the air.

The process had taken time, but he didn't mind. He wanted to make a good impression on his Captain and the others. He knew he was the outsider. He wanted to be accepted as a member of the group. It was all he asked for—although the instincts he'd developed in Army Intelligence warned him that his news would not be good.

As he peered into the monitor that was attached to the microscope, his instincts proved to be correct. To his reluctant amazement, he saw clusters of black objects in the glass, thousands of them. When he set the microscope at the highest power, the Keres' Eyes virus leapt into view.

This was sick. He had suspected the glass had been used to kill Danny, but seeing the proof was disturbing. The glass was specially designed to shatter into microscopic pieces at the slightest pressure. It allowed for the transportation of a deadly virus, safely imbedded in the glass, as well as a means to disburse it. When the glass shattered, the miniscule shards of glass would become airborne, releasing the virus. The glass shards, light as air, would even help the virus penetrate the victim's defenses, acting like tiny daggers that pierced the skin or nasal passages before dissolving—although the microscopic shards were too small for the victim to see or feel.

Whoever had planted the virus had murdered Danny. That was obvious. But why? He figured Craig could find the murderer fairly easily. It would be whoever had access to Keres' Eyes. So why would that person risk being charged with murder? What other hidden agendas were there?

"I don't know what you're talking about," Mitchell said to Craig.

"Did you send those programs out?"

"Are you working with Sebastian to take control of the lab?" Manny asked.

Mitchell's eyes darted between the two men. "I just look at porn, dammit! Sure, I've forwarded a few things from time to time, but they're all porn—"

"How can we believe you?" Jackie asked. "They're on your computer. No one knows what you send out or who you contact—and you're doing it on an illegal line."

Mitchell's panicked eyes scanned the room. "You all know I have access to the internet. It's no secret! Don't make it sound like I installed it behind your backs."

"So what *have* you done behind our backs?" Manny growled.

"Nothing!"

Craig watched Mitchell closely. Either he was an incredibly good actor or he was telling the truth—as far as Craig could tell. He wasn't too confident in his ability to read people, though. He'd trusted Sebastian and look where that had gotten him.

Tony stepped forward. "You have the means and the ability—"

"No I don't," Mitchell argued. "I don't know what the hell those programs are or where they were sent. I don't know any 'covert' military websites! I barely remember my own email address."

"They were sent from *your* computer," Manny said.

"I'm not the only one with access. A lot of people have used my computer, even you. Most of the time I'm not even here! You all know I have an open-door policy. Hell, you can come in here and use it even if I'm sleeping."

"He's right," Jill spoke up. "He hasn't done anything wrong. Sebastian probably used Mitchell's computer and sent the programs himself."

Jackie rounded on her. "How can you be sure? It's Mitchell's computer."

"He's used it, too!" Mitchell proclaimed. "Hell, all of you have at one time or another. You claim it's for research, but how do I know? I take your word for it. I didn't think I had to babysit anyone."

"If you had, maybe this wouldn't have happened," Jill said.

Craig was still trying to make up his mind when Tony burst into the room. Mouse followed in behind him. "I have a plan," Tony announced.

All eyes turned to him.

"We need to take back control of this place and reestablish communications—"

"Wow, did you think of that all on your own?" Mitchell lashed out.

Craig glared at him. "I'd watch it if I were you. You're on thin ice."

Mitchell paled as he cast his eyes to the floor.

"Like I said," Tony continued, "we need to reestablish communications—"

"How?" Jill asked. "The lines were cut, right?"

"The ones we have access to have been destroyed, but not all of them. If we can wrestle control from Sebastian, we'll have access to the lines he hasn't cut."

"So how do we do that?" Manny asked. "How do we regain control?"

"We shut down the power."

Craig gaped in amazement. "Are you serious?"

"Yeah. Mouse can kill the power to the entire level, then when he turns everything back on, we can take control."

"What about the computer system?"

"And what about the security door?" Jill added.

Tony smiled and looked at Manny. "The computer system reboots, right?"

Manny hesitated. "Yeah, it should. It would have to—"

"So you can take control when we turn the switch back on."

"Look, this is really Sebastian's area of expertise—which is the problem. He'll take control of the system again. Maybe even become more firmly in control."

Craig tried not to get his hopes up. "Is there a chance *you* could take control instead?"

Manny shrugged. "It's possible. But it's risky."

"Could you do it?" he pushed. "You used to be the lead programmer."

"Sebastian surpassed my abilities a long time ago," Manny said. He sighed. "And it's harder to establish control outside of the Computer Lab. But ... if we take him by surprise ... it's possible."

"I don't think this is a good idea," Mouse spoke up, clearly agitated.

Tony cut him off. "We don't have a choice. Besides, if we cut the power, we can manually open the security door. Right?" he asked the young man. "When I asked you, you said it could be done."

"Yeah," he said reluctantly.

Tony looked at Craig, his eyes glittering with excitement. "What do you think?"

There was a knock on the door and Trisha poked her head in. By the look on her face, Craig could tell she was troubled. "What's wrong?"

"I was in the kitchen when the phone rang. It's Brett. He wants to talk to you."

"He's on the phone?"

"Yeah. Do you want me to transfer the call here?"

"Why's he calling all of a sudden?" Tony asked, frowning.

"Good question," Jackie said. She looked at Craig. "Do you think he's in trouble?"

"You mean more than the rest of us? I don't know. Did he sound OK?" he asked Trisha.

"He sounded fine. A little excited, maybe, but fine."

"You don't think he's been eavesdropping on us, do you?" Manny asked. "If he's in on it with Sebastian, this could be a warning of some kind."

Jill looked at her husband in surprise. "Are there microphones? I know there are cameras but I didn't know about microphones."

"There aren't any," Craig assured her, "other than the ones imbedded in the phone system. I doubt Sebastian bothered installing any."

"Still, the timing is strange," Tony said.

"Who says he's on Sebastian's side?" Jill asked, nervously glancing at the phone on Mitchell's desk to make sure it wasn't on. "There's no proof, is there?"

"She's got a point," Craig conceded. "Until we have evidence to the contrary, we assume Brett is part of our team. Got it?"

"Then we definitely need to kill the power," Tony declared. "It's the only way we'll be able to get him out of there."

Craig approached the phone in the Dining Hall and picked it up. "Brett?"

"Captain. I need to talk to you."

"What is it?" He listened as Brett described the findings of the viral glass, confirming that Danny had been murdered. As he listened, Craig looked at Trisha. She gave him a reassuring smile, but her face was strained with concern.

"Do you want to come over and take a look?" Brett asked. "Jill and Manny will be back soon and I'm sure they'll be interested in what I found."

Craig was amazed. "Wait. You don't know what happened?"

Brett paused. "No," he said slowly.

"Sebastian has taken over the facility. He's sealed us off from the labs."

"What? When?"

"About an hour ago."

"I can't believe it. What gives him the right—"

"We don't know what his motives are—"

"Screw the motives," Brett seethed. "I'll kick his ass. You just hang tight. I'll take him out and then you'll get your lab back."

"Don't," Craig warned him. "He's infected us with something. He claims it's weaponized Ebola."

"Don't worry," he said in an angry tone. "I can handle him."

"No. I'm serious. Don't do anything."

"But sir—"

"Listen to me, soldier. We're going to kill the power to get through the security corridor, and hopefully overtake Sebastian. But if you rush in there you could tip him off, jeopardizing our chances. Wait until we're ready."

"I have biosuits here," Brett argued. "I can take him."

"He may also have a gun," Craig said, remembering the weapon Tony had locked up in Security Room 1. "A biosuit won't protect you against that."

Brett hung up a few moments later and looked around. The room had taken on an ominous feel, as if every shadow hid a dangerous, bloodthirsty monster. He now understood why Jill and Manny hadn't returned. He couldn't believe Sebastian had taken over the lab, betrayed the Army, and infected his coworkers.

As soon as the lights went off, he would spring into action. He stayed away from the exit, not wanting to alert Sebastian to his presence. He hoped the head scientist would be caught off-guard when Brett suddenly appeared outside his door.

Thinking about it, he turned and headed for the Prep room. He had heard Craig's warning, but even so, he was still going to put on a biosuit.

Over the course of the next twenty minutes, the team got ready to carry out Tony's plan. Mouse went to the Mechanical Room and reviewed the procedure for killing the power. Tony took up a position near the security corridor, taking advantage of the disabled video camera to make sure Sebastian didn't make a sudden appearance. Trisha left to hunt for supplies that might help them, while Manny and Jill pretended to relax in the Rec Room.

Craig didn't know how they could pretend to relax. The tension was nearly overwhelming. The air seemed to hum with energy.

He started to pace back and forth. He knew they needed to keep up appearances in case Sebastian was watching. He had debated going to the kitchen to get something to eat, but his stomach was churning with acid. He had finally decided that pacing would look perfectly natural. It wasn't the first time he'd done it since his command had been taken from him.

They only had one chance to pull this off. Nothing could go wrong.

There was still an outstanding issue: what to do with Mitchell. There wasn't much time to decide. Craig wished they had the luxury of a full inquiry, of computer experts who could track down the unknown website and look into Mitchell's past. Unfortunately, the only thing Craig had to go on was Manny's educated guess and his own instincts. He knew Mitchell was the kind of person who didn't worry about rules or restrictions. In fact, he seemed to get a thrill from ignoring them. That didn't mean he was in collusion with Sebastian, though—and he'd seemed genuinely shocked when he had been accused of helping the head scientist.

Craig decided to let Mitchell participate. It wasn't like he had much of a choice. He couldn't afford to waste manpower containing him while everyone else went after Sebastian. They needed to work as a team. If they no longer trusted each other, Sebastian would win.

Craig had to keep everybody together, whatever the risk.

He would keep an eye on Mitchell, however, just in case.

Trisha knocked softly on the door. When she was told to enter, she found Kim sitting on Danny's bed with a distant look on her face. "I didn't mean to disturb you." Trisha told her, "but you should know what's going on."

Kim looked up, the distant look fading, as Trisha described Tony's plan. By the time Trisha finished, Kim showed a spark of her former self. "What can I do?"

"Help me look for supplies: flashlight, radios—"

"What about weapons?"

"Tony said he already looked once, but if we find anything that might work, we should bring it to him."

Kim nodded and stood up. They walked into the hallway—and almost collided with Jackie. "Watch it," Jackie snapped.

"Sorry," Trisha replied, but Jackie was already on the move.

Trisha watched her disappear around the corner. "Did she seem weird to you?"

Kim nodded.

Trisha hesitated for a moment, wondering what was wrong with Jackie, but quickly decided to get moving. She started down the hallway, following Jackie's footsteps, but then realized Kim had gone the other way. "What are you doing?"

"Shhh. Come here," Kim whispered. She continued down to Jackie's room, which was next to the room Danny had shared with Brett, and tried the door.

Trisha hurried over. "What do you think you're doing?" she hissed.

"The door's locked. Maybe I can pick it."

"We don't have time," Trisha argued. "Jackie could come back any second."

Kim pulled a bobby pin out of her hair and began to fool with the doorknob. "I've always wanted to try this."

"Stop screwing around. We could get in big trouble—"

The lock popped open.

"I did it," Kim said with a muffled giggle.

"I don't believe this."

"Come on." Before Trisha could stop her, Kim slipped inside.

Trisha made sure no one was around, and then ducked into the room. "Jackie's our boss," she argued as Kim looked around. "We could get seriously busted for this."

"We'll just say we were curious about what her room looked like."

"Kim," Trisha warned.

Kim sighed as she slowly turned back around. "Fine." She reluctantly started for the door, but then spotted something out of the corner of her eye. She leaned down and reached into the trashcan.

"Now you're going through her garbage?"

Kim ignored her. The papers lying on top looked as if they had been placed there. When she pushed them aside, she inhaled sharply. "Look."

Trisha came over. To her surprise, she saw a syringe half-buried in the trash. "What the hell?"

Kim's eyes were wide. "You think Jackie does drugs?"

"I don't know," Trisha replied. Jackie had seemed really anxious earlier, then had calmed down, and now she was all jittery and flushed. Trisha had initially assumed it was due to the situation they were in, but now she wondered.

"We should tell Craig," Kim said.

"And admit we broke into her room?"

"He won't care when he hears what we found."

Trisha knew she was right. "Let's get out of here. We'll get the supplies, then I'll talk to him."

Kim replaced the papers in the trashcan.

Trisha reached for the doorknob but hesitated as a spike of fear shot through her. She thought she heard something in the hallway.

After a moment, she took a deep breath, gingerly turned the knob and opened the door to peek outside.

The hallway looked clear.

Mouse stood in the Mechanical Room, among the maze of machinery and life-support systems, wondering if he had made a mistake.

The constant roar and hum made it hard to think. Normally, the noise didn't bother him, but now, with his mind full of doubt and concern, he couldn't concentrate.

Tony had surprised him. When he had started grilling Mouse about whether they could do it, whether they could actually turn off the power, Mouse had been honest. They could kill the power, and he could turn it back on. But he didn't know if he had been forceful enough when he'd warned Tony.

Either that, or Tony hadn't listened.

Tony's plan was risky. Nothing like this had ever been done before. The facility had run 365 days a year since becoming operational. Virtually every machine had been replaced at one time or another, but the electrical power had never been shut off.

The problem wasn't the machinery, though. It was the computer system. Mouse wasn't sure if it would be able to restart everything after he killed the power. They were so dependent on computers to run the various systems that made life possible down here that he didn't know what would happen once they were shut off. He didn't know if the computer system would automatically turn the equipment back on, or if it would have to be instructed to restart everything.

What worried him the most was the air filtration system.

He would need to keep the power off long enough to wipe out the computers' current memory, but he couldn't just flip the power back on and walk away, assuming the computer would do the rest. They needed the support systems running, especially the carbon dioxide filter. Without it, if the carbon dioxide level grew too high, the air would become toxic.

Craig, Tony and Jackie huddled together in front of the two-way mirror. They reviewed their plan one last time, preparing themselves for action.

Jackie furtively glanced at the mirror. "You don't think Sebastian is in there, do you?"

"No," Tony said, "although I wish he was."

"We need to move fast, as soon as Mouse is ready," Craig told them.

"What about Manny?"

"He should be in position."

"I hope he can pull it off," Jackie said in a doubtful tone.

"It won't be easy," Craig admitted.

"With the two-prong attack, we'll overpower Sebastian," Tony assured them.

Craig hoped so. This was their only chance.

Trisha and Kim appeared. "We found these," Trisha announced, holding up a pair of two-way radios. They had also found four emergency canisters, narrow tanks only ten inches high that each contained approximately five minutes of air.

"Not great, but they might help," Tony judged, reaching for one of the canisters. Jackie and Craig each took one as well.

Kim gave Craig one of the radios, then left to rush the other one over to Mouse. "We need to be careful going in," Craig warned as he hooked the radio to his belt. "Sebastian could have booby-trapped the place."

As he spoke, Mitchell appeared.

"What about him?" Tony asked pointedly.

Craig looked at him, then at Mitchell. "Willing to help out?"

"Absolutely. You couldn't keep me away."

Tony opened his mouth to speak, but before he could, Craig said, "Good. You'll stay here and keep the security doors open once we get through."

"I'll do more good helping you get Sebastian," Mitchell argued.

"It's just as important to keep these doors open. If Sebastian manages to retain control, he could close them again. You need to prevent that. Got it?"

"What about Kim and me?" Trisha asked.

"Stay here with Mitchell. We need to make sure the passageway stays open."

She nodded in understanding.

"Are we ready?" He glanced at Mitchell. The scientist had a grimace on his face, as if he'd just swallowed a glass of sour milk, but he didn't argue. He nodded instead and turned away.

Jackie left for a minute, slipping around the corner.

Trisha gently pulled Craig aside. "I know you have a lot on your mind," she started.

He smiled. "I'll be OK, if that's what you're worried about."

"Well, I am, but that's not it."

"Ouch."

It was her turn to smile, although it quickly faded. "I need to tell you something. I don't know if it's fair even saying anything or not—"

Craig's expression cleared. "Oh, I understand. I'm not entirely comfortable with you being near Mitchell either," he confided in a low voice. He reached into his pocket and slipped her the taser gun. "Here. Use this if you have to."

She looked at the taser in surprise. "Uh, no, that's not it," she said, flustered.

He frowned, his confusion returning. "Oh. Then what is it?"

Jackie reappeared. Trisha sighed as she glanced at her. "Nothing."

"You sure?"

She nodded and turned away.

He reached out to stop her, but at that moment his radio sprang to life. "Boss? You there?"

Craig unclipped the radio and hit the send button. "I'm here."

"Ready when you are."

The air thickened with tension.

Tony and Jackie moved into the corridor and approached the security door. At the same time, Kim reappeared and joined Mitchell and Trisha by the mirror.

Satisfied, Craig entered the corridor and faced the door blocking the hallway. "OK. We're in position. Kill the power."

In an instant, they were plunged into darkness that was as deep and total as the darkest cave.

CHAPTER 16

Craig froze in surprise. Unable to see anything, he felt disoriented, confused. Next to him, Tony cursed under his breath.

After a few seconds, emergency lights clicked on. The lights were scattered throughout the level and left much of the facility in darkness, but at least they could see.

As one, Tony and Craig reached for the thick emergency door and pulled, trying to force it open. It was only when Jackie joined in that they were able to get it moving. It took longer than expected, however, the door's hydraulics fighting them for every inch, but they were finally able to push the door into the wall.

Once the door was in place, Craig, Tony and Jackie raced to the end of the hallway. There was a second security door blocking their path, which Sebastian had also engaged. Behind them, Trisha, Mitchell and Kim entered the corridor.

By the time they managed to open the second door—with Mitchell's help—Craig was dripping with sweat. He wiped his forehead absently as he followed Tony into the security office. They were inside! Craig felt an almost savage thrill—but his elation was tempered by the feeling that time was running out. It had taken longer to open the security doors than he'd expected, and he was already tired, his muscles strained from the effort.

He saw Tony look around in amazement. The security room had been trashed. Papers were scattered all over the floor and one of the computer monitors had been smashed. Wires dangled from underneath the security control panel.

Tony turned to the metal box hanging on the wall behind the desk and squatted down. "He didn't get it open," he said with relief. "The lock's scratched up but it held."

"We need to get moving," Craig said in a hurried tone.

Tony pulled out his key ring. "Let me just get the gun—"

"There's no time."

"He's right," Jackie said, edging towards the door. "Come on."

Tony stood up and followed them into the hallway. The quickest way to the Computer Lab was to the right, around the corner and past Lab 2. They immediately headed in that direction.

"What do you want us to do?" Mitchell called out.

"Find the panel for the security doors and see if you can disconnect them," Craig yelled over his shoulder. "We don't want Sebastian to close them again."

As soon as the emergency lights kicked on, Manny lunged for the computer terminal in the corner of the Rec Room. He quickly got situated and waited for the computer to turn on.

When the overhead lights kicked on, his screen lit up. He immediately hit a combination of keys, but the mainframe ignored the command. It began its startup checklist, running through a self-diagnostic.

Manny gave Jill a shaky grin as he waited. He hunched over the computer, his hands poised over the keyboard as he waited impatiently for the diagnostic to finish. He would only have one shot at this. He prayed he would be able to pull it off.

Craig, Tony and Jackie raced to the next door and began forcing it open. Sebastian had triggered all of the emergency doors, setting up as many obstacles as possible. It was a bad omen, but

Craig didn't let himself think about it. They were already running out of time.

He wedged his fingers into the tiny space between the door and the wall, jamming his fingers into the inflated seals in order to grab the doorframe. The tips of his fingers were throbbing, as was his back, but he forced his body to keep moving.

As the three of them struggled with the door, Mitchell remained in the security corridor with Trisha and Kim.

Trisha took a step towards the lab area, wanting to be with Craig, but forced herself to stay where she was. She couldn't control her anxiety, though.

Kim slipped past her, heading towards the lab. Trisha frantically grabbed her arm. "Where are you going?"

"I want to get my hands on that bastard."

"You're supposed to stay here," Trisha said, her back to Mitchell. Silently, she added, "Please?"

"I found it," Mitchell said. "Hey guys, help me with this."

With a resigned look, Kim followed Trisha over to the panel. They managed to open it and began to inspect the wiring that controlled the motorized security door.

Brett had also become disoriented when the lights went out. He'd expected it, however, and had attempted to leave the Prep area before the emergency lights came on—but ended up banging his shin on something.

When the emergency lights clicked on, he discovered he had almost knocked over a cart filled with utensils. He couldn't believe how close he had come to creating a horrific racket that would've ruined any chance of surprising Sebastian.

He had at least had enough sense to keep the Prep room doors open. As soon as the emergency lights turned on, he left the Prep room and headed across the lab. He was fully suited in a gray biohazard suit, complete with its own portable air supply.

He knew Sebastian could be out in the hallway, just waiting for him, but he didn't care. He wanted out of the lab.

Without thinking, he slapped his hand on the doorplate. Of course, nothing happened. He swore under his breath and reached for the door. It wasn't locked, but it was difficult to get a firm grip.

He debated whether to take off his gloves. If he did, he'd be able to get a better hold, but then he'd be vulnerable. Still debating, he glanced out the window—and found Sebastian staring at him from inside the Computer Lab. So much for the element of surprise.

Sebastian sneered at him—and the power came back on.

Brett tried the doorplate again. Still nothing. The plate was computer-controlled, and the system hadn't come online yet. He quickly ripped off his gloves and started to pull on the door, struggling to get it open.

Manny frantically began typing as soon as the mainframe finished its diagnostic check. He threw commands at it, trying to establish control while also instructing the computer to ignore commands coming from the Computer Lab.

The computer paused, as if deciding which commands to respond to. After a moment, it began to run the scheduled startup programs. Manny swore under his breath as he typed, using language that made even Jill—who had lived with the man for years and had heard virtually every form of curse she could've ever imagined—blush.

Craig, Tony and Jackie wearily pushed the emergency door into the wall and stumbled down to the next one. As they reached for the door, the lights went out.

"Is the power off again?" Tony gasped as he struggled for breath.

Craig shook his head. "Don't know."

The lights flickered, went out a second time, and then came back on.

"Did Sebastian regain control of the system?" Jackie asked. "We can still move the doors, right?"

Craig and Tony began to pull on the door. "No, it's OK," Craig told her. "It must be the computer reestablishing its systems. Come on. The emergency programs haven't been engaged yet."

She joined in and the three began to force the door open. They were close to the entrance to Lab 2, at the intersection of the adjoining hall. Two more doors and they would reach the Computer Lab.

Sebastian threw commands at the computer, telling it how to establish its program parameters. His fingers danced across the keyboard, moving so fast at times that they were little more than a blur.

He had seen the other commands, the ones that tried to prevent him from taking control. It had to be Manny. Sebastian wasn't surprised. He was making a valiant effort, but Sebastian countered every move he made.

Manny kept distracting him, however, forcing him to respond.

They weren't able to bypass the basic mainframe programs—they would be unable to control any of the systems otherwise—so they dueled for control in how the computer assigned priorities, user protocols and administrator settings. At the same time, Sebastian was trying to execute the programs that had been slipped into the computer network. If he triggered them, he would take over the entire system.

Brett appeared in the hallway on the other side of the emergency door. Without hesitation, he reached out and helped open the door that stood between them. As soon as it was out of the way, he stepped aside.

"Good to see you," Craig huffed as they approached the last emergency door between them and the Computer Lab.

"You too." Brett became self-conscious about his biohazard suit. The other three only had portable air canisters for protection.

Tony and Craig reached for the door. With Brett's help, they quickly wrenched it open and shoved it into the wall, slamming it into place. After the door was out of the way, Brett pulled off his helmet. He would face the same danger as his commander. It was only right.

He let the helmet slip out of his hand and fall to the floor.

Up ahead was the Computer Lab. "You ready?" Craig asked.

Tony nodded, as did Brett. Jackie gave Craig a nervous smile and motioned him forward.

Sebastian was hunched over one of the computer monitors, seemingly oblivious to their presence.

Craig reached for the door, moving to the side so Tony and Brett could help. Jackie stepped back and the three men began to pull. Unlike the emergency doors, the lab door was more substantial, heavier, which made it harder to move. The three men gritted their teeth as they pulled, struggling to get to the man who had taken over their facility.

Manny watched in growing despair as Sebastian blocked his moves. He continued to fight, battling for each system that came online, but Sebastian managed to beat him every time. A bead of sweat rolled down the side of his face but he didn't waste time reaching up to wipe it away. He had to figure out a way to beat Sebastian.

He became desperate.

He started to skip steps, ignoring some of the minor programs that popped up. He threw out commands to programs that hadn't even fully come online yet in the frantic hope of establishing control.

So far, he'd come up empty-handed. Sebastian was better at this, Manny had to admit. But he couldn't give up. He couldn't. He was their only hope of stopping Sebastian from getting complete and total control of everything.

*   *   *

Deep inside the Mechanical Room, Mouse faced the air filtration equipment, his face covered in sweat. He'd waited for the computer to turn it on, but so far, the equipment remained quiet.

He watched the gauge that measured the level of carbon dioxide in the air. The needle had been slowly creeping up for the past few minutes, causing Mouse's anxiety to increase.

He decided he had waited long enough. He reached out, grabbed the lever on the side of the machine, and pulled it down to start the machine manually.

The machinery clicked but didn't start.

Oh crap.

Mouse pulled again but nothing happened. He immediately ripped off the cover and started to check the motors and wiring inside. If he didn't get this machine going, the CO_2 level would become toxic. They would suffocate and die within hours.

The needle had only gone up a little bit, but this was a big facility. The machine had a hard enough time maintaining the CO_2 level as it was. He didn't know if it would be able to lower the CO_2 level even if it started running right now.

He'd been waiting for one of the machines to turn on him. He'd felt that way ever since he'd learned about the emergency doors, hidden from him until they'd trapped Danny, and it had finally happened. The air filtration equipment had rebelled.

As he frantically worked on the machine, checking connections, he realized the temperature was dropping. That was another problem he'd have to deal with—if he ever got this damn machine working.

With grunts, the three men managed to pull open the door to the Computer Lab a few inches. They could hear Sebastian typing away, muttering an occasional curse under his breath.

Craig switched positions, getting between Tony and Brett. He grabbed a better hold on the doorframe and they pulled the door back, widening the opening until they could slip inside.

As Craig straightened, he heard Jackie's voice behind him. "Stop right there," she warned in a cold voice.

The three men turned—and froze. To his utter amazement, Craig found Jackie standing a few feet away with a gun pointed at his chest.

CHAPTER 17

Craig could've screamed in frustration. Sebastian was right there! "What the hell are you doing?" he demanded.

"Move away from the door or I'll shoot," Jackie told him.

"Why are you doing this?"

"Move. *Now.*"

Craig prepared to lunge at her but Tony held him back. "Don't," he said, with his arm across Craig's chest. "You do no good dying now."

"Smart boy," Jackie sneered. "There's hope for you yet."

Tony glared at her but didn't reply. He backed away from the door, stepping into the middle of the hallway.

Brett watched them carefully, his eyes constantly darting to Jackie's gun. When Craig moved away from the door, he and Tony created an inadvertent shield between Brett and Jackie. Brett took advantage. He spun on his heel and raced for the corner.

"Hey!" she called out, training her gun on him. She didn't have a clear shot, though, and swore when he disappeared around the corner. She quickly retrained her gun on Craig, holding him at bay.

"Now what are you going to do?" Craig taunted her.

She cocked the gun. "You're going to go back to the living quarters—"

"And if we don't?"

"I'll shoot you."

"We're already dead," he pointed out. "We're all on borrowed time."

"Start moving or I start shooting."

As soon as he was around the corner, Brett broke into a run. He raced down the hallway to the opposite end, turned the corner, and kept going, but had to stop when he found another emergency door blocking the hallway just past the Computer Lab. Obviously Sebastian had triggered the door before the power had been cut to prevent anybody from approaching the other entrance to the Lab.

Brett frantically tried to figure out what to do. He glanced at the door to the Computer Lab, debating whether to go after Sebastian—but knew Jackie might appear at any second. She could shoot him before he had the chance to pry open the door. He had to keep moving.

With a burst of adrenaline, he wrenched open the emergency door and raced down the hallway. He glanced down the side hallway, which was blocked off with two or three emergency doors, and saw Tony and Craig being forced back towards Security Room 1.

Brett grimaced. He was worried about Tony and Craig. He'd seen the look on Jackie's face. She was tough, relentless—and it was obvious she knew how to handle a gun. They didn't stand a chance against her.

He ducked and raced across the hallway out of sight. He was forced to open another emergency door as he struggled to get away, and there was another one up ahead. Before he reached the next door, he stopped and turned to the door leading into Lab 5. He slapped his hand on the doorplate, but it didn't respond.

Gritting his teeth, he managed to pry the door open. As soon as the gap was wide enough, he slipped inside and quickly looked around. He needed to find a weapon, something he could use to fight back.

His eyes danced around the room. The lab was dark, with various lab equipment arranged neatly on the work tables.

Brett hurried to a side closet and looked inside, but there was nothing that served as a weapon.

He didn't have time for this. He had to get moving if he was going to have a chance.

When he closed the closet door, he spotted a thin metal rod propped up against the side of the electron microscope. The rod was used to push slides into the microscope's field of vision.

Brett raced over and grabbed it. The rod was about a half-inch in diameter and over two feet long. He hoped it would work. It was a pretty weak weapon.

Sweat flowed down Manny's face as he continued to type. He had tried every trick he knew, but the end was nearing. He was losing the battle.

In a sudden burst of inspiration, Manny pulled up a communication window and typed in a new command: Establish control.communications.surface04266.3. He hit the ‹Enter› key and held his breath.

After a brief hesitation, the words COMM OPEN appeared on the screen.

With a sharp intake of breath, Manny typed, "Surface control."

"Control here," came the reply.

"Help! Mayday!" Manny wrote. "We are no longer in control and need help." He hit the ‹Enter› key to send the message. He risked a quick glance at the screen, to make sure his message was sent, and then kept typing. "Sebastian has taken over the lab and infected us all. He must not be trusted."

Just as he hit the ‹Enter› key to send the second transmission, he looked at the screen. It only showed "Sebastian has". The cursor was frozen, unblinking.

"Bastard," Manny swore. Sebastian had blocked the comm link.

He minimized the window, in the desperate hope that his message would eventually go through, and continued to fight for control, but the battle was soon over. His frantic efforts to snatch control of the computer system from Sebastian had failed.

The only thing he'd managed to accomplish, besides the aborted message to the surface, was control of the security corridor, and the door that led to the elevator. Both doors operated on their own systems, and he'd modified the programs on each one to run an infinity loop. That way, neither program would respond to outside commands.

Two doors. In the entire level, Manny had only managed to block two doors.

Jill saw that it was over. "How bad is it?" she asked in a gentle voice.

"We're screwed, babes," he told her. "I tried, but he's got everything now."

Jackie stood in the hallway outside the Computer Lab, her gun trained on Craig and Tony as they slowly, reluctantly retreated back down the hallway. They shuffled their feet, facing her as she forced them towards the security corridor.

Suddenly, she sensed someone behind her. She spun, gripping her gun with both hands—and felt an explosion of pain as Brett hit her wrist with a metal rod. She felt her wrist break on impact. The accompanying pain was unbearable.

But somehow, she held onto the gun. She'd been driven downward by the force of the blow, and was bent over, but she still held the gun in her hands.

Brett froze for an instant, obviously shocked that she hadn't dropped the gun, but then spun around and raced for the adjoining hallway. Jackie lifted the gun, determined to destroy him, and fired.

The sound of the gunshot was excruciatingly loud in the confined space.

She howled in rage and pain. The gun had wrenched her broken wrist—and she'd missed her attacker. She howled again when he disappeared around the corner.

She switched her gun to her left hand so she could fire without damaging her wrist.

She started after Brett, determined to kill him, when she was tackled from behind by Tony and Craig and knocked to the floor. Craig ended up on top of her, with Tony laying a couple of feet away.

Jackie fought like a lioness. Her arm with the gun was pinned under her, but before Craig could take advantage, she rolled underneath him. She brought the gun up, jammed it into his shoulder, and fired.

The bullet shot through Craig's shoulder, painting the corridor behind him with blood and filling his mind with pain, and the force of the gunshot threw him off of her. He half rolled, half smacked into the nearby wall, causing a secondary burst of pain.

Free of her commander, Jackie lashed out at Tony with her foot, kicking him in the face.

His feet slipping on the polished floor, Brett raced around the corner. He was back in the far hallway with no time to waste. He knew Jackie would come after him; he'd seen the murderous look in her eyes. He needed to find somewhere to hide.

There was still an emergency door in his way, sealing off the hallway. He gripped the frame and began to pull, an image of Jackie sneaking up behind him playing in his mind. His fear triggered another surge of adrenaline and he managed to pull the door open.

He heard the second gunshot and wondered if Tony or Craig had been hurt. There was no time.

He ran into the courtyard and frantically looked around. The good news was that the area was clear. The bad news was that he could already hear Jackie coming for him.

The hallways were dark, as most of the overhead lights hadn't come on yet. There was only a smattering of light here and there, leaving plenty of shadows, but none of them were dark enough to hide in.

He raced across the courtyard, ducked around the corner and dashed across the hallway in front of Lab 9. He paused at the next intersection, briefly toyed with going down to Lab 8, but then scurried towards the offices.

The doors to the office area and Craig's office, like the ones in the living quarters, were ordinary doors. There was no need—theoretically—for them to seal off. All of the dangerous work occurred in the lab rooms, which necessitated the airtight doors.

Brett could hear her coming. He grabbed the doorknob, opened the door and slipped into the offices. Desks filled the large room, arranged in orderly rows, and file cabinets blanketed the side wall. There were boxes and paper all over the place, however, which made the work area appear to be disorganized and chaotic.

He didn't mind the appearance, but he instantly regretted coming in here. The room was a dead end.

He looked for a place to hide but knew he didn't have a chance. There were no major obstacles, nothing he could hide behind. She would spot him as soon as she opened the door—and she would figure out where he was.

He was screwed.

He started down the center aisle, wondering if it was even worth trying to hide under a desk. Doing that would only delay the inevitable. As he hurried down the aisle, his ears strained to hear the telltale sounds of Jackie's approach. All he heard, though, was his own ragged breathing and the helpless pounding of his heart.

As he passed the third row of desks, he turned and started across—but stopped after the first desk, suddenly making up his mind. Squatting down, he set the rod on the ground and gripped the chair with both hands to pull it out of the way. He rolled it back as quietly as he could and placed it against the back of the desk that formed part of the next row.

He turned to duck inside when the door to the office suddenly crashed open.

Before the sound died away, he spun and pressed his back against the edge of the drawers next to the opening.

He was dead sitting out here in the open like this. He only had one chance. He reached for the rod—but it wasn't there!

Jackie's footsteps grew louder as she started down the center aisle that bisected the rows, following the path Brett had taken.

He whipped his head around, searching for the rod. At first he didn't see it. The room was dark, the only light coming from a lone desk lamp a couple rows over. Desperation gnawed at him. It was gone! Then he saw it. The rod was barely visible in the darkness, gleaming dully in the shadows.

Jackie came closer.

Brett dared not move anything other than his arm for fear of giving away his location. He stretched his hand out, feeling for the rod, searching for it. She was almost here! He was going to be defenseless when she found him.

She approached his row.

His mind roared that it was over. He was going to pay for what he'd done. She would notice one of the chairs had been moved back and would know where he was.

Just as he was about to give up, and Jackie took another step forward, his fingertips grazed the metal rod. As soon as he touched it, he picked it up, gripping it tight, and whipped it back so fast it made a faint "whoosh". To his left, Jackie entered the row. With a scream of fear and desperation, Brett swung the rod, bringing it back around. At the same time, Jackie swiveled towards him, aiming her gun—but before she could pull the trigger, the rod smashed into her knee. She crumbled to the ground, the gun slipping from her grasp.

Brett scrambled to his feet, the rod still in his hand. His triumphant grin faltered when he saw the gun only inches away from her. She had seen it as well and was already reaching for it. He was still confused, disoriented. He didn't understand why she'd turned on them—but in that instant, all explanations were meaningless. She would kill him as soon as she grabbed the gun.

He spun around and raced out of the room.

He ran down a couple of hallways, then turned and stopped. As he leaned against the corner, his breathing ragged and hot, he tried to figure out his next move. He thought about going back around the Computer Lab and out to the living quarters. At least he would be able to retrieve his helmet for the biohazard suit on the way. Without it, the suit was useless.

He made his way back towards the Computer Lab, but the lights overhead suddenly clicked on. He froze. Sebastian could be coming after him. He ducked into the nearest room—and found himself back in Lab 5.

He knew he couldn't stay there. Jackie would find him in a heartbeat.

CHAPTER 18

Concerned for Brett's safety, Craig called out his name—but his voice was weak. His body was in shock.

He could feel blood slipping down his arm, soaking his shirt. His shoulder was numb, his arm useless. He feared Jackie returning—but he feared more for Brett's safety. "Brett," he called, louder this time.

"He's gone," Tony said as he got up.

"You OK?"

"Better than you," he said. He leaned over Craig. "How bad is it?"

Craig's hand covered the wound, trying to stem the flow of blood. "Don't worry about me. Where's Jackie?"

"Chasing after Brett. Need help up?" When Craig nodded, he helped Craig to his feet, careful to avoid jarring the injury. He hooked an arm around Craig's waist and turned towards the security corridor.

"What are you doing?" Craig asked.

"You need to have that checked. Too bad we don't have a surgeon down here," he added, worry creeping into his voice.

"No. We have to stop Sebastian," Craig said. He started to turn around, but was hit by a wave of dizziness. Tony helped him stay on his feet, hesitated, and then started to lead Craig back towards the Computer Lab. Before they reached the door, however, lights flickered on overhead and the door to the Computer Lab closed.

Biting back his frustration and fighting the shock that had a grip on his body, Craig lurched over to a nearby phone. He reluctantly removed his hand from his wound and punched in the extension to the Rec Room. "Manny?" he rasped as he put his hand back on his wound. "What happened?"

"Sebastian has control. I wasn't able to stop him."

Craig swore.

Tony reached over and hit the button to end the call. "Come on," he said. "You're about to collapse."

Craig let the security officer turn him around. The two started down the hallway that led to the living quarters.

Before they'd gone halfway, Trisha flew around the corner, her face pale with worry. When she saw Craig, she cried out.

"I'm OK," he tried to reassure her, although his voice was watery.

"Ohmygod," she gasped, her eyes taking in his blood-covered shirt. "I knew this would happen. I just knew it!"

"I'm OK—"

"When I heard the gunshot, I knew you'd been hit but they wouldn't let me go find you."

She was so upset her body was shaking. Behind her, Kim appeared in the hallway. "You both should get back," he said, his voice a little stronger. "It's not safe here."

"Where's your gun?" Kim asked Tony, eyeing him suspiciously.

"I didn't shoot him. Jackie did. Somehow she got a gun down here."

Craig's head rolled on his neck as he looked at him. "That wasn't yours?"

"No. Mine's a nine millimeter. I don't know where hers came from."

The group managed to get to the security corridor. Mitchell came over to help, his long face tight with concern. "What happened?"

Tony quickly filled him in, his earlier mistrust gone. "We all need to stay away from the lab area," he told the group. "Jackie's running around in there and she's armed. No one goes in there without checking with me first."

Mouse's fingers scurried over the motor resting in his lap as he quickly tried to put it back together. He was still trying to get the air filtration system to start. He knew they were running out of time.

A drop of sweat hung from the tip of his nose as he quickly reassembled the motor. He had been forced to take it apart and clean it, as it had been caked with old oil and had been unable to spin. Even after he got the motor back in place, though, he wasn't sure if he could get the equipment started in time.

He glanced at the CO_2 monitor. The needle had crept even closer to red.

Forcing himself not to panic, he finished putting the motor back together and replaced it inside the machinery. He reattached the wires that ran to the motor, and then hooked the belt over the drive train.

He prayed he'd be able to get the machine running. Breathing raggedly, he continued to work, scrambling to bring the crucial equipment back to life.

Craig tried to hold still as Kim bandaged his arm. "You were lucky," she said. "The bullet passed completely through the shoulder, just missing the bone."

"I certainly feel lucky," he muttered.

Trisha hovered close by, desperate to help.

Kim told her to move back as she wrapped Craig's shoulder. Trisha barely heard her and Kim had to push her away so she could see what she was doing.

Craig gave Trisha a weak smile to try to alleviate her fears. She didn't seem comforted, though.

Manny and Jill entered the Medical Unit. "What happened?" Craig asked them.

Manny told him how he had fought against Sebastian but was blocked at almost every turn. "I thought I had him at one point," Manny said, "but then there was a whole flurry of commands. He had to have used some sort of special program or something. I'd never seen anything like that before."

"Those programs we saw on Mitchell's computer," Trisha said.

Craig nodded in resignation.

"That has to be the case," Manny said, his voice almost hostile with impotent rage. "There's no way he could've typed all of those commands so quickly. Had to be a program."

Manny went on, describing the rest of his struggle for control. As Craig listened, he felt an overwhelming despair. He realized they had probably helped Sebastian by cutting the power. Now he had complete control of everything.

"I did manage to send off a message to the surface, but I'm not sure it'll help," Manny concluded.

"With what you're telling me, the surface can't control anything now."

"They might be able to do something," Jill said.

Craig sighed. They could get into the labs, but it had come at a terrible price. If it hadn't been for Jackie, they would have gotten to Sebastian and stopped this nightmare. Now they had to worry about getting shot as well as dying from Ebola.

Kim finished working on his shoulder, and he had to admit that it did feel better. "I put on a special bandage," she told him. "It's specifically designed for down here. It protects the wound from getting infected by any airborne particles. That's why it feels so tight."

"Isn't it a little late to worry about infection?" he asked.

She grew flustered. "I-I know. It's the best I can do."

He thanked her. He didn't mean to rattle her.

He looked up at the ceiling, his mind spinning. He felt stupid that he'd suspected Mitchell, when in fact it had been Jackie who had turned on them.

He heard Trisha consoling Kim, easing the bite of Craig's comment. He wanted to add to her words but didn't seem to have the energy. They needed to find Jackie. He would tell Tony to start looking for her. They couldn't let her roam free—and they had to get into those labs. But how would they find her? He didn't know who else he could trust, other than Trisha. Was anybody else behind this?

He wondered if he was being paranoid. Even if he wasn't, though, it was obvious the others were asking themselves the same thing. When Manny and Jill had walked in, there had been a feeling of mutual distrust in the air. His team was starting to break apart, and he didn't know how to stop it.

CHAPTER 19

Up on the surface, the communications specialist motioned to her superior. "Sir, you need to look at this."

He came over and read the message on her screen. *'Help! Mayday! We are no longer in control and need help.'* "Is there any more to the message?"

"No sir. I tried to reestablish communications but so far I haven't been able to."

"Who sent it?"

"The person did not identify himself."

The commander's eyes narrowed as he reread the message. "It sounds like they've been infected," he mused.

The young woman didn't reply. She looked at him expectantly.

"Any more word on the evacuation of Level II?" he asked.

"The entire floor has been cleared and shut down."

He frowned in concern. He wondered if the infection in Level II had spread to the lowest level. God, he hoped not. Either way, the message was ominous.

"Figure out a way to reestablish communications," he told her. "I don't care how you do it. Just do it."

"Yes sir."

* * *

"How are you feeling?" Trisha asked, pulling Craig out of his thoughts.

"Physically? I'll be OK," he said.

"Does it hurt?"

"Some."

"I ... I was really worried about you back there," she confided in a soft voice.

Before he could reply, Tony entered the room, which made Trisha tense. "I got the gun," he said, clutching it triumphantly.

Craig was amazed. "It was in your office?"

"I told you Sebastian couldn't get to it. He tried but couldn't break the lock."

Trisha turned from him and looked at Craig. "I'll leave you two alone."

"You don't have to go."

"No, that's OK," she said. "I want to check on Kim, see how she's doing."

He watched her slip away.

Tony smiled. "I heard Manny got a message out. That's a good sign. Between that and the gun, we might have a chance."

Craig frowned at him. "How? I got shot, Brett's on the run and Jackie's armed. The odds are against us."

Tony's smile faltered. "Yeah, but we didn't know that would happen. Look, we flushed Jackie out. Now we know she's on his side."

"And that seriously hurt us. Not only did she stop us from grabbing Sebastian, but she destroyed everybody's trust in each other. I gotta admit, I feel it. I've been lying here wondering who else is going to turn against us."

"I agree, Captain, but we can't give up. We just can't. We have to keep fighting."

"Oh? How, exactly?"

Tony grew quiet. "I'll think of something," he promised.

Jill and Manny walked into the room. "Are we interrupting?" she asked.

"No," Craig said. He forced himself to sit up. It was bad enough having everybody see him with his shirt off and his shoulder wrapped in bandages. He wasn't going to lie around as well. "If you're wondering how I'm doing, I'm fine," he told them with a grunt.

Jill shared a look with Manny. "We're glad to hear it, sir. We were hoping ... I mean, we wanted to ask you if we can go into one of the labs."

"No."

"But sir—"

"It's too dangerous."

Jill took a deep breath. "Sir, we need to run tests to find out what we're infected with. It's the only way we're going to know which vaccine to use."

"I am well aware of the need to identify the virus," Craig said, "but it's too dangerous right now."

"We don't have much time—"

"The answer is 'no'."

Jill stormed out of the room. Manny glared at Craig before following her out.

Brett's throat burned. He swallowed, but it didn't alleviate the irritation. He felt like he couldn't get enough air. He was starting to get lightheaded.

He had been on the run for a while; doing everything he could to avoid Jackie. He was limited, however, and was running out of space.

He had grown desperate, forced to run blindly from location to location as Jackie hunted him. He thought he had known where she was, but then had heard sounds behind him. He didn't know what was going on, but had bolted from his last hiding spot—and had run into a blocked corridor.

He had spun around and raced down a different hallway. Now he was crouched behind the Conference Room, not sure if he should make a break for the security corridor or not. He heard a shuffling gait from the nearby hallway and quickly raced back around the Conference Room.

He continued to run for a while, only stopping to catch his breath. He knew he needed his helmet. Jackie or Sebastian could unleash Keres' Eyes and he would be dead. But wouldn't Jackie get infected as well? At this point, he wasn't taking anything for granted.

He was about to take the hallway to his left when Jackie suddenly appeared. She shot at him and he dove around the corner, scurrying down the hallway.

He ran without any idea of where to go.

The gunshot echoed throughout the level. Jill heard it, Manny knew, but she didn't seem fazed.

"You can't go," he told her.

"There's no use arguing about it. We're wasting time."

"If Jackie sees you, she's going to shoot you."

Jill got that determined look on her face he knew so well. Instead of responding, she left the security corridor and headed towards the labs.

Manny gnashed his teeth as he watched her leave. He had never been this scared before. He felt helpless to protect his wife. He didn't know what he would do if anything happened to her. She was the center of his life, the reason he breathed.

He saw her pause at the first intersection. She cautiously checked the hallway, then snuck around the corner and disappeared.

There was no way she was going alone. Still gnashing his teeth, he went after her.

Mouse's breathing had taken on a frantic rasp as he scrambled to replace the filters.

He couldn't bear looking at the gauge again. The last time he'd looked, the needle had hovered just outside the red zone. By now, it would be on the line, if not into the red, and if that was the case, they were in trouble. The CO_2 level would be too high—and the filters would be unable to clear the air fast enough.

Mouse only had a vague idea of what would happen. He thought he remembered being told about brain damage and other side effects, but he wouldn't let himself think about it. He was scared enough already.

The computers had come back online, but the filtration system remained dormant. He'd gotten the equipment to run but it had locked up after only a few moments, victim to a sensor that indicated the system was clogged. It had taken Mouse precious minutes to realize that the system wasn't clogged; the level of CO_2 in the air was simply too high. The only thing Mouse could think to do was change the filters. He hoped the new ones would draw enough CO_2 out of the air to prevent the sensor from triggering.

He slid the last filter in place with a clang and slammed the door. With sweat dripping into his eyes, he pulled down the lever to start the unit.

Almost reluctantly, the machine began to cycle up.

Mouse wrung his hands. He didn't know if changing the filters would help. The old filters had been usable, and in fact weren't supposed to have been changed for another three weeks. The new filters were the only ones left. If this didn't work, or if the filters became dirty too quickly, the sensor would trigger again and the machine would shut off again.

The filtration system began to process the air. Mouse held his breath, expecting the machine to cut out at any moment.

But it continued to run.

After a few moments, Mouse let out a ragged sigh of relief. His efforts had worked. Unable to stop himself, he glanced out of the corner of his eye at the air gauge. The needle was right on the line. But the filtration system was going, and besides, they didn't have enough bottled air for everyone. They would have to breathe the CO_2-rich air for now. He just hoped the filtration system would be able to remove all of the CO_2 out of the air—but deep down, he doubted it would be able to. There were almost a dozen people down here breathing and exhaling. The new filters would quickly become filled.

The surface had replacement filters but there was no way to get them down here. They were on their own, and the clock was ticking. All he'd managed to do was delay the inevitable.

It was almost ironic that they could all die down here, not as a result of the deadly viruses they worked on, but by the air itself. There was nothing else he could do.

He thought of telling the others but feared they would blame him for their situation. He didn't know what he would do if they blamed him. He became fidgety just thinking about it.

His back pressed against the wall, Brett took stock of his situation. He was nearly out of options in a game he'd been destined to lose from the start. He couldn't escape the level—and didn't think he would get another chance to strike back.

He jerked his head to the side when he heard a faint noise from the nearby corridor. He knew Jackie was hurt, but unfortunately he hadn't broken her leg. She continued to chase him, albeit with the slow, unstoppable determination that the Grim Reaper employed with all of his victims.

Brett hesitated, not sure if the sound he'd heard had been real. But when he heard it again, he forced his body to get moving. He began to scurry down the hallway towards the central lab area. Jackie heard him and picked up speed, forcing him to break into a run.

He was near the end of the hallway. As he ducked around the corner into the intersecting hallway, a gunshot rang out. He felt the bullet slice through the air next to his head before plunging into the wall.

He raced down the hallway, forcing down the panic that rose up to grab him. He knew he was running out of places to hide.

He turned another corner, entering the hallway where Jackie had prevented Craig and Tony from breaking into the Computer Lab. The hallway was now deserted, the door to the Computer Lab closed. Brett had expected this, but he hadn't come here to get to Sebastian. He'd come for the helmet he had abandoned earlier, the crucial piece that would finish his biohazard suit. But when he turned the corner, he stumbled to a halt, his eyes frantically searching the empty corridor. The helmet was gone!

Behind him, he heard Jackie coming up fast—much faster than he would have expected. To his right, the door to Lab 2 was still open. He dove inside, keeping low and out of sight.

As soon as he entered the lab, his eyes rested on the Prep room. There were more suits in there. He could get another helmet. He anxiously hoped that Jackie would pass by the lab without looking inside, but he doubted it. His only chance was to hide—and hope she couldn't find him.

He hurried across the length of the lab and entered the Prep room. There was a large window that looked out into the lab, as did each of the individual chambers, which worked against him, limiting his ability to hide. Keeping low to stay out of view, he crawled underneath the window, across the narrow room, towards the helmets. When he was at the far end, he looked up. The helmets rested on a set of shelves next to the door to Chamber 1, as they were the last piece of the suit to be donned before entering the sealed chambers.

He reached up but the shelf was too high. Taking a deep breath, he stood up, reached for the helmet—and found Jackie on the other side of the window, glaring at him.

Brett jumped back, a yelp of surprise slipping past his numb lips. With a triumphant grin, she raised her gun and pointed it at him.

Brett instantly dove for the door to the chamber, the need to run overwhelming all else in his mind. The double doors slid open and he slipped inside before they had finished opening. The realization that Jackie knew where he was, that she had found him, throbbed in his mind. He was out of luck. The game was over.

His training, his instincts, would not let it end so easily. Before he had time to think it through, he had dashed across the darkened chamber to Chamber 2. He didn't stop until he had gone through the second chamber to Chamber 3.

He stumbled to a stop as the double doors slid closed behind him. He quickly scanned the room, his heart beating desperately in his chest, then scurried across the room and ducked down behind a metal cart.

He realized that Jackie could simply walk in after him. He jerked his head up and looked at the double doors, the only way into the chamber. The doors had identical windows, twin panes of tall, slender glass that allowed him to see into Chamber 2. He didn't see her but knew she could appear at any moment.

He leapt to his feet and ran over to the doors. There had to be some way to prevent them from opening. He looked around for a stick or something to wedge between the doors and the wall, to block Jackie from opening them.

As his eyes scanned the room, he spotted Jackie in the lab, staring at him through the large plate-glass window. His breath caught in his throat until he realized she couldn't get to him. The windows were thick plates of some specially designed material, like glass but different. Tougher. Probably some sort of acrylic blend. He didn't think a bullet could penetrate them.

He paused. What was she doing out there? She had to know she couldn't get to him through the glass.

With growing consternation, he watched as she walked away from the window. He thought she was going towards the Prep room, but she stopped after only a few yards. He walked across the chamber to the large window and peered out, searching for her.

He spotted her facing Chamber 2. She seemed to be looking at something but he couldn't figure out what it was—or why she was even interested. Then it hit him. The glass that Jill and Manny had found, the viral glass filled with the Keres' Eyes virus, was there.

He ran across the chamber to the double doors and pressed his face against one of the windows. Oh god, she had found the viral glass! He froze in horror as Jackie, using the rubber gloves, transferred the entire pile of viral glass into the grinder and closed the lid, sealing it. With an angry stab, she punched the button on the grinder.

He flinched, breaking his paralysis. His heart went into overdrive, desperately hammering in his chest as the machine chewed through the glass, transforming it into a hot weapon. Brett glanced at the door on the other side of the chamber. He wondered if he could make it in time. He took a step back, ready to open the door, when the machine turned off.

Reluctantly, he looked over to see what Jackie was doing. The grinder was like a modified blender, although instead of a graduated glass pitcher, there was a large bowl with a lid on top. To his dismay, Brett watched as Jackie undid the catch and removed the lid from the bowl. The inside of the lid was coated with a layer of shattered glass, shredded to a fine white powder. The bowl itself was also covered in glass, with a large mound of the deadly stuff in the center. Brett broke into a cold sweat when he saw the powder. He knew it contained millions of viruses.

She turned and looked at him with a smirk on her face.

With her eyes locked on his, she punched the button on the grinder again. As the machine roared to life, the whirling blades threw the powder into the air, causing a deadly plume. The air became filled with the Keres' Eyes virus.

Jackie withdrew her arms and left. Brett watched helplessly as she walked away, leaving him to his fate.

The grinder continued to run, spitting up more and more powder into the air.

He was trapped. The only way out was death.

CHAPTER 20

"What have you learned?" the surface commander began the meeting.

The communications officer swallowed as he scanned the room. The men sitting at the table were responsible for every aspect of the facility. None of them looked happy. "We still aren't sure what's going on," he said. "We haven't received any further communications from Level III."

"Are they all dead?" someone asked.

"We don't know. The message we received could mean they're still alive—"

The commander cut him off. "The fact that we haven't heard from them seems to indicate otherwise."

"What about the investigative team?" another man asked, leaning forward.

"They've been unable to get down there. The entire lab might be a loss."

There were murmurs around the table. "Sir, the message may not have meant they were dying," the communications officer said. "It depends on how you interpret it."

"It's obvious *something's* going on," the first man spoke up. "Maybe there was a leak of some kind, some event that allowed a weapon to escape."

"If that's the case," the commander said, "then either every-body's dead or they will be."

"We could send a team down—" the communications officer began.

"That'd be suicide."

"I'm bothered by the message we received," the staff psychologist said. "The wording was highly suspicious."

"What do you mean?" the commander glared.

"I wonder about their mental state. The message was desperate, alarmist. Look," he said, facing the others, "we all know there are at least three active viruses that alter a victim's perception—"

"That's just a side effect," someone argued.

"Yes, but it *is* an effect. So is living underground for long periods of time. We have to be aware of that before we overreact."

The commander forced himself to hide his disgust. "Your point is well taken. However, the fact remains that we have not received any response from the Level, even after repeated requests."

"Have we received *anything*?" a third man asked the communications officer.

"The computers report that they're operational," he admitted. "There seem to have been a few minor glitches here and there, but nothing major."

"What kind of 'glitches'?"

"Simple mechanical anomalies, that sort of thing. None of the reports are cause for concern. They happen all the time. Frankly, the fact that we're still receiving them tells me the computers are fine."

"That leaves the human factor as the problem. Unless any of you can tell me differently, I have no choice but to consider the team a complete loss."

"Do you want me to start planning a replacement crew?" his assistant asked.

The commander nodded. "Obviously, we'll need to gut the place and make sure it's clean before we establish the new team.

When we do, I want to be hooked into the security camera feeds like we've discussed before, so we can see for ourselves what goes on down there. I don't like being in the dark—"

"Sir, with all due respect," the communications officer said, "what about the team we already have in place? Those men and women are depending on us to help them."

"What do you suggest we do?"

"I don't know," the officer sputtered. "We need to do *something*. We should call—"

The commander leaned forward, his eyes blazing. "Who? Who do we call? The police? Understand something, Lieutenant. We don't exist. Those men and women down there don't exist. There's no one to call because there's no facility in trouble, no 'accident'. Do I make myself clear?" His voice had risen to the point that he was virtually yelling at his subordinate.

His words echoed in the room. No one spoke. The communications officer, his face white, risked a nod.

In a quieter tone, the commander said, "All we can do is hope for the best—and salvage whatever we can."

*   *   *

"Keep trying," Craig commanded, hovering over Mitchell. The biologist retyped the message and hit ‹Send›, even though they hadn't received a response to any of their previous messages.

Cupping his elbow to alleviate the pain in his shoulder, Craig forced himself to step back. He knew he had to figure out a way to stop Sebastian and Jackie but he wasn't sure how to do it. Without help from the surface, they didn't stand a chance. Sebastian held all of the keys and was dictating the rules of the game.

Craig hated it.

He wanted to strangle Sebastian with his bare hands. He couldn't, though. Sebastian controlled the doors, and with Jackie's gun, could shoot Craig before he had a chance to grab him. Hell, all Sebastian had to do was wait it out. The Ebola virus would kill them before too long.

They had to do something, fast, but Craig was hesitant to try anything. The last time they'd tried, their efforts had backfired. True, they had won access to the labs, but they had handed over the rest of the controls to the complex in return.

He turned to go. He couldn't stand being in here any longer, watching Mitchell's fruitless attempts to contact the surface. Before he reached the door, though, it burst open, causing Craig to stumble back as Tony walked in with a big smile on his face. Flustered, Craig barked, "Don't you knock first? What are you smiling about?"

"You'll love this," the security officer said. "When I tell you, you'll be smiling, too."

"I seriously doubt it," Craig growled.

"I realized Sebastian forgot something. Mr. Intelligent did a good job of taking over, but he didn't remember everything."

"What are you talking about?"

"He wants to take the viruses out of here, right? He forgot the most important part: how to take them out."

Craig's frown deepened. "You talking about the canisters?"

Tony nodded. "We have 'em."

"Are you sure he didn't bring his own?"

"I checked the records of deliveries over the past three months, but he hasn't received any personal shipments, and they're too big to sneak in. No, the only way he's getting those viruses out of here while keeping them viable is by using canisters—and we have 'em."

Craig felt a spark of something he hadn't felt in a while: hope.

She knocked on the glass. Sebastian glanced up and instructed the computer to open the door.

Thoroughly exhausted, Jackie limped into the Computer Lab. Sebastian closed the door behind her, and then turned as she collapsed into a chair. "About time you got here. You done running around?"

She looked at him with glazed eyes. "You done being an arrogant prick?"

Sebastian gave her a cold smile in reply.

"Brett's trapped. He's in Lab 2, in one of the chambers."

"How many bullets did you waste?"

She tried to shrug but didn't have the energy. "I didn't keep count. Don't worry. I have another clip."

Sebastian held out his hand, a hard look on his face. She hesitated before handing over the gun. She averted her eyes. "I'm hurt."

"How bad?"

"He broke my wrist."

"And your leg?"

"I can walk, but he messed up my knee." She didn't know how much Sebastian knew, but when he didn't ask her how it had happened, she assumed that either he'd seen the attack or simply didn't care.

Sebastian turned back to the computer and began to type.

"At least Brett's no longer a concern," she said. When he didn't respond, she asked, "What about the others?"

He stopped typing and turned to her with a smile. "They're doing everything I expected."

Manny hurried to the intersection and stopped, pressing his body against the wall.

From where he stood, he could see across what everyone referred to as the "courtyard", the wide-open space between the conference room and Lab 6. Behind him was the Computer Lab, just down the hallway. He could feel its proximity, radiating with evil intent.

He spotted a shadow moving down the hallway between Labs 6 and 9.

That's the route he had to take—but it would be dangerous. Just thinking about crossing the courtyard, being exposed like that, caused sweat to trickle down his back.

He peered around the corner, checking to make sure the hallway was empty. From where he stood, he could see the corner of the Computer Lab.

This was so stupid.

Gritting his teeth, he forced his feet to get moving before he could think through what he was doing. He scampered across the courtyard and plunged into the hallway, chasing Jill's shadow.

He suspected he knew where she was going—but hoped he was wrong.

He reached the door to Lab 7 and quickly entered the room. As soon as he stepped inside, he saw the door to Animal Storage close. Grumbling under his breath, he followed his wife's footsteps and went into the room.

The musky scent of animals held against their will assaulted him as soon as he entered. Cages littered the room, filled with animals of various sizes. He cringed as the animals cried out. They had spotted Jill. The monkeys, a group of seven each in their own cage, were the loudest.

Manny hurried over to the monkeys. As their handler, he had shown a deft, caring touch in dealing with them. Upon seeing him, they stopped jumping around in their cages but continued to cry out. He talked to them in a soothing voice, reassuring them. After a few moments, the monkeys quieted down, a few of them with their tiny hands wrapped around the bars of their cages. Manny quickly grabbed a bag of treats and handed them out to his tiny charges to reward them for calming down.

He spent the next several minutes going through the room, checking on the other animals. He spent a lot of time in here, much to the relief of his coworkers. He had a lightning-quick temper, but in here he had the patience and understanding of a saint. He came in here not only to care for the animals but to soothe his soul.

After he finished, he slipped out the opposite door and entered the next hallway. The far end was still blocked off from when Danny had been murdered, which left the door to Lab 4 as the only exit.

Manny gnashed his teeth as he slapped the doorplate to Lab 4. He'd been right all along.

When the door slid open, he spotted his wife—and immediately became aware of the window by the far door. That damn window allowed Sebastian to look into the room without leaving the Computer Lab.

Manny instantly ducked down. "Jill!" he hissed. "What're you doing?"

"Come here. He can't see this half of the room."

He could feel his blood pressure rising as he scurried over. He stood up straight when he reached her and grabbed her arm. "This is too risky. We can't be here."

She pulled her arm back. "Leave if you want. I'm staying."

"But Jill—"

"We need to find a vaccine," she said in a clipped voice that was much different than the voice she used when talking to the other team members.

Manny scratched the back of his head as he looked around. Most of the equipment they would need was here. And they were out of Sebastian's line of sight.

Even so, he didn't like being this close to the lead scientist.

Making sure to stay out of sight, he made his way over to the opposite door and inspected it, seeing if there was a way to block it. He reached over to a nearby cart, grabbed a metal rod similar to the one Brett had used on Jackie, and wedged it into place to prevent the door from opening. When he was done, he carefully retreated. He couldn't do anything about the windows, but at least Sebastian couldn't get in.

He guessed that would have to do.

He turned back and found Jill already at work. He watched her for a moment, mentally debating whether to try to reason with her. Why bother, he wondered. He'd recognized the tone in her voice. She wasn't going to change her mind.

His shoulders slumped in acceptance as he joined her.

*　　*　　*

Sebastian pulled up the log of door openings—the doors he had left unlocked—and quickly scrolled through the list. He was surprised at first by the number of entries, but then realized that Jackie's hunt had greatly increased the number.

He scrolled to the end of the list and found what he'd been expecting. Someone had gone the back way, ending up in Lab 4. He resisted the temptation to glance at the window. He didn't want to tip his hand too early.

Instead, he turned to the monitor next to him and clicked through the video feeds. Cameras were set up in each lab, tiny units that silently watched the top-secret operations. He pulled up the feed to Lab 4. The video filled his screen, revealing the husband and wife team inside. Sebastian smiled as he watched them.

He was struck with a thought. "Did you make sure Trisha saw the vials?" he asked, glancing at Jackie.

She nodded.

Turning back to the first monitor, he instructed the computer to turn on the lights in Lab 9. A quick check showed him that the lights were indeed on. The vials were laid out and highlighted, his trap set. "Good."

CHAPTER 21

Tony punched in the number for the Computer Lab. When Jackie answered the phone, his grip on the receiver tightened. "I need to talk to Sebastian," he growled.

The lead scientist came on the line a moment later. "Yes?"

"It's Tony."

"Ah. Our trusted security officer. What do you want?"

"Don't talk to me like that, you little piss-ant."

"What did you say?"

"You heard me," Tony said. "You think you're so smart. Well, Jethro, you're not as smart as you think you are. In fact, you're nothing more than a blowhard; a stuffed shirt who acts like his shit doesn't stink."

"How dare you—"

"You act like every thought that comes out of that swelled head of yours is some sort of mystical revelation, yet it's nothing more than the recycling of other people's ideas and hard work. You're nothing, Sebastian. You know it and I know it. That's why you pulled this little stunt. You're throwing a temper tantrum because we haven't praised you like a tribe of superstitious natives who think you're a god. You're not a god, Sebastian. You're a pathetic has-been. Hell, you're a 'never-was'."

Sebastian's voice sputtered. "I'm going to make you pay, you little—"

"Don't bother," Tony said. "You're all talk and we both know it. I can prove it. You act like you're a genius but you forgot one little thing."

"What?"

"The canisters. You forgot the most important thing, you moron. See what I'm saying? You go through this elaborate setup to take control, but how are you going to get the viruses out? You're such an idiot."

"What do you want?"

"I know what *you* want," Tony threw back at him. "You want to take the viruses out of here—but you need the canisters to do that. Now who's in control?" Sebastian didn't reply, but Tony could hear his angry breathing. "If you want the canisters, you're going to have to come and get them."

Sebastian swore as he hung up the phone.

"What is it?" Jackie asked.

Sebastian didn't answer at first. Tony's taunting cut to the core, as it evoked a memory that continued to haunt Sebastian. It had started a year ago, when Sebastian shot down one of Mitchell's requests for a new project. He'd wanted to work on a "master cure", as if he could create one master antidote that would protect against every conceivable biological weapon. It was inconceivable; insulting that he would even make the request, and was a slap in the face to Sebastian's intellect. Mitchell had tried arguing that there were certain patterns he'd seen and he wanted to pursue it further, but Sebastian had shot him down, telling him it was a waste of time and resources.

Besides, Sebastian didn't add, he had more important things to focus on. Craig had confided in him, saying he didn't think he would stay in his current position much longer. Sebastian had been surprised, as Craig seemed to enjoy his role. He eventually realized it had something to do with the arrival of the new scientist, Trisha Foster, but the reason was unimportant. The CO position was opening up.

The realization galvanized Sebastian. Within weeks he traveled to the Pentagon to meet with the general in command of all of the Army's black-ops operations. Sebastian had earned the job, he knew, and when he was done listing his qualifications and performance, he asked for the position and sat back, confident that the job was his.

Instead, he was turned down. He was told he was invaluable where he was, but there was no way the military would promote him.

Sebastian flew into a rage. He didn't recall what was said but he returned to the facility furious, ashamed and betrayed. He deserved Craig's job. A man of his intellect should report to no one.

He stormed out of Level III's entrance chamber, through the security corridor and headed straight for the Computer Lab, wanting the comfort of his lab to try to recover from his humiliation. The level was quiet, and he'd thought the others were eating dinner which suited him fine. All he wanted was to be alone. After making it through the level, he approached the Computer Lab, slapped the metal plate, and the door slid open. He immediately charged into the room—

But was grabbed by a nearly invisible force, the air in front of him turning slightly opaque, and was thrown backwards. He stumbled as he was shoved backwards, his feet slipping, tripped and fell hard on his ass. Laughter erupted nearby as he found himself sitting in the hallway outside the Computer Lab, legs spread and his hair in his face. He whipped his head around and found Mitchell and Tony at the end of the hallway, Mitchell with a video camera in his hand and Tony doubled over next to him, holding his stomach as he laughed. Sebastian was both humiliated and confused. He looked back at the Computer Lab but the door had already closed. There were others laughing as well: Manny, Kim, and Danny appeared behind the two men, laughing at Sebastian's expense.

"Welcome home!" Mitchell said, causing more laughter.

Sebastian had never been so humiliated in his life. He struggled to his feet and slapped the plate again. The doors opened and he started forward, his arms stretched out before him—and immediately found resistance. As he watched, the air seemed to coalesce around his hands, turning opaque. "What the hell is this," he roared, his confusion interfering with his thinking.

"You can't figure it out?" Tony scoffed between laughs.

Sebastian flashed him a look of anger, and then realized what it was. They had somehow filled his room with what had to be a massive balloon, so big it filled the entire room. The balloon was transparent, but when he pushed against it, the rubber contracted and turned visible. "You fools," he snarled. "This is the most ridiculous thing I've ever seen. How dare you!"

He managed to grab the rubber and started to pull. Behind him, he heard someone caution him but he didn't listen. He didn't care. He tore at the rubber furiously, straining—and it popped.

It was the wrong thing to do.

The massive balloon had been filled with a clear chemical—Sebastian didn't know what one. He'd never bothered to figure out what they'd used. It didn't matter anyway. The damage was done, for the instant the clear chemical was released, it interacted with the air and turned purple in color. It happened in a flash. All Sebastian knew was that as soon as he popped the balloon, he was showered with a purple mist. It coated his skin, his hair, and his clothes.

The laughter turned deafening.

It took hours to wash all of the pigmentation out of his hair and scrub his skin clean. He used up every ounce of hot water but he didn't care. He was furious. Hot water was the least of their worries. He'd made up his mind. They had signed their death warrants.

When he finally got out of the shower, he reached out to some of his old contacts. They'd been surprised to hear from him, but very interested in what he had to say.

Within weeks, things were set in motion. Sebastian knew there was no turning back, especially from these people, not that he wanted to. His payout would be enormous. He was pleasantly surprised to discover that his decision to reach out to his old contacts allowed him to look Mitchell and his other coworkers in the eye. They thought he took their joke in stride.

He didn't like jokes. Nor did he like threats.

Pulling out of his thoughts, Sebastian looked at Jackie. "Tony has the canisters."

"What?" she cried. "You don't have the canisters!? I can't believe it. Of all the stupid—"

"Stop it. Right now."

She sat back in her chair. "Fine. So now what?"

He looked at his watch and nodded. "Stay here. I'll deal with it."

"But do—I mean ..."

"I told you, I'll deal with it." Before she could say anything else, he left.

Craig stood against the wall by the showers, waiting anxiously. He peered around the corner, looking down towards the Computer Lab, and made sure that the hallway was empty.

He was not only anxious, he was furious.

After agreeing to Tony's plan, he had instructed Mitchell and Mouse to get into position. They needed to watch Tony's back, to make sure Jackie didn't screw things up. Again.

Trisha had returned from checking on Kim and offered to help. He set her up in the security corridor, to cover their retreat. He told Mitchell to stand at the corner before turning to Lab 2, to make sure Jackie didn't sneak up behind them. Before sending Mitchell out, though, he asked if he'd seen Manny and Jill. He could use their help as well.

Mitchell swallowed. "They're not here."

"What do you mean they're not here?"

"They, well, it's funny actually. They're in Lab 4."

Craig exploded. "What the hell are they doing in Lab 4? Did you know about this?" Mitchell tried to calm him down but Craig was in no mood to listen to his bullshit. He swiped the handle off the nearest phone and punched in the extension to the lab—but before it rang, he abruptly cut the connection. Sebastian could be keeping track of all calls made in the Level. If he didn't already know about Manny and Jill in Lab 4, calling them could alert him.

Craig swore impotently as he slammed the phone onto its cradle—which caused his shoulder to howl. "Has anybody heard from them?" he gritted.

Mitchell shook his head.

"I need to warn Tony. They could end up being used as hostages."

"Boss. Calm down. They know what they're doing—and you know Manny won't let anything happen to Jill. He's watching her back, OK? Besides, it can't be undone."

Craig muttered to himself as he went to find Tony. "Right. It can't be undone. None of this nightmare can be 'undone'."

Now, as he peered around the corner again, he couldn't help but worry. He was furious at Manny and Jill, especially as he'd expressly forbid them from going into the lab area.

But his doubt was overshadowing his anger. He didn't know if Tony's plan would work. So far, Sebastian had defeated them at every turn. Their only hope was that Sebastian had truly been surprised, that he had forgotten about the portable canisters. If so, then they might actually be able to get him.

Still, he worried.

Tony slipped out of the conference room, set the lunchbox-sized canisters in the courtyard and joined Mouse in the hallway that led back towards Security Room 1.

"Did you call him?" Mouse asked.

Tony nodded. "He should be here any minute. Ready?"

Mouse could tell Tony was nervous, but that knowledge didn't ease his own jitters. "I-I guess."

Tony placed a hand on his shoulder. "I'm depending on you. The others are making sure Jackie doesn't sneak up on me. I need you to watch my back—"

Mouse started to shake his head, aghast at what Tony was saying. His entire body started to vibrate with fear.

Tony leaned in. "Do you want innocents to get hurt?"

"I've got a bad feeling about this," Mouse admitted.

"You can do this. If anything happens to me, I need you to make sure no one else is harmed. Hold them back if you have to. More importantly, I need you to get the canisters before Sebastian does." Mouse began to protest again but Tony wouldn't listen. "You're the fastest one here. You can dash out, grab the canisters and get out of sight before he can get them. OK?"

Mouse wrung his hands. He didn't know how to keep the others back—no one listened to him—and he started to tell that to Tony, but before he could, they heard a door open down the hallway. Sebastian was coming.

Wringing his hands harder, Mouse nodded to Tony. He felt trapped, unable to back away now that Tony's plan had been initiated.

He watched with trepidation as Tony scooted to the edge of the hallway and peered around the corner, preparing to confront Sebastian. Tony acted like he was in his element, but as Mouse watched him, something didn't seem right. Mouse didn't know what it was, but his anxiety magnified.

Sebastian stepped out of the Computer Lab and glared at Jackie until she instructed the computer to close and lock the door. Satisfied, he turned and started down the hallway towards the courtyard.

The area was quiet, his footsteps the only sound he heard. As he approached the intersection where the hallway widened, he considered glancing down the intersecting hallway, but there was no need. He knew the other team members would be scattered about in defensive positions.

He entered the deserted courtyard. The canisters, two of them, sat under a pool of light three-quarters of the way down. With a faint smile on his face, Sebastian walked towards them.

Before he got halfway across the courtyard, Tony appeared from behind the conference room, his gun raised. Tony held the gun with both hands, aiming it at Sebastian's chest.

"Tony."

"Put your hands in the air."

Sebastian halted but kept his hands behind his back. "Isn't this a little melodramatic?" he asked with a faint smile. "Are you going to dare me to 'make your day'?"

"I'm serious," Tony growled. "Do it now."

Sebastian slowly brought his hands around and let them hang at his side. In his right hand was Jackie's gun.

Tony saw it immediately. "Drop the gun or I'll shoot."

"We're civilized men," Sebastian told him. "Let's start acting like it."

"Fine. You first. Drop it."

"You know I can't do that." He could tell Tony was becoming more agitated.

"Do it now. Last chance."

Sebastian was gratified to see the bead of sweat rolling down the side of Tony's face. Even so, he swallowed. "Then you're going to have to shoot me."

Tony tightened his grip on his weapon, his eyes on the gun in Sebastian's hand.

Sebastian suddenly raised his gun, aiming at Tony.

Tony pulled the trigger, his gun fired—and the world exploded.

Mouse heard the entire exchange between the two men. If it was possible, he was more anxious than both of them together. He watched Tony closely, knew the moment Tony pulled the trigger—and watched in horror as the gun backfired. The weapon exploded, torn in half by the force of the bullet. Shrapnel lanced Tony's body, hot bits of metal that swarmed over him in an instant.

Tony fell to the ground.

Mouse's eyes bulged as he saw Tony's face. It was covered in blood. He couldn't tell if Tony was even breathing.

He wanted to cry out in horror but a part of him whispered that Tony would be disappointed. He knew what Tony wanted him to do.

Before he could think it through, Mouse raced into the courtyard. He didn't give himself time to realize that there was a man with a gun at the other end, that he could get shot. He didn't want to let Tony down.

His shoes slipped on the polished floor as he shoved down with all of his might, trying to go from a dead stop to full speed the instant he committed to going for the canisters. The sharp smell of gunpowder assaulted his nostrils as he entered the courtyard, warning him of the danger his mind was starting to realize even as his legs pushed harder, faster. A faint cloud hung in the air, a grizzly reminder of the threat that hung over them all.

The canisters were just ahead, the silver-blue metal gleaming in the light.

Mouse had almost reached them when he inadvertently stepped in blood. Tony's blood. He slipped and fell, sprawling on his hands and knees, but even though he was in danger, even though he had slipped in his friend's blood, his friend who was badly hurt and maybe dead, Mouse didn't stop. He spun, reaching for the nearest canister—and Sebastian loomed over him. The barrel of his gun was pointed at Mouse's head. From his angle, the barrel looked like the gaping heart of a black hole.

He could no longer ignore the danger he was in. It slammed into his mind in an instant, the horror of Tony getting hurt, the lack of cover from Sebastian's gun.

Mouse jerked back, away from the canisters and the gun that protected them. His back hit the wall and he curled into a tight ball, whimpering helplessly.

Sebastian kept his gun trained on the young man for a moment, watching him, then turned and walked over to Tony. He leaned over, his eyes dancing over the multiple injuries Tony had sustained. The security officer was unconscious, his body in shock from the damage it had suffered.

Satisfied, Sebastian scooped up the canisters, hooking one under his arm so his gun would remain free. When he glanced at the canister's back, he saw that the LED indictor light was dark. He pursed his lips. They needed to be charged. That was easy.

He turned back to Tony, a smug look on his face. "You can't stop me," he whispered, aiming his gun at Tony's head. He had a flash of memory of Tony laughing at him and he began to pull the trigger, but then changed his mind. It was better to let Tony suffer through the pain.

Turning away, Sebastian returned to the Computer Lab, his footsteps drowning out the desperate scurrying of his former teammates as they raced to help their fallen ally.

CHAPTER 22

Craig was the first to reach Tony.

He fell to his knees, frantically hoping the security chief was still alive. At first glance, he didn't see how that could be possible. Tony's face was a mess, shredded by the shrapnel from the pistol. Blood was everywhere.

Craig struggled to keep himself together as he heard Mitchell running towards them. Trisha was a few steps behind and she gasped when she saw Tony's body.

He glanced down the hallway but Sebastian was already gone. He should have been more careful. Sebastian could have taken them out right there—

"He's still alive," Mitchell said.

Craig glanced at Tony's chest. When he saw it rise, he let out a raged sigh of relief. "We need to get him to the Med Unit."

"Mouse? You OK?" Mitchell asked, looking over. Mouse was still curled into a ball, his body shaking with fear.

Trisha hurried over to him, bent down and put a gentle hand on his shoulder. She talked softly to him, calming him down.

"We can't stay here," Craig said.

Mitchell nodded. "Grab his legs."

Craig complied and the two men lifted Tony as gently as they could. "Come on," Craig whispered to Trisha. She nodded and helped Mouse to his feet. The young man was pale, hunched over with fear—but at least he was moving.

Craig took the lead. He tried not to look at Tony's injuries too much. He looked at Trisha instead as he walked backwards, glad for her presence. He appreciated the fact that she didn't ask him if Tony was going to make it. The truth was that Craig didn't know. All he knew was that Tony was lucky to be alive.

Drying her eyes, Kim let out a big, trembling sigh. She had known it would be hard going through Danny's things, but knowing it was one thing. Actually doing it was something else. Seeing his handwriting, reading his enthusiastic comments about his work, was soul wrenching. His presence filled the room, lingering so close she wanted to reach out and touch him, but he was gone, and that fact—hammered into her over and over—pierced her heart repeatedly. She felt as if she was bleeding inside from the repeated attack.

Her hands moist from wiping away her tears, she pulled back her hair, spun it around and made a ponytail. Normally, she would have done this in a series of quick, easy moves, but she had been wrecked by Danny's death. Nothing was quick or easy anymore. She was numb inside, like an ancient tree whose center had rotted away long ago.

She returned to the stack of papers she'd found, forcing herself to keep going. Even after reading through half the stack, it hadn't gotten any easier. The pain was still sharp. But she had to do it. Putting it off only prolonged her ache.

She read every note he'd made. Some of the papers contained graphs or chemical analyses of different agents. His notes were oftentimes the only way for her to understand what the graphs even meant, as she was looking at raw data instead of a final report. He had worked on a lot of viruses, but it became apparent that Keres' Eyes had attracted the most attention. Most of the paperwork she'd found had to do with the virus and the many setbacks Danny had suffered.

It was obvious that he had spent a lot of time and effort finding an effective vaccine. After going through the stack of papers, however, she was still unsure whether he'd been successful or not. She could tell he'd kept these papers as a guide, showing him what hadn't worked so he could avoid repeating himself, but nothing showed a clear indication of success.

Staring at the stack, she realized her mistake. Of course the papers would only show the failures. If he had succeeded, he would have kept that information separate.

She closed her eyes, her body swaying from grief and exhaustion. She should leave. There was nothing to find here—but leaving would feel like she was closing the book forever on her time with Danny. She couldn't bring herself to do that. Not yet.

She went over and crawled onto his bed. She remembered the intimate times she had shared with him and hugged her knees as the memories assaulted her. She would never feel his arms around her again, his lips on hers, or his breath on her body. The pain cut deep, burning as it sliced at her soul.

She held back the tears, determined not to cry. She'd wept enough already. The situation they were in wouldn't allow it. She had to be strong now, had to figure out a way to help. She couldn't let Sebastian get away with Danny's murder, she told herself. She had to do something to stop him.

She sat up. She had held off from looking in Danny's personal locker, which she knew was under the bed, as she'd been unable to bring herself to do it. Not only did it feel like a violation of his personal space, but it would be the last barrier, the last remnant of his spirit. Once it was opened, he would no longer be a living person. He would become part of the deceased, his effects needing to be catalogued and sent away to make room for whoever eventually replaced him.

Her body trembled slightly as she knelt on the floor. She closed her eyes, took a deep breath, and lifted the sheets that hung over the side of the bed. When she opened her eyes, she saw the dark green locker, half hidden in shadows.

She swallowed, grabbed the handle and pulled. The locker was heavy but she was able to pull it out from under the bed. She dropped the sheet and, with some effort, maneuvered the locker until it was facing her.

The trembling in her fingers increased as she reached for the clasps. Her eyes began to water. She chastised herself, knowing she had to be strong. She thought of Sebastian and was rewarded with a flash of anger that hungered for revenge. It eased the trembling in her hands, and she undid the clasps. Before she could stop herself, she threw back the lid.

The inside was a mess, cluttered with papers, some clothes, a couple of small figurines and a bunch of other stuff. Seeing the clutter, Kim had to smile, although the smile was sad. This was Danny's locker all right. He left a mess wherever he went, his mind working too fast to bother with such things as cleaning up—or even keeping things in order.

She began to empty the locker, handling each item as if it was a priceless treasure. She removed a number of shirts, magazines, and other odds and ends, but there was still more.

She reached back in—and a frown creased her smooth skin. She had found a dark-covered book with the words "Ledger" stamped on the cover.

She pulled out the book, sat back on her heels, and opened it. After scanning the first page, she knew she had found what she'd been looking for. It was a detailed record of his and Sebastian's efforts to find a vaccine for Keres' Eyes.

She flipped through the pages, stopping at random places to read his notes. It became obvious that they had struggled to find a cure and had met with numerous setbacks. Certain passages, wedged within the thin lines that had been designed to hold columns of numbers, were filled with Danny's frustration, usually followed with excitement for a new vaccine they were going to try. She realized that these notes corresponded to the paperwork she'd been going through. They were summaries of the work done, tracking each attempt they'd made to find a vaccine.

Danny's notes ended abruptly, his last entry written a few days ago. The entry was typical of some of the others she'd read, filled with childlike enthusiasm for the latest potential cure. However, the more she read, the more she believed that they had finally found the right vaccine. The initial tests had been extremely positive. The vaccine seemed to work as fast as the virus. It would have to, she thought, to have a chance of fighting a virus as aggressive as Keres' Eyes.

She had to smile at Danny's enthusiasm. He even described the 'promising' discovery, which in vial form was a dark purple color. Danny wrote that the color was so vivid it reminded him of a neon light.

She closed the book and held it to her chest. Danny had been right. The vaccine had indeed worked—so well that Sebastian had killed him in order to keep the secret for himself.

Craig needed to see the book. If there was a way to get to the vaccine before Sebastian, they might have a chance of stopping him. Even if he got away, though, this was proof that a vaccine existed—and that Danny had been murdered.

Kim glanced at the locker and the items scattered on the floor. She couldn't leave Danny's things sitting out like this. She put the book down; scooped up everything she'd pulled out and leaned over the locker.

After returning the items, she began to pull her arms free and felt her forearm rub against a small, hard object. Keeping her arm still, she freed her other arm and pushed the magazines and clothing aside. Burrowing her hand under the clutter, she grabbed the object and pulled her arms free.

She sat back. She found herself holding a small box, velvet-covered with a hinged lid. She instantly knew what it was: a jewelry box.

Her heart skipped a few beats as she stared at it. She had to know.

She lifted the lid and found a ring inside, its solitaire diamond twinkling at her from its bed of black velvet.

It was an engagement ring.

Danny had planned to marry her. She hadn't known. She would have said yes, even though they hadn't really talked about marriage. Kim hadn't thought Danny had been ready—but the ring proved she'd been wrong.

Staring at the ring, she imagined the life she'd lost. She would've enjoyed being Danny's wife. She would've been so happy.

As she began to cry, her pain wrenching deep sobs out of her that shook her entire body, her world slowly faded to black.

*   *   *

The monitor let out a steady beat that mimicked Tony's heart. His rate was slow, although Craig wasn't sure how much of it was from shock. Tony had suffered a brutal injury and was still losing blood.

As Mitchell worked, Craig leaned over to inspect the damage. Tony's face was a mess. Both cheeks had been sliced open, his nose was cut and his forehead was still bleeding.

"It's a miracle his jugular veins weren't hit," Mitchell murmured.

Craig nodded. "What about his eyes?"

"Don't know yet. Haven't been able to check."

Craig leaned closer. Tony's eyelids were covered in blood and Craig thought he saw a few nicks around the edges, but couldn't tell if any shrapnel had punctured them. He moved back, hesitant to touch the wounded man.

Mitchell continued to clean and irrigate a major cut on Tony's left cheek. Trisha stood across from him, using a suction to remove the blood and water. She was hesitant, though, afraid she would cause more harm.

Mitchell's eyes flickered towards her. "It'd be better with Kim here."

"I'm doing the best I can," Trisha protested. The two kept their voices low so they wouldn't wake Tony.

"I know, but Kim's the most experienced. Hell, I just know the basics." When Trisha didn't answer, Mitchell added, "This could take her mind off of Danny."

She didn't say anything for a moment, seeming to concentrate on her task. Craig didn't think she was going to move, but after a few moments, she put down the suction. "I'll get her."

Craig watched her go. He hadn't wanted her to leave but knew Mitchell was right. He turned and looked at the tall scientist as if seeing him for the first time. Trisha had a stubborn streak in her, yet Mitchell's gentle push had been enough.

"Sorry Captain," Mitchell said without looking up. "I hope I didn't make her mad."

"You handled that well."

Mitchell's cocky grin suddenly appeared. It was the first time Craig had seen it since this whole nightmare had begun. "I knowz how to talkz to ze ladiez," he said in a fake accent.

Craig shook his head in admiration. "I bet you do—but don't let Trisha hear you being so confident."

An involuntary chuckle escaped Mitchell's lips. "She'd make me pay."

Craig picked up the suction. "Should I help?" he asked uncertainly.

"Use some gauze pads instead."

Craig grabbed some pads and carefully wiped away the excess blood from around the cheek. "How bad is it?" he asked in a quiet tone.

Mitchell risked a quick glance at him. "It's bad. He's lost almost a quart of blood. He should be in a hospital, not down here."

A nasty thought hit Craig. "The Ebola virus is going to make it worse, isn't it?"

"Don't know. People infected with Ebola—if that's what we got—usually don't live long enough to heal."

Craig's jaw clenched. They had to figure out a way to stop Sebastian. Unfortunately, their best person had been injured. "He's in a lot of pain, isn't he?"

"He will be. When he wakes up, I'll give him some pain meds."

Craig watched in silence as Mitchell carefully applied a bandage.

"He's going to require stitches."

"Can you do that?"

"I guess." Mitchell chuckled. "I'll probably end up making him look like Frankenstein."

"Maybe Kim should do the stitches."

The phone rang. "Speak of the devil," Mitchell said. Craig went over to answer the phone, but when he picked it up, Sebastian's voice came over the line instead.

"How's the patient?"

A chill ran down Craig's back. "What do you want?"

"I told you not to underestimate me," Sebastian said in a cold voice. "Did you think I was foolish enough to walk into a trap?"

Mitchell had looked up at the sound of Craig's voice. The two men exchanged a look filled with anger and loathing. "You messed with his gun, didn't you?" Craig realized. "You knew it was going to backfire."

"Of course I did. Too bad you weren't the one who pulled the trigger."

Craig's grip tightened on the phone. "You're going to pay for this."

"No I'm not," Sebastian said in a bored tone. "I'm in control whether you like it or not."

"For now."

"Let this be a lesson. Stay away until I'm done."

"Why should we?" Craig demanded. "What do we have to lose? We're already dying."

"Did you forget I have the vaccine you need? If you want it, you'll do as I say—"

"And when are you gonna give it to us?"

"When I'm done here. Not before. But if you interfere again, you'll all die a horrible death. Remember that the next time you try to defy me."

*   *   *

"Are you finished?" Jackie asked as he hung up the phone. "We need to get out of here before they figure out some way to stop us."

"Relax," Sebastian told her. "They won't. Besides, I'm not ready." He turned to the computer monitor and watched Manny and Jill working in Lab 4.

"They can't stop us. We've worked too hard to fail. America has to learn. People have to know what we're doing down here. The only way is to unleash the virus so they can see what monstrosities their government has created. You agree with me, don't you?"

"Of course."

"We can't let them get away with this any longer," she continued with a fanatical edge to her voice. "The only way to wake everybody up is to unleash Keres' Eyes. Chicago is the perfect place. No one will be able to ignore the truth once thousands die. I wish it didn't have to be this way but we don't have a choice! The government will have to face up to what it's done—and when we provide the cure that the Army will refuse to give, people will listen to us."

Jackie continued to rant and rave, going on and on about the evils of their lab. The Army had operated under peoples' noses for decades and she was determined to tell the world.

He'd heard it before. He grunted occasionally, to make her think he was listening, but his attention was focused on the scene in Lab 4.

His plan was working perfectly.

Unaware of the fact that they were being watched, Manny and Jill continued to work on isolating the virus. They worked as quietly as possible, aware of how precarious their position was.

The phone hanging on the wall suddenly rang, jarring Manny out of his concentration.

With a desperate gasp, he launched himself at the phone, grabbing it before it could ring a second time. "Hello?" he whispered, his wide eyes immediately glancing towards the door.

Craig's voice seemed to explode out of the phone. "Put Jill on."

"She, uh, she's in the middle—"

"I don't care, Manny. Put her on *now*."

Manny held the phone out. "It's Craig. He wants to talk to you."

Jill's face hardened. "Craig, I—"

"Get out of there."

"We're right in the middle—"

"You and Manny need to leave *immediately*. Sebastian is crazy and could show up any minute. It's not safe—"

"With all due respect, sir, we're staying."

"That's not acceptable."

"If we don't figure out which virus we're infected with, we don't stand a chance of fighting it," she said. "Like you pointed out, Sebastian is crazy. He's not going to tell us what virus he used. Even if he did, would you believe him?"

Craig struggled to find a response.

"As soon as we isolate and identify it, we will give you a call," she said.

He hung up and swore loudly. Maybe it was a good thing he was being transferred. He had lost the ability to control his people. They should be rallying together during this crisis, not going off on their own.

Behind him, Mitchell continued to work on Tony. Craig didn't know how much longer he could stand looking at Tony's injuries. They made his stomach queasy, although he wasn't sure if that was from looking at Tony's wounds, or if it was because of the intensity of Craig's impotent rage.

Turning away, he walked to the door and looked out. He found Mouse hovering against the far side of the hall, nervously waiting for him.

"Mouse. Good to see you," Craig said. "Come on in."

Mouse hesitated, but came when Craig waved him into the room. "You wanted to see me?" he asked in a soft voice.

Craig nodded. He could tell that Mouse didn't want to be near anybody. He was visibly uncomfortable seeing Mitchell—and turned pale when he saw the extent of Tony's injuries. "I'll make this quick," he promised the young man. "I want you to go up between the floors and tell me what you find."

Mouse, who had been unable to stop looking at Tony, whipped his head around. "Wh-what do you mean?"

"I need you to find out whether we can get into Level II. I know you can reach the space between the floors, so I want to see if there's some way to get into the level above. Maybe there's a back door or a gap of some kind caused by the plumbing system. I don't know, but I need you to find out."

Mouse nodded in understanding.

"If you can't find a way up, then see if there's a way we can get into the Computer Lab from above. There's got to be some way to get to Sebastian."

Mouse turned to go, but Craig stopped him. "Be careful up there, OK? And stay in touch."

Jill and Manny continued to work in Lab 4, keeping well away from the windows. They worked quickly, going through the steps needed to isolate the virus.

They didn't know that they were being watched. In their desperate attempt to fight back, they had forgotten all about the cameras that silently oversaw each lab.

CHAPTER 23

Brett stood in front of the double doors, his face jammed against the glass, eyeing the way out.

He was so frustrated he could scream. He was totally helpless. He'd tried to break the window between the chamber he was in and the lab—he'd beaten on the glass so hard that his arm hurt—but the damn thing was too thick. He wondered absently if he had torn the muscles in his arm.

The only way out was through Chamber 2.

He massaged his arm as he looked hopelessly through the narrow windows into the chamber. That way was a deathtrap. There was no way he could get through there alive.

He wasn't sure what to do or where to go. He was trapped—all because of a stupid helmet. He couldn't believe he hadn't grabbed another one before diving into the chambers. He was a complete idiot.

He could tell that Sebastian had disconnected the air monitoring systems; otherwise, they would have detected the Keres' Eyes virus and sucked out all of the air in Chamber 2. Same with the ultraviolet light system. The lights hadn't kicked on, which would've degraded and eventually broken down the DNA that made up the virus, rendering it inert. Instead the virus was still in the next chamber, unharmed, eagerly waiting for him.

He forced himself to turn away from the window, forced himself to face his situation. He felt edgy and uncomfortable being in here without a full biohazard suit on, but he couldn't stand around waiting for a miracle. His only hope was to find something that could help him—and it was that realization that got him moving again.

He started to search the chamber.

He had never expected to end up working in some underground laboratory in the middle of nowhere. He had excelled at school as a kid. Outgoing and athletic, he had gone to college, but after graduation he had followed his father's footsteps by joining the Army.

He'd showed an aptitude for the Army's way of life, which wasn't surprising given his upbringing, but he quickly surpassed even his own expectations. After receiving a number of commendations for his work, he had attracted the attention of the Army's Intelligence Department. They had promised him a life of challenge and intrigue. It had been an easy sell.

He was put through a specialized training program that served as his introduction into the spy business. Within a month of finishing the program, he was sent overseas and his new career began.

It took him a few months to get a handle on his job and what was expected of him. He was certainly challenged, although his life ended up being less glamorous than he'd been led to believe.

He had returned to the States two years ago, reassigned to the Department's training unit. Before he had finished teaching his first class, however, he'd wanted out. No more lies, no more games. Teaching those young men and women the tricks of the trade cheapened his experience, made him question his own actions, and tainted his view of his superior officers, so he requested to be transferred out of the Intelligence division. After a number of heated battles, his request was finally granted—but the Army wasn't too keen on letting a former Intelligence officer with his experience and training coast through the rest of his enrollment by taking a cushy desk job somewhere, so they banished him to this dungeon instead, using his college degree in biology as an excuse to bury him deep underground.

He had taken the assignment in stride. He'd had a similar assignment in the past, after all, but after he got here, he began to suspect he was being watched. He wondered if paranoia had set in; he didn't know who would be watching him. But the feeling wouldn't go away. His instincts, which had served him well in the past, warned him there was more going on than met the eye, and he stumbled across a couple of suspicious things. He was new, though, and wanted to make friends, so he kept his mouth shut.

That had been a big mistake. Not only had he held back from saying anything, he had been wrong about the threat. He should've known better. The Army had locked him up and thrown away the key. They wouldn't have wasted resources on him. No, the threat had come from the inside.

He swore under his breath. There wasn't anything useful in the chamber. As he stared wistfully at the doors on the far side of Chamber 2, he noticed a rack of vials sitting on a cart near the back wall of the chamber. He stared at the rack for a few moments before it hit him. Those vials contained vaccines. A vaccine for the Keres' Eyes virus could be in there!

Pressing his face against the glass, he strained his eyes, struggling to read the handwritten labels taped to each vial. He systematically read each label in the first row, but unfortunately, none were labeled Keres' Eye.

He'd heard that Sebastian and Danny had worked on finding a vaccine for the deadly virus. Sebastian primarily operated out of Lab 1. It was "his" domain. But there was a chance he could have done some work in this lab as well—or Danny could have. Determined not to give up, Brett tried to read the labels he could see. The rack sat at an angle, allowing him to see some of the other labels, but not all ...

He froze. One of the labels caught his eye and he strained further, not daring to blink. There was a group of letters written on the side, something "eres". He tilted his head to try to read the vials better. After a few moments, he began to feel a stirring of hope. He was positive the label said "Keres' Eyes Vac".

His training in Intelligence instantly made him suspicious. If Sebastian had created an effective vaccine, why hadn't he told anyone? And why was it just sitting out here like this?

Brett's mind raced as he tried to figure it out. Sebastian would have wanted to keep the discovery a secret given his planned betrayal, but he couldn't have hidden the vaccine without arousing Danny's suspicion. Brett thought he remembered that Danny had performed many of his experiments in Lab 2, under the watchful gaze of the lead scientist. Maybe Sebastian didn't realize a vaccine was here. The label looked like Danny's handwriting, neat and professional.

Brett spun around and raced over to one of the cabinets. He yanked the doors open, searched around and withdrew an empty syringe. He stared at it for some time, his earlier hope tempered by fear. He didn't mind giving himself a shot. That wasn't the problem. The problem was that in order to do this, he would have to enter the next chamber. He would become infected with Keres' Eyes before he even reached the rack. Ever since coming here, he'd been terrified of becoming infected, and now here he was, unable to avoid it.

He could feel his terror rising as he contemplated what it would feel like. He hastily pushed his thoughts aside. He needed to get in the right frame of mind to do this. He began to take a few deep breaths—and tried not to think about what awaited him in the next chamber.

Jill checked on the culture growing in the petri dish. She knew she should give the culture more time to grow, but they couldn't wait. She began the process of taking a sample of the culture and transferring it to a slide.

She had taken a sample of her own blood and had deposited the blood onto the petri dish. She didn't know how infected they might be, so she had wanted to increase the number of viruses, and needed to have a sufficient number of viruses in order to get a clear picture.

She grimaced. She knew she was stalling. Her blood was probably filled with the rapidly multiplying virus—a fact she didn't want to acknowledge.

The culture sample in hand, she went over to the microscope. Some viruses couldn't be seen with a microscope, but if Sebastian had told the truth, they'd be able to see this one.

"Well?" Manny asked.

She ignored him as she adjusted the settings on the microscope. "Why don't you see if you can access the computer?" she asked him. "We should verify the sample with the photo database."

"Can't," he said. "Besides, you'll know it on sight. You know every virus we work on down here."

She didn't reply. There was a lot of truth to Manny's statement, but she didn't feel comfortable relying solely on her memory.

She searched the sample. She found viruses clumped together but wanted a clear picture of a bacillus so she could identify it correctly. There was so much riding on this. She adjusted the microscope—and found it. A single strand hovered before her, revealing its deadly nature.

"It's Ebola, all right."

"Are you sure?"

She looked at him and nodded. "It's got the shepherd's hook that's Ebola's trademark."

"Is it the weaponized strain?"

She turned back to the microscope to make sure. "Yes. I can see the modified trunk." She allowed a small smile. "We got it."

"Yes," Manny growled, smiling. He gave her a big hug.

She pulled away. "You're burning up."

He shrugged. "I'll be OK."

She frowned at him. She knew better. If they didn't get the vaccine in the next couple of hours, it would be too late. "I'm surprised," she muttered. "Sebastian didn't lie about which virus he used."

"Don't read too much into it," Manny warned. "He knew we would find out one way or another. He had to play it straight with this. Otherwise, we wouldn't have believed anything he said."

"Does that mean he's going to give us the vaccine?"

Manny hesitated. "No. We're going to have to find it on our own."

Alone in one of Lab 1's chambers, Sebastian finished preparing the remote-controlled biodispenser. When he sealed the device, he let out a small sigh of relief. Of all the viruses they worked with here, he had the most respect for the one he'd just handled.

After checking to make sure the dispenser was properly sealed, he prepared to leave. He would only have one other bomb available, but this was important. It was worth the price. Besides, he was in complete control. He doubted he would even need the last dispenser.

He reached into the containment box, his hands sliding into the rubber gloves that allowed him to work, carefully picked up the bomb and placed it in the compartment at the end. When he closed the door, ultraviolet light flashed from behind the tiny door, killing any microbes that might have lingered on the canister. He removed his hands from the gloves, opened the door on the outside of the containment box and took the canister.

With the bomb in hand, he made his way through the chambers towards the Prep room. He moved slowly, as the biohazard suit he wore had been designed for protection, not speed.

Once inside the Prep room, he turned and stepped into the chemical shower to kill any microbes that might have attached to his suit, washed off the chemicals with water, then got out of the suit and headed into the main portion of Lab 1. He was pleased with the way things were going. So far, he'd only had to deal with a couple of minor surprises, nothing to worry about.

He walked over to the back corner of the lab where a small door sat in the wall. Sebastian hit a button and the door rose up out of sight. A metal tray waited on the other side of the door, connected to a conveyor belt.

The conveyor belt system was used to transfer animals from Storage to one of three labs: Lab 4, Lab 3 or Lab 1. It allowed the scientists to move infectious animals without potentially spreading the infection to the entire level.

Sebastian placed the biodispenser on the metal tray. Satisfied, he walked over to the intercom system and contacted Jackie in the Computer Lab. "I'm on my way."

"OK."

Jackie unlocked the door to Lab 1, then to the Computer Lab. Within moments, he was back in his domain. "Mission accomplished," he said as the door closed behind him.

"Nothing going on here," she said in a bored voice.

"Good. I like it quiet." He walked over to the computer terminal and she moved out of his way. He immediately sat down in the chair she had vacated and began typing, only dimly aware of her limping over to another chair. When he hit the ‹Enter› key, the conveyor belt system came to life. It began to pull the metal tray along the small, dark tunnel, dragging its lethal cargo along the outside of the level.

Jackie sighed listlessly. As he watched the computer screen, he heard her picking up one of the cryo-canisters—and detaching the cooling mechanism.

"Sebastian."

"What?"

"The canisters are damaged."

He spun around. "What are you talking about?"

"I noticed the indicator lights hadn't changed, even though the canisters had been charging for a while, so I opened them up. Look." She tilted the cooling mechanism she held in her hand, which she had detached from the top part of the canister. The components had been smashed. "Tony sabotaged both of them."

"Dammit," Sebastian swore.

"They're useless."

Sebastian turned and glowered at the computer screen. They wanted to play that way? Fine. The gloves were coming off.

"You know they're not going to give us the other two canisters."

"Yes they will. I'll force Craig to hand them over."

"How?"

"Watch and learn," he said with a dark smile as he began typing instructions into the computer.

*   *   *

Brett had gotten a hold of Craig in the Med Unit. Trying to keep his voice as calm and professional as possible, he had told his commander about his predicament. "I'm going to try to break out," he concluded.

"What? How?" Craig asked.

"I can see a vial labeled 'Keres' Eyes vaccine'. I'll inject myself with it before the symptoms start."

"No. Bad idea. We'll get you out."

"I don't want you or anyone else jeopardizing themselves for me. It's too dangerous—"

"Exactly. It's too dangerous to go in there. We'll think of something else."

The intercom issued a short ring and a light began to flash on the phone. Someone else was calling them. Mitchell went to the other phone in the Unit and answered it. "Captain. Jill's on the line for you."

"Brett, hold on," Craig said. Without waiting for a reply, he picked up the second line. "Jill? You guys OK?"

"We're fine," she assured him. "Captain, we found the correct virus. Sebastian told us the truth. He infected us with weaponized Ebola."

"Good. Now I want the two of you to get the hell outta there."

"Yes sir, we will."

Craig switched back over to Brett. "That was Jill. They've confirmed that Sebastian used weaponized Ebola on us."

"Really?" Brett glanced at the doors to Chamber 2. "Hold on." He turned on the speakerphone, hung up the receiver, and scrambled over to the double doors. "I think I see it."

"See what?"

"The vaccine for Ebola."

"Don't be rash. I told you we'll get you out of there. If it makes you feel better, this gives us another reason to help you."

Brett came back to the speakerphone. "Sir. We have a way out of this mess. Please. I can help."

Craig's heart sank. Brett wanted to be accepted by the others, to contribute, but risking his life like this was way beyond the call ...

But was he risking his life? "Are you sure you see the vaccine for Keres' Eyes?"

"Almost positive, sir."

"You really want to do this?"

"Yes sir."

Craig rubbed the side of his jaw. He knew Brett was going to do it regardless of what Craig said, but he wasn't being suicidal. The Keres' Eyes antidote worked even after infection—if what Danny had told Kim was true. "I want you to be careful," Craig told him. "Inoculate yourself before you worry about anything else. Once you've done that, grab the vials and get the hell out."

"Yes sir."

Craig could hear the nervous tension in Brett's voice. "See if you can find some goggles before going in the next chamber. If you can protect your eyes—"

"I already looked. There aren't any."

Damn. "Remember, inoculate yourself before doing anything else."

"Trust me. I will."

Silence fell between them. "Are you sure—?"

"I better get ready."

"I can't be there with you, but if you'd like, I can call into the next chamber. When you're ready, I'll hear you come in. You can tell me what's happening."

"I'd like that, sir."

"I'll go ahead and punch in. Take your time. Whenever you're ready, I'll be there."

Brett's voice thickened with emotion. He thanked Craig and quickly hung up.

Her eyes still red, Trisha kept her hand under Kim's elbow, supporting her as they approached the Med Unit.

She had found Kim in Danny's room, crying, and when she saw the engagement ring, she had joined her. Kim had clung to her, grieving Danny's death and the happiness that had been taken from her. Trisha had held her for some time, tears dripping helplessly down her face.

After she calmed down, Kim listened as Trisha explained about Tony. Agreeing to help, she let Trisha take her away from Danny's room.

Voices floated towards them as they approached the Med Unit. Hearing Craig's voice, Trisha stopped and tilted her head, straining to catch every word. Kim stopped as well, and the two women eavesdropped on the conversation.

It only took a few moments for Trisha to realize what had happened. They'd discovered which virus Sebastian had used on them. As she listened, she heard Craig and Mitchell talking about where they could find the Ebola vaccine. They suspected the vaccine was under Sebastian's control, either in the refrigeration unit inside Lab 3 or the cryo-storage off of Lab 1.

"Maybe we can get into the cryo-storage from the Mechanical area," Mitchell suggested. "We could break through the wall and vaccinate ourselves before Sebastian realizes what we're doing."

Craig argued against the idea, pointing out that it was not only risky but impractical.

Trisha pulled Kim away from the Med Unit. "I think I know where the vaccine is."

A dim spark lit in Kim's red eyes. "Really? Where?"

"In Lab 9."

"Lab 9? Why there?"

"I saw a tray of vials there, back before this whole thing began. It might still be there."

"I doubt it. If Sebastian knew about it, he'd take it so we'd be helpless." Her voice started to quiver at the end, her emotions rising up.

"Maybe he doesn't know it's there."

"Then you should tell Craig."

"No. Not yet."

Kim blinked. "Why not? Shouldn't he know?"

"I wanna see if they're still there first."

"Why don't you want to tell Craig?"

"I don't want to get his hopes up. I want to check it out first. And you can help."

"Me?"

"I need you to distract him while I check it out."

Kim shook her head. "No. It should be the other way around—"

"No. You've suffered enough. Besides, I want to contribute. I ... want to show him that I can help." She didn't add that she wanted to prove to herself that she hadn't become totally dependent on him but it seemed that Kim could read her thoughts. She stared at her intently, weighing her decision.

"You don't have to do this."

"Yes I do," Trisha said in a soft voice.

Kim sighed. "What do you want me to do?"

"Just distract him for a few minutes. I'll go to the lab. If the vials are there, I'll bring them right back. If not, I won't even stop. I'll come back immediately."

"Be careful."

"Just make sure Craig doesn't find out." She turned and hurried towards the labs before Kim could change her mind.

CHAPTER 24

"You ready?" Manny asked, heading towards the door. He stopped when he realized his wife wasn't following him. "What is it?"

"I ... I'm still not sure I identified the correct virus."

"Babe, come on. You know your stuff. Everybody knows—"

"This is too important to rely on my memory alone, OK? We need to verify the sample, to make sure."

Manny felt a surge of anger, but it dissipated when he saw the doubt on her face.

"Do you think you could try the computer? For me?"

Manny flexed his jaws as he thought. "There might be a back door I could use," he murmured to himself.

"If it doesn't work, we'll leave."

He went to the computer terminal and reached for the keyboard. "This is really risky."

"We have to know."

Without replying, Manny began to type. His initial effort was blocked, as Sebastian had initiated a program that blocked all terminal access to the mainframe. Manny suspected it was a blanket program, however. He typed quickly, utilizing the flaws in the system's programs to maneuver past the block.

He began to feel more confident as he moved deeper into the system. His idea seemed to work. Hell, they could even contact the surface if they wanted.

He typed in the command to access the archives—but then the computer froze. "Uh oh."

"What is it?"

"He knows we're here. We have to go *now!*"

They ran for the door. Jill reached it first and slapped her hand against the doorplate, but it wouldn't open. Manny grabbed the door and pulled, but it wouldn't budge.

"Try the other one," Jill called out. She raced across the room, her husband on her heels, heading for the door near the Computer Lab. She slapped her hand on the doorplate as Manny kicked the metal rod out of the way, but the door didn't move.

Manny cursed under his breath. He glanced out the window towards the Computer Lab, his hands curling into fists.

Jill heard a noise behind her. She turned around and saw the conveyor belt door lift up. "Oh my God."

Brett took a deep breath, then another. He wasn't sure if he could do this. He tried to convince himself to follow through, to do what was required, but that was easier said than done. The next chamber was full of hot agents, millions of microscopic copies of Keres' Eyes ready to attack the moment he stepped inside.

He shoved the image away. He had to do this. He was not the type of man to let his commander down, to let his team down. Besides, he didn't have a choice. Sebastian would eventually decide to kill him. All he had to do was instruct the computer to open the chamber doors. There was nowhere for Brett to run.

He continued to take deep breaths, pulling in large quantities of air that filled every corner of his lungs. It was time to see how well he danced with the devil.

With a trembling hand, he reached for the doorplate.

Trisha crept quietly down the corridor past the conference room, stopped at the edge of the courtyard and looked down the adjoining hallway. She knew Sebastian was down there. If he walked out of the Computer Lab, he'd spot her. The image of him appearing in the hallway, a gun in his hand, locked her muscles for a moment. She fought the image, wrenching her head away to defeat the paralysis.

Forcing herself to move, she skittered across the courtyard to the hallway on the other side. She tried not to make a sound, afraid Sebastian would hear her like some sort of preternatural creature. She entered the hallway and stumbled to a stop, giving herself a moment to catch her breath.

She hoped Craig would forgive her for doing this—but he shouldn't be so protective. It was sweet and all, but it was really starting to bother her. His attitude was insulting. She'd taken care of herself long before he'd entered her life, swooping down to protect her like some dweebish knight in shining polyester.

She smiled as the image of Sir Craig, Knight of the Round Lab, popped into her head. She was being mean, she knew, and untruthful to herself. He might be a nerd to a degree, but she'd come to look at him as *her* nerd. He was smart, handsome and immensely sexy. He was also tougher than he looked—which only added to his appeal, dammit. But he could also be overly protective, demanding and inconsiderate.

She turned the corner and approached the door halfway down the short hallway. When she looked through the window into Lab 9, she spotted the vials immediately. A tiny sigh of relief escaped her lips. At least the journey, and the deception, had been worth it.

The area was quiet. It felt like she was the only person here. Even so, she looked around to make sure no one was sneaking up behind her.

Satisfied, she triggered the doorplate.

The door slid open—and she suddenly became wary. It was one thing for Sebastian not to know about the vials, but he would have locked the doors to all of the labs, right? She hesitated. But if that was the case, how had Jill and Manny gotten into Lab 4?

As she weighed her options, the door closed. She frowned, still unsure. She knew she should be glad the door was unlocked, but what did she expect? That it would be locked, and she'd have to run back to Craig like a helpless ditz?

Her face hardened as she pressed on the doorplate and walked inside. Trap or no, they needed those vials—and she was not about to surrender her independence to a man ever again. Not even Craig.

"I trust I have your attention," Sebastian said, his voice harsh over the intercom. "You weren't going anywhere, were you?"

Jill and Manny stared in horror at the biodispenser sitting on the conveyor belt's metal tray. "What do you want?" Manny demanded.

"We are going to perform an experiment. Go over to the conveyor belt. There's a gift for you."

"We already see your 'gift'."

"Not the bomb. The gift I'm referring to offers salvation— for one of you."

Manny started towards the rectangular hole in the wall. Jill grabbed his arm and silently pleaded with him, but he knew they had to do as Sebastian ordered. He walked across the room, his footsteps the only sound.

He approached the opening hesitantly, reluctantly.

When he leaned over, he spotted a syringe lying on the tray next to the remote-controlled biodispenser, filled with some sort of purplish liquid.

"Go on, take it," Sebastian said.

"Why don't you come in here and make me?" Manny asked, angry that Sebastian would even think to endanger Jill.

Sebastian laughed. "In your dreams. Now take it."

Manny took the syringe and returned to Jill.

*   *   *

Sebastian reached over and turned on the recorder to film the events in Lab 4. "The experiment will be straightforward, although I must admit I don't believe you will like it. As you have already discovered, the doors are locked and you cannot communicate outside this room. It's just you and me."

"What's the syringe for?" Jill asked.

In the Computer Lab, Sebastian smiled at her image on the computer screen. "That's what I like about you, Jill. You always go to the heart of the problem.

"I have filled the biodispenser with the Keres' Eyes virus. In a moment, I will trigger the dispenser to release the virus into the room. The syringe I have provided contains the vaccine; however, it is only enough for one of you. The syringe is a single-dose dispenser and will automatically release the vaccine once you inject the needle into your arm. That person will be protected. As for the other, well, I will go ahead and say 'goodbye'."

"You can't do this," Manny roared.

"You have one minute to decide who gets the vaccine."

The computer screen next to him was divided into four quadrants, each showing the video feed from a different camera. The bottom right quadrant showed Trisha as she entered Lab 9.

Sebastian watched Jill and Manny as they argued over the syringe. He thought it was sweet, really. Both insisted that the other take the vaccine. It was almost enough to make a cynical person like himself wonder if there really was such a thing as love.

Trisha walked into the lab.

As the door closed and the seals inflated, she went to the tray of vials sitting on the table. She almost didn't believe they were real, her disbelief causing her to reach out and lightly touch them. Only when she felt them did she accept their existence.

Her eyes danced over the vials, inspecting the seals to make sure they were intact. Satisfied, she looked around for something to carry them in and spotted a canvas bag on a nearby shelf. After retrieving the bag, she carefully transferred the vials and zipped the bag closed. Taking the handles in her hand, she gingerly lifted the bag, cringing when the glass vials clinked together.

She needed to get out of there. She'd pushed her luck already. She couldn't help smiling, though. She had done it.

She approached the door and triumphantly slapped her hand against the doorplate. Nothing happened. Her smile faltered as she tried the doorplate again. The door wouldn't open.

With rising panic, she grabbed the phone and dialed the Med Unit—but the line was dead. Dropping the receiver, she looked around the room. There was no way out, not even a window other than the one in the door. She was trapped.

Sebastian smiled at Trisha's image. He had his ace in the hole, the bargaining chip he needed. He'd originally set up Lab 9 as an additional insurance policy, in case things got messy—and to watch his beloved commander grovel—but with the damage to the canisters, his trap now served a higher purpose. Craig had become his slave although he didn't know it yet. The delicious irony. Trisha had taken the bait Sebastian had left for her. He knew she would. They were all so damn predictable.

He turned back to the other computer monitor where Manny and Jill were still arguing. "I insist you take it," Manny told his wife. "There's no way I'm going to let you die just so I can live."

"Don't you think that's how I feel?" she shot back. "I can't live without you. You're my entire life."

"And you're mine."

Sebastian rolled his eyes.

After hanging up with Brett, Craig had opened the intercom in Lab 2's second chamber. He wanted to be there, to somehow help Brett escape, but he couldn't. Being on the intercom, letting Brett know there were people who cared about him, was the only thing he could do.

He snapped out of his thoughts when he heard the doors open. Crap. Brett was in the room. He heard Brett scurrying across the chamber, followed by a loud sound. "Brett. I'm here. Are you OK?"

He heard a nervous chuckle. "I almost crashed into the table with the vials. Thank God it's on rollers."

"Forget about that. Focus on the vaccine. You don't have much time."

"I'm already on it," Brett said. "I'm filling the syringe now."

Craig shifted his weight from one foot to the other as he waited anxiously. "You almost done?"

"Yeah. Almost."

"You have enough to fill the syringe?" He waited for a reply. "Brett?"

Brett sighed. "Yeah, there was enough. I just injected the vaccine."

Craig echoed Brett's sigh. "Thank God."

"Do you know how long it takes? My eyes are already starting to burn."

Craig struggled to keep his voice level. "It shouldn't take long. Get out of there, just in case." He heard the sound of the cart being pushed. Brett said something, but he couldn't hear it. "What?"

"I said I'm taking the whole damn cart with me."

Under ordinary circumstances, Brett's comment would have caused a smile. These were nowhere near ordinary circumstances. They were so unordinary that Craig had to struggle to keep his sanity.

He heard a moan. "Brett? Are you all right?"

"I don't feel so good."

"Get out—" He heard a loud thump. "Brett?" He didn't hear the cart moving anymore. Pressing the receiver harder against his ear, he heard a low thumping noise, and realized Brett was in convulsions. "Dammit Brett, fight it! You can fight this thing! Concentrate! The vaccine will kick in any second!"

The only sound was the low thumping. When it suddenly stopped, Craig felt like crying. Mitchell and Kim, who stood close by, assumed the worst when they saw the horrified look on his face.

"Brett?"

No answer.

"Brett!" Craig nearly yelled.

The former Army Intelligence officer never replied.

"The bomb will trigger in five seconds," Sebastian announced. "Make your decision."

Tears streamed down Jill's face as she looked at Manny. "Don't do this," she whispered.

"I have to," Manny said in an emotional voice. "I can't let you die."

He took her arm and inserted the needle into her flesh. The syringe released the vaccine and the purplish liquid entered her bloodstream.

Jill never felt the needle. Her heart hurt too much for her to feel anything.

She didn't know if she would ever feel anything again.

As soon as Manny removed the needle, Jill threw her arms around his neck and cried against his shoulder. He wrapped his arms around her and held her tight.

Behind them, the biodispenser jumped to life, spraying its deadly contents into the room.

Craig was still in shock when an alarm began to buzz. He had continued to hold the receiver to his ear, unwilling to abandon Brett even though it was obvious he was already gone—but the alarm forced him to react. "What now?" he muttered under his breath. Reluctantly hanging up the phone, he followed Mitchell and Kim into the hallway. They split up to find the source of the problem.

Mitchell was the first to locate the alarm. It was in Security Room 1, an alert that warned of a problem with the electrical systems. Mitchell frowned at it as Craig and Kim entered the room. "I have no idea why it's going off," he told them. He reached over and pushed the button acknowledging the signal, silencing it.

Craig opened his mouth to reply but before he could say anything, Sebastian spoke to them from the intercom. "I'm glad I have your attention." The computer monitor, the one Sebastian had left undamaged, flickered on. "This is what happens when you displease me."

He sent the video feed from Lab 4 to their monitor, and Craig, Mitchell and Kim watched in horror as the events unfolded before them.

Manny pulled away from Jill to rub his burning eyes.

"Don't," Jill whispered, gently taking his hands. "It'll only make it worse."

"I'm sorry. I haven't been a good enough husband."

"Don't say that!" She threw her arms around his neck again. "You dumb, stubborn man," Jill sobbed. "You should've taken the vaccine."

"No. You're more important."

"That's a lie."

"No it isn't. The best parts of me were because of you."

She pulled back and kissed him. His knees buckled and he fell to the ground, inadvertently pulling her down with him.

"Manny!"

"I-I love you," he told her, his body beginning to convulse.

She tried to stop his body from shaking but he was too big. She ended up holding his head in her lap, stroking his hair. She could barely see him through her tears. "I love you so much," she whispered. "I don't know what I'm going to do without you."

"I love you," he told her, looking up at her. She tried to stifle the gasp that tore out of her throat when she saw the growing splotches in his eyes. They darkened, quickly turning black.

"I love you, too. I always have."

"I. Love..."

He never finished the sentence. She'd heard him say it a thousand times—and had taken it for granted at times—but she knew she'd never hear it again. Manny died in her arms, his eyelids slowly closing over his black eyes.

She was alone, now and forever, in this room and in the world. Her sobs were the only sound, the only presence there to comfort her.

CHAPTER 25

Mouse aimed his flashlight to the right, highlighting a nearby tank. He tried to see behind it but the shadows blocked his view.

He muttered to himself as he picked his way towards the tank. It would undoubtedly prove to be another dead end, but he was determined to inspect every square inch of this place.

It wasn't easy. The space between Level II and Level III was inhospitable and dirty. He'd been up here before but he didn't like it. He felt like he was crawling around inside a buried coffin.

He used his flashlight to slice through the oppressive darkness, which breathed down his neck from all sides. The only other light consisted of a faint glow from the open access door. He was on the far side of the facility, however, and the curved sides of the central shaft blocked the feeble light.

He checked the area behind the tank but there was nothing useful—just a few pipes and a small motor. With a frustrated sigh, he turned away and continued his search.

Even though it was cold in here, he was sweating. The place gave him the creeps. Wedged between the ceiling of Level III and the floor to Level II, he was forced to crawl as there was only a four to five foot gap between the two levels.

He scrambled over a bracing beam that was connected to two support beams, tripped and fell. The flashlight slipped out of his hand as he fell, skittered away, and disappeared.

The darkness crashed down on him and wrapped its cold hands around his face. Mouse began to scramble away, blindly trying to get somewhere safe, unable to think—and the flashlight came into view. A cord of pipes had shielded the beam from him.

Whimpering, he clawed his way to the flashlight and gripped it tight in both hands.

He sat on the cold concrete until he calmed down.

When he could think clearly again, he looked up at the floor hovering overhead. He knew he was supposed to find a way up there but he didn't think there was one. Without an access of some kind, they were screwed. The floor had been made with reinforced concrete. It would take a jackhammer to puncture a hole in it.

Picking himself up, he continued his methodical search. He'd never really checked out this area before because it frightened him. The few times he'd been up here had been to fix an equipment malfunction, and he had always scrambled back to the access door as soon as he'd finished. Now that he was here, though, he forced himself to check everything. It was a futile search, but at least it enabled him to get a better idea of the equipment, pipes and tanks that were here. In fact, there were more tanks than he'd thought. Some of the tanks held reservoirs of gas, air or water. Other tanks, though, were the storage tanks used by the vacuum systems. They stored contaminated air that had been sucked out of the chamber rooms, as well as regular air that had been drawn out to create negative air pressure. Mouse wondered if the tanks had ever been cleaned out. How much could they hold before they reached their limit? The metal tanks were huge, but this facility had been around for a long time. He made a mental note to inquire about it—if he managed to somehow survive their current predicament.

He wiped more sweat off his face. He was burning up, and he started to hiccup. He dry-swallowed a few times but it didn't help.

Doing his best to ignore his hiccups, he continued on into the darkness, using his flashlight to search for something, anything, that could help them.

Craig sat in the Rec Room, completely mortified. The lights had been turned low, which matched his mood. Manny was dead. Brett was probably dead as well. Why? Why did they have to die? What was the point of all of this?

He was ready to cede defeat—hell, he'd already been defeated. He had been in denial for too long and Manny and Brett had paid for it with their lives.

He was so tired. And angry. The vaccine should have worked for Brett. Was Sebastian wrong? Did his antidote not work? It would be ironic if Sebastian had risked his life and trashed his career for a cure that didn't actually work.

No, Sebastian was too smart for that—and Jill had survived becoming infected. So what was going on? Brett had said Jackie had ground up the glass found in the bathroom. It had to be Keres' Eyes. But what if she had switched the glass?

He didn't know what the truth was. He might never know, for they were running out of time. The Ebola virus was inside him, rapidly copying itself—and destroying his body in the process.

Brett's death really bothered him. Either the vaccine hadn't worked for some reason or Jackie had switched the glass. She could have used a different strain of Keres' Eyes, or a different virus altogether. There were all types of weapons in this facility. He'd never thought about it before, but this place was a candy store for psychos and mass murderers. They could find everything from flesh-eating viruses to Ebola—which liquefied a person's insides—down here.

The lights switched on overhead.

He looked up in surprise and found Kim standing by the door. "What's wrong?"

"Nothing. I just wanted to check on you."

He blinked a few times. "I didn't even hear you come in."

She knelt beside him. "How long have you been in here?"

"I don't know."

"Have you seen Tony? I think he's better."

"Really?" Craig sat up a little straighter.

She nodded. "I thought you might like to see him. It's the first good news we've had in a while."

Craig had to agree. "Do you know where Trisha is?"

"Uh, I think she's in the ladies room. Come on, let's go see Tony."

When Craig walked into the infirmary, he found Mitchell checking Tony's blood pressure. "How is he?"

"Better. His vitals are stable and the bleeding's stopped."

Craig joined him next to Tony's bed. The security officer was still sleeping, but his body seemed more relaxed. "You took off some of the bandages."

"I didn't want to restrict his face too much. He's not going to be happy when he wakes up. I figured being wrapped up like a mummy would only piss him off more."

A ghost of a smile appeared briefly on Craig's face. "Has he woken up yet?"

"Once. Briefly. He was in a lot of pain, so I gave him a shot of Demerol." Mitchell hesitated. "That was an hour ago. It's probably worn off by now. Should I give him another one?"

| "Good idea." Craig wasn't surprised Tony was in pain. He looked like a mess. Craig's shoulder hurt from getting shot, but luckily the bullet had gone clean through. It hurt, but he could function.

"I'll get working on it."

With a series of quick, efficient moves, Sebastian stopped recording the scene in Lab 4, removed the videotape and turned off the recorder.

He returned to his chair and glanced at the video monitor. Jill was still on the floor, cradling her dead husband's head. His eye twitched as he watched her cry. With an effort, he reached over and turned off the monitor.

He took a deep breath and then quickly looked behind him. Of course, Jackie was watching him. "Starting to feel guilty?" she asked. "Better be careful. People might think you're human."

"Shut up," he snapped before turning back around. He didn't deserve to have any regrets. He'd known the cost before he'd started all of this.

He wished he could do something for Jill—and immediately crushed that idea. He couldn't let her leave the room, not with Keres' Eyes in there. He looked at Trisha on the other monitor pacing around the room. Maybe he could somehow trap everybody in separate rooms. Nah. Not worth the effort.

He grabbed the videotape and stood up. Holding the tape in his hand made him feel better. They were ready to collect their stuff and get out. After all, they had a deadline to meet.

"Why are you smiling?" Jackie asked suspiciously.

"Because we're almost ready to leave this hellhole."

"We still need the other canisters."

His smile turned cold. "Of course we do. It's time for Craig to dance for me."

"He's not going to help you," she argued. "He's too much of a Boy Scout, a good little soldier who does what he's told. That's what's wrong with this place, and this government—"

"Not now." He was in no mood to hear her sermon.

She huffed at him, her face so distorted with surprise and hurt that she looked like a B-movie actress trying to emote. He had to stop himself from rolling his eyes.

He turned away, but as he did, her face changed, dropping the ridiculous façade. He continued his turn and put his back to her, but he no longer trusted her. He knew what he'd seen. He'd always suspected she would turn on him at some point, but he'd assumed she would wait until after they'd escaped the facility.

His suspicion grew the more he thought about it. When he'd come up with the solution for the canisters, she had been upset. He had believed it was because they had been duped, but now he wondered. She could have damaged the canisters herself.

Maybe she had a different plan, one that didn't include him. If so, she was making a fool's mistake. She was no match for him.

Kim approached the door to Security Room 2 but quickly turned away. She wandered back towards the Med Unit, couldn't go there, and found herself in the Dining Hall. She frowned as she looked around the deserted room, gnawing nervously on her thumb. She realized what she was doing and pulled her hand away from her mouth, but it didn't help her nerves.

She was worried. She had kept her promise but couldn't stand it any longer. She didn't know which was worse: having Craig confront her and demand to know what was going on, or having something bad happen to Trisha.

Her guilt finally grew too big for her to ignore, looming over her like some sort of winged monster, its teeth dripping with slime as it bent down to chomp her. She turned and left the Dining Hall, her face set in a mask to hide her concern—and fear.

When she walked into the Security Room, Craig was typing a message to the surface. "Can you get through?" she asked.

He shook his head. "I thought I'd try. Just in case."

"Oh."

He stopped and looked at her. "Something wrong?"

She nodded, her mask starting to crack.

"What is it?"

The intercom buzzed. "Craig."

Craig tensed when he heard Sebastian's voice.

"I, um—" Kim started.

"Hold that thought," he said. He turned and jabbed the intercom button with his finger. "What do you want, Sebastian?"

"The other two portable cryo-containers. I need them."

"You already have two."

"It appears that Tony has damaged them. They're useless."

Craig smiled. "Good for him."

"Bad for you. You're going to get them for me—"

"Fat chance, Sebastian. You need them so badly, go get them yourself." Craig turned away.

"You *will* get them for me."

Craig stopped. "And why's that?"

"Because I hold Trisha's life in my hands. Those containers are the only thing that will save her."

Craig frowned at the intercom. "What are you talking about?"

"Your dear sweet woman has gotten herself into a bit of a mess, I must say. Seems she went somewhere she shouldn't have. Now she's trapped, with only the biodispenser I hid in there earlier to keep her company."

"Oh my God," Kim whispered.

Craig threw himself at the phone. "You harm her and I'll kill you!"

"Strong words," Sebastian said. "Too bad you can't back them up."

"Let her go, Sebastian."

"After you give me the containers. You better hurry. You know what I'm capable of—and my patience has worn thin."

Craig's worst fears had come true. Trisha was in danger! He had to do something.

His mind flashed back to that fateful night in Dallas—her catching him sneaking out of the conference, their long talk in the bar where their admiration for each other and their physical attraction drew them closer, the amazing night in her room—and he found he could barely breathe. He hadn't stopped thinking of her since that night. When she'd arrived here, he'd been shocked to see her, stunned that she would be reporting to him, and scared of his feelings towards her. He had battled those feelings ever since, even as he grew closer to her, depended on her and confided in her. Now with her life in danger, he faced the truth, what he'd known deep down inside for some time: he was in love with her and had been ever since that night. Even though her presence caused an internal battle between what he wanted and what he fought against, he had grown to love her more and more with every passing day. She was all he thought about, all he wanted.

But now she was at the mercy of a homicidal maniac.

In a panic, Craig raced down the hallway towards the Med Unit. "Mitchell!" he yelled. "Don't give him that shot!"

He was so focused on getting to Mitchell before it was too late that he took the corner too sharply and slammed his hurt shoulder against the doorframe. He cried out as the force of the blow spun him around. It took a few seconds for the world to come back into focus.

"Jesus, Captain, what the hell's going on?" Mitchell asked, clearly startled.

Craig saw the syringe wavering in Mitchell's hand. "Did you give him that? Did you?"

"Huh? No. I was about to but you started screamin' your head off."

Craig bent over in relief. He struggled to catch his breath as he gripped his throbbing shoulder. When he was able to speak, he straightened. "We need to wake him."

"Who? Tony?"

Craig nodded.

"I don't know ..."

"Just do it."

Mitchell put down the syringe and reluctantly turned to the patient. After some prodding, Tony slowly came out of it. "How long have I been out?"

"Too long," Craig said in an abrupt voice. "Where are the other two cryo containers?"

Craig's voice had the desired effect. "The portables? Security Room 2. Why?"

"Sebastian's got Trisha trapped. He's threatened to kill her if I don't give him the containers."

Tony forced himself to sit up. Both Mitchell and Kim rushed over to stop him, but he swatted them away. "I'm fine," he told them. "It's bad enough you knocked me out. What'd ya give me?"

"Demerol," Mitchell said.

"No wonder I feel out of it. Dammit, you shouldn't've given me anything."

"Oh come on," Mitchell argued. "You're not supercop, no matter how much you like to believe it. Your body needs rest—"

"I'll rest when this is over. Until then, I'll deal with the pain."

Craig's eyes narrowed as he watched Kim. "You know where Trisha is, don't you?"

She yelped as if she'd been pinched. Her cheeks burning red, she nodded, unable to look at him. "Lab 9."

Mitchell groaned. "You knew about this?"

"I didn't know about the bomb! She swore she'd be careful."

Tony got to his feet. "You have a plan to get her out?" he asked Craig.

Craig tore his angry gaze away from Kim. He hadn't thought that far. "Not yet."

"You better."

Craig's eyes drifted around the room as his mind raced. As he tried to come up with a plan, he kept thinking about the biodispenser. He knew Sebastian would have filled it with Keres' Eyes. It was his weapon of choice.

He found himself staring at a cluster of tall oxygen tanks sitting in the corner of the room.

His fear regarding the biodispenser intermingled with the layout of the floor and the image of the oxygen tanks—and he was struck by an idea. "Where's the two-way radio?" No one knew. He realized he'd left it in Security Room 1.

He took off at full speed. He snaked through the checkpoint, spun around the corner and skidded to a halt inside the security room. Scooping up the radio, he called Mouse. "You there?"

Mouse's voice came back choppy. "Yeah, I'm here."

"The emergency doors, the ones that seal off the hallways. Is there a way to close them off manually?"

He strained to hear the answer. "I think so," came the faint reply. "You'd have to hotwire the motors."

"How do I do that?"

"Access the panels next to ... doorways."

"Thanks."

"... need me ... back?"

"No. Keep trying to find a way to stop Sebastian."

He hurried back to the Med unit. He had a plan.

As he approached the Med Unit, Sebastian's voice erupted from a nearby intercom. "What are you doing?"

Craig fumbled for a reply. "What do you mean?"

"There's no way to beat me. Where are the containers?"

"Tony's the only one who knows," Craig said, thinking rapidly. "We're trying to wake him up."

"You have five minutes."

Craig heard the intercom shut off. Without a moment to spare, he raced to join the others.

"Do you really think this is going to work?" Jackie asked.

"Aren't you Miss Optimism today?"

"Can you blame me?"

Sebastian shook his head. "You keep doubting me like this and I'll develop a complex."

"It's obvious you didn't plan for this to happen. What else haven't you thought of?"

"Very little. Besides," he said, turning to glare at her, "if I haven't thought of it, how could I tell you?"

She pursed her lips but didn't reply. He turned back to study the monitors, switching from one camera angle to another. So far, he'd been unable to locate them.

"You believe him?" Jackie asked.

"Of course not." After a moment of contemplation, he pulled up a new window and began to type.

"What are you doing?"

"Seeing if I can move the security cameras. I know there's a way. I just haven't bothered to try before."

She crossed her arms. "How long will that take?"

He shot her another glare. "A lot longer if you keep inter-rupting me."

"OK, everybody got it?" Craig asked in a breathless voice. He'd been talking for the last minute, explaining his plan to what was left of his team.

"Yeah," Mitchell said, only slightly confused. "I think so."

"Why bother?" Kim asked.

Craig blinked. "What?"

"I don't mean about Trisha. I wanna save her too. But why bother? I mean, what do you think is going to happen? We're all gonna die."

"You're shitting me, right?"

"Don't you see—?"

Craig lunged at her. Hands grabbed him from behind, holding him back, but Craig could feel his anger exploding. "How dare you!" he roared. "I know you lost Danny but if you're too goddamn selfish to help out a friend, a woman who'd bend over *backwards* to save your life, then you can go to Hell."

"Boss," Mitchell said as he held onto Craig.

"He's already won," Kim cried. "Can't you see that?"

"Don't you dare give up," Craig yelled at her. "Trisha wouldn't and neither will I!"

Tony broke the tension between them. "Come on," he growled, stumbling between them and heading towards the door. "Enough talk. You all need to get a move on." He shot a sharp glance at Kim. "Right?"

She nodded, her cheeks red. "Sorry, Captain," she said in a soft voice. "I—"

Craig's voice was still heated although it lost some of its edge. "The man's right. We need to move." There was no more time. He grabbed the handle of the two-wheeler, tipped it back and pulled it towards the door. Mitchell and Kim followed, pulling a second two-wheeler along behind them.

They had little time to put Craig's desperate plan in motion.

Trisha paced back and forth, nervously glancing around the room. She berated herself for getting trapped in here, but her self-loathing was nowhere near as strong as her fear.

She had spent the last ten minutes trying to think of a way out but nothing she came up with had worked. The worst part was the fact that she was being watched. She'd spotted the video camera a few minutes ago; its all-seeing eye unnerved her.

She couldn't get out of the room, but there was something she could do about the camera. She abruptly turned and walked towards it, intent on pulling out the wires. Before she could reach it, though, Jackie's voice issued out of the speakerphone. "You touch that and Sebastian unleashes the bomb."

Trisha froze, her worst fears confirmed. "Bomb? What bomb?"

Jackie didn't answer.

She looked around the room, really looked this time. She now knew why she hadn't searched the room very thoroughly. She'd been afraid of what she would find.

She spotted the bomb almost immediately. It sat on one of the shelves, almost hidden among a clutter of beakers, bowls and other equipment. Once she saw it, though, she was unable to see anything else. It was the same kind of remote-controlled bio-dispenser Sebastian had used on them earlier—but she knew that this time it would be filled with Keres' Eyes.

Her heart rate accelerated as she stared at it.

Her protective instincts suddenly rose up. She didn't want to die, not like this. She began to search the room, hoping to find something—a mask, a portable oxygen canister, anything—that might help. She checked under the cabinets and rifled through both supply closets, but couldn't find anything.

Despondent, her eyes drifted back to the biodispenser. All Sebastian had to do was push a button and her life would end. She wanted to cry, scream, pound her fists against the wall, but nothing would change the facts. She'd survived a sadistic ex-husband, and for what? To die in a secret underground lab in the middle of rural Illinois? That was so pathetic she could cry.

And she'd never had a chance to tell Craig how she truly felt about him.

Mitchell's feet slipped and shuffled as he tried to stop abruptly, pushed forward by the momentum of the dolly he pulled behind him. When he regained his balance, he glanced down the courtyard towards the Computer Lab. The area was clear—but there was a video camera at the far end. Unfortunately, there was nothing he could do about it. The camera was too far away. He'd just have to chance it.

He took a deep breath to steel himself and then raced across the courtyard as quickly as possible, dragging the dolly behind him.

Once on the other side, he pulled the dolly down the hallway, turned left and went past the door to Lab 9. He skidded to a halt at the next intersection and looked up at the video camera that hung from the ceiling. The small camera was angled to the side, covering the other approach to the Lab.

Mitchell ripped the wires out of the back of the camera before pushing the dolly back down the short hallway.

Dragging the other dolly, Craig arrived in time to see Mitchell disable the camera. "Don't you think he'll notice?" Craig whispered harshly between jagged breaths.

As he tilted the tank upright, Mitchell shrugged. "Better than him watching us do this. It's not going to work, you know."

Craig glared at him but didn't reply. Behind him, Kim stumbled to a halt. "Where do you want this?" she whispered. On Mitchell's direction, she had grabbed the toolbox out of Security Room 1. Her face was flushed, her eyes wide with fear.

Mitchell took the toolbox, returned to the intersection with the disabled camera, and spotted the panel for the emergency door. "Go find the other panel," he said, setting down the toolbox. He opened it and pulled out a screwdriver. "You'll need this."

Kim took the screwdriver and dashed back through the small hallway, passing Craig along the way. As she turned the corner, Mitchell began looking for the telltale panel that would allow him to get to the motor that controlled the emergency door.

While Kim and Mitchell worked on the doors, Craig focused on the oxygen tanks. He and Mitchell had grabbed the three large oxygen tanks that had been in the Med Unit. Each one had to weigh at least a hundred pounds. In his rush to try to save Trisha, however, he had managed to carry two of them on a dolly, even though his shoulder pounded from the strain.

He set the tanks on the floor, pointing them towards the door to Lab 9, and then hesitated. He didn't know if they would be enough. He was taking a tremendous risk.

He glanced up. Trisha stood on the other side of the door, staring at him through the glass. His heart cramped at the thought of her dying. He would not let Sebastian kill her—not if he could help it. He didn't know if his plan would work but it was all he could come up with.

He realized Trisha was staring at him. He motioned for her to turn away, but she didn't seem to notice. She continued to stare in wonderment and fear. Craig knew Sebastian would be watching her. He didn't want him figuring out what they were doing or their efforts would be in vain. Craig shook his head at Trisha and waved his hands again, his sense of urgency making his gestures frantic, confused.

She noticed his efforts, and his urgency. Even though they couldn't talk through the door, his message finally registered. She turned away and began to pace the room again—but she stayed close to the door.

Craig's suspicions were correct. Sebastian focused his attention on the video feed for Lab 9 and watched in silence for a few seconds. He began to experience a nagging worry in the back of his mind. Rather unpleasant. With a frown, he widened the picture, but couldn't see anything other than Trisha pacing the room.

The monitor next to him beeped. When he turned to it, he found that his program had succeeded. The screen asked him if he wanted to open the available source.

He nodded in satisfaction. Good. It was time to get this show on the road. He grabbed the phone, opened the intercom and punched in the code to broadcast throughout the facility.

"Craig. Where are you?"

In the hallway outside Lab 9, Craig jerked up at the sound of Sebastian's voice. He hadn't expected Sebastian's call to come so quickly.

"I'm losing patience," Sebastian announced. "You have ten seconds to tell me where the canisters are."

"Go," Mitchell whispered. "We'll keep working on these."

Craig took off around the corner and raced down the hallway towards Security Room 1. As he ran, a voice inside his head ominously counted down the seconds.

"Time's up," Sebastian's voice echoed.

Craig dove into the Security room and jabbed the 'Talk' button on the intercom. "No, wait! I know where they are."

"Where?"

Craig hesitated. Catching his breath, he tried to figure out a way to avoid answering him, but he realized there was no way to get around it. "Security Room 2."

"Good. Bring them to me immediately."

Craig's breath caught in his throat. He didn't know what to do. There was no way to get to Trisha in time—and when he glanced out the two-way mirror towards the open area on the residential side of the facility, he saw a security camera swivel around towards him. Sebastian now had control of the security camera, and was waiting expectantly. He was going to watch Craig retrieve the canisters.

CHAPTER 26

Craig stared at the video camera through the two-way mirror, locked in indecision, when a figure suddenly appeared in the doorway behind him. Craig spun around at the sudden noise, expecting to find Sebastian leering at him with a devil's grin. "Tony!" he said in surprise. "What are you doing?"

"I'm here to help," the security officer growled.

"How? You can barely walk. You should be resting."

"No, dammit. You need my help."

Craig's frown deepened. "Tony—"

"No time. Give me your jacket. And your shirt."

"What?"

With a burst of energy, Tony pulled his shirt over his head. "Give me yours. I'll fool Sebastian."

Tony looked worse with his shirt off. There were bruises and burns across his chest. "There's no way—"

"Look, I know where the cameras are," Tony said, glaring at him with one good eye. "I can fool him."

Still skeptical, Craig took off his lab jacket and quickly unbuttoned his shirt. "He's going to notice. You're shorter than I am and half your face is covered in bandages!"

"We don't have time to be choosy," Tony said in a raspy voice as he grabbed Craig's shirt and put it on. "Get going. I'll stall as long as possible."

Craig hesitated, Tony's shirt in hand. He didn't think Tony could walk straight. Craig wasn't sure how he was even standing. It had to be from sheer willpower.

He felt a stab of fear at the thought of what they were all sacrificing. Tony could re-injure himself, and Mitchell and Kim were risking exposure to Keres' Eyes.

He knew he needed to get back. There was no other choice. Throwing Tony's shirt over his head, Craig ran out of the security room.

Kim's breath escaped in short, hot bursts as she fiddled with the wires. She could feel the time pressure like a weight constricting her chest, making it difficult to breathe.

When she had pulled off the panel, she had been confronted with a large set of wires running into the motor. She had spent the last couple of minutes trying to make sense of them but had made little headway. Most of the wires ran into the back of the unit, with a few sticking out here and there near the front.

Going through the bundle again, she told herself to concentrate, but it didn't help. No matter what she did, she couldn't decipher the layout.

"Kim," she heard Mitchell call out. He spoke just loud enough for her to hear, and at first it didn't register. "Kim."

She leaned over and looked around the corner. Mitchell was leaning over as well, his head visible on the far side of the hall. "Try the red one," he whispered.

"What do I do with it?"

"It should provide juice for the motor."

His head disappeared and Kim straightened. At first, she didn't even see the red wire, and had to push other wires out of the way in order to find it. When she did, she ripped it out of the motor—but wasn't sure what to do with it. With a mental shrug, she began to touch it to different spots on the motor. Nothing happened.

She knew they were running out of time. The hand holding the wire was slick with sweat and her heart was pounding in her chest.

She pushed more wires aside and touched the power line to the node where the large group was attached. Still nothing. She ran the wire along the motor—and when it grazed a small node sticking out, the motor suddenly made a noise.

With a gasp, she looked up, but the door hadn't moved. She put the wire back to the smaller node, touching the metal prong that stuck out of the back of the motor, and the machine shuddered with energy. Keeping the wire in place, she turned her head, but the emergency door didn't appear. What was going on? When she removed the wire, the motor stopped running. In the ensuing silence, she heard Mitchell swearing quietly. Obviously, he didn't understand it either. The wire should have worked. So why didn't it? She could have screamed in frustration—but didn't think she could get enough air into her lungs.

Sebastian cycled through the video feeds on the monitor to his left, relentlessly switching from camera to camera. At the same time, he watched the video feed from the security monitor out of the corner of his eye. It had been gratifying to watch Craig walk towards Security Room 2, but that feeling had faded. He wasn't sure why. He couldn't explain it. The nagging doubt he'd had earlier had returned—and it was making him uncomfortable.

He continued to switch from one video feed to the next, but so far, nothing seemed out of the ordinary. He didn't buy it. He knew Craig was up to something. He just didn't know what.

Sebastian really didn't think Craig could outsmart him, but he was bothered. Craig was supposed to have died with Danny. Sebastian had timed it out but Craig had been late—a rare occurrence. Sebastian's doubts whispered to him, telling him Craig would slip out of this trap as well. Sebastian pushed his doubts aside, but they continued to pester him, warning him that

something was wrong. Sebastian knew he'd figure out the problem, but he wished he would do it quickly. He was getting
agitated.

He grabbed the remote detonator. His eyes drifted back
over to the monitor. Trisha was still pacing. That was good. She
knew she was going to die.

His smile faded as Jackie shifted behind him. He could tell
she had grown uneasy but he didn't care. She could screw off.

"You're going to kill her, aren't you?" she asked.

He refused to answer.

"You know where the canisters are. They can't stop you.
Why don't you just go get them?"

Sebastian spun around in his chair to face her. "I don't trust
Craig," he spat. "Besides, I enjoy making him work for *me* for a
change."

"This isn't necessary—"

"Becoming squeamish, my dear?" he asked. "It's a little too
late for that. What about our great plan to unleash Keres' Eyes on
the world?"

Jackie's eyes darted away as she tried to come up with an
answer.

He turned back around, effectively dismissing her. He
focused on the monitors, switching through the various feeds
available to him. He decided to focus on four feeds in particular, to
make sure things went as planned.

Jackie said something behind him but he ignored her. He
could care less about whatever pathetic excuse she'd come up
with. It didn't matter anyway. What was done was done.

He switched the monitor on the left to show the four
specific feeds he'd selected. Almost immediately, he spotted
someone approaching Security Room 2.

Sebastian tensed. He knew Craig was retrieving the
canisters, but as he watched the figure shuffle down the hallway,
his instincts screamed that something was wrong. The picture on
the monitor only reinforced his suspicion.

He was being played with.

Craig ran up to Mitchell, who was still working on the door. "How's it coming?"

"I got the motor working but the door won't close."

"Let me try," Craig said. He snaked his hand into the wall, even though both of Mitchell's hands were already inside.

"Captain—"

"We've got to close the doors. If we can't, we could all become infected—"

"I know. Captain, *please.*"

Craig stopped and looked at him.

"I can do this," Mitchell said. "Really."

Craig removed his hand and stepped back. He clenched his jaw, knowing he had to trust Mitchell—and Kim—to get the doors to work. He glanced down the hallway to Lab 9 when he was hit with a thought. What about the door to the lab itself?

Time was running out. Craig spotted a hammer sticking out of the toolbox, grabbed it, and ran over to the panel next to the lab's door. With a surge of adrenaline, he used the hammer to rip the panel off of the wall.

Trisha forced herself to continue pacing, to act like no one was in the hallway. It was so difficult to do. She wanted to throw herself at the door but she couldn't. Sebastian was watching.

She spotted the bag she'd filled with the vials. As nonchalantly as possible, she picked up the bag and put it closer to the door. If Craig managed to get her out, she didn't want to leave them behind.

Sebastian gripped the arm of his chair as he leaned forward. Craig was moving way too slowly. He was up to something. His moves seemed off, his walk different. Sebastian's grip tightened until his knuckles turned white. He didn't trust this.

He wondered if Craig was trying to stall. Of course he was. But why? It wouldn't bring him any closer to Trisha, and if he was hoping Sebastian would suddenly feel guilty or remorseful about threatening her life, he was wasting his time. All he was doing was pissing Sebastian off.

Sebastian opened the intercom. "Craig," he said. When the figure didn't respond, he grabbed the remote control. "Last chance, Craig."

The figure on the video screen seemed to be focused on something. As his body stumbled along, approaching Security Room 2, he continued to stare straight ahead.

Sebastian lost his patience. Craig was walking like some sort of zombie, playing a childish game. Sebastian toggled the intercom button again—and saw Craig scratching the back of his neck. He continued to scratch as he walked into the Security Room.

Tony reached the Security Room with a sense of relief. His journey here had been a dance, carefully shielding his face as he'd moved from camera to camera. He was exhausted from the effort and was burning with fever, a sign that the weaponized Ebola was spreading fast, but he knew his work wasn't done.

He squatted down, opened one of the cabinets and removed the last two canisters. Urging himself to get moving— he'd heard the impatience in Sebastian's voice—he left the office, keeping his head down to shield his face from the camera. For good measure, he halted outside the room, hooked one of the canisters under his arm, and with his free hand scratched the back of his neck.

He hoped his ruse would be enough.

At the sight of the canisters, Sebastian relaxed. Everything was going as planned. Craig had tried to delay the inevitable, but he had obviously realized that the only way to save his beloved woman was to retrieve the canisters.

Sebastian saw Craig stop outside the room and scratch the back of his neck. Of course! He had a rash, one of the signs of infection. Sebastian smiled to himself. Craig was dying and didn't want to show it. Nice try, but it wasn't good enough.

He was worse off than Sebastian had realized. Tough break for him, but it wasn't Sebastian's problem. He toggled the intercom. "Bring the canisters to the Computer Lab right away."

The figure on the monitor gave a weary nod as he began to shuffle back down the hallway.

"Move it, or Trisha dies. You have thirty seconds."

He watched with satisfaction as Craig began to shuffle a little faster.

Sebastian had broadcasted his threat throughout the entire level.

Kim had heard everything and knew they were running out of time. That fact made her frazzled nerves even worse.

She was so frustrated she was almost in tears. She had tried using the red wire but the door still wouldn't open. No matter where she touched the wire to the motor, the door wouldn't move. She'd found the one spot where the motor would activate, but it wasn't enough.

Not knowing what else to do, she kept the wire on that spot. The motor ran, churning in its hidden compartment, but she realized it hadn't been designed to run very often. Afraid that she was burning out the motor, she glanced inside to make sure it wasn't smoking—and noticed a tiny arm sticking out from underneath the machine. It was a gearshift.

She removed the red wire to stop the motor, and then reached for the arm. She inadvertently grazed the underside of the motor as she pulled the gearshift down, burning her fingers. She jerked her arm back, whimpering with pain. Still hurting, she reached in with her other hand and carefully touched the wire to the motor again.

The motor sprang to life. With wide eyes, she saw the emergency door suddenly appear, sliding across to block off the hallway to Lab 9.

The door closed the gap and the tubing around its edged inflated. The hallway was sealed off.

Craig was fiddling with the mass of wires that controlled the door mechanism when the emergency door suddenly closed at the end of the hallway. Kim had done it! Craig raced over and peered through the glass, but he couldn't see her. OK, that was fine. She could help Mitchell close the other one.

He went back to the lab door. With a renewed sense of purpose, he reached in and began to clear the wires out of the way to get to the motor.

In what seemed like an instant, Tony found himself past the security corridor and inside the working half of the Level. He could feel time slipping through his fingers, racing towards a conclusion he dreaded.

He turned left and shuffled along the hallway that followed the contour of the central shaft.

As he started along the wall of the conference room, he cleared his throat a few times in a feeble attempt to warn Craig and the others. They only had seconds left.

In the Computer Lab, Sebastian watched the figure shuffling past the conference room. He turned to Jackie. "He's heading for the courtyard. Go out there and meet him. Make sure the canisters are in good condition."

"I can't move very fast," she reminded him.

He held out the gun. "Take this."

She stood up, took the gun and limped towards the door.

"Jackie." When she looked at him, he said, "Be careful. Craig might try to pull a fast one. Tell him Trisha won't be freed until after we get the canisters and make sure they work."

"In other words, lie to him."

Sebastian's eyes narrowed. "Get moving."

*　　*　　*

Kim quickly replaced the panel, barely securing it to the wall, and turned to circle around the lab. She didn't think Mitchell had seen the gearshift. He would need help closing the other door.

She scooted down the hallway and stopped at the intersection. The coast was clear. She took a deep breath, preparing to dash around the corner, when the door to the Computer Lab suddenly opened. Kim jumped back, ducking out of sight, as Jackie exited the Computer Lab and began to limp towards her.

A sound to her right caused Kim to look across the hallway. Tony was approaching the intersection, his head down as he carried the two canisters. He was going to be spotted the instant he turned the corner. Kim froze, aware that any warning she gave would be heard—and then Jackie would know they were trying to rescue Trisha.

CHAPTER 27

Craig struggled to make sense of the mass of wires in his hands. The mechanism for the lab door was much more complex than the ones for the emergency doors. It would take him forever to figure out how it worked. He wasn't an engineer. He didn't know which wires to use.

He grabbed the two-way radio. "Mouse? You there?" he asked as loudly as he dared. There was no answer. He swore and shoved the radio back into its holder. Either he was too far away or the batteries were too low.

He and Mouse had done this once before. A couple of years ago, a door had malfunctioned and Mouse had hotwired it open. But that had been a long time ago. Craig couldn't remember how it had been done.

Tony's body thrummed with exhaustion. The canisters were dead weights dragging him down. It was all he could do to keep moving, but he had to. He refused to let his body give up.

As he neared the courtyard, he thought about Craig and the others. Right before he turned the corner, he glanced over to see if he could spot them—and saw Kim staring at him in terror. He froze, his exhaustion temporarily forgotten.

Kim jerked her head to the side, warning him that someone was down the hallway. With trembling hands, she waved him to go back the way he had come.

He nodded in understanding and turned around. Drawing on a well of strength he didn't know he possessed, Tony pushed his body to get moving. He picked up a little speed as he shuffled back down the hallway, intentionally making as much noise as possible. Past the conference room, he turned and started down the hallway that led past Lab 5 to the Computer Lab. In a burst of inspiration, he coughed a few times, his voice echoing down the cold hallway.

Kim anxiously peeked around the corner. Jackie was still by the Computer Lab waiting for Craig. Kim wanted to scream at her to move. There was no time!

Jackie's head whipped to the left when she heard a noise. Holding the gun out in front of her, she turned and began to limp down the hallway that ran along the back side of the Computer Lab. Within moments, she disappeared.

Kim took off the moment Jackie was gone, racing around the corner. She circled Lab 9 and joined Mitchell by the other emergency door, a voice inside her head screaming that they were too late.

"Did you get the other door closed?" Mitchell asked.

She nodded, out of breath. She looked at Craig. "Tony's going to be spotted any second."

"Seal up the hallway," he ordered frantically.

They got to work. As Kim showed Mitchell how to activate the emergency door, Craig began to release the gas from the oxygen tanks. He turned the valves on the first two tanks and the pressurized oxygen began to fill the hallway. The valve on the third tank wouldn't budge, so Craig left it for now. He didn't have time.

Standing up, he noticed the door to the showers. The doors themselves were sealed, but there were slats on the upper part of the door to allow steam from the showers to dissipate into the hallway. With a hurried slap, Craig pushed the slats closed, sealing the door. When the emergency door slid closed a moment later, the oxygen became trapped in the hallway and began to build pressure.

Craig turned to the panel once more. He saw Trisha staring at him desperately. He tried to give her a reassuring look, but she didn't seem comforted. He didn't realize his face was too pale for her to believe him.

Tony slowed down, trying to delay the inevitable. He'd played his hand, dragging it out as much as possible, but he was out of cards. He slowed down just past the adjoining hallway, reluctant to continue.

He saw a shadow at the far end of the hallway. The next thing he knew, Jackie appeared around the corner with a gun in her hand. The two froze as they stared at each other.

Tony moved first. With a surge of adrenaline, he dove back and ducked around the corner, holding the canisters in front of him as shields. He disappeared around the corner and almost fell when he stumbled to a halt. At least Jackie hadn't opened fire.

Quickly overcoming her shock at seeing Tony instead of Craig, Jackie lunged for one of the phones scattered throughout the facility, dragging her stiff leg behind her. "Sebastian," she screamed into the speakerphone. "It's a trick!"

Movement out of the corner of his eye warned Craig that time had run out. He hadn't heard Jackie screaming, but Mitchell and Kim had. Their frantic waving told him all he needed to know.

He could have cried. He didn't think there was enough pressure in the hallway to ensure they'd be safe—and he still couldn't open the door. He grabbed the wires, desperately trying to remember how to hotwire it. He thought he remembered something about a sequence, but he wasn't sure. He knew he needed to disengage the locks to open the door. No, wait. There weren't any locks. Sebastian "locked" them by ordering the computer to ignore the command to open the door. Craig remembered how the doors sealed when they closed and unsealed right before opening. He had to somehow deflate the seals and then open the door. If he manually tried to wrench it open, he'd ruin the seals—and all of their efforts would be in vain.

Sebastian quickly scrolled through the camera feeds. When he found the right one, he saw the figure crouched in the hallway between the conference room and Lab 5. He had the canisters—but it was Tony!

Sebastian swore. He grabbed the remote and toggled the intercom button. "That was a nice try, Craig," he said, his voice echoing throughout the Level, "but it didn't work. You failed. Say goodbye to Trisha."

With a savage look on his face, he jabbed the button on the remote detonator.

Craig and Trisha stared at each other in fear. They'd heard Sebastian's announcement—and Trisha heard the biodispenser begin to hiss as it released its deadly contents. Craig saw the light on the biodispenser begin to blink. Looking at her, he pantomimed for her to close her eyes and hold her breath.

As she mimicked his instructions, Craig spun back to the panel. He wanted to scream. The pressure in the hallway wasn't strong enough yet! Glancing at the oxygen tanks, he eyed the third tank. The tank was pointing towards the door, the butt of the tank pressed against the far wall. In an act of desperation, Craig grabbed the hammer and struck the valve, hoping to knock it off. The force of the blow raced up his arm, jarring his teeth, but the valve remained intact. He tried again—and the second swing did the job. The valve flew off, the end of the tank virtually exploding from the pressure of the oxygen inside. The oxygen roared out of the tank, increasing the pressure in the hallway.

Craig turned to the door, ready to use the hammer to pry it open, when he spotted the unresponsive doorplate. He suddenly remembered. The key was the set of wires from the doorplate!

Dropping the hammer, he snaked his arm into the wall, grabbed the wires attached to the doorplate and ripped them off. Pulling them out of the wall, he touched the wires together, finishing the connection. The seals around the door deflated and the door quickly slid open.

Trisha stood just inside the lab, shaking uncontrollably. She'd never been this scared before in her life. Never. Her past experiences were nothing compared to this. The hissing from the biodispenser sounded like the doors of Hell opening up to unleash the demons God had trapped inside.

She held the bag with the vials in one hand and was covering her nose and mouth with the other. When she felt a push of air, signaling that the door had opened, she was hesitant to move—especially with her eyes squeezed shut.

His body flooded with adrenaline, Craig lunged for her and pulled her into the hallway. "Stay there. Don't move, don't breath," he said as he quickly grabbed the wires again. The lab door closed behind her and the seals re-inflated.

"Keep your eyes closed," he said as he took her arms. His hands were shaking with fear and adrenaline so it took him a few seconds to realize she was also shaking. Trisha had been pale before, but now her face was drained of all color. "Hold your breath a few more seconds."

He pulled her across the hallway and into the shower room. A faint breeze followed them in as he led her into the tiled room and pulled her to the group of showers. There was a small changing area, complete with a stack of temporary clothing, and then a row of three showerheads. The first two were normal showerheads, but he ignored them. He pulled her past them—and she stumbled. He wrapped his arms around her, keeping her on her feet. Her body convulsed from the lack of air as she struggled not to breathe.

He knew she was going to pass out at any moment. "Almost there," he said, his voice thick with fear.

Holding her body against his, he continued to the shower in the corner. It was a chemical shower, designed to kill any lingering microorganisms that clung to the skin. Still holding her up, he reached past her and turned on the chemical spray. "Keep your eyes closed," he warned. He knew he only had a few seconds. Her body was growing limp, her face turning a slight shade of blue. He pulled her under the chemical spray, squinting to protect his eyes as the chemical mixture washed over Trisha's body.

He tilted her head back, to make sure her face was clear of any lingering virus, and then brought her head down, away from the spray. "OK, breathe."

Trisha took a deep breath, greedily sucking in as much air as she could—and immediately began to cough from the chemical fumes. As she struggled, he pulled her away from the chemical shower and turned on one of the other showerheads. He maneuvered her under the water and helped her wash off the chemicals as she continued to breathe in deep waves. After she caught her breath, she looked up at him.

He stared into her eyes, fearfully searching for signs of dark splotches that would indicate she had become infected. Her eyes were red, but so far, they were clear.

As he continued to look into her eyes, his feelings pounded through him. He realized he had almost lost her, that he'd taken a tremendous gamble that had threatened both of their lives—but it had been worth it. He continued to stare into her eyes, taking in their beauty as he searched for signs of infection.

Her soft, full lips began to curl into a smile.

Aware of the fact that their bodies were still touching, Craig took her back under the chemical shower. He had planned to let go of her but found he couldn't.

She continued to watch him as the chemical spray washed down her back.

He opened his mouth, hesitated, and then said, "You need to take your clothes off." He saw the surprise that flashed in her eyes. "We need to make sure you don't have any virus on you," he tried to explain.

She continued to look at him for a moment. Then she slowly pulled her arms back, sliding them across his shoulders and down his chest before taking a small step backwards. With her eyes still locked onto his, she reached up and slowly, sensually, began to undue the top button of her blouse.

Trying to convince himself that his intentions were still honest, he reached over. She moved her hands out of the way and let him unbutton the rest of her blouse. It slid to the floor. She raised an eyebrow and unhooked the top of her pants. She pulled the zipper down and then looked at him expectantly. Craig tried to keep his face a mask as he hooked his thumbs into the top of her pants and slid them over her hips. They fell to the floor and she faced him in her underwear, the chemical spray making her skin glisten.

Still not saying a word, Trisha reached over and grabbed the hem of Craig's shirt. She pulled it over his head, and then let it drop to the floor beside them.

Craig's body was on fire. He looked into her eyes, painfully aware of how close her nearly naked body was to his, how incredibly beautiful she was. He swallowed and reached for his pants. He undid them and pushed them down his legs. Within moments, Craig and Trisha were in their underwear, their body only inches apart.

She took his hand and led him back to the other shower. The water ran over their bodies and turned to steam from the heat.

As the water washed away the chemicals, Trisha finally spoke. In a raw voice, she said, "You saved my life."

Craig tried to think of a response.

Before he could, she reached up and kissed him. It was a hot, passionate kiss that his body responded to immediately, the memory of their passionate night together exploding in his mind. He found his arms around her waist—and knew he couldn't remove them even if he'd wanted to. He was helpless, raw with emotion. Their passion escalated and he couldn't think straight as their mutual desire grabbed hold of them both.

The room continued to fill with steam, blocking out the rest of the world. There was nothing else except for her, and his passion for her.

CHAPTER 28

"Give me the canisters or you're dead," Jackie said.

Tony glanced around the corner. Jackie was at the far end of the hallway, resting her weight on her good leg as she pointed the gun at him.

He pulled his head back and rested it against the wall. He knew he couldn't move very fast. His body had grown numb from exhaustion and his face was burning. At least she couldn't move very fast, either. If she had, she would have chased after him.

"Drop the gun or I destroy the canisters," he said. "You know I can do it."

She snarled at him but didn't reply. She realized the situation she was in. With a sigh, she dropped the gun.

Tony risked another glance around the corner. He spotted the gun lying by her feet. "Kick the gun away. Down the hallway."

"I'm not kicking it to you."

"No kidding," he said in a tired voice.

Still grimacing, Jackie turned and kicked the gun down the adjoining hallway. Tony heard it slide along the outside of the Computer Lab and hit the far wall.

He hoped Kim saw it. From where she was, she should be able to spot it easily. All she had to do was run down, grab it, and back Jackie off.

"Give me the canisters," Jackie said.

Tony hesitated. He looked back down the other way but didn't see Kim. Crap. He couldn't wait any longer. He set one of the canisters on the floor and with a shove slid it towards Jackie.

She picked up the canister, leaning over with difficulty. "Where's the other one?"

Tony struggled to his feet. He stepped into the hallway and dropped the other canister. "Come and get it," he said before backing up as quickly as possible. He began to shuffle over to the security checkpoint, disgusted with himself. If he'd felt stronger, he would have attacked her—but he didn't have the energy.

He stumbled into the Med Unit a few minutes later, totally exhausted. He just wanted to lie down. He felt like he could sleep for a month.

When he walked in, he spotted Kim and Mitchell. "How did it go?"

"He got her out," Mitchell said. "Not sure how she's doing, though."

Tony looked at Kim. "Did you grab the gun?"

"What gun?"

He sighed in defeat and shuffled towards the bed.

*   *   *

With a grunt, Mouse shoved his body over the thick pipe, his back scraping against the bottom of Level II. He felt like he was trapped in a maze created by a psychotic lunatic. He'd been in here so long, he no longer thought of the obstacles as tanks, pipes, etc. They were merely obstacles, malignant objects that tried to block him in and trap him. If they succeeded, they would slowly devour him, burning away his flesh and consuming his ripe, wet organs while he screamed in pain.

He turned the flashlight on himself to wake him up. The light pierced his eyes, sending a bolt of pain into his brain. He closed his eyes and took a few deep breaths. It worked. When he opened his eyes again, he saw the tanks and pipes that occupied this dark cavern, rather than the monsters he'd been imagining.

He found himself near the far wall of the complex. Unable to resist, he reached out and ran his hand over the rough wall of rock that encircled the underground facility. It must have taken a lot of dynamite and hard work to carve into this rock. It had been an amazing feat of engineering, one the world would never know about.

It was made even more impressive by the way they had dug the facility. From what he'd learned, they had dug straight down at first, creating a hole as wide as the facility. After they had reached the planned depth for Level I, however, they had stopped. They had only dug a smaller shaft from then on, down to the bottom. This was now the central shaft that ran from the bottom of the facility all of the way to the surface. To dig out the space for Levels II and III, they had started from the bottom of the central shaft and carved outwards, until they had the rough dimensions they needed for the other two levels.

Mouse had been surprised. It seemed like a ridiculously inefficient way to create this facility, but obviously there had been a reason. The space between Level I and Level II was occupied by the original rock, untouched except for the shaft and the small hole needed for the elevator.

Mouse felt discouraged. Even if he made it to Level II, the only way to get past that was either through the central shaft or the elevator. It didn't make sense.

Craig believed there was a way to reach the surface from Level II. Mouse hoped he was right. So far, however, he hadn't found any way to get into the next Level, even though it was so tantalizingly close. Mouse sighed. He told himself to keep looking. They had to get to that level, to warn the authorities. It was their only hope.

*   *   *

Once again, Trisha's voice echoed in Craig's mind, taking him back to that incredible night in Dallas.

"We could get in trouble for this, you know."

"Who'll find out?" he asked.

"I think everyone in the entire hotel knows, with the amount of noise we've made."

"And that's my fault?"

"Actually, yes, it is. I would've been sleeping if it wasn't for you. You've been ravaging an innocent girl."

"'Innocent'? Then what do you call that thing you did—"

"Shut up and kiss me," she laughed.

The door to the shower room opened, bringing him back to the present.

He tensed as Trisha stepped into the hallway.

Sitting against the wall near the emergency door, he watched her walk towards him. They both wore the temporary clothing that had been stacked in the changing room, although she looked good even in wrinkled clothing, Craig thought ruefully.

He shifted uncomfortably as she sat down next to him. He tried not to look at her.

The two sat in awkward silence, waiting to see if they were free of infection. Craig knew he'd never forget what had just happened—and would never look at a shower the same way again—but he was hesitant. Their time together had been amazing. It left him craving more. But it wasn't right. Even though he was being transferred, he was still her boss. Craig's guilt was nearly overwhelming as he'd had sex with her while he was her superior, which he'd sworn to himself he would never do.

He knew Trisha was waiting to see how he would act, which only increased his awkwardness. To ease his guilt, he told himself not to read too much into what had just happened. He had saved her life, and she had been grateful, but it had been a heat-of-the-moment kind of thing, a last reminder of what they'd once shared.

A part of him hoped that's all it had been. The irony was that she was the reason he'd stayed here so long—and the reason he'd asked to be relocated.

He had been uncomfortable around Trisha—while also attracted to her—and that conflict had created a strange push-pull combination that had been driving him out of his mind. He had tried to ignore her, tried to balance his emotions, but had been unable to. She was the proverbial forbidden apple, dangling tantalizingly within reach. He couldn't give in to his desires, though. He was her boss! Not only did the military have strict guidelines against it, but he would not turn into his father, dammit.

And yet, she was worth the punishment and the ramifications, his heart had whispered. She was Helen, drawing the fatal desire of the Prince of Troy.

He'd finally decided to end his struggle—only not in the way he truly wanted. He couldn't have her, didn't deserve her. So he had asked to be transferred. It was the best thing to do. He'd walk away from the temptation ... no matter how painful that was.

Besides, he told himself, he'd already blown his chance long ago.

He heard a noise next to him and looked over. Trisha was rifling through the bag she'd brought out of Lab 9 with her. "What's in the bag?" he asked.

"Oh," she said, startled that he had spoken. "They're, um, vials. That's why I went in there."

Now it made sense. Sebastian had used them to lure her into Lab 9, to trap her.

"I think the vaccine for Ebola is in here," she said, bending her head so she didn't have to look into his eyes.

"They could be fake."

She flashed him a dark look. "Why would they be?"

"After what happened with Brett, I'm suspicious, OK?"

She pulled a couple of vials out. "They don't look fake."

He frowned in reply. It was a little too convenient that right after verifying they had been infected with Ebola, they had the vaccine—even if Trisha had almost died for it.

Jackie gave the canisters to Sebastian, who took them with greedy hands. "Are they damaged?"

"Didn't get a chance to look," she confessed.

He undid the clasps and inspected the mechanism. Jackie leaned over and nodded. "They seem fine," she said.

"Good." Sebastian reattached the mechanism and turned them around. When he flipped the switches, only one light of the LED display turned on. "They need to be charged," he told her, handing them back.

Satisfied, he began to gather the videotapes. All he needed now was to get the vials and transfer them to the canisters. By the time he got them together, the canisters would be partially charged, enough to keep the vials cool until he got away.

He stuffed the tapes into his canvas bag. He would have preferred to send Jackie to get the vials, but she was nearly helpless. At least this was almost over. Then he could get out of this hellhole once and for all.

CHAPTER 29

Mitchell hung up the phone. "That was Craig. He wants me to let 'em out."

"Are they OK?" Kim asked.

"He said they were."

"How long has it been?" Tony spoke up.

Mitchell glanced at his watch. "A half hour or so. I guess Craig's plan worked."

Tony watched as Mitchell left the Med Unit. He was lying down, but his mind wouldn't let him sleep. He couldn't give up, not while there was a chance—however slim—of stopping Sebastian. He wondered if there was some way to contact the surface. It was really their best bet.

He found himself scratching the back of his neck.

He stopped scratching and lightly glided his fingertips over the spot that itched, feeling a series of tiny bumps like brail on his neck and upper shoulder. Great. The Ebola virus was spreading.

He tried to force it out of his mind and focus on the problem of stopping Sebastian instead. If they couldn't get a message to the surface, the only other way would be to block the exit. Sebastian would have to come through this part of the level, and he couldn't wait forever. The longer he stayed down here, the greater the chance that he would be stopped.

Tony wanted to take a final stand against their adversary. He knew they were all weakening, but if they could hold out long enough, they just might have a chance.

He turned when he heard a soft groan. "You OK?"

Kim looked at him with bleary eyes. "God it's hot in here. I don't remember it ever being this hot."

Tony got up, forcing his aching muscles to move, and grabbed a small towel. He wet it and put it on the back of her neck. He knew it wouldn't help much. The weaponized Ebola was really affecting her. It was spreading rapidly through her body—as well as his own—and soon it would overwhelm their immune systems. Once that happened, it would all be over.

Alone in the Computer Lab, Jackie scrolled through the video feeds, stopping when Jill's image appeared on the screen.

She was still cradling her dead husband's head in her lap, which was really morbid. Her husband was dead. What, did she have a thing for dead bodies? Jackie never knew Jill was into necrophilia.

She watched the image from Lab 4 in mute disgust. She couldn't turn away, even though the image irritated her. It wasn't right. She needed to stop Jill from touching the body. Jackie felt unclean just watching her. She tried to think of a way to stop her. She wanted to hurt Jill, smack her, and drag her away from her husband's moldering corpse. She'd love to go in there and shoot Jill in the head. Then they'd both be dead. But no, she couldn't. The air was infected with Keres' Eyes.

Jill might never get out, which would make this place her grave. It certainly was appropriate. A giggle slipped out of Jackie's mouth, although she didn't hear it.

She shifted in the chair, carefully moving her damaged leg. She was in a lot of pain—had been ever since Brett had broken her wrist. She didn't have access to pain medication, so she was forced to feel every ounce of injury he had inflicted on her. Served him right to die. She wished he was alive so she could kill him again.

She didn't realize it, but the pain was making her lose her mind. She'd danced with it for too long, unable to escape from it, and it had grown inside her mind until it warped her thoughts. She couldn't remember a time when it wasn't there, suffocating her with its stinging touch.

The vaccine she'd taken had protected her from the weaponized Ebola, but it didn't protect her from the pain.

She giggled again and continued to flip through the video feeds. She wanted to find Lab 9, to see if their delusional Captain had saved his damsel in distress. Jackie really hoped so. If he'd succeeded, she knew Trisha would have brought the vials out with her. And then Jackie would have the last laugh. Yes she would. After all these years, Jacqueline DiScoli would get the last laugh on these pasty-faced losers.

Jackie continued to chuckle as she scrolled through the video feeds. She didn't even notice when she found the feed to Lab 9. She kept scrolling instead, giggling to herself in the empty room.

Christopher Banks, former scientist assigned to Level III, cautiously slipped past the door to the control center and continued down the hallway. He didn't want to be seen here. Someone might realize that the timing of his arrival with the "accident" in Level III was too much of a coincidence.

Sebastian had accounted for that. After today, Banks would keep his nose clean. The authorities would certainly watch him closely, to see what his involvement was in the accident, so he would stick to his cover story, would continue at his new job like a good boy and avoid any contact with Sebastian until things settled down. They already had plans to meet up a year from now, outside the country, where Banks would collect his portion of the payout. Banks would never be able to return to the U.S. after that, but that didn't matter. He'd be glad to get away. Besides, he had a feeling the U.S. was going to become a dangerous place to live.

He snaked his way through the building and entered a side corridor. He walked as quietly as possible, his sneakers muffling the sound of his footsteps, and stopped before turning the corner.

Glancing behind him to make sure he was alone, Banks opened the bag he carried and removed a small gas bomb. The bomb was made of metal, so Banks had wrapped a couple of rubber bands around the top and bottom so it would roll quietly.

The former scientist crouched down, pulled the pin and then rolled the bomb down the adjoining hallway. As soon as he let go, he stood back up, careful to stay out of sight, and reached inside his bag for a gasmask.

The cylinder rolled down the stark hallway towards the desk at the end, where a guard was stationed. The guard was unaware of the danger, however, as he was bent over his desk listening to a basketball game on his portable radio.

The rubber bands cushioned the cylinder, masking its presence as it rolled towards the desk. Before it reached the guard, the cylinder began to release its contents, the clear, odorless gas filling the end of the hallway. Seconds later, the guard's head smacked the top of the desk. He was out.

Banks approached the desk, stopping to pick up the empty canister on his way, and looked at the sleeping guard with a satisfied grin. The mask he wore hid the grin, but it didn't matter. There was no one else around to see it. The guard would be out for hours.

The scientist grabbed the keys hooked to the guard's belt, opened the door and entered a large, windowless room. In the center of the room, rising up from the floor, was a massive dome that dominated the space, the capstone to the underground laboratory's central shaft. The dome, consisting of two large, curved pieces of metal, slid back when the shaft was opened.

Banks walked over to a small computer screen set off to the side and punched in the code Sebastian had given him. After a brief moment, the computer unlocked the dome. Sebastian could come up at any time—and Banks rather wished he would come now. The longer he waited, the greater the chance that he'd get caught.

*   *   *

Craig and Trisha walked out of the hallway as soon as Mitchell opened the emergency door. "Hey guys," he said with a big smile. "How you doing?"

"Close the door," Craig snapped.

"Huh? Wha—Oh, OK." Mitchell spun back to the panel, flipped the gearshift, and closed the emergency door.

Trisha saw the fear in Mitchell's eyes. "It's just a pre-caution," she said.

"Oh. Yeah, that's cool." Then his grin reappeared. "So, uh, how was it?"

Craig's eyes widened. "Excuse me?"

"I mean, you two feeling OK? With the oxygen and all?"

"We seem to be fine," he said in a flat voice. Trisha could tell he was embarrassed. Mitchell and Kim had seen him pull her into the showers, and it was easy to jump to a rather unprofessional conclusion—especially since Craig and Trisha now wore different clothing.

The tall scientist looked at Trisha for support, but she wasn't about to upset Craig. She gave Mitchell a small smile instead and turned down the hallway.

Her smile faded as she walked, however. Craig had been withdrawn ever since they'd gotten out of the shower. It concerned and infuriated her. So what if everyone knew they'd been together? They could think the absolute worst—about her, about him—and she wouldn't care. But it obviously bothered Craig.

She could understand his being a little embarrassed—she'd felt that way, too, before he'd rescued her, before she'd almost died—but she didn't think he regretted it. He certainly hadn't complained at the time, she thought with a ghost of a smile. But she wasn't sure what would happen next, especially considering what had happened the last time, and what she'd recently found out. Her smile faded as she thought about it.

They walked into the Med Unit, where Kim and Tony waited anxiously. "Thank you for helping Craig save me," she said, hugging them both. "I don't know how to repay you."

Mitchell leaned forward. "It was our pleasure," he said, emphasizing the last word with a twinkle in his eye.

Trisha could feel Craig tense beside her. Before he could respond, she turned and rested a hand on his arm. "I'm going to go change," she said.

Heading towards her room, she believed she might finally be free of the scars that had been inflicted on her by her ex-husband. He had called her a slut, a whore, all kinds of vicious names that made her question her sexuality and her desires. But no longer. She was her own woman. She knew what she wanted and she'd taken it. She smiled as she walked towards her room, her body still tingling from having been awakened.

But she didn't know if she could get over what she'd learned. It might finally be the thing that broke her heart for good.

She hoped there was some way to salvage things with Craig, for being with him would certainly be magical. It already was. Because of him, she had freed herself, and she no longer cared what anyone thought.

Sebastian gathered the vials as quickly as possible. He had to be careful, as he couldn't afford to drop any of them. He needed enough viable samples to complete his plans.

He adjusted the air on his biohazard suit and reached for another vial.

Craig would have been shocked to discover how much there was. Sebastian had grown a large supply of the Keres' Eyes virus, much larger than any of his coworkers would have ever suspected. It was a perk of being Lead Scientist. He'd taken Lab 1 as his own and had used the facility's resources to generate billions of copies. There was enough in here to wipe out the Northern Hemisphere—but he wasn't interested in exposing this place to the world or any of the rubbish Jackie had talked about. No, his intentions were more basic, he told himself. He was doing it for money.

He knew he was one of the top scientists in the world, yet his compensation didn't reflect it. The salary he drew was an insult.

He thought it was fitting that he was using the government's facility to rectify their failure.

He'd known since he was a child that he'd be the best in whatever field he chose, but the riches, the rewards and accolades had been denied him. Some might say that it had been his own doing, but those people were daft. No, he had been used and manipulated by the Army, approached only when no other opportunity had been available.

But now he would get the money he deserved, that his talents demanded.

He had a meeting next week with a group of gentlemen who would buy Keres' Eyes—but they wanted proof that the virus worked. Sebastian would use the videotape of Danny's death to show the weapon's power. His other videotape, of Jill and Manny, would assure them that the antidote worked as well.

For his troubles, Sebastian would receive one hundred and fifty million dollars.

He smiled to himself as he gathered the last of the vials. His buyers didn't know that they were just the first group. He had three other meetings set up—which was why he needed all of the vials he'd created.

Sebastian had no illusions about his buyers' eventual target: the United States. In that respect, they would complete Jackie's dream, although not in the way she might have liked. These vials were weapons of mass destruction and would be used as such. His buyers didn't care about what would happen to the global economy if they destroyed the most powerful nation— except for one particular buyer. He wanted to align his country to replace the United States as the world's leader. The other groups were religious fanatics who believed that the United States went against God's will.

Sebastian didn't care about God or His will. After being rejected by the Army and humiliated by his coworkers, he was getting what was due to him.

He planned to set up a secure compound that would become his castle when the dark times came. He had enough vaccine to protect himself and a core group of people he'd already selected to surround himself with—and none of those people included the degenerates he worked with. They had made their bed when they'd laughed at him. No, there were others he would protect, men and women who recognized his greatness and would contribute to the survival of the group, thankful that he'd saved them from certain death. That would come in time, though, well before any of his buyers could unleash Keres' Eyes. For now, he needed to execute his escape plan.

He picked up the metal tray and walked out of Chamber 1.

Each portable container could hold a total of forty vials. He would fill both containers, mostly with the virus. It was enough to wipe out tens of millions of people—and would generate more money than any one man could spend in a lifetime.

CHAPTER 30

Mouse crawled dejectedly towards the trap door. He'd checked every inch of this place but had come up empty-handed. There was no way to get to the level above.

He was exhausted, covered with dust and grime, and he had a throbbing headache, but he was more upset than anything else. He felt as if he'd let his commander down. There was no way to get up to Level II. He shouldn't have been surprised, though. The Army had designed each level to be sealed from the other. Of course they wouldn't have installed a trap door or anything that would've allowed him to sneak inside.

He stopped at the opening to the Mechanical area. He didn't know if he had the energy to climb down the ladder, so he plopped down next to the opening to rest. He wished there was some way to get to the next level. He was so frustrated he felt like crying.

Admitting defeat, he turned to climb back down. He put his foot on the first step, and then paused. Something had flashed in the darkness. He moved his flashlight around for a few seconds before he spotted it again. Frowning, he shuffled over to the object.

He found himself staring at a bronze grill three feet wide and two feet high. He gaped at it for a few seconds as he tried to figure out what it was. He knew the central shaft didn't have a ventilation system. It was sealed off. So what was this?

The grill was set in the side of some sort of curved wall that stretched up to the floor above. He scooted along the wall, following its contour, and found himself back at the beginning after a few moments. It was a shaft of some sort, between four and five feet in width. Mouse was stunned, amazed that it was here and that he'd missed it before. When he bent over to inspect the mysterious grill, he discovered that it was attached with a set of screws that looked older than him. He pulled out a screwdriver and tried to turn the rusted screws, but it took both hands and all of his strength before they finally budged. By the time he removed all six of them, he was covered in sweat and his body was pounding with fatigue.

He pulled on the grill and was rewarded with a shower of dust that had accumulated over the years. He stumbled back with the grill in his hands, coughing as the dust swirled in the air around him.

After clearing his lungs, he put the grill aside, bent down and stuck his flashlight into the opening. When he angled the light upward, he felt a surge of hope. He was staring at a shaft that stretched up into the darkness, possibly all the way to the surface!

Mouse couldn't believe his luck.

He angled the flashlight down and discovered that the strange shaft stopped at his feet. No wonder he'd never known about it before—it didn't penetrate his Level. He wondered what it was for. It must have been part of a ventilation system of some kind, maybe back when they first built the facility.

Eager to get started, he contorted his body as he struggled to get into the shaft. Once inside, he pulled in his legs and looked up. The sides were virtually smooth. Undeterred, he pressed his back against the side of the shaft, lifted his legs and began to push himself up. He found that by using his hands to lift his body upwards, while using his legs to support his weight, he was able to climb the shaft. It made for slow progress, inching his way skyward, but Mouse didn't care. He was determined to reach the top no matter what.

"Are you OK?" Craig asked, resting his hand on Kim's shoulder.

She tried to shrug. "I guess."

He rubbed the side of his jaw as he watched her, unconvinced. It was obvious that she was weak. He could feel the heat emanating from her.

"We're running out of time," Tony muttered under his breath.

"I was just thinking the same thing," Craig said. Tony looked terrible—and Craig didn't feel that great himself.

Mitchell finished laying out the vials Trisha had brought out of Lab 9. "Then I say we get going with this. The sooner we get the antidote, the better. Right, boss?"

Craig hesitated.

"What's wrong?" Tony asked.

Craig sighed. "I don't know."

Mitchell tried to reassure him. "We're all set. Jill and Manny identified the right virus so we know it'll work. We actually have a total of four vials worth of antibodies, more than enough for all of us."

Craig continued to stare at the vials. Something didn't seem right about them.

He was still trying to figure it out when Trisha came into the room. The moment he saw her, he forgot about the vials. She had combed her hair and put on a very flattering outfit. She had even put on a touch of makeup.

The effect was mind-blowing. She looked totally amazing.

She sauntered over, glided to a stop next to him, and smiled. "Hi."

"Hi." He blinked a few times when he realized he'd been staring at her. It was as if he'd been whisked out of time, pulled out of the stream of life that governed them all. It was an amazing, disorienting feeling.

He wrenched his eyes away from her. To his shock, Mitchell was already filling a syringe. "What're you doing?"

"Healing ourselves."

Surprised at Mitchell's disregard for authority, Craig glanced down—and caught his breath. "Wait. Stop."

"But Captain—"

"The labels are starting to peel."

Mitchell looked down. With a perplexed frown, he asked, "So?"

"Look, I've got a bad feeling about them. Don't use them yet." Mitchell and Kim began to argue but he cut them off. "I know we don't have time. If we wait much longer, the vaccine won't be effective even if it's the right one."

"What do you mean the 'right one'?" Tony asked.

"Brett should've been fine, but he wasn't. He died. Something's funny with the vials. We need to find out what it is."

"So what do you suggest?"

An inspiration hit him. "Wait here. I'm going to check something out. I'll call as soon as I know."

"I'll go with you," Trisha piped up as she started to follow him to the door.

"No," he snapped at her.

Her confidence faltered. "What?"

"I said 'no'. You've already risked your own safety too many times."

She could feel her anger starting to rise. "Are you saying I can't come with you?"

"Exactly. End of story," he said as he walked out.

She felt as if her head was going to explode. That was the same thing her ex-husband used to say to her. That bastard "laid down the law" and never wanted to hear a word of disagreement. She felt her cheeks warm with embarrassment when she saw Mitchell, Kim and Tony looking at her.

Gritting her teeth, she stormed after him. "Craig! How dare you talk to me like that." And in front of the others, she didn't add.

"I'm not going to get into this now. It's too important and we don't have time."

"Oh, like you don't have time to tell me you'd *asked* for the transfer?"

He blinked in surprise. "What does that have to do with anything?"

"Everything! Were you even going to tell me?"

"Of course I was—"

"And what did you think I would do? Throw you a party?"

"I'd hoped you'd go with me," he admitted in a soft voice.

"Go with you? What, as your secretary?"

"No—"

"Did you ever think that maybe I've stayed in this god-forsaken place because of you? And now you're abandoning me?"

He stepped towards her. "Trisha, I'm not abandoning you, I mean, not—"

She pushed him back, her eyes filling with tears. "Why would I go with you?"

"Uh, well, it could, um, help your career. I could pull some strings—"

"And what do I have to do in return?"

His cheeks instantly warmed as she took his words the worst way possible, obviously thinking he was just like his father after all. It hit him so hard he could barely speak for a second. "You don't understand," he started. "That's not..."

"Save it, you bastard."

She stormed off. He found himself alone in the hallway, confused and angry. He felt hollow inside as his childhood fear roared through him, her words echoing over and over. Swearing to himself, he spun and raced towards the lab area as if he could escape his past.

*   *   *

As if in a dream, Jill resurfaced from the ocean of despair that had drowned her. She found herself in the lab with Manny's head lying in her lap, its weight cutting off the circulation to her feet. She grew more aware of her surroundings, and as she did, she began to feel the pain in her feet more and more as they screamed for oxygen.

Reluctantly, she lifted Manny's head, scooted back and carefully lowered it to the floor. She stared at his unmoving body for a few moments, feeling the pull of her heartbreak calling to her like a siren.

The pain in her feet was the only thing that kept her from answering the call. She forced herself to stand up, wincing as the blood flow returned to her feet, and turn away. She knew she needed to do something. Her despair was drying her up inside, leaving her an empty husk. She was afraid of what would fill the emptiness if she stayed here any longer.

She knew she couldn't leave, though. Not only were the doors locked, but the air was filled with that bastard's murderous spawn. She was protected from Keres' Eyes but her coworkers weren't. She would infect them all if she left.

She spotted a row of Bunsen burners. She stumbled over to them, her feet tingling with pain, and lit all six to create a negative pressure in the room. It was crude, but she guessed it might help. She didn't know. Her efforts were half-hearted.

When she turned back around, her eyes locked onto Manny's body. She had thought her anguish had started to ease, but then she remembered the plans they'd made together. Her grief hit her all over again and she dissolved into tears.

Exiting the checkpoint, Craig cautioned himself to be careful. He stopped, pressed against the corner and glanced down the adjoining hallway. The area looked clear, but he was painfully aware of how close the Computer Lab was to where he wanted to go.

He knew he needed to get his people vaccinated. The argument with Trisha aside, it was the most important thing on his mind. But like the argument, he didn't totally understand what was going on. He knew he was missing something—but with the vials, he suspected the answer could be found with Brett. He had taken the vaccine for Keres' Eyes. It should have worked, but it hadn't. Craig needed to understand why. He hoped that when he did, he would understand what bothered him so much.

He began to sneak down the hallway towards the door to Lab 2. He stayed low, pressing his back against the wall. They didn't have much time. The Ebola virus, which had been ravaging their bodies, was on the verge of spinning out of control. Once that happened, no medicine on Earth would save them.

"I say we take it," Mitchell argued. "If Craig wants to check something out, that's fine, let him. We'll take our chances."

"Don't you ever listen?" Kim shot back. "The Captain said to wait."

"He's just being careful. Too careful, I say."

Kim seemed to waiver. She was too tired to argue with him. "Are you sure it'll be OK?"

"It's labeled right here. Come on, we don't have much time—"

"No," Tony said. "We wait until Craig comes back."

"But Tony—"

The security chief glared at him, effectively cutting him off.

"Fine," Mitchell muttered under his breath. "But he'd better hurry up."

Craig slipped into the lab and quickly ducked down as the door shut behind him. He paused for a second, struggling to catch any telltale sign that he'd been spotted. When he was satisfied, he hurried across Lab 2 and peered through the window into the second chamber.

It was dark in there. Craig couldn't see much—although he didn't dare turn on a light. He could just barely make out Brett's body, but he couldn't see any details. Not from out here. The glass was tinted just enough to obscure his view.

If he wanted to see Brett, he would have to go into Chamber 1.

Clenching his teeth, Craig turned and went into the Prep room. He reached up, grabbed a biohazard suit, and began to put it on when he noticed a large gash in the side. Someone had sliced the material with a blade, rendering the suit useless.

He quickly went through the other suits, but they were all torn. His heart pounding in his chest, he turned and glanced through the door into Chamber 1. If he wanted to learn the truth about Brett's death, he would have to enter the chamber unprotected.

The others quieted as Trisha walked into the room. Keeping her head down, she walked to the table where the vials were laid out. "Don't mind me," she said in a soft voice without looking up. "I didn't want to be alone, that's all."

Mitchell exchanged a glance with Tony. Trisha played with the vials, putting them into neat rows according to the type of microorganism stored inside. After a few moments of heavy silence, a crooked smile exploded onto Mitchell's face. "Wouldn't that be ironic?" he said. "Watch Craig be right, and instead of what the label says, all of these vials have viruses in them."

"My God, Mitchell," Kim sputtered. "What a horrible thing to say."

"Hey, it could happen. It'd be just like Sebastian to try to trick us."

"We don't know anything yet," Tony said, trying to mediate the two.

"Yeah, just shut up," Kim said, shoving Mitchell.

Trisha lifted one of the vials and frowned at it. Something *did* seem wrong. She couldn't put her finger on it, though. As she held the vial, the handwritten label began to peel away from the side of the glass.

"See?" Tony said, watching the label. "Craig was right to question it."

"Come on, I was kidding," Mitchell scoffed. "You washed those off, didn't you?" he asked Trisha.

She lifted her head and gave him a distracted look. "What?"

"When Craig pulled you out. You sprayed them off, right?"

"Yeah. In the chemical shower."

"See? That's why they're peeling. I don't see what the big deal is."

No one answered him.

Kim finally spoke up. "Speaking of showers, what happened after Craig rescued you?" she asked Trisha.

"Yeah," Mitchell said. "Did Craig wash your back, so to speak? Come on, tell us all the dirty details."

Trisha blushed but didn't reply.

He sighed. "Too bad. You know, it would be easier to die knowing *someone* around here had had one last fling." He eyed Kim and wiggled his eyebrows.

A tired laugh escaped her lips. "In your dreams."

Craig took a deep breath as he prepared to enter Chamber 1. The air should be clean. His team was always careful, and the room was lined with sensors that monitored the air, but still, nothing had been normal today, and he knew better than to trust anything down here anymore. Yet, he was about to take a huge leap of faith, walking in there without a biohazard suit.

His thoughts turned to Trisha. He knew he'd pissed her off. If they managed to somehow make it out of here alive, he'd do whatever it took to make it up to her. He hated her being angry with him, even though he deserved it in more ways than he cared to admit. He also wanted to show both her and himself that he wasn't his father.

He reached for the doorplate, hesitating one final time. This was a dangerous move, but it was the only card he had to play. He could feel his body fighting the Ebola virus. He was burning up inside and a headache had started to form at the base of his skull. If he could save the others—especially Trisha, he admitted to himself—it would all be worth it.

Taking another deep breath, he pressed his hand against the doorplate. The doors slid open and he walked inside.

His eyes darted nervously around the chamber as the doors closed behind him. It was strange being in here without a suit. He felt off-balance.

He forced himself to get moving. He walked across the chamber and approached the double doors to Chamber 2, where he was greeted by a horrific site: Brett's body lying on the floor, his black eyes locked open in a final, terrified gaze.

Brett's corpse confirmed the fact that the chamber was filled with Keres' Eyes. It would be suicide to go in there. Craig glanced over and saw the cart that held the mix of vials. It was tantalizingly close, but he couldn't get to them. Not without a bio-hazard suit. As his eyes traveled over the vials, the vague disquiet he'd felt earlier settled over him again.

He leaned down and inspected the body through the glass. He saw all of the signs of death—and then he saw the empty vial in Brett's hand. Even from this angle, Craig could see the label. It identified the vial as holding the antidote for Keres' Eyes. Tilting his head, he could see a small amount of clear liquid still residing in the bottom.

Craig glanced at the cart. His eyes drifted among the rows of vials and rested on one near the front. The label said "Anthrax B-83". That wasn't right. He'd worked with that strain of anthrax and knew that the contents should have a yellowish tint. The label was even written in his own handwriting. But the liquid in that vial was purplish.

The labels had been switched.

He spun and ran to the phone, picked up the receiver and quickly dialed the number to the Med Unit. "The labels are wrong," he announced when Kim picked up. "Don't use the vials!"

She put him on speaker so they could all hear the news. Craig quickly explained what he'd found. "Sebastian must have switched the labels around," he concluded. "We don't know which one to use."

In the Med Unit, the four survivors were stunned. "The vials are as good as wasted," Trisha said.

"And we're as good as dead," Mitchell agreed.

"So what do we do now?"

"We'll think of something," Craig assured them. "I don't know what yet, but we will."

"What about the barcodes?" Kim asked in a hesitant voice.

"What about them?"

She had been staring at the vials while Craig had told them about his discovery. "Sebastian wouldn't have bothered to switch the barcodes, would he? We never use them."

"I'm not sure," Tony said. The barcodes were required by the Army but none of the scientists followed them. They always went off of the handwritten labels that they stuck on the vials, sometimes over the barcodes. "It's a stretch, isn't it?"

"Can you get into the computer database?" Craig asked from the chamber. "That's the only way we'll be able to read them."

"I forgot about that," Kim said, embarrassed.

"No, we can't get into any of the computers," Tony said. "The last time I tried, we were still locked out."

Craig rubbed the side of his jaw as he thought. "What about Jill? She might be able to access the computer where she is."

"I don't know if that's such a good idea, boss," Mitchell said.

He sighed. "I know what she's suffered but we need her help. I'll talk to her. Put me on conference and call her."

As Mitchell reluctantly dialed the number, Kim glanced at Trisha. "I know the Keres' Eye vaccine is purplish, but that doesn't help us, does it?"

Trisha put an arm around her shoulders. "Let's hope Jill can help."

The mournful air was disturbed when the phone suddenly rang.

Jill looked up in surprise. She hadn't known that her phone was working again—not that it would do any good. Sebastian must have unblocked it as a cruel gesture.

Her surprise heightened when she realized she had slipped back into despair. She had been lost in her thoughts for what had seemed like only a second, but as she stood up, she found that her muscles were stiff and her stomach ached from crying.

"Hello?" she asked guardedly, expecting to hear Sebastian's sadistic voice on the other end.

"Jill," Craig said. "How are you holding up?"

Tears began to reform in her eyes. "I'm here. Of course. Nowhere else to be."

"I hate to ask this, but we need your help."

For the first time since Manny's death, Jill felt a spark of life. "What do you need?" Craig quickly explained their situation. By the time he'd finished, she had already moved over to the computer. "Hang on. Let me see what I can do."

A minute later, her frustration seeped into her voice. "I can't do a thing. The computer's totally locked up. It doesn't even respond when I move the mouse."

"How about if you hit the Escape key?"

"Tried it. Manny told me that Sebastian had control of everything. This just confirms it, I guess." Her frustration was turning to anger. She wanted to make Sebastian pay for Manny's death.

She was brought back into the conversation when Trisha asked, "Do you know what the vaccine looks like at least?"

Jill nodded. "It's a whitish liquid, almost like hand soap, only dirtier."

In the Med Unit, they started to go through the vials, pulling out the white ones.

"Does that help?" she asked.

"Not really," Trisha said in a quiet voice. "There's at least a dozen vials filled with white liquid. What do we do?"

Jill sighed in defeat. They didn't have time to test the vials. "I'm not sure."

Jackie watched the video screen with an intensity that bordered on insanity.

She had rotated the camera in the hallway in order to look into the Med Unit. She couldn't see very well, but from the angle of the camera, she had been able to spot the vials a few times. Mitchell moved over a little and blocked her view again, causing her to growl under her breath. At least the idiots hadn't bothered to close the door. Then she wouldn't have been able to see anything.

When Mitchell moved out of the way, Jackie spotted Trisha examining one of the vials. As Jackie watched, Trisha pulled off the handwritten label.

Jackie pounded her fist on the desktop. Dammit! They'd figured out her trick. She wanted them to die. They were sanctimonious assholes who had lost their right to live the moment they'd agreed to come down here and work in this godless place.

Her view of her job and the people who sacrificed to work down here had grown warped over the past few months by Ricardo, her lover. They'd met three months ago seemingly by chance. Ever since she'd joined the team she'd known that other countries might try to seduce her with good looking spies to get her to divulge secrets. Ricardo definitely was good looking—hot as hell was more like it—so she'd kept her guard up ... only, he'd never asked about her work. Not once. She kept expecting it, but when it never happened she dropped her guard as they grew closer, and quickly fell for her charming Latino lover.

Once he gained her trust, he started to manipulate her, gradually filling her head with derision towards the United States, then outright hatred. From there, it had been easy. She had actually been the one who had approached Sebastian, quickly becoming a willing accomplice.

She didn't know that one of Sebastian's buyers had set the whole thing up, using information the Lead Scientist had given them to gain her trust.

Unaware of how she had been manipulated by both Sebastian and the man she loved, Jackie continued to watch the monitor. After a few moments, she noticed Tony leaning over to speak. She jerked her head back in surprise, not understanding. Then she saw the light on the phone. They were talking to someone!

She jumped out of her chair and lurched to the telephone console at the back of the room. An indicator light told her that the phone was in use in the Med Unit. She spotted two other lights as well. One was in Lab 4, and the other was in Lab 2.

She gasped in surprise. Someone was in Lab 2? She rechecked the diagram to make sure she had read it correctly, and then spun back around. She knew who was in there. It had to be.

She grabbed the nearest phone and dialed into Lab 1. "Sebastian. You there?"

"What is it?" he asked in a curt voice.

She arched an eyebrow. "Just thought you'd want to know Trisha's still alive."

"*She is?*"

"I guess her loverboy got her out in time."

"That insufferable—"

"If you wanna talk to him, he's in Lab 2, in one of the chambers."

Silence. "Are you sure?"

"Yeah. He's on the phone with the others right now."

"I'll take care of it."

Sebastian hung up the phone and continued to undress. He was pissed. Leave it to Craig to ruin a beautiful moment. Fine. He was almost out of here. He had his vials; all he had to do was transfer them to the canisters and he was done. But he'd make one stop first. He had unfinished business to attend to.

CHAPTER 31

Jill gripped the sides of her head. She hated that she couldn't help her friends. They were in mortal danger—yet she couldn't reach them, couldn't rescue them. She'd been sitting here like an old woman, crying over her husband while her friends had been fighting for their lives. She didn't have the right to mourn. Not now. She could do it later, if she ever got out of here.

Besides, she was sick of mourning, sick of being helpless. She needed to *do* something. She knew Sebastian would try to leave any time now, if he hadn't already.

In desperation, she went to the door and tried to open it. The door didn't respond, and neither did the other one when she tried it. Energized, she looked around for a way out, checking the ceiling, the walls, everything. After a few moments, it was clear she was stuck.

She gripped the sides of her head again, trying to think.

When she dropped her hands, she spotted the small door set in the wall, the one for the conveyor belt. The biodispenser still sat on the metal tray, facing her, but the dispenser didn't concern her anymore. She was interested in the door. Sebastian had closed it, but when she went over, she found that it opened easily.

She had a way out.

*   *   *

Craig's footsteps echoed in the small chamber as he hurried to the double doors, wanting out.

He reached out to slap the doorplate ... when he hesitated. They needed to identify the correct vaccine—and when he saw the vials in the next chamber, he suddenly remembered. There was a computer printout of the barcodes. The printout, which served as a backup for the computer system, was supposed to be updated weekly. He didn't 'know the last time it had been printed, however, or even where it was.

If Craig remembered correctly, the printouts should be in one of the chambers. He couldn't check the other two chambers, but he knew he should check the room he was in. They could be here.

He knew he should leave but he couldn't pass up the opportunity. There was a chance, however slight, that the printouts were here.

He was not about to give up.

He turned away from the door and quickly began to search the room. Being as quiet as possible, staying away from the window, he searched the nearest cabinet, looking for the printout, but came up empty.

Squatting down, he shuffled over to reach the next set of drawers, located underneath the window—and was hit with a wave of dizziness. He grabbed the edge of the counter and waited for it to pass. As soon as it began to ease, he forced himself to move, to ignore the signs of his sickness. He knew it would only get worse—and if he failed to find the cure to the Ebola infection, he would experience a viciously painful death.

With a grunt, Mouse pushed himself higher. He quickly moved his feet up and paused to catch his breath. He wiped his hands on his pants, then placed them on the cool metal skin of the shaft and pushed upwards.

His shoulders had never ached like this before. He felt like he had been climbing for days, even weeks. A part of him hoped he was near the surface, but he knew that was only a dream.

He risked glancing down. The flashlight, clipped to his belt, aimed downward towards the bottom. He was surprised and dismayed to see he had only gotten about twenty feet. It was impressive—and discouraging.

Gritting his teeth, he lifted himself up another few inches and adjusted his feet. He didn't know what else to do. He had to get to the surface and warn everybody of what Sebastian had done.

Ignoring his aches and pains, and the fever that ravaged his body, Mouse continued to inch his way towards the darkness above.

Swearing under his breath, Craig closed the last drawer. He had checked the entire chamber but the printouts were nowhere to be found. They were probably in Chamber 2.

He had pushed his luck far enough. Struggling to his feet, he walked over and said a silent goodbye to Brett.

As he turned to leave, he heard the door to Lab 2 open. He immediately ducked down, his heart hammering in his chest. He scooted over to the window, using the row of drawers to shield him from whoever was in the lab.

He squatted in silence for a few moments, straining to hear the door open again. The room was silent, however, and he wondered if he had imagined the sound. No, it had been real.

He hoped that he hadn't been spotted—

The lights suddenly switched on overhead. He blinked in the harsh light, his eyes burning from the suddenly illumination. He realized he only had one chance. He scrambled to his feet and dashed for the double doors

Before he reached them, Sebastian appeared on the other side, blocking Craig's escape. Craig slapped the doorplate anyway, but the doors didn't respond.

Sebastian smiled at him, reached over and turned on the Prep room's intercom system. "You were stupid to go in there."

Craig's jaw tightened. "I didn't have a choice."

"You mean the vials? Bravo, Captain. You were right. Jackie switched the labels. At least you figured out that much."

"You're not going to get away with this. The Army'll hunt you down."

"They couldn't find their own asses if you gave them directions."

Craig blinked in surprise. "How are you going to get out of the complex? There're guards all over the surface."

"Don't worry about that. It's my problem, not yours. Besides, you won't be around long enough to find out."

"What do you mean?"

"I mean that this is goodbye, Captain. I would say it has been a pleasure working for you, but then, we both know that'd be a lie, wouldn't we?"

"I thought we were friends."

Sebastian laughed. "Please. Any last words before you meet your end?"

"Are you going to come in here and shoot me?"

"No. Something better than that. You'll get to experience the chamber's vacuum system first hand—although I've heard that suffocation is a brutal way to die."

"You bastard."

Sebastian smiled. "Fitting choice for your final words." He reached over, turned on the vacuum system and walked away.

In the chamber, Craig heard the system kick on, the twin turbine engines swiftly cycling up to speed. Two small, circular vents opened overhead and the system began to pull the air out of the room.

It would only take about two minutes for the system to suck out all of the air.

CHAPTER 32

"Stop it," Trisha said. "This is ridiculous."

They had been snapping at each other for the past few minutes, their fear and discouragement causing them to lash out. They had been trying to figure out what to do, but their discussion had turned into an argument, and then had degraded into a petty fight.

Mitchell sighed as he tried to calm down. "If only we could access the damn computers. I could strangle Sebastian for doing this to us."

"Wait," she said, holding up a hand. "What about the terminal in the Mechanical Room?"

"What about it?" Kim asked in a tired voice.

"It runs the life support equipment, which is overseen by the mainframe, right? He wouldn't risk cutting that off. Otherwise, the life support equipment might stop."

A ray of hope illuminated Mitchell's face. "My God, woman, you might be right."

"Let's go."

The three of them grabbed the vials and raced down the hallway to the Mechanical Room. Trisha wrenched the door open and they shot inside, scrambling to find the computer terminal. As soon as they found it, Trisha grabbed the keyboard and opened a search box. She typed in the name of the database program that contained the information on the barcodes, took a deep breath, and hit ‹Enter›.

Within seconds, the program popped up. Not wasting any time, she double-clicked on the link to start the program.

"Quick, give me one of the vials."

Mitchell handed her one. With trembling fingers, she typed the number into the computer and hit the ‹Search› button. The information popped onscreen, listing the contents of the vial, when it was created and the supervising scientist.

"Thank God," she whispered. It wasn't the right vial, but after a few more tries, they found one. Giddy with excitement, they went through the rest of their supply. They discovered that they had three vials worth of vaccine for weaponized Ebola.

Trisha was almost in tears. They all were. "Let's get back to the Med Unit," she said. They agreed and headed back with big grins on their faces.

She couldn't wait to find Craig. Now that they knew the correct vials, she wanted to cure him ... and apologize. She had been wrong, she now realized. She had thought he was acting like her ex-husband but, unlike that monster, Craig had reacted out of concern for her, not because he wanted to control her. She'd thought she was no longer affected by what her husband had done to her, but at least she recognized it now. She would make it up to Craig. And as for the transfer ... well, they'd figure something out.

With a spring in her step, she followed Kim and Mitchell back through the Mechanical Room. Finally, the end of their journey was in sight.

Sebastian walked into the Computer Lab and set the vials down.

"How did it go?"

"He's dead—or, will be in another minute."

"You're really twisted, you know that?"

"My dear, your hands are just as unclean as mine."

"Yeah, but I don't enjoy it," Jackie said.

He shook his head. "Denial is a dangerous thing. Embrace your true self and you will be much happier." He reached for the phone. "Where are our trusty coworkers?"

Jackie almost didn't reply at first. "The Med Unit," she finally said.

He punched in the number. "I have an announcement to make."

Tony sat up at the sound of Sebastian's voice. "What do you want, you bastard?"

"Interesting choice of words. It's the same phrase Craig used a moment ago."

Tony felt a chill run down his back. Sebastian had seen Craig.

Mitchell, Kim and Trisha walked into the room with big smiles on their faces. When they saw Tony's fear, however, their smiles faltered. "What's going on?" Mitchell asked.

"I have an announcement," Sebastian said. At the sound of his voice, they tensed. "As I speak, your trusty leader is departing this Earth. He met a rather nasty end, I'm sad to say. Suffocation."

"*No!*" Trisha gasped.

"Oh yes. If you want to hold a wake for him, he's in Lab 2. But at least you won't have to bury him. We're already well over six feet below ground."

The intercom clicked off. They stared at each other, devastated by the news. Crying uncontrollably, Trisha headed for the door, obviously wanting to save Craig, but she collapsed after only a few steps. Burying her face in her hands, she dissolved into tears.

Tony saw that Mitchell was struggling with tears of his own. They all were. It was all so goddamn useless.

He watched in a daze as Mitchell grabbed four syringes, filled them with the vaccine for weaponized Ebola and administered the shots to himself and the others. Trisha didn't seem to even feel it, she was so devastated. Kim was crying openly, her tears streaking her face as she watched Mitchell give her the shot that saved her life.

Tony couldn't even muster the words to thank Mitchell. He didn't think he could talk. He felt so empty inside. There was so much death here.

He knew it would take a few hours for them to start feeling better. It wasn't like the vaccine for Keres' Eyes, which worked supernaturally fast. It would take time for them to recover, for the vaccine to stop the spread of the Ebola virus, but at least they should start to regain their strength.

The irony was that sleeping would help them heal quicker, but he didn't feel like sleeping. He didn't know what he felt—or what they should do next.

As the vacuum roared overhead, Craig frantically trashed the room, looking for something he could use. He found a rod, which was thin enough to slip through the slats, but he couldn't reach high enough. Stretching to his limit, he could stick the end of the rod only an inch or two into the vent, not enough to affect the engines.

He dropped the rod and continued to scour the room, looking for anything that might help him. He only had a few seconds left. It was already becoming difficult to breathe.

Sebastian snapped the canisters closed. Both were filled and ready to go. Moving swiftly, he placed the canisters in a large satchel bag and threw the videotapes on top.

After closing the bag, he reached under the counter and pulled out a biodispenser. When she saw the bomb, Jackie froze. "What's that for?"

"To cover our tracks. Our coworkers have probably figured out which is the correct Ebola vaccine, so this will take them out permanently. That way, all of our problems will be solved."

"Oh," she said nervously. "I guess."

"You 'guess'. So unoriginal—and unintelligent. Any moron could have come up with that response."

She frowned at him. "What's your problem? We're home free."

"That we are."

She got to her feet. "Do you think we have enough vaccine to protect ourselves? The virus will spread quickly when we unleash it in Chicago."

"Ah yes, your little scheme. I meant to mention it earlier, but there's been a change in plans."

"What change?"

Sebastian pulled out the gun and pointed it at her chest. "This one."

The shot echoed loudly in the small room.

His ears rang for a few seconds afterwards as the sharp smell of gunpowder assaulted his nose.

Sebastian slid the gun back into his pocket, hooked the bag over his shoulder and stepped over Jackie's dead body as he headed for the door. He entered the hallway, set the biodispenser on the floor and then started down the hallway towards the courtyard.

The twin engines continued to roar overhead, pulling the air out of the room.

Craig knew the chamber was sealed tight. He would die a torturous death, as if he had found himself in the deepest reaches of space without a spacesuit.

He spun around, ready to throw himself at the glass window between the chamber and the lab, when he spotted a stack of empty Petri dishes. A wild thought came to him and he lunged for the stack. Clutching the top dish, he looked up at the circular vents. It just might work. No, it probably wouldn't, and his chances of pulling this off were in the thousands, but he didn't have any other option.

He hurried over until he was directly beneath the first vent. With a silent prayer, he threw the empty dish, bottom-side up, towards the ceiling.

The dish flew up, rotating slightly as it sailed towards the vent. The throw wasn't high enough, though, and the dish reached the apex of its journey a few inches below the ceiling. It hovered for a moment, caught by the air being sucked into the vent, and then continued to rise up, increasing in speed as it flew upwards.

The dish slammed into the vent, held there by the powerful suction, covering the vent completely.

Craig yelped with triumph. It was a perfect throw. His years of playing darts had come through.

He grabbed another dish and raced over to the other vent. He knew it had to be a perfect throw or the dish wouldn't cover the vent. There was no room for error. The dish was almost the exact same size as the vent.

Taking a deep breath, he tossed it into the air.

In his excitement, he threw the dish too hard and at too much of an angle. It bounced against the ceiling and crashed to the floor. Craig could hear the engine on the blocked vent straining. If he could block both vents, the automatic shutoffs would engage, but not before then.

He raced over, scooped up a handful of dishes and ran back to the uncovered vent. He threw the next one, but it was too short. He wanted to scream in rage. He could feel the seconds flying by. The air was thinning out, which interfered with his next throw. The dish smacked into the vent at an angle and bounced away.

He took the last dish in his hand, swallowed, and tossed it up. The dish sailed into the air, was caught in the current and adhered to the ceiling—but it wasn't on perfectly. Air was still able to get through, shrieking as it was sucked through the crescent-shaped gap. The dish was off by a few millimeters—and he couldn't get it to come back down.

He suddenly remembered the rod.

He spun around, frantically scanning the floor, and spotted it a few seconds later over to one side. In desperation, he dove, scooped it up and quickly positioned himself underneath the vent. Extending his arm, he hit the dish, but it scooted too far to one side, opening a wider gap as it shifted over the vent to the opposite side. Craig moved over a little and tried again, ignoring the sweat that ran down his face as he desperately swatted at the dish.

The rod hit the dish just right, perfectly covering the vent. Both engines screamed in protest—

Then shut off.

As the fans cycled down, the Petri dishes dropped to the floor.

Craig bent over and put his hands on his knees in relief. He could tell there was very little air in the room. But it'd be enough.

He turned to the doors that led to the Prep chamber, determined to get to Sebastian.

Jill snaked her way along the conveyor belt. Her progress was slow, as the tunnel was smaller than she'd realized. She didn't even have enough room to crawl.

She pushed the small container ahead of her and continued to wiggle her body forward. She had grabbed a couple of items before leaving, and wanted to get the chance to use them. Her rage burned inside of her, pushing her forward, and she used that rage to keep going. It also kept her warm, which was good, for it was cold in the small tunnel.

She knew she had to get to the other end as quickly as possible. She had heard Sebastian shoot Jackie. Obviously, she hadn't been useful to him anymore, which meant he was leaving. In a burst of inspiration, Jill rolled over onto her back and used her arms to pull her forward. She began to pick up speed as her body slid along the metal track, pushing the small plastic container ahead of her.

Sebastian strolled through the courtyard, turned past the conference room and approached the central shaft. He walked into the niche created by the two supply rooms, pulled out a set of keys and unlocked the door set at the end of the niche.

He opened the door and ducked inside.

The central shaft, which was over fifteen feet in diameter, was illuminated by two sets of lights that ringed the shaft at intervals between here and the surface, the light reflecting off of the smooth, metal skin.

Sebastian shut the door behind him and turned to the control panel set in the wall. When he punched in the code he had programmed earlier, the control panel beeped, signaling that the program would commence in five seconds.

With a confident air, he stepped up onto the mechanized lift that serviced the Levels. The lift, basically a metal platform that could be raised or lowered as needed, was ten feet square. Beams stuck out of each corner of the lift, each one ending in a group of four wheels that pressed against the sides of the shaft.

Sebastian set the bag down and made sure it was secure. There was enough time. The viruses were cooled. They weren't frozen, but it was winter topside, wasn't it? No matter. The viruses didn't need to be frozen to stay viable.

He heard another beep and the lift started to rise. He craned his neck and looked up towards the dome at the top of the shaft as the lift rolled upwards, carrying out of this hellhole. He was on his way out.

He had to smile. His rebellion had gone better than he had hoped.

CHAPTER 33

Craig wiped the sweat from his brow and gripped the doorframe again. Wedging his fingers in as far as he could, he pulled, but the doors wouldn't budge.

Exhausted, he dropped his arms and looked around. He had to get to Sebastian.

His eyes scanned the debris scattered throughout the air-tight chamber, hoping to find something that would help him. He'd tried the metal rod but it hadn't helped.

Suddenly remembering, he stumbled over to the row of drawers to his left. He had seen all kinds of items during his quick, desperate search for the printout, and after pulling open a few drawers, he spotted a scalpel nestled in a small safety case. Scooping the case out of the drawer, he flipped the case open, removed the scalpel, tossed the empty case over his shoulder and hurried back to the double doors. Gripping the scalpel tightly, he slit the rubber seals of both doors, deflating them. Now he had a good place to grip. He tossed the scalpel aside and wedged his fingers into the gap between the doors as the seals continued to deflate, ready to pull with all of his strength. But even with the better grip, the doors still wouldn't budge.

Swearing to himself, he turned back towards the room— and noticed the doors at the opposite end. There was a small metal bar between the two doors, locking the two together. Craig raced over, kicking debris out of his way as he ran, and inspected the bar for a catch of some kind but couldn't find one. On closer inspection, he saw that the bar held the doors closed magnetically, a locking mechanism that engaged to secure them.

With a burst of inspiration, Craig raced back to the drawers, began wrenching them open, and found what he was looking for in a drawer filled with a collection of small bottles. He quickly read the labels and selected one that contained a powerful acid. Returning to the doors that blocked his escape, he pushed aside the deflated seals and searched around until his fingers touched the metal bar on the other side. He quickly unscrewed the cap, dropped it, and shoved the bottle into the gap. The acid poured over the bar and down the two sides of the door, hissing as it began to eat through the metal.

When the bottle was nearly empty, Craig put it on the floor, reached up and wedged his fingers into the gap. He pulled, straining with all of his might. At first, the door wouldn't move—but then the bar broke with a strange pop and the door slid open.

Craig would've yelled with triumph as air washed over him, rushing to equalize the pressure between the two rooms, but he didn't have the energy. He took a few deep breaths instead, almost intoxicated by the air that filled his lungs, and felt a little of his energy return. Fortified, he shoved the door the rest of the way open and stumbled into the Prep room.

He didn't waste any time. Moving as fast as he could, he went through the Prep room, across the lab and into the hallway. He headed straight for the door to the Computer Lab, looked inside—and froze when he saw Jackie's dead body.

Then he heard the distinctive sound of the lift in the central shaft start to rise. He spun and raced for the shaft, barely able to contain a howl of despair.

Mouse continued to climb up the tiny shaft, his breath coming out in short, hot bursts. Every inch of progress was a struggle; every muscle ached.

He passed a row of small dots, but in his agony, he didn't notice them. His face was angled straight up. His entire mind was focused on going up, reaching the top.

Mouse rose a few inches past the dots when he heard and felt a rumble. It took him a few seconds to identify it, as the cylinder he was in distorted the sound. With a gasp, he realized it was the lift. Sebastian was escaping through the central shaft!

With a flood of adrenaline, Mouse began to climb faster, his arms and legs churning as he rose higher and higher. His eyes were closed as he fought his way upwards, his back and neck screaming in pain. He ignored his body's protests and continued on.

But he wasn't a machine.

His body had limits.

His hands shook with exhaustion.

They were also sweaty—and when he tried to lift himself again, he lost his grip. He slid down a few feet before he managed to stop his fall. Whimpering, he jammed his body against the sides of the cylinder as hard as he could and tried to catch his breath.

He couldn't believe he had fallen. All of that effort had been wasted.

He grabbed his flashlight and pointed it upwards. He had to see how far it was to the surface.

When the beam of the flashlight showed the view above, he frowned at first, confused. The shaft ended abruptly about seven feet above him. He didn't see a door or anything. The shaft simply stopped, the end capped off.

He groaned. He knew the facility well enough to realize that above the cylinder was nothing but dense rock, then Level I, then two hundred feet of compacted rock and dirt. He must've climbed high enough to either reach Level II or had already surpassed it. Either way, he realized he had reached a dead end.

Sebastian kept his eyes trained on the top of the shaft as the lift carried him towards the surface. His smile widened. A few more feet and he'd be able to reach up and touch the domed top.

Banks would be on the other side, waiting for him. As soon as the lift stopped, he would open the doors and they could get out of this hellacious facility. An hour tops and they'd disappear. No one would find them. Sebastian was too smart for that.

He was pleased. His rebellion had gone as well as he'd expected, and with the biodispenser he'd left down there, he wouldn't have to worry about survivors. By the time the Army figured out what had really happened, he'd be out of the country, richer than most people even dreamed.

It was a great day to be alive.

Craig scrambled towards the door to the central shaft, the same door that Sebastian had used earlier. He grabbed the handle and pulled, but it was locked. Unable to get in and unsure what else to do, he put his ear against the door and listened. The sound was very faint, which meant the lift was near the top. There was no way to stop Sebastian in time.

Craig wanted to scream. He couldn't believe Sebastian was going to get away with this—but obviously, he was.

The realization hit him with blinding clarity: Sebastian had someone on the surface waiting for him. Of course. That was how he was going to get away—and there was nothing Craig could do to stop him.

His legs gave out and he slid to the ground. They had lost. Sebastian was gone and so were the viruses he had stolen. Whether Craig and the rest of his team eventually survived or not no longer seemed to matter. He had failed to stop the man who was about to put the entire world in danger.

CHAPTER 34

In the darkness of the shaft, Mouse exhaled.

His breath contained thousands of strands of weaponized Ebola. The virus had infected his entire body and had duplicated itself tens of thousands of times. His body tried to fight off the attack but it spread too quickly. Unless he received the vaccine, a specially modified antibody, it would only be a matter of time before his body was overwhelmed.

When he exhaled, copies of the pathogen were pulled out of his lungs and released into the air. This strain of Ebola did not have the ability to spread after the initial infection, so it could be used in a contained manner in times of war. Even so, his breath still contained strands of the virus, which died moments after leaving his body.

The dead agents floated in the air as his breath expanded in an invisible cloud, filling the tiny shaft, adding to the other dead microbes Mouse had already exhaled.

Strands of the virus seeped into the tiny holes that formed a ring of dots around the shaft and attached themselves to the sensors hidden inside. The sensors were part of a backup system that the Army had installed as a last line of defense. The designers had known the dangers of this place and the cataclysm that could occur if their defenses ever failed. This was a last, final protection against the unthinkable.

The contact caused a brief electrical charge, and the mechanical device quickly scanned the intruder. When it identified the intruder as a derivative of the Ebola bug, it sent a signal down to the mainframe computer in Level III.

The signal routed its way through the mainframe computer at the speed of light, snaking deeper and deeper into the computer to its core programs.

From there, it triggered a series of steps that was imbedded in the mainframe's basic design. Commands were sent out, initiating the final countdown.

Throughout the facility, on all three Levels, a new alarm began to sound.

On the surface, alarms went off as well, mimicking the warning.

People listened in shock and horror—then broke into a mad scramble for the exits. They had to get away from the complex, as far away as possible. They recognized the alarm. They knew they had only a short amount of time before the entire facility was destroyed.

Sebastian reached up, his fingertips splayed as he reached for the dome. He was there. He'd made it. Time to climb back onto the surface, rise from the grave so to speak—and become a very rich man.

The lift continued to rise and his fingertips brushed against the underside of the dome. In another few seconds, the lift would complete its journey and he could open the dome.

Suddenly, an alarm rang out, the sound piercing in the massive, metal-lined shaft. The lift jerked to a halt and then abruptly began to descend. Thrown off balance by the sudden reversal, Sebastian fell to his hands and knees, landing hard on the metal grate.

No! He turned and looked back up at the dome, which quickly rose up away from him as the lift dropped. Within moments, it seemed as distant and unreachable as the stars in the night sky.

Sebastian pounded his fist on the metal grate. He was furious. He knew what the alarm meant. He couldn't believe it. He had been so close!

Now he had this to worry about. For the first time, he felt a flicker of fear. He would have about fifteen minutes once the lift reached the bottom of the shaft. It was a ridiculous amount of time, further proof that the designers of this dungeon had been sadistic. It was meant to give the survivors time to escape and the surface to clear out. But it also killed the lift in the central shaft, ordering it to the bottom. It had to, as the shields would activate in a few moments.

He had one chance to get out—he hoped. He would have to play his last card, a chancy backup plan that he'd wanted to avoid. But now he would have to do it, he thought as the lift swiftly plunged towards the bottom. It was the only way to escape in time.

Craig rushed to Security Room 1 as soon as he heard the alarm. Mitchell, Kim and Trisha were already there, trying to find out what the warning meant. When he burst in, they spun around in amazement.

"My God, you're alive!" Mitchell yelled.

Kim gasped in astonishment and Trisha's mouth dropped open.

"Yeah, I'm alive," he started to say, but he had his breath knocked out of him as Trisha threw herself into his arms. He held her for a few moments, enjoying the feel of her body against his. His feelings burst forth, momentarily wiping out all else, his issues with his father be damned, and he squeezed her tight as her tears wet his shoulder.

"What's the alarm for?" Mitchell asked.

Craig reluctantly pulled away from her. "I don't know—"

He was interrupted by an enormous rumbling overhead. The rumbling doubled in intensity—and ended with massive clangs as thick metal slammed together.

"What the hell?" Kim whispered in the ensuing silence.

Tony hobbled into the room. "We've got a problem," he announced. "The nuke's been activated."

"Nuke?" Mitchell asked in amazement. "What nuke? Wait, you mean a nuclear weapon!?"

"Yeah."

"There's a nuclear weapon down here?"

Tony nodded and turned to Craig. "We need to disarm it."

Everybody began talking at once, shocked and scared. Craig tried to calm them down. "We don't have much time," he said, talking over the noise.

"Did you know about this?" Trisha asked him.

"Honestly, I'd forgotten. They mentioned it when I was first assigned to the facility, but that was years ago."

"It's a defense mechanism," Tony explained. "The Army designed it as a final backup in case more than one level became infected. The theory was that a nuclear blast was the only way to ensure an outbreak never reached the surface."

"Oh my God," Mitchell whispered in terror.

"What was that noise we heard?" Kim asked.

Tony turned to her. "The shields. There are two sets of thick lead shields that were activated along with the nuke. The idea is to contain the blast. It's a small nuke—enough to wipe out both levels down here—and they wanted to try to contain it. The shields closed off the central shaft between the first and second levels. The theory is that the natural rock between the two levels, and the shields, will contain the blast."

"How much time do we have?" Trisha asked.

"Not enough," Craig said. He looked at Tony. "Where's the nuke?"

"In here. I'll show you."

The lift hit bottom.

Cursing under his breath, Sebastian stumbled off the platform with the satchel bag, unlocked the door and quickly exited the shaft. Not bothering to close the door behind him, he hastened through the courtyard to the Computer Lab. Before entering, he reached down and reluctantly turned off the biodispenser's timer, then quickly unlocked the door and ducked inside.

Jackie's dead body was still there, waiting for him. He sneered at it. She'd been a delusional pain in the ass, and dumb enough to fall for "Ricardo", but if she came through for him, he'd forgive all of her flaws.

When they had made their plans, he had suggested a few items for her to smuggle into the Level. The most important was the gun, but he had requested a couple of other items as well. He hadn't bothered to follow up, but now he prayed she had done as he'd asked. If not, he was going to be seriously screwed.

Using the computer, he unlocked the doors to Labs 1 and 3, and then quickly left the Computer Lab.

His Italian shoes slid on the polished floor as he spun around the corner and triggered the door to Lab 3. As soon as it opened, he raced inside and went over to the supply closet next to the refrigeration unit. Jackie had told him she would hide the items he'd requested in the supply closet, in one of the boxes labeled 'packing materials'.

He put the satchel bag containing the canisters on the floor, threw the closet doors open and began to riffle through the boxes.

In war, nothing happened exactly as planned. But he could adapt.

He'd better hurry.

He ripped open the first box, but it didn't have what he wanted. He grabbed the next box marked "packing materials", wrenched it open, and shoved his hand inside. After a few moments, his shoulders relaxed. The wench had come through after all.

With a smile, he pulled out the plastic explosives. There were four long bars, more than enough power to serve his purpose. He was impressed. He set the bars aside and searched for the detonators. He found them at the bottom of the box, along with a digital timer. Perfect.

꜀ He placed the bars, detonators and timer in the bag with the canisters, threw the bag over his shoulder and headed for the door.

At Tony's direction, Craig and Trisha moved the computer monitor, the printer and the phone off of the wide filing cabinet nestled in the back corner of the room. As soon as they cleared the top, Tony reached down behind the cabinet and undid a couple of hidden catches.

"Wait, that's not a filing cabinet?" Kim asked behind him.

"No. Just supposed to look that way."

Craig nodded in understanding. He'd never seen Tony open those drawers and now he knew why.

Tony gingerly removed the top of the cabinet.

"You have got to be kidding me," Mitchell muttered.

The false cabinet, which was lead-lined to protect against radiation leakage, hid the nuke. The sophisticated bomb rested on the floor, with wires that connected it to the mainframe leading into the wall. The display on the nuclear device read just over twelve minutes.

"I shouldn't be here," Kim said in a watery voice.

Mitchell glanced at her. "Where would you go? Once that thing blows, we'll all be vaporized. Might as well have front row seats to our death."

"You're really sick sometimes."

Tony ignored them. "We'll have to try to defuse it," he told Craig.

Craig frowned. "Do you know how?"

"I was given a class once."

"Oh great," Mitchell muttered.

Tony shot him a look. "We have to try."

"He's right," Craig said. "Help me take the cabinet apart. We need to be able to get to the nuke."

Mitchell came forward and the three men began to unhook the lead-lined sides that made up the hidden compartment.

* * *

Sebastian strode purposefully through Lab 1, through the Prep area and—after only a moment of hesitation—into Chamber 1. He had never been in one of the chambers without a biohazard suit before, but he couldn't spare the time to put one on. As a result, he experienced the same unsettled feeling that Craig had felt earlier. Sebastian forced himself to ignore his disquiet, though, and get to work. The clock was ticking.

He grabbed a stool, pulled it over and climbed up onto the table. Opening his bag, he pushed the containers aside and grabbed the first bar of plastic explosive. He turned, ripped off the adhesive cover and pressed the bar against the ceiling, directly underneath the tank that serviced the room. The bar adhered to the smooth surface and he quickly attached the other three bars next to the first. When they were in place, he inserted the detonator caps and carefully attached the wires to the timer. After a brief argument with himself, he set the timer for ten seconds, hit "start" and jumped down from the table. He grabbed the bag, raced out of the chamber and crouched down in the far corner of the Prep room, throwing his arms over his head for good measure.

He had sucked the air out of the chamber a dozen times over the past couple of weeks, increasing the air pressure inside the tank until it greatly exceeded the recommended limit. When the timer detonated the plastic explosives, the explosion should tear right through the tank. If he'd planned it right, the secondary explosion would be cataclysmic.

Mouse slid a couple of feet down the shaft, forced to return to Level III. He felt as if he was missing something, though. Going back to the bottom would admit defeat. He'd be right back where he started.

He held his weight, his muscles shaking from the strain. Working quickly, he grabbed the flashlight and moved it around, looking for anything that might give him a sign.

That's when he spotted a grill similar to the one he'd used to access the shaft. It was only a couple of feet below and to the side of him. In his struggle, he'd been so focused on reaching the top that he hadn't noticed it. The metal grid seemed to sparkle in the darkness, reflecting the light from his flashlight.

Mouse stared at it for a few seconds. It was the missing piece.

Moving carefully, he slid down until he was level with the grill. He almost moaned at the thought of getting out of the shaft. He couldn't stand to be in here any longer. He felt claustrophobic and his body was drained. He'd never been this tired before in his entire life. His muscles were Jell-O and his back was on fire.

Marshaling the last tattered remnants of his strength, Mouse cautiously turned his body until he faced the grill, then brought one foot back and kicked the grill with as much power as he could muster. It rattled but didn't move. He kicked it again, and then again, hoping to break his way through.

The top part of the grill popped loose, and a two or three inch gap appeared at the top as the grill leaned back. He knew a couple more kicks would do it, but he couldn't. He was drained, his body completely played out. He would start to slide at any moment.

Desperate, he pushed his foot against the grill instead of kicking it. Using all of his strength, he bent the grill back as he straightened his leg. With an ear-scraping shriek, the grill tilted back and disappeared from view.

He stared at the dark opening, his breath coming in short, frantic bursts. All he had to do now was somehow get inside.

He reached out with one hand and grabbed the top of the opening, his leg still sticking straight out. He began to pull himself forward—and the metal's edge bit into his hand. At the same moment, his body began to slide.

Letting his other leg dangle, ignoring the pain in his hand, Mouse grabbed the metal's edge with his other hand, and with a last surge of energy, pulled his body towards the opening. He ducked his head and teetered for a moment between the shaft and the dark opening. Then his weight shifted forward and he fell into the darkness.

CHAPTER 35

Twisting her body, Jill reached over and pulled open the clear door. After some wiggling and shoving, she got her head and shoulders through the opening and then used her arms to pull her body the rest of the way through.

She collapsed on the ground, took a deep breath—and was assaulted with sharp animal smells as the caged creatures hollered and shrieked at her. They didn't know that the strong ultraviolet light that bathed the room, installed to prevent infected test subjects from spreading viruses to the other animals, protected them from any strands of Keres Eyes that might've managed to follow her all of the way down the conveyor tunnel to their room. They didn't care. They just wanted out.

Picking herself up, Jill lifted the door, grabbed the small container she'd transported and hurried off, weaving through the maze of cages towards the exit. When she reached the door, she slapped the doorplate—and sighed when the door opened. Obviously, Sebastian hadn't bothered locking all of the doors in the lab area.

After passing through Lab 7, she entered the hallway. With single-minded purpose, she dashed down the hallway, past the emergency door that sealed off the side hallway to Lab 9, and entered the courtyard. Without pausing, she turned left and raced through the courtyard towards the Computer Lab.

She heard a door close up ahead. She didn't see anyone, but she suspected Sebastian was around somewhere. Reluctantly slowing down, she stopped next to the door to the Computer Lab and peered through the window.

Other than Jackie's body, the room was deserted.

Jill scooted to the end of the hallway, saw that the path was clear, and turned the corner. Proceeding down the hallway, she glanced at the windows into both Labs 1 and 3. They were empty.

She felt herself drawn to Lab 1. That was Sebastian's domain, his own little fiefdom. She didn't know what he would be doing in there, so she hesitated for a moment. Then she saw a shadow move somewhere deep inside the room.

That decided it. She opened the door and boldly entered the lab, preparing to confront the man who had killed her husband. Before she could, though, her surroundings suddenly exploded in a flash of light and a blood-shaking roar of sound.

Sebastian crouched in the corner as the timer counted down. When it hit zero, the bomb exploded, filling the chamber with fire. The force of the explosion blew out the window as well as the doors to the second chamber.

The initial blast was tremendous—but it was the secondary detonation that rocked the facility as the force of the plastic explosives ripped the tank in half. The pressurized air, suddenly freed, shot out in a massive burst that ripped through concrete, steel, and everything else in its way—both above and below.

Even though Sebastian was crouched down in the far corner of the Prep room, his body was slammed against the wall.

He found himself lying face first on the ground, his ears ringing from the dual explosions. He was covered in a layer of dust, as was the floor around him. Looking up, he found that the metal chamber doors had been ripped apart. The chamber beyond was thick with smoke and concrete dust, occasionally backlit by sparking electrical wires, and there was a mountain of debris caused by the destruction. Behind him, hoses from the damaged cryo-chamber released its contents, hissing in anger.

*   *   *

Craig held onto the metal covering of the nuclear device while Tony carefully removed the screws. As soon as the last one was removed, Craig gingerly lifted the cover and turned to set it aside.

They were far away from the location of the blast, with four walls protecting them from the devastating explosions. However, the force of Sebastian's bomb and the resulting secondary blast shook the Security Room, the roar filling their ears.

"What the hell was that?" Mitchell cried.

Craig made sure everybody was OK. From where they were, they didn't see the blast, although the force was so strong it kicked up the dust in the room.

Craig whipped his head around and locked eyes with Tony. "Sebastian. He's getting out."

"What?" Kim yelped.

Trisha understood. "The exits were sealed, so Sebastian must've created his own."

"He must have blown a hole through the damn ceiling," Tony added.

Mitchell frowned. "Even if he gets to the next level, isn't he still trapped?"

"No. The elevators still work, even though the nuke's been activated. Don't ask why."

"Sebastian's destroying everything in his path, isn't he?"

Craig's heart hammered with adrenaline. If Sebastian succeeded in creating a way to the level above, he could get to the elevators and take them straight to the surface. "I'm going after him," he said. "Everyone else stay here and help deactivate the bomb."

Tony nodded. He looked exhausted and there were deep, dark circles under his eyes, but he didn't complain. He turned back to the bomb.

Craig raced for the door.

He started down the hallway when he heard someone behind him. He spun around and held up his hands. "No, you stay with Tony."

"The hell I am," Trisha told him. "We can argue about it later if you want, but don't even try right now. I'm coming with you."

CHAPTER 36

Sebastian clawed his way up the mountain of debris into Level II. As he reached the top, the debris began to shift under his feet, forcing him to grab a piece of rebar sticking out of the damaged floor above him as the mountain shifted and threatened to collapse. Using the rebar as support, he managed to pull himself up onto the floor, scraping both knees on the rough edge of the hole the blast had carved, and climbed to his feet.

The level was dark as most of the lights had been blown out, and the air was thick with smoke and dust. Looking around, he didn't see anything familiar, just a couple of damaged walls. He could barely see the walls, though, in the haze of destruction.

Coughing, Sebastian began to make his way forward. He had only gone a couple of steps, however, when he heard the sound of cloth tearing and felt tugging on his shoulder. He spun around as a sharp piece of jagged metal, sticking out from the edges of the hole blasted by the tank explosion, tore through his bag. He dove for the first canister that tumbled out and caught it before it could fall into the hole. Cursing under his breath, he lowered the bag to the floor. The second canister was still inside the bag, but the bag had been rendered useless.

He tucked the gun into his belt and grabbed both canisters. One more goddamn hassle. At least he'd cleared out this level earlier with that fake alarm. No one was around to stop him.

Getting to his feet once more, he turned and started towards what he thought was the exit. The layout on this floor was different than Level III, but he knew the general location of the elevators. It would only take a couple of minutes to find them.

Craig approached Lab 1 cautiously. He knew Sebastian still had a gun, so he had to be careful—especially with Trisha tagging along. When he looked through the window into the lab, he discovered that the air was filled with dust and smoke. "This is the place, all right," he muttered.

He slapped the doorplate. The door began to open but jammed after only a few inches.

"The blast must've warped it," Trisha said.

Craig could tell she was right. Grabbing the doorframe, he pulled the door open wide enough to squeeze inside. They slipped into the lab—and had to stop.

"My god," she whispered.

Craig nodded in agreement. The devastation to the room was amazing. The only thing that appeared to be intact was Chamber 3. The windows of the first two chambers had been blown out, and the one at the far end of the room was obviously the place where the bomb had been detonated. Squinting through the thick haze of dust and smoke, Craig saw a massive pile of broken concrete and steel that rose up past the ceiling. The ceiling, and the floor above, had come crashing down.

They picked their way through the broken glass and debris to the Prep room, and then stepped over one of the doors and into Chamber 1.

The smoke was even thicker inside the chamber. The air was so dense with dust that his throat quickly became coated and every breath turned painful. He coughed a few times as he tilted his head to look up at the damage.

The hole in the ceiling was easily a dozen feet wide. There was another, smaller hole above it, and he realized he could see into Level II.

"You think you can climb this?"

She nodded as she coughed.

He turned and started up, cautiously picking his way as he began to climb the mountain of destruction.

"Careful," Tony warned. "Remove it slowly."

"I am," Mitchell said through clenched teeth. He lifted the timing device straight up, careful not to jostle the bomb.

There was a mass of wires connected to the timing device. In theory, one of them would stop the timer.

Kim raced back into the room with a pair of wire cutters. "Got 'em."

"Good," Tony said, taking them from her. "Appreciate it."

She frowned in concern. Tony sounded weaker. She didn't know how long he would last.

Mitchell sighed as he finished setting the timer on top of the bomb's outer casing. "Man, that's the most nerve-wracking thing I've ever done."

Tony leaned in and inspected the wires. "Great."

"What?"

"I don't recognize the layout."

"What do ya mean you don't 'recognize' it?"

Tony looked at him with bleary eyes. "They must've redesigned it. It's nothing like I remember."

Kim gnawed on her thumb helplessly. "What do we do?"

"Only thing we can," he said with a weary shrug. "Go through it step by step, try to figure it out."

Mitchell's eyes darted to the timer. He hoped they'd figure it out soon. They were literally running out of time.

With a canister in each hand, Sebastian stumbled over the last of the debris and found himself in a long hallway.

He was covered in grime, his lungs ached, and he wanted nothing more than a weeklong shower. His structured world was falling apart, his articulate plans getting all jumbled and fucked up.

He pressed on with a growl. He wasn't about to stop now.

He went down the hallway, paused at the first intersection, and then turned to his right.

The bomb had caused an extensive amount of damage. Overhead light fixtures had been knocked out of place and now dangled by their wires. The few that still worked threw light in different directions, creating a strange pattern of shadows. Windows had been shattered all over the place and a steam pipe whistled somewhere in injured protest.

After snaking his way through the hallways, he realized he'd become disoriented. He stopped at the next intersection and tried to estimate where he was. After a moment, he turned left and proceeded towards the center of the facility.

He felt his confidence return when he found the central shaft. The elevators would be just on the other side. There was a decontamination room, but with the nuclear bomb activated, the system would allow him to go straight to the elevators, in the theory that he could be decontaminated after he got to the surface.

He walked down the deserted hallway, his footsteps echoing in the silence. He felt like breaking into a run but restrained himself. He was still in control. His backup plan had worked! He'd made it to Level II. The elevators would take him straight to the surface, a thirty second ride at most. Then he'd be gone.

He turned at the next intersection and spotted the door to the decontamination room up ahead. A smile broke out as he picked up his pace, hurrying towards the exit.

Suddenly, a shadow leapt at him from a nearby doorway.

Caught unexpected, Sebastian was unable to react in time. Mouse crashed into him, slamming him against the wall, then took a step back and slammed him into the wall again. The blow caused Sebastian to lose his grip on one of the canisters, although he barely noticed. He shoved back, throwing Mouse off of him, but Mouse punched him in the face before he could react.

Struggling to recover from the blow, he scooted back down the hallway. Mouse raced after him, his normally sweet face darkened with hatred. He leapt at the scientist, wrapped his hands around Sebastian's neck and began to squeeze.

A shot rang out.

Sebastian felt Mouse's grip loosen as he slid to the floor, his eyes wide with shock and pain. There was a hole in his side from where Sebastian had shot him.

Sebastian stood up, took a step towards the young maintenance worker and aimed at his head. "People should know when they're bested," he snarled as he squeezed the trigger.

"Well?"

Tony wiped the sweat from his face. "I don't know. It doesn't make sense."

"It's gotta," Mitchell insisted. "Just think. Which wire did they tell you to cut?"

Tony shook his head as he continued to finger through the wires. Behind him, Kim shot Mitchell a worried look.

He grabbed another set of wires and spread them out for Tony. "These run to the second motherboard."

"Motherboard? Oh, yeah," Tony said, his voice losing strength.

Mitchell looked up at him sharply. Tony's eyes fluttered closed and he started to lean forward. Mitchell grabbed him and held him up. "Jesus, he fainted!"

"Do something," Kim said.

Lightning-quick, Mitchell slapped Tony's damaged face.

Tony snapped awake. "Ow!"

"Keep focused," Mitchell warned. He glanced at the timer. "We have a minute left. After that, we're all dead."

Tony nodded, took a deep breath and refocused on the wires.

Kim wrung her hands as she hovered over the two men and watched the timer count down towards their doom.

Before Sebastian could finish pulling the trigger, his body jerked as he felt a sudden piercing pain in his back. The gun went wide, the bullet ricocheting away, but he didn't notice. The pain in his back intensified and he cried out.

Jill shoved the needle the rest of the way in. "Got a present for you, you sick bastard," she breathed into his ear. She was covered in dust from the explosion, her face twisted in retribution. Holding his shoulder to keep him from getting away, she plunged the contents of the syringe into his body. "You like infecting everybody so much? Here's a gift for you: a dose of my blood. Now *you're* infected with Ebola, just like the rest of us."

Sebastian spun around. The move was so fast, so unexpected, that she lost her grip on the syringe.

Before she could react, he smacked her.

She cried out as she stumbled back, but grabbed Sebastian's wrist before he could bring the gun around. He involuntarily pulled the trigger and the gun fired, the bullet harmlessly imbedding itself in the wall nearby. Jill launched herself at him, her fury giving her strength that Sebastian didn't possess. She clawed his face, shoved him back and kneed him in the groin.

The fight went out of him as he bent over, groaning.

She stepped in to knee him again when he suddenly whipped his arm holding the canister around. The metal-covered canister slammed into the side of her head and she fell to the ground.

With a snarl, Sebastian forced himself to stand up straight. He was furious, his pain adding to his rage. He aimed the gun at her, determined to finish her off, but then decided not to put her out of her misery. She wouldn't be bothering him anymore.

He inspected the canister and was pleased to see it was intact. A small dent in the side, smeared in blood, was the only sign of damage. The vials would be fine. They were well insulated.

But now he was infected. He wavered. He thought of going back to Level III to get the vaccine. Before he could decide, he heard a shuffle behind him and turned to find Mouse clawing towards him. "You just don't give up, do you boy?" he asked.

"Sebastian," Craig suddenly cried.

Sebastian spun and pulled the trigger. The shot flew down the side hallway, but Craig was already gone.

Sebastian swore under his breath and started down the hallway after him. He had such loathing for his commander that he forgot about the vaccine, forgot about the elevators—and forgot about the nuke. His mind became consumed with a desire to kill Craig once and for all.

He stopped at the corner and looked down both sides of the intersecting hallway. He didn't see anyone at first, so he turned to the left.

He'd only gotten a few feet when something flew at him.

He pulled the trigger again, but this time there was only a click. The gun was empty. The piece of debris landed harmlessly nearby and skidded past him.

The realization that his gun was empty swept through his mind, clearing away his blinding anger. The elevators. The nuke would go off any second.

The hallway he was in would also take him to the elevator. He continued forward, done with the games. It was time to get the hell out of here.

Craig peeked around the corner of the next hallway, and then ducked back. "Go to the elevator," he whispered to Trisha. "Get upstairs."

"No, I'm staying with you—"

"I'm serious. Take the elevator so he can't. When you get up top, tell the base commander what's happened."

She nodded, impulsively kissed him and then took off down the hallway. Craig watched her go for a moment before turning back around. He'd heard the pistol click. He knew Sebastian was out of bullets. He smiled darkly. The playing field had been leveled. It was time to take a final stand against the monster who had killed his team, who had tried to kill Trisha.

Clenching his fists, he stepped into the hallway to face him.

"Thirty seconds," Kim intoned, her eyes riveted on the clock.

"OK, OK, we can do this," Mitchell said, hovering close to Tony.

"You're not helping," Tony growled, nudging him back. He continued to finger through the wires, searching for the right coding. The wires had been sheathed in an array of colors and some even had stripes. There seemed to be thousands to choose from.

"Twenty seconds."

Tony pulled one wire aside, not sure if it was the right one. He kept going, searching through the rest of the stack. His vision was blurry, he was so tired, but he forced himself to keep going. He couldn't give up.

"Ten seconds."

"Come on, come on," Mitchell whispered urgently.

Tony spotted another wire. It was between that one and the one he'd previously selected. But which one?

"Five seconds!"

As Kim counted down, Tony held the wire clippers to the first wire. He hesitated, switched to the other one, and then quickly returned to the first one. "Always go with your first instinct," he muttered under his breath.

"Two seconds! One!"

He snipped the wire—

and the clock stopped.

"Ohdeargodinheaven," she whispered. Her legs gave out and she fell to the floor.

Mitchell turned to Tony with a crooked grin on his face. "Certainly know how to make it dramatic, don't you?"

"You just wait 'til I feel better," Tony warned. "I'm gonna get you back for slapping me."

Mitchell laughed. "After what you just did, you can take a free shot whenever you want."

Craig stood motionless as Sebastian approached. "Well well, why am I not surprised to see you?"

"Your gun's useless."

"So you heard. Fine," Sebastian said, tossing the gun away. "You don't think I'm helpless though, do you?" Craig started towards him—then stopped when Sebastian held up a vial. "This is my insurance, my 'Get out of Jail Free' card. I'd watch it if I were you. I drop this and you'll be dead within a minute."

"You wouldn't dare."

"No? You think I didn't vaccinate myself? You always were two steps behind. It must be difficult going through life so slow."

"We settle this here and now."

Sebastian shook his head. "No we don't. You get out of my way and I get out of this cesspool."

"The elevator's gone."

Sebastian's confidence faltered. "What?"

"Trisha already took it up to the surface." Craig smiled at the look on Sebastian's face. "Who's two steps behind now?"

Sebastian cocked his arm back. "I'll enjoy watching you die."

Craig caught a blur behind Sebastian the instant before he heard Trisha's scream, "NO!" She jumped onto Sebastian, grabbing his arm before he could throw the vial.

Her sudden weight caused him to stagger to the side. His body slammed into the wall, jarring the needle still lodged in his back. He cried out in pain—and the vial containing the Keres' Eyes virus slid out of his hand.

Craig gasped. He launched himself at them, Trisha's safety the only thing in his mind. Before he'd taken two steps, though, the vial hit the floor and shattered, releasing a wide spray of the deadly virus.

Sebastian whipped his body around, throwing Trisha off of him. She landed on top of the broken vial, getting a healthy dose of

Keres' Eyes. Sebastian loomed over her, lifting the metal canister in his hand like a club, but Craig dove into him before he could swing. The two men fell to the ground—and instantly started to fight.

Sebastian had the advantage. Craig's body was tired from fighting the Ebola infection and breaking out of the chamber. Sebastian was better rested. He began to pummel Craig, who was trapped underneath.

Craig heard Trisha calling his name and he got a sudden surge of energy. It would be his last—and he knew it. He threw Sebastian off of him, spun around and gripped the man's head in both hands. With a savage twist, he wrenched Sebastian's head to the side, breaking his neck.

He let go and Sebastian's body thumped to the floor.

He didn't have time to savor his victory. Trisha was in mortal danger.

Frantic with worry, Craig scrambled over to the canister. He fumbled with the lock, not daring to waste time looking over at Trisha. "Hang on," he said in a breathless voice. "Just hang on."

He undid the lock, wrenched open the lid and peered inside. Trisha said something to him but her voice was thick, unintelligible. The virus was spreading quickly. He had to hurry.

His fingers raced over the vials, looking for the vaccine. He spotted a vial that was filled with a purplish liquid and pulled it out. The liquid gleamed in the light. To him, it was one of the most beautiful things he'd ever seen.

He flipped open the upper compartment and was relieved to find three small syringes tucked inside. He grabbed one, inserted it into the rubber top of the vial and began to fill the syringe with the vaccine for Keres' Eyes.

Behind him, he heard Trisha begin to thump on the ground—and he could feel his eyes burning. He was infected, too! Grabbing the other syringe, he scrambled over to her.

"I'm here," he said. "It'll be OK."

She looked up at him in terror.

Gray splotches appeared in her beautiful eyes. Her body started to tremble uncontrollably as the deadly virus invaded her brain.

Craig was in a panic. She was too important to him. She couldn't die.

He blinked a few times as the pain in his eyes intensified. He had one shot at doing this right. He leaned over, ready to jam the syringe into her, but her body was moving too much. He was afraid the needle would break off.

He leaned on her, using his body's weight to hold her down. He could feel her body trembling underneath his. The world slipped and his hand began to tremble. Oh God. He knew the vaccine had to be administered immediately. Time was running out.

There was only one place he could put it.

He reached forward, and then stopped, looking at the syringe stupidly for a moment. He'd forgotten what he was doing. The virus was already attacking his brain, interfering with his thinking.

His brain recovered long enough for him to remember.

Taking a deep breath, he grabbed Trisha's head, pushed it to the side, jammed the needle into her neck and squeezed. The liquid entered her jugular vein and went straight up to her brain to attack the virus at the source.

He pulled the needle out and sat back. He hoped it would be enough.

The burning in his eyes intensified as he began to experience tunnel vision. Moving quickly, he reached for the other syringe and grabbed the vial. His hands were shaking so badly it took him a couple of tries before he could even get the syringe into the vial. Once he did, he filled it up, pulled the vial free and pointed the needle at his neck.

He had trouble focusing, though. He didn't know why he had a needle pointing at his neck. It was supposed to be important, but he didn't know why. His vision continued to fail—

and he suddenly lost control of his body. The syringe slipped out of his hand as he started to convulse, his vision fading to black.

His last thoughts were of Trisha and their magical moments together.

CHAPTER 37

EPILOGUE

Banks huddled in the darkened motel room, ready to bolt—but he didn't know where to go. No place would be safe.

Hell, he'd already been running. The moment the alarm for the nuke had gone off, he'd taken off.

That had been the plan. If the nuke activated, he was to leave and meet up with Sebastian later. Only, Sebastian had never shown up. Banks had lingered at the rendezvous point a lot longer than he should have. He didn't have a choice. Without Sebastian, he was screwed—and he didn't want to face the reality of his situation.

He had to face it now. No escaping it. No sirree.

Sebastian was either dead or had been captured. Regardless, Banks had to run, to get away.

He knew he wouldn't get far. Either the U.S. military or Sebastian's buyers would find him.

His days were numbered.

The bastard. He'd drug him into this. He'd never wanted this. With trembling hands, he twisted off the cap, tipped the bottle—and the last few pills fell to the floor.

He dropped to his knees to scoop them up. He couldn't help it if he'd broken his hand and gotten addicted to pain killers. He'd been in agony. Even when the doctors had said he was all better, his hand had continued to hurt. Banks had been forced to get the pain killers any way he could, and quickly found himself at Sebastian's mercy, pulled into all of this when all Banks had wanted were the pills that made his pain go away. It's all he wanted still. Helpless to his addiction, Bank spotted one of the pills, grabbed it, shoved it into his mouth and dry-swallowed, then searched for more.

As he picked up another, a tiny motion caught the corner of his eye, and he froze. It was the doorknob. It was starting to turn.

*   *   *

"You're wrong. I don't regret any of this for a second."

"I'm glad."

"Have you ever done something you've regretted?"

Craig turned to look at her. "What do you mean?"

"Don't play coy. So have you?"

"Already having second thoughts?"

Trisha smiled. "No. I just ... I'm not like this."

"Neither am I."

"What is it about you that makes me feel this way, like I can't think straight?"

"Come here and I'll show you."

"I'm serious," Trisha said. "What is it?"

"Always the scientist?"

She laughed. "So, Dr. Leland, what makes you happy?"

He stared into her eyes. "You do."

She lowered her head onto his chest. "How long do you think we could get away with staying here? They'd kick us out after a few days, wouldn't they?"

"Probably. We should move the dresser in front of the door so they can't open it."

"What about the conference?"

He smiled. "Let's just stay here."

"We could get in trouble, you know."

"Who'll find out?"

"I think everyone in the entire hotel knows, with the amount of noise we've made."

"And that's my fault?"

"Actually, yes, it is. I would've been sleeping if it wasn't for you. You've been ravaging an innocent girl."

"'Innocent'? Then what do you call that thing you did—"

"Shut up and kiss me," she laughed.

Feeling returned to him slowly, reluctantly, as the memory of that incredible night in Dallas faded. He was disoriented, not sure where he was, but the disorientation was faint at first. It grew as he slowly rose out of the deep sleep that had taken a hold of him. He tried to remember what had happened but his thoughts were disjointed. Images flashed through his mind that didn't make sense. When he saw Trisha in his mind, her beautiful green eyes turning dark, it was so jarring that it woke him up. He opened his eyes and discovered that they hurt for some reason. Then he remembered. His eyes widened and he found himself staring at a white ceiling.

His gasp brought someone over. He tried to turn his neck but it was stiff. In fact, his whole body ached.

He felt the bed shift as the person he'd sensed sat down next to him. His mouth opened in amazement as Trisha came into view, smiling down at him. "Hi."

"Hi," he croaked. He cleared his throat and tried again. "What happened?"

Her smile widened. "You saved my life. Again."

"But," he protested, his memory returning, "I was dead."

She nodded gravely. "You almost were. Jill saved you."

"Jill?"

"Yeah, surprised me too. She told me she came up right as you collapsed. You already had a syringe filled and ready, so she injected you with the vaccine."

He was too overwhelmed to speak.

"You want to sit up?"

He nodded. He tried to move on his own but found that he needed her help. "God, I feel like I've been beaten up. How long have I been asleep?"

"Four days." She giggled when she saw the shock on his face. "It serves you right. Not only did you get infected with Keres' Eyes, but you were still fighting Ebola. The doctors didn't think you would make it. You gave us all a real scare."

He looked around the room in bewilderment. "Where are we?"

"Solitary confinement. We're back on the surface, but we've been quarantined."

He blinked at her. "Oh." He wasn't sure what to say. Seeing her alive and healthy triggered a heavy wave of emotion. "So I gave you a scare, huh?"

"Yeah."

"I'm glad I took my vitamins."

She gave him a lopsided grin. "Don't joke. It was real close for a while. But you made it."

"What about the others?"

"They're fine. Besides you, Tony was the worst. It took so long to get the doctors down to Level III he almost died, but Kim managed to keep him going. I think they might end up an item."

"Really?"

"Maybe. Jill's fine, although still recovering from the concussion Sebastian gave her."

"What about Mouse?"

"He's stable. He's on dialysis right now, needs a new kidney, but they tell me he's going to be fine. And Mitchell's healthy. He claims he's gonna write a book about everything that happened."

Craig snorted. "Good luck with that." He forced himself to stand. He took a few steps and grimaced. "I can't believe how stiff I am."

He looked around the room. There was a cheap dresser, two beds and a table with two chairs. The far end of the room was sealed with a thick, steel door. He noticed that the door's windows had been covered with pieces of paper, and the video camera in the corner had been unplugged.

The disabled camera and the paper covering the window made him edgy. He turned to her and swallowed.

"Trisha, I need to apologize for what I did before ... back when we first met." He took a deep breath. "I know I hurt you."

"I *was* hurt," she said. "You walked out without even telling me goodbye. I felt used."

"It was the biggest mistake of my life." When he bolted from the conference, he knew he'd blown any chance of finding out whether anything more permanent could've developed between them.

When she showed up at the facility a year later as Craig's newest subordinate, the very air seemed to change. He had been horrified, excited, embarrassed and conflicted, echoes of his childhood rising up to hound his every thought. The rest of the team immediately suspected that something was up by the way they reacted when they first saw each other, and it only took them a few hours to pry the information out of both Craig and Trisha. For weeks afterwards, Craig was inundated with suggestions from the men—and dark looks from the women.

He knew he had to do something. Pulling Trisha aside, he tried to explain why he'd ditched her. She didn't help when she told him she'd tried to find him but couldn't, as if he'd disappeared. "I was already working here," he admitted. "It was stupid to go to that convention, but my superiors decided that the organizers would've gotten suspicious if I didn't show up. I ... I couldn't get into any sort of relationship."

"That's crap and you know it. You could've at least had the decency to tell me *something*. Hell, lie to me. You wouldn't have been the first man to do so."

Things had turned uglier from there. For Craig, it had been even harder, as he'd not only battled his guilt, and desire, but also his fear of becoming a leech like his father.

"I've wanted to tell you how sorry I was for so long," he now told her, "but I didn't think I had the right. So I tried to establish a working relationship with you."

Her eyes were locked on his. "And?"

"I think I failed. I mean, you're a great scientist but I can't ... crap, I can't concentrate around you! I've been torn between wanting you and not being able to have you, and worried I was taking advantage of you—or would take advantage, forcing you or something—"

"You didn't force anything—"

"When it got to be too much," Craig pressed on, "I asked for the transfer."

"I got over the hurt. Haven't you realized that? I've been waiting for it to hit you."

He paused, stunned. "... You got 'over' it?"

She nodded. "When I got to know you. The real you. And in the process," she swallowed, "I think I've fallen in love with you."

He didn't know what to say. He was thrown, confused. He'd expected her to be pissed, revolted, pushing him away and cursing him out. Her words cut through his internal accusations, his old judgments, and not only granted forgiveness, they granted his deepest wish. His heart went into overdrive. The air thickened—not with tension this time but with possibilities, a luscious weight that seemed to push him towards her.

He looked at her this time with the love he'd carried for her, the love he'd so longed to let forth but had felt unworthy of giving. Love that not only was good enough but was accepted, was desired, was worthy.

After a few moments, he found his voice. "So we're quarantined in here?"

She nodded.

"I thought 'solitary confinement' meant splitting everybody up, each in their own compartment."

She smiled. "You don't mind, do you?"

"Not at all," he quickly assured her. "What about you? Do you mind being locked up with me?"

"I think I can survive. It might even be ... fun."

He glanced pointedly at the door, then back at her. "Fun?" he asked, cocking an eyebrow.

She bit the side of her lip. "Yeah," she whispered. "It could be a *lotta* fun."

ABOUT THE AUTHOR

Michael Curtis is a writer masked as a business professional. An ambidextrous, music-loving Sicilian who created a set of comic books when he was 10 years old, he has lived in St. Louis, Cincinnati, Dallas, New York, and St. Petersburg, Russia. He currently lives and works in Chicago under an assumed name.

You can find out more about him and his next novel, and find exclusive content, at www.mcurtis.net.

You can also visit www.kereseyes.com.

Email him at michael.curtis@live.com
Follow him on Twitter (@MCurtisAuthor)

www.ingramcontent.com/pod-product-compliance
Lightning Source LLC
Chambersburg PA
CBHW060949030726
47503CB00003B/788